SOLACE

SOLACE

CAT AUSTEN

I dedicate this book to the girls who weren't loved nearly enough and now enjoy stories where the heroine is loved in abundance. Please know that I love you, too (though, I have significantly less dicks).

And, as always, I dedicate this book to stay-at-home moms. This book was written after bedtime, during naptime, waiting outside karate, while dinner was cooking, or with Blippi on in the background. I see you; I am you.

Content Warning/ Disclaimer

This book is a work of fiction. While it has humorous elements, there are also things you may want to know. Below is a list of potentially uncomfortable content within *Solace*.

Infidelity (not committed by any main characters), divorce, kidnapping, violence (including blood/gore), violence with weapons, scenes of torture, mmf sexual content, mf sexual content, mm sexual content, aspects of BDSM (including but not limited to restraints, spanking, blindfolds), exhibitionism, voyeurism. Also contains human trafficking, drug use and distribution, murder, and injury.

The BDSM in this book is occasionally done in an unsafe way. I encourage you to learn how to do it safely before attempting.

This book begins with the FMC wanting to be a mother. Her desire to be a mother is discussed but there is no pregnancy or pregnancy loss in this book. Emily begins with a very cookie cutter, suburban mindset. This book is part of a three book journey that challenges this mindset in what I hope to convey in a respectful, growth oriented way.

Solace takes place in a fictional version of Cleveland, Ohio. None of these characters are real. References to political or official individuals are fictional. A few of the places are real but used in a fictional manner. I know you know this, but, like, I don't wanna get sued.

Some of the characters within *Solace* are not good people. This is, at its core, a mafia romance with dark themes. They may say something offensive. They may do something offensive. These are not the views of the author.

Oh, and if you know me- no, you don't.

Titles By Cat Austen

Convergence- *August 2022*- a polyamorous, contemporary, romantic suspense.

Aisle 5- *November 2022*- a contemporary, erotic, romantic comedy.

Solace- *Aug 2023*- book one in a mafia why choose trilogy. Dark romcom.

Spite- *November 2023*- book two in the Solace series.

Check out catausten.com, subscribe to newsletter at catausten.com/subscribe, and follow on amazon.com for all new releases.

I

Emily

A thrill ran through me when the chilled November wind swirled up my bare legs and caressed the area normally covered by my panties. I tightened the belt on my tan trench coat and shut the door to my car. When Gregory had gifted me the beautiful J Crew coat, I bet he didn't imagine me showing up to his office wearing only it and a sultry red lipstick. Looking around in the sparse parking lot, I took a breath and headed into the building. Inside the heavy doors to City Hall, I nodded towards the always present security. The sheriff's deputy sat up with a start as I entered. His phone, still playing a show, clattered on the desk in front of him. I smiled and greeted him happily. Our suburb had almost zero serious crime and my husband, the mayor, was beloved by his people. The presence of security was more for appearance's sake than actual security.

"Happy Thanksgiving, Charles," I said to the deputy as I passed him. My black leather heels clacked on the shined marble floors, and I worried that the reflection of my bare sex would be visible if he looked down. But I kept moving towards the elevator. It opened almost as soon as I pressed the button and the chime echoed in the all but empty lobby. It was the day before Thanksgiving, and many of the people who worked in city hall had taken the day off.

Gregory and I had been so busy the past weekend that we had not discussed our plans for today, including my day off. In the past, I had not always gotten the day off from my job as a kindergarten teacher. Sometimes it was a teacher in-service day and sometimes it was a regular school day. But we'd gotten a new superintendent this year, and she had made the day before Thanksgiving a holiday even for teachers. I was certainly thankful for the extra time to get things ready for tomorrow and the opportunity to seduce my husband at his workplace.

I used the mirrored wall of the elevator to check my hair and makeup. I usually wore my mousey brown hair in a conservative bun at the nape of my neck, as it was easiest to keep while chasing five-year-old children all day. And make up was often skipped other than a quick swipe of foundation and mascara. Today I wore a dramatic and sexy look, false lashes and contouring included, and my hair was down in frizz-free barrel waves. My blue eyes looked wider and more expressive and my lips more kissable. I felt confident and sexy.

Gregory and I had been together since high school, and

we were each other's first and only lovers. We stuck together through college and even shared an apartment as soon as we could as students. While our sex life was active and plentiful, it was rather vanilla. And that was okay. I loved him dearly and didn't need anything more. A quick tryst at his office was as scandalous as I could dare to try.

Above the city worker's and supervisor's offices was the mayor's office. The elevator chimed as the doors opened on the small, but well-decorated lobby. His secretary's desk was empty as I approached. I couldn't recall her name. She had worked for Gregory for a few years now and I could not think of her name. Gregory didn't talk much about her, now that I thought about it. She must have taken the day off. Today was a notoriously slow working day, and Gregory was a generous employer. I peeked into Gregory's office and saw his chair empty, but a Starbuck's cup was on the surface and his computer was on. He must have been in the bathroom or breakroom. I sat in his leather desk chair and crossed my naked legs.

I spun in the chair and figured I would hear his footsteps as he came down the hall. The windows behind his desk over-looked the street below and let in some beautiful sunlight. I looked at the curtains for a moment before deciding to close them. I didn't want a scandal now that Gregory had been re-elected for a second term earlier this month. With the curtains firmly closed, I sat back in his chair and fiddled with the hem of my coat. I didn't hear him coming, but his coffee still felt warm in its paper cup.

Fifteen minutes went by without a single sound on the floor. My mind strayed to the things I still needed to do to get ready for Thanksgiving. The house was clean and tastefully decorated for the holiday. The turkey was brining, I had located the roasting pan in the basement storage, and I had washed and cut the green beans for a casserole. Gregory's mom preferred a tart cranberry sauce. I would have to remember to lessen the sugar in my recipe....

Where was Gregory?

I straightened the pictures on his desk and rubbed a spit moistened Kleenex over the frames to shine them as I continued to plan Thanksgiving dinner in my head. Mashed potatoes, sweet potatoes... oh, the salad. My mom would be upset if I didn't have a regular salad at dinner. I would need to pick up some spinach today....

I sighed and looked at Gregory's computer. Maybe he had a lunch meeting that he had left early for, and it would be in his calendar. Nothing. But his secretary had emailed him, so she was there at least this morning. Maybe there was a meeting in the conference room?

I stood from the leather chair, feeling silly now. Gregory was in a meeting and I was naked under my trench coat. I could probably sneak back to the elevator and get to my car before anyone other than Deputy Charles saw me. In the hallway, I heard a sound like a feminine laugh. It wasn't abnormal to hear people laughing when working with Gregory. He was very charismatic and funny. He was a born politician.

But something had my feet moving down the hall towards that sound and away from the elevator. I moved as if in a daze as I walked down the hall, my fingertips grazing the wall on one side. The staff room didn't have a door, and I peeked in to see it empty. The bathrooms across the hall were also empty. The conference room had frosted glass windows so I couldn't see in. There wasn't a sound as I stood there, only an awareness of another person nearby. I could tell that there was someone in the room, but I didn't hear anyone talking or moving. Until I heard a loud smack and an accompanying feminine moan. My heart leapt to my throat, and I reached out for the door handle. It swung open silently and it revealed the horrible picture to me.

Gregory's secretary- Lily? Annie? Betsy? What *was* her name? was naked on the conference room table. Her wrists were tied to her ankles with red rope, and she was face down, ass up on the table. She looked alarmingly-upsettingly like a Thanksgiving turkey set to be carved. Behind her was Gregory. His suit jacket on a chair, the button down I had pressed for him yesterday evening was unbuttoned and hanging open on his torso. Sweat gleamed on his lean physique as he lifted his hand to spank his secretary once again.

I wish I could say that I gasped. Or made a sound of righteous fury. Or sobbed in despair. No. No, I audibly gagged. Gagged like I had just done two rounds on the Tilt-o-Whirl at the county fair and was trying to suck down a cold chili dog doused in tequila. I put a hand to my mouth reflexively as they both looked up and saw me. The scene before me was horrifying, but it wasn't particularly *disgusting*- I was an emotional gagger. Bile simmered in the back of my throat, threatening a dramatic display, as I stepped into the room.

"Emily," Gregory said, shock clear on his face. He lowered his hand from where he was poised to smack the tanned, pert ass of his secretary. Bethany? Julie? Fuck, I'd sent her a

Christmas card last year and a birthday card in June. How could I *not* remember her name?

"Gregory," I said, but it came out gargled and thick.

The little secretary struggled against the ropes for a moment before Gregory looked down and tugged the knots loose with two quick snaps of his wrist. He knew exactly what he was doing. That was a practiced move. My heart sank even further and felt like ice falling into my stomach. One of those fancy ice balls that you get with bourbon in a trendy bar, specifically. The woman looked up at me and attempted to cover her breasts and crossed her legs. As if I was invading her privacy as she screwed my husband on their workplace conference table. A taxpayer funded conference table.

Gregory's jaw was tense as he tucked his now flaccid penis back into his slacks. "What are you doing here, Emily?" he asked, his voice low and melodic, like he was trying to soothe a wild animal.

"I-" *was coming to seduce you in your workplace* "- it doesn't matter. I'm leaving. I'm... done," I said and met his ice grey eyes on the last word. I turned on my heel to leave before he could say anything, but the belt of my coat caught on the door handle. I was leaving with such speed that when the coat hooked onto the door handle, it was ripped back from my body. Stupidly, I hadn't buttoned the coat, thinking it would have been sexy to undo the belt and let the material slide over my shoulders and to the ground. Preferably, while he was sitting in his big leather desk chair, on the phone, and he'd have had to say, "I'll call you back... something came up," and that something was supposed to be his erection. *Not* the finish line flag of our marriage.

Instead, I was hooked to the door handle of the heavy wooden door with my ass as exposed as Talia's- Britney's? Sheila's? - though significantly less spanked. The door came with me as I continued to run. As the door slammed shut behind me, I ran fully out of my coat and was now naked in the hallway. I stopped, turned to pick it up, and put the coat back on as I ran to the elevator. I did up the buttons and bound the belt in the brief elevator ride to the lobby.

My heart was in my stomach still- that trendy ice ball present and accounted for, and I gagged again in the silent elevator. I pressed the back of my hand against my mouth as my teeth chattered in my revulsion. I shuddered as the doors slid open and I stomped my way past Deputy Charles and out the front doors. Blood was rushing in my ears, so I didn't hear my own shoes on the marble floors or Charles' cheerful farewell. I needed to get out of the building. I needed-

I didn't know what I needed.

I needed my husband to tell me what to do. But he was the one who hurt me.

Thankfully, I got to my car and drove out of the parking lot before the tears started. I kept my sobs to short hiccups until I reached the driveway of our house.

Our house.

Well, of course he would have to leave. There was no way that I was the one who would have to leave our home when he was the one who cheated.

My house.

Stumbling and crashing into the front door, I sobbed and crawled up the stairs to my bedroom. And it was going to remain *my* bedroom. He would never enter it again. I wanted nothing more than the comfort of my bed. I crawled in, rumpled coat and all, and tried to get comfortable. Sobs wracked my body and tears soaked the pillowcase.

The bed smelled like him. I screamed into my pillow and rage took over. I opened the window of our bedroom and started throwing out his stuff. His pillow, the pajamas he'd left in the bed, his entire tie rack, his collection of movie tickets, and his box of cufflinks. Anything that was his that wasn't bolted down and wasn't too heavy for me to lift was hefted out of the bedroom window with a screaming sob.

I was parched and my throat burned from screaming. In the kitchen, where we had danced and made pancakes every Saturday, I found a bottle of red wine. I had been hoping to pair it with Thanksgiving dinner tomorrow. Instead, I wrenched out the cork with the corkscrew and started chugging.

That's how Gregory found me. Still in the damned trench coat, one breast out from the effort of throwing all of his belongings out the window, and frat boy chugging a fifty-dollar bottle of wine. He waited as I chugged a considerable amount of wine. Gregory leaned against the kitchen island, arms crossed and head down. He looked like a father about to scold his teenaged daughter.

I pulled off the wine bottle with a sucking pop and said in a rasping tone, "Get the fuck out of my house." Wine dribbled down my chin and landed on my coat.

"No," he said in a calm, even tone.

"Yes," I spat out.

He shook his head. "I know you're angry, confused. But this is something that we need to work out."

"Work out?" I screeched. "I just caught you screwing your

secretary on the conference room table! There is nothing we need to work out!"

He uncrossed his arms and rested his palms on the granite island behind him. He was disgustingly calm about this. Why wasn't he ashamed? Why wasn't he *groveling*?

"You should be begging me to forgive you," I said in a whisper now, realizing he wasn't fighting.

"Is that what you want? For me to embarrass you?" He asked and cocked his head to the side.

I opened my mouth to respond, but he continued.

"You want me to get on my knees and tell you she's nothing to me? That *you're* everything to me? You want the people of this town to know that their mayor is weak? That he has to beg his *wife* to let him be a man and a husband? You want me to cry and simper because *you* thought to come to my workplace naked and disrupt my day?" With every question he got closer and closer to me. "Emily, I don't beg."

I sucked in a sharp breath that almost made me choke. Crossing my arms over my chest, I was still clutching the neck of the wine bottle in my left hand. I gripped it so tight my wedding band and engagement ring pressed uncomfortably into my skin.

"Almost twenty years," I whispered, looking at a button on his shirt rather than his face. We'd started dating in high school. We were the all-American dream even now in our early thirties. The mayor and the kindergarten teacher.

"It got a bit stale, didn't it?" he asked just as quietly.

I refused to answer him. I turned my head away, looking down at the tiled floor. He stroked a hand over my hair like he was petting me. I bristled. "Why?" I asked.

"Why what?" he asked after a moment.

"Why did you cheat on me?" I clarified, trying to keep my tone even.

He exhaled and stale coffee breath washed over me. Gregory stepped back but didn't respond.

"We were talking about having a baby, Gregory. Why would you let me get my hopes up?" I asked in a hoarse whisper. My voice would have been weak and unreliable.

Gregory looked at me for a long time and I knew he was trying to find a diplomatic answer. "You, Emily, are my wife. Our town knows you, loves you, respects you. A family like ours would be the perfect picture to get me to Senate. I don't want to lose my career over..."

"Divorcing your high school sweetheart for your secretary," I finished for him.

He didn't say anything.

"Was I going to be in the dark forever?" I asked. I wanted to look up at him and see his face, but I couldn't bring myself to see him. I was sure to cry again if I saw the face I knew almost better than my own.

He rubbed a hand over my biceps and fixed my coat, so my breast was no longer out. "I was never intending to hurt you," he said finally.

"So, I was going to find out when I randomly got an STD or something?" I said harshly.

He shook his head, and I looked at him now.

"No, I would have found out when she got pregnant," I continued.

"We're careful, Emily," he said as if he was reassuring me.

I pushed him away from me and moved towards the stairs

with my bottle of wine. "Leave my house, Gregory. I'll see you when we sign divorce papers."

"Emily-" he tried to call after me, but I was already stomping up the stairs, and drinking from the bottle of wine.

Three weeks later, I sat in a room at Gregory's lawyer's office next to my lawyer. Even though we were indoors, I wore a pair of huge black sunglasses to hide the puffy bags under my eyes. My hair was back in its typical low bun, and I wore a simple dark grey sheath dress and a navy cardigan. I was sat up straight and unmoving with my legs crossed at the ankles, channeling my inner Queen of Genovia. My lawyer argued with Gregory's lawyer across the table. Gregory leaned back in his seat and watched me with a furrow in his brow. I had not moved since we sat down, and it probably looked like I was asleep at the table.

The past weeks had been difficult, to say the least. I had broken the news to both of our parents when they all showed up for Thanksgiving dinner to find me incredibly hungover and with no cooked turkey. Gregory ended up showing up with a pre-cooked meal he picked up from a restaurant minutes after my parents broke down in tears at the news. Gregory's parents were defensive rather than apologetic for raising a cheater and had questioned my part in the scandal.

Gregory had swooped in with a full Thanksgiving feast and assured everyone that there was no divorce coming. He told them all I was just upset over a misunderstanding. My parents were so relieved to hear his blatant lie that they stuck with his story even after I insisted they listen to me.

"Let him get it out of his system, Emily," my mother had *tsked* when I tried to confide in her later. She had waved her hand dismissively and told me to buy nice lingerie to get him interested again.

My friends had been more interested in the idea of a scandal than they were with the actual relationship that had crumbled, and my coworkers perpetuated the rumor mill and accusations. The public did not know the reason for our divorce. I had agreed to keep Gregory's infidelity a secret as part of our divorce agreement. He had only agreed to a divorce on those grounds.

And apparently that he got to keep the house and my car.

Just after we were married, we had bought our home together. Our wedding gift money and the bulk of our combined savings went towards the down payment. But when we were buying a house, I had student loans that limited our ability to finance our home in a way that fit our salaries as a new teacher and bank manager. My name was not on the loans or the deed to the house. A bit of information I had not been fully aware of the ten years we had lived in our home. My lawyer argued that half of the money in the down payment was mine and half of the mortgage came from my paycheck and therefore the house was half mine. This, unfortunately, would prove insufficient to get me anything other than entitlement to a small percentage of the selling of the house if Gregory sold it.

It also did not guarantee that I could keep the vehicle I was living in and driving to work every morning. Since it had been a gift for my thirtieth birthday, it was purchased and registered in Gregory's name.

I left the building a divorced woman. I had handed back over my wedding and engagement rings, the keys to my car and the house, and our shared credit cards. Gregory handed me a wad of cash as I left, and I had to take it. Until my next paycheck hit my new bank account, I was fully broke. Swallowing down my shame at accepting money from my ex-husband, I left the office quietly and stoically.

I was on my own.

2

Emily

The kindergarteners in my class were refreshingly uncaring about my personal life. They did not care about my public divorce one bit. They only cared about earning their extra recess in the afternoon and the upcoming Christmas holiday. I enjoyed their presence more in the days post-divorce than I had on my first day of teaching. Most of my time was spent in my classroom and as little in the teacher's lounge as possible. I didn't want to encounter the pitying looks or the intrusive questions.

When I went to the teacher's lounge, it was always with dual purpose. While my students were at music class one Friday morning, I made a quick stop in the lounge for a fresh cup of coffee and to use the teacher's restroom. I set my mug under the Keurig and lined it up to brew while I was in the restroom. Just as I was finishing up in the bathroom, I heard voices entering the lounge and I cringed.

"He's so handsome, of course he called it off," a voice said with a laugh.

"Yeah, there's just no way *she* asked for the divorce. Who would give up that beautiful home and the chance to be married to a future Senator to live in a motel?" a second voice reasoned. I heard them shuffling through the PTA provided snacks.

"Wait, he's running for Senate?" the first one asked.

"He wants to. He talked about it at the last Christmas party," the second said.

They were fifth-grade teachers. I didn't have much to do with them since I taught kindergarten, but I knew who they were. My stomach felt sour at their words and my lip quivered.

"Do you think they disagreed politically?" the first asked.

I rolled my eyes and pressed my forehead against the bathroom door.

"No, I think he wants an updated model for the campaign trail," the second one chuckled.

Rage curled through my limbs, and I yanked open the bathroom door. The two teachers quickly stopped gossiping and looked at me. I couldn't stop my mouth from opening and breaking my agreement with Gregory. But this rage was unfamiliar to me. I had felt nothing like it before. There had always been someone protecting me and helping me through difficult situations. I knew everyone had coddled me and the new awareness of my naivety added fuel to my rage.

"He was screwing his secretary. I caught her hog-tied and naked on their conference room table during a workday. He was inside another woman and spanking her. So yeah. I asked for the divorce." My voice was steady and without intonation as I stirred creamer into my coffee.

The women gasped, and I realized my mistake in that moment. What did I win by telling them the truth? Their sympathy? I wanted no sympathy from people who were so quick to gossip behind my back. Did I think I would win the divorce? There's no win in divorce. I had literally nothing except for the boxes of clothes and other items that had been dropped off at my motel room a day after the official divorce. Did I feel better after telling the truth? No, I felt even worse for breaking the agreement.

The day at work ended with a sinking feeling of dread and the awareness that I had royally messed up. I knew I was going to be faced with the consequences of telling the truth. I looked at my phone once I got to my rented car to see three voicemails and ten missed calls from Gregory. Frowning, I looked at the transcript of the first voicemail. I didn't want to listen to his voice. I had only read two words "Emily, what-" before my phone lit up with an incoming call. I knew better than to answer the unknown number. It was likely a local news reporter and if I didn't have a prepared response, I would be in for more public humiliation. It was better to not return the call than to speak out of turn or officially decline to answer. Throwing my phone into my bag, I left and headed back to my motel.

Sitting alone in the cold motel room as snow steadily fell outside, I let myself be consumed by the grief and sadness of my situation. I was alone. Gregory was gone. My parents still wanted me to work things out with him and were still in regular contact with the beloved mayor. I couldn't trust them to help me. My friends were now non-existent. My colleagues would not help the disgraced ex-wife of the mayor. It was just me.

Self-pity got no one anywhere good, so I switched on the TV for a distraction. I watched reruns of a makeover show while I ate a sad microwavable meal on my motel bed. It was Friday night, and I could hear people outside laughing as they headed to their cars. Doors slammed in the distance, and I felt the sting of being alone again. The show I was watching had a well-coiffed woman state that to change your life is to change your hair.

Maybe she was right. Maybe I needed to change my hair. I surely needed to change my life, so why not start with the easiest option? I scrolled through my phone to find a salon in the city. A brand-new credit card of my own had arrived at my motel door yesterday, so I could stand to pamper myself a little. I booked an appointment online for tomorrow morning and settled in for a depressing evening alone with the crappy TV.

The salon was bustling with people getting last-minute cuts before Christmas and the New Year. I had only booked an appointment because someone canceled, or so I was told when I checked in. I hung up my North Face coat on a hook the busy receptionist pointed out. Grey slush covered the Cleveland streets and salt crunched under the boots of every customer who came into the salon. I had lived in a suburb of Cleveland my entire life and had always loved to come to the city. Today was no exception because not a single person in the building knew me as the mayor's wife or ex-wife. They had their own mayor and their own drama. I settled in for a shampoo with my stylist before she started chatting with me. The salon smelled like hair products and bleach, with a hint of a Christmas candle.

"What's inspiring such a big change?" she asked as she massaged my scalp under the warm water.

"Um, well, I just need something new," I mumbled, wishing she'd just be quiet and massage my scalp. I didn't mean it rudely, I just wanted a singular moment of bliss before I had to go back to dealing with my wreck of a life outside this salon.

"Oh yeah? Bad break up?" she asked sympathetically.

"You could say that," I grumbled.

She hummed and spent extra time massaging shampoo into my scalp. "What a bad time for it." She clicked her tongue disapprovingly.

I snorted. "Yeah."

"Do you need a revenge look?" she asked, a grin clear in her voice.

I smiled. "Heck, yes."

"Ever been blonde?" she asked as she rinsed the soap from my hair.

"No," I said. His secretary was blonde. Clara was her name, as I had finally learned. She was in her early twenties, too.

"Wait, you said that, and I know *everything* now. *She's* blonde. You're going red," the hairdresser said.

"Red, keep the length," another woman's voice said from my left. I peeked to see an older woman getting her hair washed by one silent stylist, while another silent stylist massaged her hands. The two exchanged glances, and I knew that this woman was important and scared them.

"Thank you," I said quietly.

"He's a piece of shit. She's too young for him, anyway. He'll figure it out soon enough," the woman said without looking over at me.

There was no way she even knew who she was talking about. She was likely generalizing. What cheating man didn't cheat with someone younger?

"Yeah, well, I don't intend to be around to watch it happen. I... I'll be somewhere else with a new life," I said instinctively, inspired by the feeling of change.

The older woman didn't say anything else, and my stylist took me back to her station. We chatted while she worked, and it was about an hour later before I saw the older woman again. She was wearing a structured black dress, her black hair pressed into a voluminous style a la Jackie Kennedy, and a swipe of blood red lipstick. She was beautiful and exuded power. I froze as she approached me, and every stylist's head turned to watch her. She held out what looked like a business card for me to take. I took it into my hand, and she leaned down to be eye level with me in the salon chair.

"If you were serious about starting a new life, call this number. No woman should feel like they're being left in disgrace. Leave in power," she said in a quiet voice, so only I heard her. I slid the card in my palm under the salon cape and nodded to her. She lightly pinched my chin in her thumb and forefinger and lifted until I was sitting tall again. She smiled down at me as she stood to full height and walked out of the salon.

The salon was silent for a moment before everyone resumed their tasks. My stylist made no comment about the exchange and continued to do my hair. I gripped the card in my hand and relaxed into my seat. The woman was probably a lawyer or a realtor or sold cosmetics. I would look at the card later.

While I was getting my hair done, my mom texted me an invitation to dinner tonight. I didn't want to see my parents and hear more about how I should try to get Gregory back, but I was sick of fast food and microwavable meals. I wanted proper food. And comfort. And maybe... my childhood room back for a bit. Just until I could get an apartment. A down payment for a new place would be easier to save for without having to pay for the motel.

I arrived at my parents' house ready to weep into my mother's embrace and beg for her to take my side and let me stay with them for a few weeks. For my entire life, there had been someone by my side or leading me. It was my parents until it was Gregory. And now, with Gregory out of my life, I only knew how to go back to my parents.

My mother did embrace me when she opened the door, but it felt stiff. I did not cry into her hair like I had wanted to. "Hey, Mom," I greeted her in a quivering voice.

She stood back from the door and said, "Come in, come in. Oh, your hair looks lovely! Red suits you. Dinner's almost ready. I made lasagna."

I stood in the entryway for a moment and reveled in the feeling of coming home. The warm stained wood of the door and staircase was polished but didn't hide all the cuts and dents from the life of a family home. One stair still had spatters of blue nail polish from an incident when I was in sixth grade. After slipping off my boots, I met my mom in the sunny kitchen. It smelled of tomato sauce and starchy noodles. She poured me a glass of wine and didn't look me in the eye. I sighed and took the glass with a murmured thanks. I took a long gulp.

"You know, I talked to Gregory's parents today," Mom said as she pulled plates from the cabinet. I leaned against the counter and listened, ready for the lecture. It was the price I would pay for lasagna and a glass of wine, apparently.

"I did not know," I replied simply.

"We all agreed that you should work harder to get Gregory back and interested in you again," she started her lecture, but I interrupted.

"Mom, we're divorced. Fully. Legally," I insisted, trying to keep the annoyance out of my voice.

Mom was quiet as she stared at her aged hands on the countertop. I waited patiently for her response. "Nobody in our family has gotten divorced before you."

"I'm the first woman in our family to go to college. The first person to get their belly button pierced. What do you-" I started to snap but Mom *tsked* me and shook her head. "I'm the first to find their husband fucking his secretary."

Mom whirled around to face me. "Don't use that language in this house, Emily Catherine," she scolded, her eyes alight with outrage. She had middle named me like I was a child.

And that's when it hit- I was an adult, but everyone had treated me like a child for my entire life. My parents never taught me how to survive on my own, only how to wait for a man to come around and help me. Gregory never even had my name put on the deed of our house. Or on the registration of my car. Hell, he never shared his more intense sexual desires with me because he saw me as someone who couldn't handle it.

I took a step back and set my wineglass down. My eyes strayed to the stack of four plates on the counter. Mom, Dad, me... Gregory. The back door opened, and Dad and Gregory came in, chuckling together. Dad was wiping his hands on a shop rag, still clad in his oil-stained clothes, while Gregory's shirtsleeves were rolled up to his elbows and a streak of grease marred the skin of one forearm. I looked at mom where she was looking uncomfortable and anxious.

"Mom," I whispered, and even I could hear the hurt in the word. Even I could hear the betrayal in my own damned voice.

"He's a good man, Emily. He's going to be a Senator one day. Don't you want to be a senator's wife? He would make a great father, too," Mom was saying to me in a soothing tone that felt more patronizing than anything.

Gregory looked up to see me and his smile settled into a closed mouth, smug look. He looked like he thought I was about to beg him. "Hello, Emily," he said in a smooth, low voice.

"Where's Clara?" I spat.

Gregory had the audacity to share a look with my father like I had just whined about not getting a pony for my birthday. "She's not here," he said in a reprimanding tone.

"No, taking her to your ex-wife's family's home would be a bit much," I said sarcastically, though breathlessly.

Gregory shook his head disapprovingly.

"I imagine I'm supposed to beg for him to take me back? Promise to be kinkier in bed? Pretend like I've learned my lesson?" I asked the three of them.

Dad huffed in disbelief at my harsh words. Gregory put his hands on his hips like I was a child that needed scolding.

"No," I said and stomped my way to the front door. I shoved into my boots, grabbed my coat and purse, and rushed out to my rental car.

I heard the raised voices of my parents and Gregory, but... I didn't care anymore. Slamming the car into reverse, I took off out of the driveway. I looked up before I sped away and saw all three of them standing on the front porch looking shocked and confused. Raising my middle finger out the window, I gunned it down the street away from them.

I truly hoped that I never saw any of them again.

3

Emily

Bursting into the motel room, I ran around and packed all of my things. First thing Monday morning, I was going to get my name changed at the Social Security office, and then I was out of here. I was leaving this town. Maybe even the state. I felt bad when I thought of my students. But I knew that they would be in excellent hands with whatever substitute was pulled in before the school hired a new teacher for the remainder of the year.

It was nine o'clock on the dot Monday morning when I entered the Social Security office with all of my important paperwork. The girl at the desk was young and smiled at me as I approached. I was her first customer, so she was still in a good mood.

"Hello, I'm here for a name change," I said and placed my paperwork on the counter.

"Okay, please fill out this form. Have your birth certificate and marriage certificate, social card, and proof of address all ready for when you come back up," she said and slid me a clipboard.

"And divorce paperwork?" I asked.

"Oh, uh, yes. That, too," she added.

I sat and completed the required paperwork as more people filed in and out. When it was my turn to return the forms to the clerk, her smile fell when she saw my married name.

"Emily Ambrose?" she asked.

I nodded.

"Um, I think I'm missing some paperwork," she said and glanced behind her. I could only see a row of offices against the back wall and a few other clerks.

"No, I have it all here. I looked online before I came," I said confidently. I was very good at following lists.

"I'm missing your proof of residency. It says on your license that you live somewhere other than the address you've provided," she said calmly, but again glanced over her shoulder.

"I gave you my parents' address because I do not have a permanent one. The address on my license is my ex-husband's home," I explained. Two other clerks were watching me now. I wasn't being loud; they were just nosy.

"I'm sorry. I'll need an address for *you*," she said sympathetically.

I had a feeling that this was incorrect, but I didn't want to make a scene. I grabbed my papers in my hands and rushed out the doors, only to see Gregory's car parked in the lot. Tears and rage bubbled at the surface as I got into my car.

I let out one quick scream of frustration before I backed

out of the parking spot. What was his angle? What did he want from me? Surely, he could present an all-American picture to the public with Clara instead of me. There had to be something else. But I didn't care anymore.

My phone had been switched off to avoid the calls from my school, wondering where I was. Once I was back at the motel, I turned it back on and dug out the business card that the beautiful woman in the salon had given me. It was a simple white cardstock with black writing on it. It said, "Harold 555-0806" and I hesitated only a moment before I dialed the number.

"Deniro's Delicatessen," a gruff man's voice answered.

"Um, hi. I was told to call and ask for Harold?" I said, suddenly shy. Had that woman been offering me a job at a deli?

"This is he, hold on-" there was a muffled sound like he was holding a hand over the phone and talking to someone. "Yeah, is this the newly minted redhead from the salon?"

My heart leaped to my throat. "Y- yes, it is."

"Alright, girlie," he said in a more comforting voice than when he had answered the phone. "Come to the deli this afternoon. Can you do three? It's after the lunch rush."

"Oh, yes I can," I said, relief pouring over me.

"Good," he said, and I heard a bell above a door tinkling.

"Do- do I need to bring anything?" I asked. "I'm... not sure what exactly I'm getting into."

"Ah, we'll explain as soon as you get here," he said assuredly and warmly. "Just bring a bag of your most important things. The stuff you wanna run with."

"Got it," I said, and my heart pounded in excitement.

"See you at three," he said happily before hanging up.

I packed up the rest of my belongings into boxes and left a small stack of cash that I hoped would cover the inconvenience of having to trash all of my stuff after I left. My motel room was paid until Friday, so they likely wouldn't even know about my departure until they came to clean the room. I had nobody to say goodbye to, so I stared at the door of the motel room before I went to my car with one stuffed duffle bag and my purse.

It was kind of crazy to be doing this. Who even was Harold? Who was that woman in the salon? Deniro's Delicatessen sounded Italian- was this a mafia thing? Or was it a mob? What's the difference between them? I shook my head, dispelling my thoughts. This was *Cleveland.* There was no mafia here. That's just ridiculous. Maybe Harold and that woman ran a program that helped women get out of abusive relationships. While my situation was not the same, I would appreciate the help to get out. I would donate to their cause as soon as I was able, if that was the case.

Deniro's Delicatessen was in the heart of Cleveland and had only street parking. I parked down the road and fed the meter. The sidewalk crunched with salt as I hurried to the glass front deli. I opened the door and the rich smell of oregano, tomato sauce, and cured meats wafted over me. My stomach growled, and I hoped I would have time to grab a sandwich. To the right of the door was a standing refrigerated case with a selection of drinks for sale and to the left was a small cluster of formica top tables and chairs. This was primarily a takeout place, but three men were seated there. I didn't look closely at them, as I was eager to meet Harold.

My boots squeaked wetly on the tile, and I stepped carefully around the Wet Floor sign.

A man in a white apron came out of a swinging door behind the counter. He was probably five foot eight inches tall, portly, and with pockmarked olive skin. "What can I get for you?" He asked.

"I'm here to meet Harold," I said.

He looked me over and settled on my hair. It was still very red, but in a low bun. I turned my head so he could see it better. I saw one guy stand up from the table out of the corner of my eye. He was very tall and had the lapels of his black peacoat up to cover his face.

I paused for a moment before looking back at the man at the counter. "Are you Harold?" I asked.

"I am. You the new red head from the salon?" he asked me, but was looking at the man that stood up.

"Yeah," I said as I turned to look at the tall man again.

Bright grey eyes framed with thick black lashes looked back down at me, closer than I had expected. I went to step aside so he could order something from Harold, but a hand stopped me.

My spine stiffened as I sensed a threat. Another man stood up and came to my other side. I looked up at him. He was wearing a black Columbia coat and had glasses over his blue eyes. An auburn beard covered the bottom half of his face, and he wore a beanie hat. I looked back at the first guy, and he also wore a beanie hat over his hair, but I could only see his icy eyes over his coat lapels at this angle. Hands grabbed at my elbows, and I immediately dropped to the ground in a crouch.

That semester of self-defense I took in college was coming to use as I yanked my arms back to my sides. One man cursed and then reached out to grab me again. "No!" I screamed and kicked with my right leg into the knee of the second guy. He cried out in pain and the first guy scrambled to get to me. I grabbed the Wet Floor sign and swung it at him. I hit him across the head with a *crack* and he stepped back. Harold was yelling, and I remembered a third man had been sitting at the tables in the shop's front. I kicked out again from my crouched position and hit one man as I scrambled on my hands and knees to the door, trying to stand up and run as fast as I could.

"HELP!" I screamed as my hands hit the cold glass of the front door. Cleveland was a busy enough city. There was bound to be someone right outside the door.

Someone grabbed at my shoulders, and I employed the drop to the ground trick again. It only worked because the man had not grabbed my coat, but held around my shoulders. Had he grabbed my coat, I would have been hanging from his hands like dry cleaning. I was crouched in front of the door and pushed at it. But it was locked.

"No," I choked out as multiple sets of hands grabbed me. They pulled me towards the counter and around the back. As I kicked and punched and scratched at the men, I reached blindly for something to use as a weapon. I screamed as loud as I was able as I fought. I could tell that the three men and Harold were also yelling, but I was not listening to see if they were yelling at me or each other. Something solid met my palm, and I grabbed it and wielded it as a weapon. I had hoped it to be the handle of a knife that I had grabbed, but it was, in fact, a stick of pepperoni.

I swung that pepperoni like it was a sword, a wild scream ripping from my throat. I hit at least two of the men in the head with the pepperoni, with little to no effect other than Harold yelling about his merchandise. A white-hot pain seared into my side where my skin was exposed in the struggle and then all was black.

Christmas was my favorite holiday in the classroom. The bright and wondrous faces of my kindergarteners as we read Christmas books almost erased the stress of the constant colds and student absences and the rush to get work completed before break. Every year I strung up lights in our reading corner and made cocoa with marshmallows for after the first snowy recess. The sounds of their little boots squeaking on the linoleum in the hallway and their snow pants swishing as everyone walked with a finger to their lips in the single file line was music to my ears.

I smiled as I listened to the sound of boots squeaking on the floor. Though, this time it didn't sound right... it seemed to echo. And the squeaks were lower pitched than with little kindergarten feet. More awareness came back to me, and I realized I was being carried over someone's shoulder. A muscular arm held me around my thighs, and I dangled like a rag doll along their back.

Oh shit, that's right, I was being kidnapped. I remained limp as I assessed my surroundings. Cracking an eye open, the first thing I saw was a denim clad ass. I fought the urge to pull away in disgust because it would ruin the illusion that I was still unconscious. Gross. I turned my head the slightest bit and saw that we were in a large garage, walking past multiple high-end cars. The ground beneath us was a painted cement and was swept clean of any debris. There were two other men walking with us. The one I was dangling over was wearing the black peacoat I had seen earlier. Another was wearing the black Columbia coat, and the third I had paid little attention to was wearing a long, dark gray wool trench coat.

Was I being trafficked? Was there really a demand for thirty-year-old, mid-sized, divorced kindergarten teachers? I fought a gag at the thought. I needed to keep a cool head if I was going to get out of this. I had wanted to run away and disappear, sure, but I definitely didn't want it like *this*.

"She going to wake up soon?" a man's voice asked quietly.

"Yeah, it was a small dose," the man carrying me replied, his voice rumbling under my thighs.

"Did you get her phone?" another man asked.

"Yeah, I trashed it."

"Any Air Tags or other GPS?"

"Not on her, no. Harold just texted and said there was an Air Tag on her rental car."

"The mayor's?"

"I think it's safe to assume so."

"Have him drive it back to her motel. Leave it clean."

"Already on it."

Gregory had been tracking me? I was actually relieved to hear this. That meant he could find out I was missing and come back to the deli where I got taken. He would surely figure it out and get the authorities involved. My heart raced at the prospect of Gregory saving me. I would even consider taking him back if he rescued me.

A door opened, and a burst of cold air washed over me. I fought a flinch as the icy wind stung my eyes. Snow and ice crunched under their feet as they walked. I peeked around and saw we were alone and heading towards an enormous house. It was a mansion in the Greek revival style with white pillars around the front door. There was a red brick path peeking through the snow and ice as we walked towards the house. The stillness of the surrounding air had me thinking we were rather secluded for typical Cleveland area homes. I wondered where I could have been taken. One man said I was given a small dose of a drug that knocked me out, so I must not have been out long, and we must not have gone far from town.

We approached the front door, and one man opened it. The air inside was warm and smelled like lemony wood polish. The men all toed off their boots and even mine were tugged off my feet and placed by the front door. I would need to grab them before I made a run for it. There was no way I'd make it very far on foot in the snow.

I was carried through to a formal looking room where I was deposited gently onto a couch. I peeked through my lashes and saw the men taking off their coats and one of them bringing the coats to the rack by the front door. From here, I could see into the foyer and the dining room. The walls were painted a warm cream color, and the doors were all framed in a dark, ornate wood. I could see a curling staircase leading to a second floor opposite the front door. Everything was clean and ornamental.

There was the sound of a cork coming out of a bottle, a

quiet glug of liquid being poured, and then murmured thanks between the men. They were quiet and I was sure they were staring at me, waiting. There was no point in staying fake unconscious when I could feel their eyeballs glued to me. But I would need to sell the wake up. I fluttered open my eyes and looked around for a second.

I gasped and then shrieked, "HELP!" as I stood up from the couch, almost tripping over a low wooden coffee table. The men jumped into action and rushed at me. I kicked and punched wildly at them as they grabbed me.

"FUCK! Again, with the fucking kneecaps! FUCK!" one of them said and collapsed onto the couch.

The bigger, more muscular one got me into a hold with my arms held over my head and unable to move against his body. I tried kicking back at him, but he dodged each blow. The third man stood in front of me, arms outstretched like he was trying to tame a lion. He was trying to talk to me as I screamed and kicked.

"We're not trying to hurt you," he was saying in a placating tone, trying to soothe me.

"You kidnapped me!" I snapped, my voice cracking and hoarse.

"Technically, you asked for it," the guy on the couch said in a snide tone. He was rubbing at his knee through his jeans.

The guy standing in front of me shot him a look. "What he means is that you called Harold to disappear."

"I thought he was getting me a new ID or something," I said breathlessly. "I thought he, like, rescued battered women, or something. Not trafficked them."

The two guys in front of me stared at me, expressionless.

"Right, well, that's not the case. So, welcome. You're not being trafficked, you were hired," the man standing in front of me said. He was tall like his friends and was lean and muscled. With his hands in his pockets, he had a natural power and ease to his body. He was wearing dark blue jeans, a burgundy Henley with the sleeves pushed up, and a gold watch around his wrist. His hair was a rich brown, his skin tan, and his eyes an amber brown. He looked me over warily as he spoke.

The guy behind me slowly relaxed his hold on me, and my muscles sagged in relief. He settled me on my feet and waited a moment to see if I'd run before standing next to his friend. He crossed his beefy arms over his even beefier chest and glared as if he didn't trust I wouldn't try to make a break for it past him and to the door.

"Hired?" I asked, aghast. "You need me to teach kindergarten?"

Injured guy on the couch snorted.

"Who are you?" I asked when nobody answered my question. Obviously, this was not a teaching position at all, and I was actually in trouble.

"I'm Devon," Mr. Amber Eyes said smoothly.

"Sterling," Mr. Muscles grunted out, still glaring suspiciously. His hair was jet black, and he had gray eyes that pierced as they glared. His skin was a pale white and tattoos peeked over the neckline of his black t-shirt and decorated his biceps and forearms. When he uncrossed and recrossed his arms, I saw tattoos on the backs of his hands.

Silence fell as I looked at the guy on the couch. He was massaging his knee and looking irritated. His auburn hair and beard were disheveled but clean. Blue eyes behind thick-rimmed glasses glanced up at me. "Milo," he said un-enthusiastically.

"Emily," I said back, quietly.

"We know," they said in unison, though with different inflections.

"Why?" I asked and tried not to gag.

"Harold and Victoria," Devon said, his eyes pinned on mine.

"Victoria was the one at the salon?" I asked.

"Yes," Devon replied.

"She hired me?"

"Yes."

"Why?"

"You applied."

"No, I don't think I did," I said with a soft chuckle.

"You said the magic words. You said you wanted to disappear."

"Do *all* magic words work with you? Can I click my heels and say, 'There's no place like home' and get to leave?"

Devon smirked at me, having not ended our eye contact. "You are home."

"This is not my home," I insisted.

"Oh, and Shady Pines Motel room 4 was home?" Milo asked condescendingly.

I glared at him and crossed my arms. "I'm not staying here, and I don't think I want this job."

"The job is yours and you don't get a say over whether you stay. You're staying," Sterling said, his voice cool and quiet though no less demanding than if he were yelling.

I swallowed. "That's literally kidnapping."

Devon shrugged, his hands still in his pockets. "Call it what you will, but you're not leaving."

A sob broke from my lips, and I trembled. "Gregory's going to-"

"Nothing. Impotent Mayor Ambrose is going to do *nothing*. Your divorce has gone viral in your town. Everyone knows you caught him screwing his secretary. People are calling for him to step down as mayor. He's got enough to worry about without tracking down his scorned ex-wife, who left signs of running away to Europe," Devon said calmly, but his words left me anything but soothed.

"Europe?" I asked, feeling a new blood rush of panic sweep through my veins. I clutched both of my hands around the neck of my cable knit cream turtleneck sweater like it was choking me. And it felt like it was- like I couldn't get enough air past my neck. Nobody was going to find me if they thought I ran off to Europe as part of a post-divorce public scandal crisis.

Devon shrugged again, and then checked his watch.

"Wait, how do you know so much?" I asked as a few of my brain cells not zinging around in panic came together.

"Emily Catherine Ambrose, maiden name Gardener, thirty-two years old. You're a kindergarten teacher, graduated from OSU with your master's in education nine years ago. You married your high school sweetheart. He then became the mayor of Shady Pines. You've recently stopped taking your birth control because you were trying to get pregnant-" Milo listed boredly on the couch.

"Okay, I get it. You're stalkers," I said exasperatedly and looked to the front door again.

"Not us, just him," Sterling said, gesturing to Milo. "And stop looking at the door. You're not going anywhere, sweetheart."

"Everyone gets a background check before they work with us," Milo said, slightly defensively.

Submitting for now, I sat down on the couch. I would wait until they thought I was comfortable and then I'd run for it. The couch was stiff, and the fabric design was bold stripes of jewel tones. There was no way this house was theirs.

"Who lives here?" I asked.

"Us," Devon said, and reclaimed his drink from the coffee table. Sterling took his and Milo's from a marble-topped bar that stood in the room's corner where they had been standing when I woke up.

"And who else?" I asked as Sterling handed Milo his drink and gestured for him to see his knee.

"Just us," Devon said, his voice echoing in his glass as he sat in a stiff-backed chair across from the couch. He crossed a leg over the other, his ankle atop his knee in a relaxed pose that still exuded power. Was he the leader of the three?

Sterling kneeled before Milo as Milo lifted his pant leg over his knee. His right knee was already bruised and swollen. Sterling pressed his fingers into the bruised flesh and Milo hissed at the painful contact. "You're benched," Sterling murmured.

"And it looks like your first day on the job is today," Devon announced with a furrow in his heavy brow. "Since you've injured one of the team, you get to work."

I stood by that injury. In fact, I'd injure the other two

as well, if given the chance. I stared at him, wide eyed and confused. "And who do I now work for?"

He closed his eyes with a brief sigh. "We work for... a family."

"No, not the mafia," I groaned and leaned back against the couch in a defeated slump.

Milo stared sideways at me as Sterling gently pulled his pant leg back down. "What do you know?"

"Literally nothing. Are you guys even Italian?" I asked, thinking only of the Godfather movies.

"Baby, it's twenty twenty-three. That's racist," Devon said with a cocky grin over the rim of his glass.

I flushed. "Sorry," I muttered. "I just figured... Deniro's Deli... the pepperoni."

"The fucking fifty-seven-dollar pepperoni," Milo snapped at me.

Devon shot him a look again before answering me. "Harold's family owns it. They've been around forever, but he's not our boss."

"Who is?" I asked.

Neither of them answered. Sterling went back to the bar and poured a glass of sparkling water. He handed it to me, and I set it on the coffee table. I had watched him break the seal on the glass bottle, but I still wasn't going to touch a single thing they gave me.

"Well, what is my job, then?" I asked hesitantly.

"Today? Driving," Milo grumbled.

4

Emily

A quiet Sterling led me up the stairs and down a hall. He walked close to me to ensure I wasn't about to turn and bolt. I was smarter than that, though. If we were going to be out of the house later and driving, I would have an opportunity then. The hallway overlooked the foyer and had potted plants in golden vases and gold framed artwork on the walls between doors. It was a long, wide hall, lit with chandeliers.

We passed two doors on the right and two on the left before Sterling stopped. "This will be your room," he said and opened the door.

"Not a locked room in the dungeon?" I asked sarcastically, my arms crossed over my chest.

He looked me over. "My suggestion for it was outvoted."

"Wait, there's- there's a dungeon?" I asked hesitantly.

He didn't reply, only opened the door and gestured for me

to enter. If I walked into that room, I was going to be locked in. I knew it. He knew it. I let my eyes meet his black lashed gray ones as I passed him into the room.

Sterling didn't say anything as I entered the room, only quirked a brow. Once in the room, I broke eye contact to look around. The room was beautiful and lavish. A large four-poster bed stood in the room, dark ornate wood like the rest of the house, with soft white linens and pillows. The floor was a light gray carpeting and felt plush beneath my socked feet. A huge TV was mounted on the wall across from the bed and a long dresser stretched beneath it. The far wall was all floor-length windows with a door leading out to a balcony. I could easily get out of the house and over the balcony at night. I walked to the door and found it to be nailed shut.

"Yeah, I wasn't going to risk it," Sterling said in a falsely apologetic voice.

"I... just wanted to see the view. This is a lovely house," I said through a dry throat.

"We're on almost six acres of property, most of it is wooded. Our neighbors also have multiple acres surrounding their homes. You would be lost in the woods in the freezing temperatures before you would ever stumble upon someone willing to help you," he said in a voice with no feeling.

"Understood," I whispered.

"There's a bathroom through there. Someone will give you a tour soon. Don't kill yourself while I'm gone," he said in the same unfeeling voice, and then left the room.

"Wait!" I said and dove towards the door, but he had it closed before I got there. I heard the click of a lock, and I whirled around back towards the room with a panicked sob and a gag.

My heart and lungs constricted in my chest, and I felt like I couldn't breathe. With a hand clutching at the neck of my sweater, I looked around the room for anything I could use as a weapon.

The room was bare of anything that wasn't a piece of large furniture or bed linen. The drawers were empty and clean. Two doors stood closed on either side of the large bed. I had been too distracted by the door to the balcony to notice them there before. Rushing to them, I found one to be for a large, empty, walk-in closet and the other to an ensuite bathroom. It was large, containing a toilet, sink, a spacious shower, and a soaking tub. The walls were a white marble with black and gold veins throughout, making the room feel like a luxurious spa. Glass mostly surrounded the shower, as much of the far wall was floor to ceiling windows like in the bedroom. The tub and shower were in front of the window, and I cringed at the thought of showering or taking a bath in full view of the back patio and yard. There was a mirror above the sink, and I thought about breaking the mirror to use the glass as a weapon when I ran tonight.

I shut the door behind me and pulled my sleeve over my fist. I took a deep breath and swung at the glass. I hit at it with all my strength three or four times and the only thing broken was the skin on my knuckles. Tears of frustration and pain gathered in my eyes, and I leaned against the sink. I let myself wallow for a minute while I regrouped. Lifting my head, my eyes settled on the shower head. It was one that could be handheld on a hose or stationary. I could probably unscrew it from the faucet and swing it to break the glass and as a weapon itself. I rushed into the shower and found where the head was attached and started unscrewing the metal fittings with my hands.

I almost had it detached when there was a sound at the door, and it swung open. Milo stood there looking irritated and disappointed, his weight on his good leg. "Nope. Back away."

"How'd you know?" I asked, my hands dropping to my sides.

He held up his phone. On the screen was the video feed of a camera somewhere above the door in this bathroom. The back of his head was visible on the bottom of the screen. I looked up and saw a small camera above the door frame.

"That's disgusting!" I snapped at him.

He shrugged. "Well, if you were going to use it to break glass to hurt me or my brothers, then it's a necessary part of our security."

Sterling appeared at the door holding the duffle bag I had put in my car before I was taken. "Harold dropped this off. Do you have anything... dark?"

"Um," I said and took the duffle bag with a jerk. I thought about what I had packed. "I have a green shirt and black leggings."

Sterling rolled his ice gray eyes and gestured for me to follow him. Sliding past Milo, I followed Sterling out of the bathroom, through my room, and down the hall to the next door. He opened the door and led me into what I assumed to be his bedroom. While the rest of the house was ornate and very traditional, Sterling's room was dark and cold. He had thick black curtains over the windows, a balcony door along the back wall, and a bed in the same spot as my room. His bed had a black metal headboard peppered with dents that made the room feel aggressive. Black and navy linens and clothes littered the bed and the floor. The only personal items in the room were his clothes, a small jewelry box, a few books and magazines on the nightstand, and a black satiny box on the entertainment table below the tv. He went into his closet and quickly came out with a black long-sleeved t-shirt. "Wear this with the leggings. Get changed and we'll give you a tour," he said and walked me back to my room.

I rummaged through the duffel on my bed, wondering if there was anything in my bag that could be a weapon, while feigning to look for the leggings. I could spray my perfume in someone's eyes, or my razor could slice, I realized, as I located my toiletry bag. My hands shook as I unzipped the bag. I felt eyes on me as Sterling watched me look for my leggings.

"Do you think I would have left anything in there that could hurt us?" Milo scoffed at me as he came out of my bathroom with the shower head attachment in his hand.

He was right. My perfume and razor were both gone. I sighed and pulled out the leggings as Milo left the room, leaving me and Sterling.

I carried the leggings and shirt into the bathroom and as I moved to shut the door, Sterling caught it with a slap of his hand to the wood. Fear made my breath catch in my throat as I spun to look up at him. He leaned down to see me almost eye to eye, and he smirked down his nose at me. His eyes squinting into a self-satisfied expression. "Keep the door open," he said in a low voice.

"What does it matter? You creeps have cameras in here anyway," I said with a trembling voice.

His smirk deepened as his eyes darted between mine. His lashes were long and in stark contrast with his pale skin. If I wasn't able to see every single lash this close, I may have wondered if he was wearing mascara. "Like you were told earlier, Milo is the creep, not me."

I stepped back from him. "Can you at least turn away?"

He turned his body so his side was to me. I swallowed and quickly changed into the new outfit. He took my discarded clothes from me. "Now you can't hang yourself," he said and shut the bathroom door, giving me some privacy. I used the toilet and washed my hands, hoping Milo wasn't watching me but desperate to empty my bladder.

When I emerged from the bathroom, Sterling was going through my duffle. I opened my mouth to argue with him, but snapped it shut. There was no use in fighting him. There wasn't anything super personal in there, anyway. I had been prepared to disappear, after all.

I was silent, hugging myself around my middle until Sterling walked me through the house. He didn't tell me where Milo or Devon's bedrooms were, but he showed me the gym and sauna at the end of the same hall as the bedrooms, and then back down the stairs to the formal dining room, the hearth room we had been in earlier, the living room, and then the kitchen. The home was built on a hill and had levels like a split-level home where two floors walked out onto a ground level patio. There was a lower floor with a game room and an enormous office. The grounds were snow covered, but an in-ground pool and a large red brick patio spanned the back of the house. An outdoor fireplace stood along the side, with couches and chairs covered with tarps. The yard was large and surrounded by thick trees. Sterling explained each room and area of the property, letting me know I could go to the gym if I preferred, but the sauna was off limits. I was not shown the basement, but if Sterling hadn't lied about dungeons, then I definitely had no interest.

We ended the tour, going into what he had pointed out to me as the office. Milo and Devon were there, talking already. Milo sat at the large wooden desk in the bookshelf lined, maroon painted room. It felt like a set from an old movie, and I wondered again why the house was decorated how it was. Devon was leaning over the back of Milo's chair as they both looked at one of two computer monitors.

They both looked up when Sterling and I entered. I tugged awkwardly on the too long sleeves of Sterling's Irish spring soap scented shirt as Devon's eyes slowly looked me over. When he got back up to my face, he glanced at Sterling and quirked a brow.

"She owns nothing dark," Sterling grumbled as he crossed his thick arms over his chest.

Milo and Sterling were both now wearing long sleeve black sweaters to match Sterling's, and I realized this was a uniform of sorts.

"Are we burglars?" I asked, horrified.

Neither one answered me, but I swore Sterling's lips twitched as if fighting a smile.

"We're set. He sent the list," Milo said to Sterling.

"You sure you want her to drive?" Sterling asked.

"I'll stay in the car with her," Milo replied, and leaned back in his chair, the top of his head brushing Devon's chest.

"Am I the getaway driver?" I asked, trembling again. I fought to stifle a gag.

"We'll take the van," Devon said to the others. "We need extra cover."

The van turned out to be a small, presumably stolen or fake, Amazon box truck. They shoved me into the back of the truck with Sterling while Devon drove, and injured Milo claimed the passenger seat. I sat criss cross applesauce on the metal floor of the truck with my back to the front wall of the truck and Sterling sat beside me, legs outstretched. Devon drove for about twenty minutes before he stopped and opened the door at the back.

"Come here," he said and let me out.

I was shaking as I followed him to the driver's side door of the truck. He opened it and shoved lightly until I was climbing in. Milo handed a loop of chain over my lap to Devon and my throat constricted in panic. "I don't want to do this, but I need you to not run away," Devon muttered to me as he wrapped the chain around my lap and around the car seat.

I didn't know what to say, so I remained quiet and trembling. Devon looked me over and rolled his eyes like this was the worst idea ever before shutting the door. If this was so terrible, then why were they making me do this? It was clear none of them desired this so like... maybe let me go?

Devon and Sterling went into the building they parked us in front of. I didn't recognize it, as we were in a part of the city I'd never been to. There were no streetlights and it looked like a row of storage garages. I rolled down the window and tried to listen to hear if I was near the highway or Lake Erie. But I couldn't hear much other than distant traffic sounds. Was that enough traffic to be the highway? Could I make it to the highway if I could slip out of the chains?

"We will do multiple stops, but you and I will wait in the truck," Milo said and scrolled on his phone. I couldn't see what he was doing on the glowing screen, but I hoped it distracted him enough for me to slip from the chains.

I hesitated for too long, and soon Sterling and Devon were returning to the truck. One of them knocked on the van wall, startling me.

"Drive to this location," Milo said, and pointed to the GPS screen on the mounted tablet between us.

Slowly and extra carefully, I navigated the truck to what appeared to be a mechanic's shop a few blocks over. Devon and Sterling hopped out of the van and went in. I listened out the window to hear the definite sound of the highway. My heart pounded in my chest as I slouched in the seat so I could slide out of the bottom of the chains. If I could get out of the truck, I could outrun Milo on his injured knee. I sucked in my belly and slid halfway out while Milo scrolled on his phone again.

"Stop," he said in an annoyed tone and then brandished a gleaming black gun.

My blood ran cold, and I got back into my seat properly. I didn't see Sterling or Devon get back into the truck, and the sharp knock against the wall made me yelp. Milo swore under his breath and rubbed his ear.

Without needing to be told, I drove to the next location. This time, I froze while we waited. The fear of seeing the weapon in Milo's hand made my body lock up. He wrapped his long index finger around the trigger guard of the gun on his dark denim clad lap. I tore my eyes away from his hand just as Devon and Sterling came sprinting out of what looked like an office building this time. Sterling was holding a backpack and a gun. He was running and shooting backwards, much like Devon was as they approached the truck.

"Go, go, go!" Milo shouted, looking into the side mirrors. I heard the back door slam shut, and I stomped on the gas. The tires squealed as I sped away from the bullets that were peppering the truck.

I screamed as a bullet smashed the glass of the passenger window and planted itself in the dashboard. Panicking, I took a hard right. I heard two thumps on the side of the truck.

A roaring engine was catching up to us as fewer and fewer bullets hit the truck. I took a hard left turn and heard two thumps against the truck again. I heard screaming from Devon or Sterling. Were they shot?

"Go straight," Milo directed me.

I followed his instruction as the sound of the engine pursuing us advanced.

"Right, coming up... don't signal you *dumbass!* Now right!" Milo shouted.

Thump thump.

"Never driving again!" shouted Devon, his voice muffled through the truck's walls.

I realized with a start and a gag that the thumping sounds were Devon and Sterling being bounced around the back of the truck like bowling balls. Over six feet tall, lethal, and bossy bowling balls. If they weren't dead back there, then they were for sure going to kill me. I gagged a few times, my eyes watering, and swiped at the moisture on my face. I glanced at Milo, who was aiming his gun out of the window and firing shot after shot. His muscular back was stretched and his braced knee was still in place with his leg extended.

A few more erratic turns, vicious cursing from the van, and a reload for Milo later and they declared us to have lost our pursuers. Milo directed me back to the mansion, and I learned it was just outside of Cleveland, hidden away from sight. He typed on his phone the entire time and barely looked up to give me driving directions.

I parked outside of the garage and shook the chains anxiously and impatiently. Milo snorted a rude laugh at my expense. Furious, and rather disheveled, Devon and Sterling appeared at the driver's side door, and I locked it on impulse.

"You're just going to make them madder," Milo advised, as one of them tugged on the door.

"Well, it slowed them down," I muttered.

"Keep playing with fire and see what they do to little brats," Milo said, his voice deep and teasing.

I slid my eyes over to him. "What's that supposed to mean?"

Sterling pounded on the glass and shouted for me to open the door. His angry breath fogged the glass like a bull.

Milo only shrugged with a mocking grin.

Sterling's eyes were blazing with anger, the gray like a high heat flame. Devon's eyes were thunderous and threatening, like he was just waiting to dole out a punishment. I let out a breath and unlocked the door. Sterling practically ripped the door from the hinges. His anger was palpable and made the air taste like metal. Devon's anger simmered and scared me more. He approached me with the key to the chains as Sterling walked around to help the injured Milo out of the van.

Devon unlocked the padlock near my waist and the anger was coming off of him in waves like summer sun off asphalt. It made my entire body feel hot. His skin was smooth and caramel colored, black stubble on his jaw, and he wore a woodsy cologne. His composure made him seem more dangerous than the explosively mad Sterling. "Please don't hurt me," I whispered through a quivering jaw.

He looked up, mildly shocked. His honey eyes were startlingly bright in the garage lights. "Why do you think I would listen to you?"

He yanked me out of the van and into the house and a whimper caught in my throat. Devon stomped us into the kitchen, his hand clamped on my biceps in a tight hold. He practically threw me down to the floor in the kitchen and I stumbled to regain my footing. "Make us dinner."

"No," I insisted and crossed my arms. "And don't touch me like that."

"If you don't cook, you don't eat," he gritted out just as my stomach growled. I had been hungry going into the deli this afternoon and that was now almost six hours ago.

I sighed and opened the refrigerator to find it full of ingredients. Maybe being forced to cook wasn't as bad as being locked in a dungeon or killed. I wondered if I could poison them. Not to kill them outright, but maybe some salmonella to keep them sick so I could run. "Who normally cooks?"

"We had a cook."

"Where are they now?" I asked and opened the walk-in pantry.

"Elsewhere. We don't need them now that we have you," Devon said coolly as he sat at the bar seat of the kitchen island.

I whirled around. "Am I your cook or your getaway driver?"

A corner of his mouth twitched up. "You're surely not driving again. You almost killed Sterling and I."

Oddly, I felt embarrassed, and I shifted on my feet. "That wasn't intentional."

"I know, that's why you're alive," he said in that same cool voice.

Exhaling, I turned to the refrigerator again. If I was going to run or fight my way out of here, I would need to eat. And I would like to be the one that cooked the food I ate. There were some fresh chicken thighs in the fridge, and I took out the package. I rummaged around the kitchen and found a heavy cast iron pan, the spice cabinet, and utensils. Lifting the skin on the chicken, I shoved in some salted butter and a few sprigs of fresh thyme. I got the pan heating on the stove under the scrutiny of Devon. I didn't see Milo or Sterling, but I heard their voices somewhere in the house.

With Devon watching so closely, I wasn't able to poison the food. But my stomach growled, and I fell into the comforting domestic tasks of cooking and preparing a meal. I finished the meal in the pristine oven with some fresh asparagus and some small roasted potatoes.

As I was setting the table, my heart clenched in sadness. I had wanted this comfortable domesticity with Gregory. I had wanted to be cooking his meals and setting his table for the rest of my life. But here I was, kidnapped after a nasty divorce, making dinner for my mafia captors. I set four spaces at the table, hoping I'd be allowed to eat with them. Did I enjoy their company? No. Did I need to learn about their organization so that I could report it to the police when I escaped? Yes. So, I set the steaming cast iron on a trivet on the dining table, straightened the silverware, and called out, "Dinner's ready!"

Milo and Sterling came into the room, eyeing me and Devon warily before they sat at the table. They took the sides, leaving Devon and me to take the host and hostess seats. I hesitated before sitting down after the men. It was possible they were not aware of the etiquette of seating arrangements, but it was odd to be kidnapped and then sat at the hostess place at the dinner table.

The men fell into coded talk about their work almost instantly as they served themselves from the food. I served myself and settled into my seat to see Devon watching me as he cut into his food. He took a bite and then they all looked at me. Okay, maybe they understood some etiquette. I took a bite of the food and while it all smelled fantastic; I tasted none of it. Nerves, exhaustion, and adrenaline had it tasting like paper in my mouth. Once I had taken my bite, Milo and Sterling ate as well.

I was silent the entire meal, only observing them and listening. The people who were shooting at us were upset about paying their dues after a financially hard month. The truck I had been driving was to be dumped as it was damaged and was seen speeding through town. The rest of the pickups were being handled by another team since this team was busy indoctrinating a new employee. Me.

When dinner was done, I packed up leftovers and did the

dishes. All while being watched by Sterling. "Am I just going to be your maid and cook now?" I asked him.

"Isn't that what you were to the mayor?" he asked.

"I was a kindergarten teacher," I corrected him with a blush of shame.

"We're trying to figure out where you fit. You can't drive for shit, but you can cook and clean. Can you shoot?" he asked.

I shrugged. "I've never done it."

Sterling looked amused. "Cooking and cleaning it is."

"You could always let me leave," I muttered.

"Apparently, that's not an option," he replied, his un-enthused tone the same as mine.

I finished my task in silence and set the dishwasher to run. Sterling grabbed my arm as soon as I finished. "No," I said instinctively in the same demanding Teacher Voice I used on my students when I meant business. "You will remove your hands from me."

Sterling hesitated and glanced back to where Devon stood in the doorway. "It's time for you to go to your room," he said in explanation.

"I can walk on my own," I insisted. "Hands are not for grabbing others."

Sterling curled his hands into balls at his sides and he looked very much like someone who was literally made to use his hands for grabbing others. His jaw clenched, and he glanced back to Devon, who gave a small shrug and shake of his head. "Fine, let's go," he grumbled.

"Let's go, *please*," I coached as I started walking to the stairs.

Sterling followed me up the stairs and to my room, where he locked me in. I wanted to shower, but the shower head was still missing. A bath would have to suffice. I didn't want to bathe when I knew there was a camera up in the corner, so I took a washcloth and tried tossing it to block the lens. After a few tries, I was successful, and I turned to get undressed and fill the tub. There was an assortment of lovely smelling soaps in a cabinet, and I chose one with a calming lavender and vanilla scent. Maybe the men would be calmed by the aromatherapy and wouldn't be so mean when they were around me.

I was just sinking into the bubbles when the door opened. I shrieked and dropped all the way under the suds to hide my body. Sterling stood there, a cruel grin on his face, while I panicked and the water sloshed.

"Milo says you covered the camera. I'm here to make sure you don't drown yourself," he said.

"I- I'm not. Get out!" I insisted.

"Either I watch you here, or Milo watches you on the camera," he said.

I shook my head. Sterling scared me and Milo could record me and exploit images of my body or something. Neither one felt safer than the other.

"You're both creeps," I said and slid down further in the bubbles so only my head was visible.

Sterling shrugged and then leaned against the sink.

"I will not kill myself. I would feel much better if you removed the camera from the bathroom," I said evenly.

"I'll run your request past the guys," he said simply.

I sighed and washed quickly, dunking my head back to get my hair wet. I washed my hair and was rinsing when Sterling spoke. He was facing the wall and not looking at me directly, and I appreciated his privacy. His phone buzzed, and he looked down.

"What is your clothing and shoe size? Milo is shopping," Sterling said.

"Why?" I asked.

"Because you work with us now and we have an image to uphold. And Miss Frizzle-chic is not part of that image," he explained.

"So, you think I look chic?" I teased. I knew my clothes were a cross between 90's schoolteacher and Hillary Clinton pantsuits with a splash of kid patterns- I was a kindergarten teacher and the wife of a mayor after all.

Sterling shot me a not amused look before settling back on his phone.

I answered the questions and finished bathing. It seemed like they responded more favorably to me when I wasn't showing my fear. When I responded to their bossiness rather than cowering, they reacted less aggressively. I would have to remember to keep my genuine emotions hidden.

Sterling remained respectful as I changed into my pajamas and brushed my hair and teeth. I let my damp hair tangle around my shoulders since they did not trust me to use a hair dryer yet. When I went into the bedroom, I turned to say goodnight. But Sterling was pulling a high-backed, uphol-stered chair from the small sitting area to be between my bed and the door.

"What are you doing?" I asked warily.

"You're not allowed to be alone," he said dryly as he plopped into the seat.

"Why?"

"Because you'll run."

"What if I pinky promise not to?"

Sterling smiled but it was far from kind. "Cute."

"The door is locked, why do you have to stay?" I questioned.

"A precaution," he said bitterly, like he hated this as much as I did.

I rolled my eyes and got into bed. I faced away from him and looked out the windows. The windows overlooked the back patio below and framed the trees on the property. I watched branches sway and listened to Sterling's even breathing as he scrolled on his phone as I fell asleep.

5

Sterling

Fucking Bambi-eyed housewife. That's all she was. A naïve, big eyed, damsel in distress with no spine. The sun streaming into her room woke me before it woke her, and I stared at her sleeping form. She wore a soft gray pajama set with an actual collar and buttons down the front. How sleeping in business casual wear was comfortable, I'd never know. The only pajamas I'd ever seen on a woman were silky lingerie that I promptly ripped off. Did the mayor douche have a kink for formal wear?

My phone buzzed where it was wedged between my thigh and the chair I still slouched in. Picking it up, I rolled my stiff neck and reveled in the pops and snaps. It was Milo asking if "she" was awake.

"Not yet," I typed my reply and stood up to stretch.

"Devon wants her to make breakfast," Milo's lighting quick

reply came. All of his replies were inhumanly quick. The man typed like the keys were connected to his brain and not being pressed by his fingers.

I stood and stretched out my muscles, and my stomach rumbled. Bambi had made us a good dinner last night, but I didn't trust her with breakfast. If she made some egg white omelet or granola bullshit, I would drop her off at Victoria's myself. I bet the mayor ate fucking oatmeal.

"Hey!" I barked out in a rasp. "Wake up."

She sat upright with a start and a gasp. Her hand fluttered to her chest like a fucking Disney princess. "Sterling!" she gasped in shock as her big blue eyes landed on me. A weaker man would apologize for scaring her.

"It's time for you to make breakfast," I demanded and strode to her door.

"Wait, let me..." she said and looked to the bathroom.

"Fine," I grunted out and shook my head to show I was annoyed.

I let her do her business alone, realizing with a bit of a shock that I had trusted her to go somewhere unattended. It was her big dumb eyes, making her look trustworthy and innocent. Fucking Bambi.

In the kitchen, Dev and Milo were already sipping coffee, and Milo slid a mug towards me. I nodded my thanks, but he didn't see me because of his precise cataloging of Emily. Dev and Milo were both sitting at the kitchen island bar stools, and I sat on the remaining one. Emily rubbed her eyes and looked around the kitchen.

"What-" she started and then cleared the sleep from her voice. "What do you normally eat for breakfast?"

I snorted and trusted the guys to tell her what to make, and I headed to the bathroom. When I came back, she was already busy cracking eggs, and a slab of bacon sat on the counter. As I reclaimed my seat next to Milo, I bumped my thigh against his. He looked up from his ever-present laptop and quirked a questioning brow from behind his glasses. I pretended to pop the imaginary collar on my black t-shirt with a pinched, haughty expression. Milo's full lips curled in a smile, and he glanced at Emily, who was concentrating on her cooking. He mouthed words at me instead of speaking, "What the fuck is that? Is that suburban lingerie?"

I snorted into my coffee mug. "The mayor has a matching pair," I mouthed back to him.

Milo huffed out a laugh, his blue eyes crinkled at the corners. "Do you think she's wearing panties under all that?"

I was about to answer that yes, she was, and they're tastefully beige, when a throat clearing caught my attention. Emily and Devon were both looking at us. Milo's thigh pressed hard into mine as he looked down at his laptop with a serious expression, as if he was looking at the stock reports and not the front page of Reddit. I pushed my thigh back into his more forcefully and took a sip of my coffee while making direct eye contact with Emily.

"If you two are done giggling about my pajamas, could you please tell me which cheese you like in your scrambled eggs?" Emily asked, as if it hadn't bothered her.

"Whatever you have," Milo grumbled, his eyes still on the screen.

Dev looked at us in warning. He loved to pretend to be our leader at every opportunity. Just because his parents were alive, he'd been bred to take over the family business. Milo's uncle, Matthew, and Devon's dad, Anthony, were the leaders of our family. Matthew had argued that since he adopted Milo and Milo's sister when they were toddlers, they should be equal to Devon in the business. But Anthony's connections and strength had squashed that notion from the beginning. I, on the other hand, had never been one to want leadership. Anthony and Stephanie adopted me when my parents were murdered and I was only a few months old. I was raised as Devon's brother in every way but blood and rank in the business. It was never an option to believe I was equal to Devon in the business, so I never felt the conflict like Milo did. I owed my life to Devon's parents, but that didn't mean I had to put up with his superior attitude bullshit. I gave him the finger, and he turned back to watching Emily cook like she was about to poison us at any moment.

As she cooked, I watched Milo's screen as he pulled up my account on Personal Cameras, a paid subscription-based content website. While the family business had paid me well, all of my success had been paved by Anthony and Stephanie's connections and influence. The only thing that was mine was my body and the work I put into it. So, I used it to make money on the side. Money nobody else could claim as theirs.

Except maybe Milo, because he edited, posted, and managed my content pages. But I paid him for his work. He grinned over at me as he highlighted the number of new subscribers my last video brought in. Three hundred new subscribers paid the first month of ten dollars a month subscription to my content based on a video I made jerking off while wearing a Santa Claus outfit.

"Dude, no way!" I whispered excitedly to him.

Devon looked over to see the website and shook his head and returned to his eagle-eyed watch of Emily. Devon knew about my content and didn't care much about it. Milo clicked on the Santa video and scrolled, muted, to the exact moment in the video where I was leaned against the fireplace in the hearth room, bare chest heaving, and my cock in my fist shooting come into my fake Santa beard. "Ho, ho, ho," Milo said with a chuckle. Of course, he knew the timestamp for the video. He was the one who edited it and posted it. It wasn't as if he'd been watching it on his own.

I chuckled back and finished my coffee. "I'll film another today," I whispered.

"Another Santa one?" Milo asked.

I shrugged. "Maybe an elf?"

"You should ride this wave and do some more marketing shots for social media, too," Milo said, and signed into a few of my accounts.

"Hm," was all I could say while I watched Emily plate up our breakfast. She slid the plates on the island toward each of us. A proud little smile played on her lips. I frowned and accepted the silverware she slid over next.

Maybe I was the worst person to judge, but did she really want to be some douchebag's housewife for the rest of her life? Sure, she was a kindergarten teacher before coming to us, but something told me that was just until the mayor knocked her up. Devon's mom, Stephanie, and Victoria were the only adult women I'd known growing up, and they were just as involved in the business as the men. They weren't involved with the more violent parts of the business, but they were still integral to the operations. I remember Stephanie had taken a step back while Devon and I were young to care for us, but once we were in school, she picked back up. Emily probably wanted an easy life where her husband made all the decisions and all she had to do was raise babies and cook and... grow flowers or some shit. I had yet to see the value in her working for us other than to replace our cleaning and cooking staff.

"What did you cook Mr. Mayor for breakfast?" I asked her as she stood at the counter and nibbled on a piece of toast with jam.

Emily winced, like thinking of him was painful. "Um, well, he normally made his own breakfast. He liked to make a green juice."

"A what?" Milo asked with a scowl.

"You know, a juice made with celery and spinach and fruit." Emily shrugged.

"The man *juiced*?" I asked, appalled.

Emily let a little smirk through. "The man *juiced*."

"No wonder he couldn't knock you up. He was too weak from the lack of food," I scoffed and took a big bite of eggs and bacon. The girl could cook.

"If a man empties himself of sperm too often, he doesn't produce enough strong swimmers to impregnate a woman. More than likely, he was probably fucking his secretary too much," Milo said matter-of-factly, without taking his eyes off his computer. He took a bite of his food and continued to type in a comment section.

Emily dropped her toast to her plate, and her eyes filled with tears. They didn't fall, but her lower lip trembled. She bit it and blinked away the tears from her Bambi eyes. Nice job, Milo.

Devon slid his empty plate back towards her on the island as he stood up. He was already dressed in a suit, and he tugged it into place as he spoke to Emily. "I have business to attend to this morning. I expect to find the gym cleaned, and the laundry done by the time I return."

Emily nodded forlornly as she gathered his dishes.

"Who are you meeting with?" Milo asked, his eyes detaching from his screen to cock an eyebrow at Devon.

"An associate," he replied, and glanced at Emily.

"I understand, but what is it regarding?" Milo muttered to Devon while Emily was running water at the sink, rinsing off Devon's plate.

"There's a new family in town and my father wants to discuss our next steps," Devon said under his breath.

Milo's spine stiffened next to me, and I took a deep, steadying breath. "Do you think it's going to be a war?"

Devon gave a small shrug and shook his head. "I don't know yet."

"We should go with you," Milo insisted.

Devon glanced at Emily again in answer.

Milo shook his head angrily and went back to his computer, typing furiously.

"I'll fill you in when I get back," Devon said, and left.

"Is he your leader?" Emily asked, breaking the angry silence encompassing me and Milo.

"No," Milo snapped at the same time I said, "Sort of."

Emily raised her eyebrows and put her hands up like she

could tell she said the wrong thing before clearing the rest of the dishes.

Sensing more tension in Milo, I clapped a hand on his shoulder and squeezed as I stood up. He sighed and his shoulders relaxed a bit at my show of affection.

"So, um, do I just go into your rooms and get your laundry?" Emily asked hesitantly.

"No," Milo said tersely. "I'll set it outside my door."

"You can go into my room. I locked all my weapons up." I shrugged.

"I wasn't going to look for a weapon," Emily insisted.

Milo snorted.

"I wasn't!" she insisted again, more forcefully.

I left them to squabble and got ready for my workout. There was a tripod in the gym to use when I filmed in there or took some muscle shots. My muscle pictures and videos did well on social media and brought people to my Personal Cameras page. I heard movement in the house when I was headed to the gym from my room. Emily was supposed to clean in there, so I figured I'd just watch for her when she came in. Milo was with her and wouldn't let her out of the house. Or his sight, for that matter. Whether he was in the room with her or watching her on the cameras was another story.

I set my phone up on the tripod in front of my bench and I was posing with a weight when Emily came in. My phone snapped a picture of my steel gaze and bulging muscles.

"What are you doing?" she asked like she was about to laugh.

"None of your business."

"Are you taking... selfies?" A giggle escaped her, and she

pressed her little fingers to her lips like she could hold the sound in.

I glared as my phone snapped another. "Aren't you supposed to be doing laundry?"

She held up the cleaning caddy in her hand. "Cleaning the gym."

"Stay out of my shot," I grumbled and posed for another timed picture.

She pulled her pink lips into her mouth like she was fighting another giggle. Fucking hell. She moved towards the far side of the gym, out of my shot, and got to work.

I put on some music while I worked out and took pictures and videos. While I worked out, my mind was focused on what Devon had said this morning about another family business moving into town. If it was direct competition for our businesses, legal or otherwise, we'd have huge issues, and it would end up in war. If we didn't have direct business competition, then we'd probably still have beef with them because we'd be sharing resources. And as far as I was aware, this family didn't share well. After being lost in thought, I glimpsed Emily in the room and was startled to remember she was there. She was idly wiping down a bench, but her eyes were on me.

Emily's eyes were slightly hooded, and she was licking her pink lower lip as she watched me. I smirked and decided to take a turn in the mood of the pictures I was taking. Nobody was entirely immune to my show of muscles and tattoos- even prim, suburban bitches with broom handles up their asses. I sat up on my bench and took a long drink of water from my water bottle before taking off my t-shirt. I used the cotton to mop up my sweat while smoldering at the camera. Moving to the mats and angling my phone down, I did a round of push-ups, complete with grunts and a few growls of effort. The mirror was in front of me, and I could see Emily staring at me, no longer wiping down the bench.

Her mouth was open as she watched me with lust in her eyes. I doubted she even knew what she was doing. Getting her all worked up was... exhilarating. I wanted to push it even further. I picked up my boxing gloves and moved to the punching bag. There was no need to bring the camera this time because she would be in my shot. It didn't matter; I had enough content for a few days. She shuffled around a little as she realized she'd stopped cleaning. She moved over to the treadmill and started wiping down the machine. I still felt her eyes on me. After swinging a few punches, I glanced over to see her standing with her legs crossed. Like she was desperate for some pressure on her pussy. Desperate for contact. Seeing her like that had my cock twitching, and I adjusted myself with my boxing glove. Fuck.

I swung a few more punches before my cock was straining against my boxer briefs. This pair was tight enough that she likely wouldn't notice, but I was uncomfortable. I ripped off my gloves and went to my phone. My videos and photos had been automatically uploading to my cloud storage, so Milo already had the footage I shot. I sent him a message telling him I was headed to the sauna and then a shower, so he was on Emily duty. When he replied to say he was on it, I stripped out of my shorts and boxer briefs, flashing my ass to Emily. I walked and then acted like I'd just remembered her there. "Oh, Emily," I said and looked over my shoulder. "Milo's watching you while I'm in the sauna and shower."

Her eyes were glued to my ass, and her cheeks were flaming red. "O-okay," she said hoarsely, and then turned back to her work.

I grinned and headed into the sauna with my phone and tripod, sure to keep my ass to her so she couldn't see my erection. After quickly setting up and hitting record, I entered the shot in only a fluffy white towel. I sat down with my legs spread in front of me, eyes intense on the camera. "Hey baby, that was a great workout. It really got my blood pumping," I said and rubbed my hand down the towel over my aching cock. "I'm so glad you chose me to be your personal trainer."

Typically, I planned out my role plays, but this one came naturally to me. I needed to come soon, so a quick video was on the table. "After a good workout, I like to come in here and relax. Sometimes I even touch myself. Is it okay if I do that now? Oh, you're going to watch? That's okay, I like an audience."

Opening my towel, I took my cock into my fist and squeezed with a groan. I stared directly into the camera as I spit into my palm and used it as lube. Going slow wasn't an option today and my fist pumped faster and faster. The slick sound of my hand on my cock and my breathing filled the sauna. I moaned, deep and long, and tried to slow down. But I was heading towards a huge release. There was no stopping now. I felt my abs contract as I was nearing my orgasm. I had dropped the role play at this point and was just chanting "Fuck yes," and grunting. My head tilted back, and I thought about Emily coming in and seeing me like this. Fuck. It had been a few weeks since I'd gotten laid, and I didn't think I would be able to stop myself from telling her to get on her knees while I finished in her pink mouth. Her blue Bambi eyes would look up at me with a shocked lust as she swallowed me down.

My hips were coming off the sauna bench with every thrust, and the arm that was behind me, holding my weight, was trembling. I gave three more straining thrusts into my fist, accompanied by deep growls, before I came all over my chest. It felt like it just kept coming and coming, my abs contracting and releasing over and over as come coated my sweaty skin. I let out one last grunt as I fell back against the bench, my chest heaving. My body trembled, and I laid down along the bamboo. As my come dripped down my sides, I chuckled. I blinked at the camera. "I, uh-" my voice was raspy and I cleared my throat. "I forgot what the roleplay was. Oh well, that was fucking huge." I laughed and reached up to hit stop so it would upload to the cloud.

I sent Milo a quick text that there was new content and then wiped up with the towel. When I exited the sauna, I tossed the towel in the laundry basket with a smirk before heading for a shower.

6

Emily

I could hear water starting in the shower that I had cleaned while Sterling was working out. He had been so focused on what he was doing that he didn't hear me move around. Of course, that was before I got distracted with watching his muscles bulge and flex under his glistening, sweaty skin... I shook my head. This was ridiculous. This man was essentially holding me hostage, and I was staring at his body like an animal. I sighed in irritation and finished wiping down the equipment that he had used and picked up the few towels that were in the laundry basket outside the sauna. The one Sterling was going to use after his shower would have to wait until the next load.

Carrying the used towels and cleaning caddy with me, I looked around the room for Milo's camera. I located one above the mirrored wall. "Milo, I'm headed to the laundry," I called out to him in case he was listening. One towel under my arm felt wet and warm and I shuddered, thinking what could be on that towel. I tossed the towels into a basket and headed to the laundry in the basement. Milo had shown me to the dark basement and told me to stick to the laundry room if I knew what was good for me.

The laundry room was down a hall in the basement. Three metal doors lined a metal wall on one side and the entire space emanated a horror movie-like chill. Something deep within my brain stem said that horrible things happened in those three rooms. A fourth room was an outdated bathroom, and the fifth was the laundry room. Both the laundry room and the little half bath had normal walls and floors and doors- furthering my suspicion that the metal rooms were not part of the original floor plan. I bet a family would love to have this space as a den with a pool table or something. I put the laundry in the washing machine and then made a quick stop in the bathroom.

As I sat on the toilet, I looked around for Milo's camera. I didn't see one anywhere in the small space. They probably didn't think about this room much if they had a cleaning staff before me. I swiped a finger over the toilet tank, and it came back dusty. My heart pounded in my chest as I washed my hands. The sink was on top of a small cabinet and the mirror above the sink was the front of a medicine cabinet. I didn't know what I was looking for- a weapon, a clue of these guys' crimes to tell the police, a key to get out, *anything*. Ripping open the medicine cabinet, I shuffled through the old and yellowing packages of bandages and antiseptics. Nothing I could use there. I dropped to my knees and opened the cabinet below the sink. There was a plunger, an old bottle of toilet bowl cleaner, a stack of toilet paper rolls, and a few yellowed boxes of laxatives. I sat back on my heels and stared disappointedly. They didn't care about this room because there was nothing of value to me in here.

Finishing up in the basement, I headed upstairs and was met by Milo in the kitchen. He was grinning in a way that said Trouble as he handed me a package. "What's this?" I asked.

"Your new uniform." His grin didn't falter as I hesitantly opened it.

It was a maid costume. Complete with miniskirt, fishnets, and a cleavage showing top. I looked at him over the fabric. "Are you kidding?"

"Dead serious."

"Well, I'm dead serious when I say I'm not wearing this," I said, and shoved the costume back at him. "Halloween is over."

He laughed, and it was anything but a friendly sound. "Halloween may be over, but we'll be much scarier when we're not listened to."

He stepped towards me until I was backed against the counter. His body was barely an inch away from mine, his body heat tickling at the edges of my awareness. As he looked down at me with an intimidating expression, I paused and stared at him again. He did not intimidate me though. I've stared down the most disruptive children and learned that you never blink first. Keeping my eyes on Milo, I sighed and set down the package on the island and crossed my arms over my chest. I pursed my lips and cocked my hip to the side like I would while waiting for a child to finish spilling his

Goldfish snacks on the story time carpet. Milo's eyes pinched at the corners and his feet shuffled as if he was unsure what to do now.

The soft slapping of bare feet on tile was the only clue that Sterling was coming into the kitchen. Out of my peripheral, I saw him stop in the doorway when he saw us. "Uh, what's up?"

"I got Emily here a new uniform, and she's refusing to wear it," Milo replied, not taking his eyes off me still. The air was dry from the heater running all winter and it was admittedly difficult not to blink. Milo's eyes were watering just the slightest.

Sterling picked up the uniform off the island and snorted. "Wait, she can have this after I use it for something."

Milo's eyes snapped to Sterling, and he blinked. "That one won't fit you. I'll get one in your size."

Sterling smirked. "Good boy, Milo." He went to the fridge and didn't see the bloom of a blush over Milo's beard. "Emily, if we're going to be using you as a maid, you might as well dress the part."

"It's humiliating," I said and watched as he chugged straight from a half gallon of chocolate milk.

He put the lid back on and belched as he shut the fridge door. "Nah, Bambi, I think the most humiliating thing is that you begged to escape your little domestic life and here you are- you're essentially useless."

I stood up straight as rage coasted through my veins. "I am not useless!"

"Hmm, well, I'll be sure to call you when we need business negotiations or someone to lead an interrogation, or wait- a driver. Oh, fuck! You can't do any of that! Shit, I guess you're stuck cooking our food and cleaning up our jizz towels. Put the fucking uniform on, Emily." Sterling stood before me, leaning down so he was in my face with the last sentence.

I felt my lower lip tremble, and I bit it to keep it from giving away my emotions. I was not used to being demeaned by a grown man and I didn't know how to handle it. His gray eyes caught my bitten lower lip, and a look of satisfaction crossed his eyes as he straightened back up. I swiped the package off the island and stomped to the basement. In the little dusty bathroom, I felt safe from their words and watchful eyes. I shuddered again when I remembered the wet towels I cleared out of the sauna earlier. He hadn't been kidding. Stripping off my clothes and wriggling into the demeaning maid costume, I remembered the expired laxatives in the cabinet.

This type of medication lost its potency after it expired, but it might still work if I used enough. I finished dressing and popped the little pills out of their foil pack and hid them in my bra cup. If they asked me to cook dinner tonight, I could slip the pills in somehow. Maybe if there was enough of the drug in there, the men would be busy in the bathroom, and I could sneak out. Maybe even steal a car.

I spent the rest of the day mostly alone while I vacuumed and mopped the gym and did more laundry. I only saw Milo and Sterling in passing and refused to make eye contact with them. I knew I was being watched on cameras, so I didn't bother doing anything out of line.

Devon returned to the house in the late afternoon and stopped and wordlessly stared at me while I unloaded the dishwasher. I sighed and turned to see his eyes on my fishnet clad legs and his hands in his pockets. "Milo provided me with a uniform."

"I see that."

"I don't want to wear this."

"One would imagine so."

"Would *one* like to call off his dogs?"

"No." He strode out of the kitchen casually and then called back, "Dinner is to be on the table at six thirty."

I kept my smirk to myself and checked the time. It was already four thirty, so I rummaged through the pantry and fridge. My eyes settled on the bent pepperoni in the refrigerator. I pulled it out and let my smile play across my lips as I set it on the counter and planned the rest of dinner. I made a dough with flour, egg, salt, and olive oil and used a pasta maker to roll it out. I easily fell into the task and lost myself in the steps to make some fettucine noodles, a red sauce seasoned with red pepper and the grease from the pepperoni, a green salad, and a plate of laxative stuffed brownies.

Dinner time came around and the guys left the office to my call that food was ready. They all had the same furrowed brow, pinched expressions on their faces as they sat at the table. I had placed sparkling water on the table, and they all helped themselves. They ate in almost complete silence with troubled expressions on their faces, and I wondered if Devon's meeting had gone poorly earlier.

"Is dinner tasting alright?" I asked to break the silence.

"Yeah," Sterling said as if startled out of his thoughts. "It's great."

"When someone cooks for you, you say 'thank you,'" I coached them.

Sterling and Devon both distractedly murmured their thanks and Milo grunted. They gave me no attitude, no snark, no mean comments. Something must really be brewing in the mafia world. I wasn't sure if I was supposed to feel relieved they were potentially facing trouble or worried that I was about to be dragged into it.

"Is this the...?" Milo asked, and gestured with a piece of pepperoni on his fork.

"Yes," I said with a little huffed laugh.

"You cooked it?" Milo pressed.

I shrugged.

"I've never had it cooked in pasta before," Milo said in a voice that sounded like a complaint.

"I'm sorry, I thought you guys *weren't* the Italian mafia?"

Milo rolled his eyes and Sterling snorted a laugh. Devon remained stoic, watching everyone.

"Well, I'm stuffed," I said and pushed my mostly clean plate away from me. "But I made you guys dessert."

They were quiet again as I set freshly cut brownies on the table. They each grabbed a gooey chocolate- and laxative filled- brownie and began to eat. I hoped the expired medication was potent enough to at least give them stomach aches.

"You two will go on tonight's pick ups with Harold. I'll stay here with Emily," Devon said after checking his phone.

Milo took in a long breath and sat back in his chair, not looking at Devon. Sterling raised an eyebrow at Milo like he was reminding him of a previous conversation and Milo replied with a shake of his head and pursed lips. They clearly had some communication and leadership problems within their "family."

"Emily, you will clean the kitchen while I work," Devon instructed me, and wiped the last bits of chocolate off his fingertips on his napkin.

"Milo, want an espresso before we head out?" Sterling asked as he stood up.

"Yeah," Milo muttered and went with him, leaving me and Devon to stare at each other in silence.

I wondered if mixing espresso with an expired laxative brownie would improve its effectiveness.

"Can I change out of this outfit?" I asked Devon and gestured to my maid's costume.

"No."

"Why?"

"It's your uniform. I expect to see you in it every day."

"This is ridiculous," I sighed and got up to clear the table.

Sterling and Milo left the house while I was doing the dishes and Devon sat at the kitchen island with a sleek laptop. Devon put on music while he worked, something classical and brooding. I internally rolled my eyes at him. He was so moody and pretentious.

It had been about four hours since dinner and I was waiting on a loaf of bread to rise while flipping through an old cookbook that had been on display in the kitchen when I heard it. The first rumble of Devon's stomach. I bit the inside of my cheek as my heart raced at the idea of making a run for it. My shoes and coat were in the hall closet and I knew I could get to them in less than twenty seconds and be out the door in another five as soon as Devon went into the bathroom. I tried to play it cool as Devon shifted on his stool as if he were trying to shuffle and make a sound that would cover up his stomach.

Another hour later and the bread was just about to come out of the oven, the dishes were done, and I was making a shopping list of ingredients for upcoming meals. As if I wasn't planning on running tonight. And soon. Devon was visibly sweating now and checking his phone. He muttered a curse under his breath and looked up at me. He was probably going to suspect me if I wasn't also acting sick. I wrapped my arms around my stomach and scrunched up my face just a little like I was in pain. I pretended to breathe through a cramp and wiped away some nonexistent sweat from my forehead.

"Take the bread out," Devon's tense voice cut through the classical music.

"It'll be done in five minutes."

"Get. It. Out," he said through gritted teeth. He was visibly paler now.

"Okay, okay," I said and took the bread out of the oven and set it on a trivet on the island. I held my stomach again and let out a little miserable moan.

"Go to your room," Devon snapped.

"What?"

"Just fucking do what I say!" Devon yelled, sounding more frantic than he likely meant.

"Let me finish the bread and then I'll go. You seem sick. Maybe you want to go to bed?" I asked him in a worried voice.

"No. Go."

"Want me to make you some ginger tea?" I scrambled as he stood up, gesturing for me to leave.

"Go!" he screamed at me and reached for me just as his stomach made a sound of great distress.

I rushed past him and towards my room, casting a longing glance at the front door as I passed. He followed me up the stairs. "Here, I'll help you to your room. It seems like you're sicker than I am."

He didn't respond, only shoved me into my room and slammed the door shut behind me. I stumbled to the ground and whipped around just as the door locked. No! I banged on the door and screamed for Devon to let me out. But there was silence in the hall. Devon must have gone to his room. Tears slid down my face as I realized that there was no escape tonight and my plan had failed. I was stuck here. I'd been here for a day and tomorrow was Christmas Eve. There was nothing I wouldn't give to be watching sad re-runs in the motel again.

I was still leaning against the door, crying, when I heard a commotion downstairs. Sterling and Milo's angry voices got closer and closer as they came crashing up the stairs.

"Fucking hell, we'll count in the morning. I need to get to a bathroom like yesterday," Sterling was groaning.

"Devon said he and Emily are sick, too," Milo said, and I heard his door open.

"Fuck, Harold said he's calling in Doc," Sterling said and I heard his door slam shut, followed by Milo's door.

I hadn't even been able to grab a phone to call for help. My plan got me nothing other than more time locked in this room. Defeated, I got up to make sure the camera in the bathroom was still covered, took a bath to clean the day off of me, and then climbed into bed.

7

Sterling

Waking up feeling like every drop of moisture left my body like the worst hangover of my life after not drinking a drop of alcohol was not a fun time. I groaned and sat up in my sweat-soaked sheets and glared at the streak of sunlight that was shining through a small opening in my black curtains. A glance at the clock on my nightstand said it was just after nine in the morning. The doorbell was ringing, and I groaned again. I sat at the end of my bed and stretched. Whoever it was would have a key and was ringing it out of courtesy. All of our mail and deliveries were left at the gate with the grunt we hired to stand guard. As if anyone dared to find us. But it was a good, undemanding job for gangs that owed us small amounts of money.

I heard the clip of shoed footsteps on the floor in the hall. "Hello, is everyone alive?" came Doc's voice. He sounded too happy for a man who was potentially finding the sick or dying bodies of men he had delivered into this world. I shuffled over to my door and opened it, and nodded at Doc as both Milo and Devon did the same from their rooms. Emily's room remained shut and silent. Milo leaned against his door frame across the hall from Emily's room, looking disheveled and sweat soaked. His sweatpants hung low on his hips, leaving a gap of skin exposed below his white t-shirt.

"Gentlemen," Doc greeted us and stopped between all of our doors, large medical bag in hand. "Who am I treating first?"

"Emily," Devon grunted and ran a hand through his greasy hair.

Doc looked at the three of us. "Did one of you change pronouns and not inform me?"

"No, we have a girl," I answered gruffly through my dry throat.

"A girl," Doc repeated and quirked an eyebrow.

"A woman," Milo clarified.

"Oh? In the cells?" Doc asked, referring to one of the locked metal rooms in the basement that we used for interrogations.

"No, on our team. Did my father not tell you?" Devon asked.

I pointed to Emily's room next to mine. Milo stepped forward to unlock the door with the key from his pocket.

"She's locked in?" Doc asked as he approached the door.

"Yeah, she's... new and unsure about her place here," Devon explained.

"Understood," Doc said, and steeled himself before knocking lightly on the door.

I heard Emily's voice on the other side invite him in. "Emily, I'm Doc, I'm here to help," he said gently as he slowly opened the door. "I'm coming in alone."

He shut the door behind him and left us in the hall.

"You both good?" Devon asked, and leaned his body against the railing that overlooked part of the foyer.

Milo nodded, and I grunted in response.

"Do you think she did it?" Milo asked.

"She was also sick. Besides, the house is clear of any poisons, and we've all watched her the entire time," Devon said and waved away the concern.

"Do you think it was poison, though?" I asked.

"I don't know," Devon said, and yawned. "Dad said nothing happened last night, so our illness wasn't a distraction. Your meeting will still happen tonight as long as you're healthy."

My stomach dropped at the reminder, and I glanced at Milo. He pushed up from the door frame and stood up straight. "I didn't think our ability to do our jobs was in question," Milo said with a glare.

Devon rolled his eyes. "You know what I mean."

Milo and Devon glared at each other, and now it was my turn to roll my eyes. I went into my room and hopped into a scalding hot shower.

Doc had the three of us line up in the hearth room on the couch for IV drips after taking our vitals. "Some hydration and a simple diet today should get you back on your feet. No alcohol for a few days and limit your coffee. Don't stress your system."

"What do you think it was?" Devon asked.

"It could have been a stomach bug or something you all ate.

I don't believe it to have been poison or any other malicious activity," he replied as he typed into his laptop at the bar. "It will probably be out of your system today or tomorrow. Let me know if there are any more bouts of sickness and I can come back with some more fluids."

"She can't even cook right," Milo grumbled.

"If you're thinking salmonella or anything from her negligence, you'd be mistaken," Doc said. "You'd be much sicker. So, don't blame her entirely."

Milo sighed, and Doc shifted to face us in his seat. He studied us for a moment before speaking. "You know, boys, I don't know if Emily is a good fit for your team."

Devon bristled at being addressed as a boy. I could tell from the other end of the couch. He hated being demeaned, as if he hadn't worked hard at the job. "What makes you say that?"

"She asked me to let her out. She said she's being held here against her will and that you drugged her and kidnapped her," Doc said, looking us each in the eye for a moment before moving to the next.

Devon scoffed. "She'll come around."

Doc shrugged and turned back to his computer. I had to agree with him. She was a liability to our team. Emily had not grown up in this life like we had. She was not accustomed to the violence and the way we did things around here. She was a wildcard that could hurt us or herself before any enemy. I shifted in my seat and Milo nudged me with his elbow. I was confident he felt the same, but there was no changing Devon's mind.

"She seems in great health other than some dehydration,

much like yourselves, and her mental distress," Doc said as he finished typing. "The medical records Milo sent me suggest she was married and trying for children."

"She was," Devon replied with finality.

While Doc was the only medical professional that our family trusted, there were limitations to his knowledge of our business. He knew enough to be dangerous, but not enough to completely fuck us over. He'd been around back when he was still in medical school and Devon and Milo's grandparents were in charge and was the one who oversaw their moms' pregnancies and births. I knew Doc wouldn't try to do anything with his information about Emily, but I didn't want to push it, knowing that she was the wife of a mayor.

Doc looked between the three of us again and then went back to typing with a sigh. "Well, let me know if she needs birth control."

"She *works* with us," Devon bit out defensively.

I pursed my lips. I mean, she was hot... in a suburban housewife kind of way. Shaking my head, I dispelled the thought.

I spent the rest of the morning in bed and browsing comments that people left on the recent social media posts that Milo had made on my behalf. Nothing amped up my confidence and simultaneously creeped me out in quite the same way. Milo entered my room in the afternoon with his laptop under his arm. He was wearing a clean pair of sweatpants and a t-shirt, and his hair and beard were groomed. His glasses sat low on his nose as he came in.

"What's up?" I asked him and sat up in my bed.

Milo sat next to me and pulled his laptop open on his legs. "Our meeting tonight."

"Yeah, what do you know so far?" I asked, and peered over at his screen.

"Alright so, Devon had said they're new in town, but that's not quite the case," Milo said and brought up a page of scanned in property deeds. "The people who run the business owned property in Cleveland until the late eighties, early nineties. Two houses, an apartment complex, and a strip mall. The people they sold to are civilians, nothing out of the ordinary. This family, though, sold all of their Cleveland area assets and strongholds and moved to Akron all around the time our parents and my uncle came into power. We'll have to ask Anthony and Matthew if it had anything to do with that transfer, but I didn't find any known conflict in our records or any police records," Milo said, and showed me his screen.

"So, this guy we're meeting-"

"Giovanni."

"Right, so Giovanni must be a good guy because Anthony and Matthew would remember him if he wasn't. They're sending in you and me. They wouldn't send us in if they thought it was a dangerous situation," I assured him. The stiffness of his shoulders suggested he was more worried than he'd let on.

Milo let out a controlled sigh. "I'm not convinced."

"Matthew would never send you somewhere he thinks you'd be in danger. And Anthony should fear the wrath of Devon if anything happened to us, the only people that tolerate him," I elaborated.

"I didn't actually hear the assignment from Matthew. He's unreachable until the party tomorrow night," Milo countered.

"Still, I don't think it's as big of a deal as you think. Besides, I've got your back," I said so quietly I almost whispered it, hoping it would calm his nerves.

He tipped his head back against my metal headboard and rolled his head side to side as he stared at the ceiling pensively. The sound of his hair against the metal was a soft shushing. His blue eyes were moody, and the computer light shone through his auburn eyelashes. He swallowed and his bearded throat bobbed. I looked away quickly.

Milo, Devon, and I had been born best friends. We were all about three months apart in age. Our parents had all made a plan to have kids at the same time, and they were successful within six months. Milo's sister, Marie, came two years later and is the only sibling of the three of us. She wasn't raised like we were and had little to do with running the business and married one of our family hired lawyers. Milo and Marie's parents died in an accident about a year after Marie was born and two years after my parents were killed.

With the loss of our parents at very young ages, we bonded in a way that I couldn't with Devon. While Anthony and Stephanie were the ones who took me in as a baby, it was always very clear that Devon was Anthony's son, and I was not. This had been confusing as a child and I bonded with Milo, who also had to learn and accept that his uncle Matthew was not his dad. We both felt the "otherness" of our lives and had grown up with the agreement to never be outsiders to each other. We were family, more than the court documents that determined our real legal families.

"I know you do," he whispered in return.

"Go get dressed, get armed to the teeth, and we'll be on our way to get this over with," I said, and slapped his thigh.

He reluctantly stood up and put his closed laptop under his arm again. "You know I have your back, too, right?"

"Yeah, but I'm more of a top," I joked, to lighten the mood.

Milo stared down at me on the bed, his bottom lip tucked into his bite, and his eyes flickered over my body. "Figured as much," Milo said in the same quiet voice as before, and turned and left.

A laugh burst from me as the door shut.

I drove to the meeting with Milo playing passenger princess in my 1990 Cadillac Brougham. The restored engine purred beneath us, and Milo fiddled with the portable Wi-Fi device he had rested on the dash. His brow was furrowed, and he kept flicking his hair away from his eyes. He was nervous. I was, too, but I felt comforted knowing we had an objective for the meeting. We were to gather information about why this family was in Cleveland, what their business was, and what they dealt in. We were to welcome them, but also calmly warn them that we didn't want any problems.

"Mi, chill out," I scolded.

"I'm trying," he grumbled, and ran a hand through his hair. He'd used a product in his auburn hair that was supposed to keep it back, but it kept falling into his eyes behind his glasses.

"Put the tablet down, take a hit off a joint, sit back and relax. We've got time before the meeting. I was going to say let's stop for a coffee, but I don't think you need any more jitters," I instructed him.

"I don't want to smell unprofessional," Milo grumbled.

"That's fine, I've got edibles," I said, happy to problem solve.

Milo huffed out a sigh like he was annoyed with me, but when we stopped for burgers, he bit off half of a weed gummy. I grinned at him and held out my hand for the other half. It would do nothing for me, but I wasn't going to waste it. "Good boy," I joked as he handed me the rest of the gummy.

He startled and took his hand back quickly. "So," he snapped. "I was thinking about our approach to the meeting. I was thinking if we walk in with a casual air, they'll think we're relaxed and not looking for a fight."

"Yeah, I figured we would, since this is more of a social call than official business," I said and finished my burger and leaned back in the vinyl booth.

Milo's knees knocked against mine as he rested back in his seat, almost mirroring me. His blue eyes finally met mine after bouncing around the diner. It would be a bit before the edible kicked in and he relaxed. For now, I'd have to deal with his squirrely ass.

"If they offer us a drink, it'll be a social call for them," Milo said.

"Then we accept." I nodded.

His knee bounced under the table, and he bit at the corner of his bottom lip.

"Damn, I should have brought Emily. Maybe she would have been calmer," I said sarcastically.

He let go of the bite he had on his lip and smiled. "Sorry, I don't think you and I have ever been in charge of a meeting like this. Matthew or Anthony is always there."

Milo was right, but this meant we were being trusted with

more responsibility because we could handle it. Anthony and Matthew wouldn't intentionally put us in a situation that was not safe. They were doing this because they trusted us.

"No, you're right, but we should be happy about it, not anxious as fuck," I replied.

Milo shrugged and didn't respond as our server came over with the bill.

Pulling into the hotel's parking lot, Milo looked around for their surveillance detail. "Two men and three cameras," he mumbled as I parked. His body was no longer vibrating with anxiety, but I knew his hesitance. They weren't going to kill us tonight, but that didn't mean we shouldn't be on our guard.

I parked, and two guys in suits met us at the hotel lobby door. "Evening, gentlemen," I greeted. The men nodded in response and gestured for us to follow them past the front desk and to the elevator. The heater above the doors blew hot air that smelled of disinfectant and dust over my shoulders and hair. Milo shoved his hand through his hair again, taming it back into place. Despite it being below freezing outside, Milo and I had left our coats in the car for a better range of movement. Milo wore a dark green sweatshirt and khakis, and I wore black turtleneck and black slacks. We discreetly carried our guns and knives under our clothes, and they were the only reasons I felt safe walking into this meeting.

The elevator ride to the top floor was silent, other than the faint classical music and floor chimes. I bumped Milo's shoulder with mine and he stood up straight and tightened his jaw. I quirked my mouth at him in the smallest of smiles as the door opened. They led us into a lavish hotel suite that opened into a formal living room with views overlooking the city. Lights shone and flashed in the darkening sky and a plane was descending into the airport.

Two men were standing in front of the cream plush couch that faced a marble fireplace and two light leather armchairs. They were dressed finely in suits and gold jewelry. The men both appeared to be older than Anthony and Matthew, maybe mid to late sixties, but in good health and grooming. They both held rocks glasses of amber liquid and had calm expressions. "Good evening, boys," one man said. His skin was olive toned and wrinkled, and his hair and smooth beard were almost entirely gray. He had a friendly enough expression in his dark brown eyes as he held out a hand to shake. "It is so lovely to meet you. I'm Giovanni and this is Taz."

The man he gestured to also held out a hand. He was pale and had thinner wrinkles around his eyes and mouth and had short white hair. His expression was tighter than Giovanni's, but not unfriendly.

"I'm Sterling," I said and shook their hands.

"Milo," he said, as he gave a firm shake to both men.

"Sterling... Hawthorne?" Giovanni questioned. "And Milo... Holden?" His eyes flickered with question and a little shock before he settled back into his neutral, calm expression.

"Correct," I said, figuring he'd done his own research before reaching out.

He and Taz exchanged a glance before he spoke again. "I'm just shocked to see you both. We... we knew your parents."

"You seem to have left just before they were all killed," Milo said evenly.

Giovanni's eyes bounced between me and Milo, like he was

figuring us out just as much as we were studying him. "You are right. It was a tragic story," he said and seemed genuine enough.

Milo and I remained silent and stoic. We'd done our fair share of lamenting the deaths of our parents and didn't need to do it with a stranger.

"Come in and sit down. Can I fix you a drink? Taz and I are on a Manhattan kick as of late," Giovanni said, and went to a silver bar cart.

"Sure, thank you. I'll have a whiskey neat," I said and sat on the couch, leaving room for Milo.

"Make that two," Milo said, and sat next to me.

Taz sat in one armchair facing the couch and sipped his drink. Once Giovanni served us our drinks, he sat in the remaining chair.

"It is so good to see you two grown. I think I had only seen you, Sterling, once when you were just a bundle in your mother's arms," Giovanni said with a smile. "And Milo, I saw your mother just before she gave birth."

"What had you leaving town so quickly?" Milo asked abruptly.

"Oh, I understand now. You are worried we had something to do with their deaths," Giovanni said, almost startled, and set down his drink on an end table. He glanced and Taz who was also quickly putting down his drink and shaking his head. "No, boys, that was not our doing. Now... I wonder what you think this meeting is about."

"You're trying to take the rest of our business out so you can take over," Milo said, and I swallowed down my urge to elbow him. I sipped my drink.

Giovanni tipped his head back and laughed. "You are so much like your father. No, boys, we're not here to kill you. We asked for a meeting, thinking we would get to see our old friends Anthony and Matthew again. It is a pleasant surprise to get to meet you two as men."

Milo relaxed a fraction in his seat and took a sip of his whiskey.

"So, why are you here?" I asked.

"We're expanding our businesses back to where most of them began, Cleveland," Giovanni said and waved a hand towards the large window overlooking the city. "There's just something about returning home that had me feeling like a move was necessary in my old age."

"And you're still going to be running the same business here?" I continued.

"Yes, and I believe we can work out a deal," Taz spoke up.

"A deal for what?" I asked. "We don't know much about your current businesses."

"We work mostly with fighting and some weapons. We also work in protection for locals and their workplaces. I understand that is our overlap. And we will come to an agreement on that," Taz explained.

"What kind of agreement?" I asked and set my empty glass down.

"I need fighters to get the games going here," Taz said. "If you guys help us get the fights going we won't sell protection to your jurisdiction."

"Also, get us a meeting with Anthony and Matthew. As much as I enjoy seeing your faces, I want to see them, too," Giovanni added, and his face took on a more tense expression.

"What kind of fighting?" Milo asked.

"MMA mostly," Taz said.

"You want us to fight, or recruit?" Milo continued.

"We want you to fight. Isn't there another one of you? Anthony's son," Giovanni asked with a hand gesturing vaguely between us.

"Devon," I said with a nod.

"Good, that's three to add to the few that came with us from Akron," Taz said to Giovanni.

"Before we agree to anything," Milo started and leaned forward. "We need to come to an agreement about resources, locations, and trades."

Giovanni smiled, but it didn't reach his eyes. "That's why I want to meet with Matthew and Anthony."

"They're going to ask the same questions," Milo said. "So, what are your goals in Cleveland? Are you hoping to usurp our position and our businesses?"

Giovanni's unfeeling smile didn't change. "Your first fight is on Friday. You'll meet Mack here at ten and he'll take you to the location. If I get that meeting."

There was a note of hard finality in his voice, and I stood up. We weren't going to get more information without a fight. And we didn't exactly come prepared for one. Milo stood next to me and smoothed his sweater casually. "We'll be seeing you," I said curtly, and led the way to the door. The same men who walked us up to the room walked us back down to the front doors of the lobby.

Milo and I were silent the entire way to the car and then out of the parking lot. I drove to make sure we weren't being tailed before we were comfortable enough to talk freely.

"I didn't like any of that," I grumbled.

Milo had whipped out his cellphone seconds after getting in the car and was typing away at a message for his uncle. He looked up as I spoke, and his bright blue eyes were sparked with apprehension. "No kidding," he said and set his phone on the armrest. "Something is going on and we should not be entering any deals."

"They had me in the beginning until they were asking us to fight," I said and turned towards home.

"Yeah, I'm not fucking fighting," Milo said, and looked out the window.

"If Matthew and Anthony want us to fight, then we'll be fighting," I reminded him.

Milo was silent for a moment. "What do you think they trade in?"

"It must be more than protection, fights, and weapons. There's no way that they made much money doing just that. There's gotta be drugs in there- which we have a handle on. Or something else, like prostitution. Which Anthony and Matthew won't tolerate being gang controlled in their juris-diction," I thought aloud to Milo.

"Hopefully it's just that," Milo sighed and then said, "I don't know how much of this we bring to Devon."

"All of it. Why wouldn't we?" I asked and glanced over at him as I drove.

"You and I have a bad feeling about them, and Anthony was the one who sent us. Devon is going to follow what his dad said and not our *feelings* on the deal," Milo reasoned scornfully.

"Maybe you're right, but we have to tell them. We can do

it at Christmas dinner," I said. "And then Devon can see his dad's reaction in real time and decide."

"And then we can start our MMA training," Milo said in a quiet, disdainful tone.

"I'll train you. You're not too far off, I'm sure," I said encouragingly. Milo, Devon, and I had been trained in many forms of martial arts and self defense for years. But Milo had long preferred technology over hand-to-hand combat. We still sparred as part of our workouts, but that's as far as Milo and Devon's fighting capabilities went. We had gangs below us to do our dirty work. I, on the other hand, was the one who most often needed to fight. I was head of security and that often came with times of combat and defense.

"Merry fucking Christmas," Milo grumbled.

"Merry fucking Christmas, My-My," I said cheerfully and slapped his thigh as I pulled onto our street.

8

Emily

I woke up on Christmas morning to a soft snowfall outside. It was the first morning I hadn't woken up and been afraid of my surroundings. I knew where I was and who to expect to see. While I wasn't afraid of my room, I wasn't so sure about the guys. They hadn't done anything to hurt me, but I didn't trust them. Begrudgingly, I pulled on the maid's costume and stood in front of the camera in my room. "Milo, I'm ready to make breakfast."

A few moments later, Milo was unlocking and opening my door. Tablet in hand and low-slung gray sweatpants on his hips. He didn't even look up at me before he left. I was used to their bad attitudes at this point.

Christmas morning called for cinnamon rolls, so I had prepped a homemade batch last night that just needed to rise and then bake this morning. I put on some coffee while Milo had both his tablet and laptop open before him. He furrowed his brow as he studied what looked like video surveillance footage of a hotel lobby.

"Is everything okay?" I asked him as I put the cinnamon rolls in the oven.

"Yeah, you'll hear about it later," he grumbled with only a glance over my maid's costume.

"Is it about your meeting last night?" I pressed.

"Sort of," Milo said shortly. Even though he was being abrupt, his tone wasn't as condescending as it usually was, so I considered it an improvement.

I went to the fridge to look for some inspiration of what to pair with the cinnamon rolls. Bacon or sausage would be a good choice. And if I made that entire package of bacon, there would be enough for BLT sandwiches at lunch. I detected movement behind me that derailed my train of thought. The hum of the refrigerator had deafened me to his approach. I spun around with a gasp. Milo was so close I could smell his clean soap and the beeswax scent of the product he must use in his beard. His blue eyes darted all over my face and he licked his bottom lip. My vision zeroed in on that little movement unintentionally.

"I'm just getting the cream for my coffee," he said, his voice gruff and low as he reached over my head for the half and half carton on the top shelf. My heart pounded in my chest with anticipation as he leaned. The back of my head knocked lightly against a shelf as I pressed away from him. My body hummed with awareness as his front just barely grazed mine. He pulled back with the carton in hand and paused a moment, his eyes back on mine. "Why are you so afraid of us?" he asked quietly in a rare moment of softness.

"Y- you kidnapped me," I whispered.

"You called Harold. Emily, *you* asked for it," he said and stepped back now, his eyes confused despite his sure words.

"I didn't know what I was in for," I replied. "I didn't know it would be like this."

"And is this so bad?" he asked, his head cocked as he gestured to the house.

I sighed. "You three are rude. I have no access to the outside world, and I'm being forced to wear a demeaning costume. Milo, you literally have cameras in my bathroom and bedroom, and you lock me in my room at night. We were *shot at* my first day here!"

A little smirk covered his lips. "If the door was unlocked, would you run to the police and tell them you were kidnapped by the *mafia*?"

I crossed my arms over my chest. "Maybe."

"We're not doing it to hurt or punish you. We're protecting our family and businesses. All of us have cameras in our rooms, not just you. And that costume is only demeaning if you want it to be." He moved away to the coffeepot and poured himself a cup. With his absence, I noticed the cool air of the open refrigerator behind me. I shut it and stopped him from putting cream in his coffee. "Wait, I wanted to serve you guys frothy coffees."

He stopped and stared. "What?"

"I wanted to froth little Christmas trees on top," I explained and gestured for him to walk away.

He obeyed and returned to his seat. I poured the half and

half into a little cup and used the milk frother I had found in the cabinets to make the creamy liquid fluffy. I used a teaspoon to layer it onto his coffee. The closeness of his body from before had left a slight tremor in my hands, so the tree looked less tree-like and more like a carrot.

"Well, it looks more like Frosty the Snowman's nose than a Christmas tree. Still festive, though," I said and slid the mug on the island before him. As it came to a stop before him, it drooped to the side a little, looking more like a wilting carrot.

"Festive," Milo repeated without intonation, and the tops of his ears reddened.

"Do you not like it?" I asked.

"I'm not sure how to drink it now," he said and was biting the inside of his cheek like he was trying not to laugh.

"Ugh, fine," I said and hopped up to lean across the island to his mug and slurped up the froth so it would be a normal cup of coffee.

In the less than two seconds that it took me to get up there, Sterling and Devon entered the kitchen. I was leaned across the island in a way that my toes were off the tile floor, my bare ass was exposed under the costume's miniskirt, and I had my mouth around a carrot shaped froth mountain. Everyone froze. I gulped my mouthful of foam and wiped my mouth as I slid off the island with a screech of skin against shined granite.

"Why are you- was that a dick in his coffee?" Sterling guffawed as he came around to sit next to Milo. He squeezed Milo's biceps as he sat down. Milo shook him off.

I looked at the remaining base of foam. Oh, my god. I had just served Milo a penis-shaped foam coffee. It hadn't even occurred to me. Oh, my *god*! I had my mouth around it as I slurped it up basically in Milo's face. I felt my skin turn as red as Milo's ears.

"It was a- uh, Christmas tree," Milo murmured. "It's festive."

"Merry Christmas," I whispered, not trusting my voice.

"Emily, where are your panties?" Devon asked, finally speaking.

"Oh, in the dryer. I did all of your laundry yesterday first," I said and smoothed down my skirt.

"Her clothes will be here in two days," Milo said, seemingly happy for the change of subject.

Devon nodded. "I'll have a dress and some appropriate underwear brought over before the party."

I nodded back at him and turned towards the coffee pot to pour them their mugs.

"I'll take a dick coffee, too. But I think mine should have more girth than Milo's," Sterling said, and I heard someone punch him. He laughed and said "Ow!" but said nothing more.

The guys had a quiet Christmas morning, but they didn't exchange any gifts that I saw. It made me a little sad that they didn't have anything to open on Christmas. There wasn't even a tree in the house. I loved decorations for any season and holiday. My home and classroom were always decorated for something. I missed my silly Christmas sweaters that the kids in my class always loved, and the dancing Santa figurines. With a sharp clench of my chest, I remembered the hand knit red stockings that Gregory and I would hang on our mantle. Last Christmas, I had put a new designer watch in his stocking with his favorite imported chocolates and he had put a new diamond tennis bracelet and my guilty pleasure cookies'n'crème Hershey's bars in mine. I didn't miss the gifts, but I missed that feeling of warmth and love on Christmas morning.

There was no warmth or love in the delivery of my dress by Devon that afternoon. He had knocked on my bedroom door and handed me a garment bag and a handled Sephora bag before leaving without a word. I thanked him as he walked down the hall, but he didn't respond.

The dress was an emerald bodycon with a deep V neck and thin spaghetti straps. A black, fitted blazer was paired with it. In the bag was a fancy looking black box with a matching white lace bra and panty set. I tried hard to not think of which man picked them out. The bottom of the bag contained a pair of closed toe, shiny black pumps. The Sephora bag held more makeup and hair products than I had ever owned. With a sigh of surrender, I went to the bathroom to get ready.

While nothing but the blazer and the shoes were something I would have worn previously, I had to admit that Devon had a good eye. I looked great. My hair was styled in barrel waves that shined with the hair oil I'd been given. My makeup was dramatic with lashes, contour, and a bold lipstick. I was ready for whatever this party entailed. I had spent years socializing with people I didn't know and even didn't like because of Gregory's job as mayor. None of those people were mafia leaders, but they couldn't be much different. Everyone liked compliments and being asked about themselves.

I was putting on some small gold hoop earrings when Sterling darkened my door. I glanced at him in a black suit and styled hair. "I'll be done in a second." When I finished,

I picked up the gold clutch that only contained my lipstick and a hair tie and turned to him.

He stood up straight from his leaning position on the door frame. His eyes slowly trailed over my body and back up. I felt the fire of his silvery flame gaze everywhere it touched on my skin. Shuffling my feet, I looked over my dress. "Does it look alright? It's not something I would have worn on my own."

"You look..." his eyes burned over my skin again before he seemed to remember himself. "Passable."

I snorted. "Hey thanks. Just what every woman wants to hear." I pushed past him out the door.

He grabbed my arm and whirled me back towards him. I hit his chest and then bounced back against the door frame. A small, startled gasp left my painted lips.

"Would you rather hear that I'm glad I just spent twenty minutes jerking off in the shower? Otherwise, I'd be forced to bend you over that bed and fill you with come so it dripped down your legs all night," he taunted, his voice gravelly and deep.

"P-passable is good," I stuttered, staring wide-eyed up at him.

He smirked and then headed down the hall towards the stairs. I took a moment to gather myself with a long breath before I followed him. He was just trying to rattle me to show he still had control over me. He couldn't mean anything that he'd said, so I ignored the warmth that had spread through my belly.

At the bottom of the stairs, Milo and Devon were grabbing coats from the hall closet. Milo looked up first, like he was going to say something to Sterling, but his eyes caught and stayed on me. The heat that had bloomed in my belly traveled throughout my body at the burning ember expression in his eyes. I bit my lip as I got to the bottom of the stairs and held out a hand for my coat. Devon handed it to me before looking up. His eyebrows shot up for a second before returning to their normal glower. "I see the dress fit."

"It does, thank you," I said and looked up at him through my lashes.

"Good, because our family has an expectation for grooming and clothing," Devon said cooly and closed the closet with a snap.

I wanted to roll my eyes, but I took a steadying breath instead. The garage was heated, and Devon's car took a prime space. A brand-new black GMC Yukon Denali shone with a fresh coat of wax under the garage lights. Sliding into the back seat with Milo, it still smelled like new car leather. I was fairly certain nobody had sat in the back seat yet; it was so new. I stroked my fingers over the buttery soft light beige leather. Devon and Sterling spoke quietly in the front seat. I was behind Devon, so I couldn't see him, but I could see Sterling smiling as he spoke to Devon.

"Do you know who you're meeting?" Milo asked me while he scrolled on his tablet.

"No, not really," I admitted.

"Anthony and Matthew are the leaders of our family," Milo explained. When he wasn't being condescending, his voice was smooth and deep and easy to listen to. "Anthony is Devon's dad, and was Sterling's guardian for most of his life. Matthew is my uncle and was my guardian throughout my childhood. Stephanie is Anthony's wife and Devon's mom.

Marie is my younger sister, and Brendon is her husband. Marie chose not to be involved much in the family business at large and mostly runs the salon where you met Victoria. Brendon is a lawyer for our businesses, and also our link to the Irish families in the area. Harold, you met him at the deli, was the right-hand man for Anthony's father back when he merged his business with my family. Harold is married to Victoria, and they are mostly retired from the business. They still have some projects and help us out when we need it. I don't think anyone else will be there. This is just a party for the family. Which, apparently, you are a part of now."

My head spun a little with the information thrown at me, but I knew I'd figure it out when I got there. This wasn't my first time meeting new people I needed to impress. "Sounds like a big, happy family," I said.

Sterling snorted from the front seat, and I realized that they had stopped talking to listen.

"Is there anything I should definitely not bring up? Any hard limits on conversation?" I asked them all, since they were all listening.

"Politics," they all chorused.

"Heard," I acknowledged with a small smile.

Devon's parents lived in a beautiful brick mansion not more than twenty minutes from our house. I didn't pay attention to where we were going, and I realized with a start that I had forgotten to escape. I hoped the guys would drink and talk to their family enough that maybe I could sneak away later. We parked and walked up the salted and well-cleared driveway to the brightly lit front door. The door swung open before anyone could knock. A beautiful woman with Devon's mouth and nose stood at the door with a wide smile. She beamed and hugged the guys as they each walked in.

When she came to me, I smiled and held out a hand for her to shake. "Hi, I'm Emily."

She laughed and moved around my outstretched hand to hug me. "Emily, it is so good to finally meet you."

Sterling mouthed "Stephanie, Devon's mom" over her shoulder to me, and I nodded. I had recognized his features in her immediately.

"You, too," I said as she pulled away.

"We will have to talk woman to woman tonight. These boys need a lot of work," she joked as she linked her arm with mine and led us through the grand foyer.

"Mom, we're thirty-two and thirty-three. You can stop calling us 'boys," Devon complained.

"When I can no longer remember the feeling of your gigantic head bursting from my body, I will stop referring to you as a boy. Now, *boys*, could you please fix our newest member a drink?" Stephanie said as we entered a large formal dining room that had a full bar along one side.

Devon turned to me with an expectantly cocked eyebrow.

"Chardonnay, two ice cubes," I said with a sweet smile.

"Disgusting," he mumbled as he walked away.

The large room was decorated in sleek black and white. Large abstract paintings hung on the walls and the furniture was minimalistic. A few other people were in the room, and I spotted Harold and the woman from the salon, Victoria, talking to a man with Devon's skin tone. Stephanie led me to them while Sterling and Milo followed us. I looked back at them, and Sterling raised his eyebrows encouragingly.

Devon handed me my drink just as Stephanie pressed a hand to Anthony's arm to get his attention. He turned to her with love in his eyes before he looked up to see us standing there. "Oh, hello, boys. A newcomer! I'm Anthony Bilal. You're...?"

"Emily Ambrose," I replied with a smile and shook his hand.

"Right, right. The mayor's wife," he said warmly.

"Ex-wife. But yes, you're correct," I reminded him.

"My apologies. This is Harold and Victoria Deniro. I believe you've met them both?" he said and gestured to the familiar faces.

"Yes, Harold, I'm sorry about the pepperoni," I said, and reached out to shake his hand.

He guffawed and shook my hand. "All is well, all is well."

"It's good to see you smiling," Victoria said and grasped my hand in hers.

I smiled back at her, knowing that this was a mask I had perfected years ago. I would talk to the important people, be seen and heard amid a few great conversations, be photographed twice, and then leave to grade papers while Gregory did the rest of the politician's duties. I was queen of being seen, making an impression, and then leaving without notice.

"Milo!" a feminine voice called.

"Come meet my sister," Milo said, and I excused us before walking with him to the other group of people mingling with drinks.

"Marie, this is Emily. She's working with us now," Milo said smoothly.

I shook her hand, and she looked me over like she couldn't figure out how I fit in with this family. Well, she was not wrong.

"This is Brendon, my husband," she said and pressed a possessive hand to the chest of a lanky man with incredibly red hair and freckles. She beamed up at him as he shook my hand.

"And this is Matthew, our uncle," Milo said, and gestured to the remaining person in our circle. He was quietly assessing me but smiled as we shook hands.

He looked vaguely like Milo, in the way an uncle would have a few features in common with his nephew. Marie looked nothing like Milo except for the shape of her smile and her posture.

I mostly listened to their light conversation before a staff member of the house, wearing a suit and a blank expression, informed us that dinner was ready to be served. They sat me between Sterling and Milo and across from Victoria and Stephanie. The dinner service was formal and nothing I wasn't used to. Anthony stood at the head of the table to give a toast as the staff set down our first course and topped off our drinks. "This year was a prosperous one for us. It was all because of the work of the men and women at this table tonight. And for that, I want us to clap ourselves on the back, and enjoy a fantastic meal and holiday. To new alliances and old ones made anew, *salute!*"

The table all raised their glasses and chorused "*salute!*" or "*cin cin!*" On our plates were three oyster shells stuffed with ingredients. It was oysters three ways, and I followed suit to eat them while everyone around me continued to talk.

"This is oysters. Fish number one!" Stephanie announced happily.

"Wait, is this the feast of the seven fishes?" I asked Sterling next to me.

"Yeah," he replied.

"I thought you weren't the Italian mafia?" I half joked quietly, so only he could hear.

"Harold is Italian," Sterling whispered to me and shrugged.

"Anthony?" I questioned.

"Bilal is a Pakistani name," Sterling informed.

"But why is everything Italian?" I asked and gestured to the prosciutto wrapped scallops being placed on my plate. "And don't tell me what year it is. I know anyone can enjoy and celebrate anything. I'm just trying to learn."

Sterling grinned at me like I had caught him in what he was about to say. "Anthony's dad was Pakistani, and his mom was Italian. So sure, our family has some Italian mafia roots. But the Italian mafia is different from the way we operate. Anthony's family story is very beautiful, if you ever get the chance to hear it."

"Beautiful stories and the mafia don't typically go hand in hand," I said and sipped my wine.

Sterling smiled coyly at me again. "So, you've got a lot of experience with organized crime?"

They settled the main dish in front of us, and a fresh glass of wine replaced my empty one. I hated to admit it, but I was truly enjoying myself. Stephanie was laughing and regaling us with memories of Devon and Sterling both potty training at the same time while she was trying to negotiate terms for protection with a local business and she had to stop to bring both little boys to the establishment's bathroom. Victoria's voice was loud and jovial as she shouted down the table to Anthony and said he should have paid nannies better and they would have stuck around. Anthony laughed and shouted back that there was no salary that could keep a nanny with Devon and Sterling as toddlers.

The table was loud and happy, and I was laughing with them as they practically screamed over each other with memories and recent stories alike. I found I didn't want to run anymore. Sure, the men I lived with were total dicks to me, but their family loved them and had silly stories like any other family. It felt... normal and inviting. Maybe it was the second glass of wine talking, but I felt like I could work it out with the guys if I tried.

9

Emily

It wasn't until after dessert and coffee that the business was mentioned. Matthew announced that a Giovanni and a Taz were in town from Akron. Victoria and Harold looked worried, but Stephanie nodded seriously. I imagined she already knew.

"They have moved into our territory and have met with Milo and Sterling," Matthew said. His voice was like Milo's where everything had a slightly condescending note to it. "They claim to have differing business interests than our own and have asked for a meeting with Anthony and myself. Giovanni and Taz claim to have built their fortunes on MMA and boxing, and have demanded that Sterling, Milo, and Devon aid in building their audience here by fighting next week before they discuss any actual business."

My head snapped to Sterling and then Milo on either side of me, who both sat stoic now in their seats. Sterling swirled the remaining whisky in his glass. This was the first I was hearing about this fight and Milo's stiff posture told me that this was not a preferred tactic to making alliances.

"The meeting seemed like it was a social call, but they had been expecting Matthew and Anthony, not us," Sterling spoke up. "They were not forthcoming in their business dealings and claimed that our only overlap was protections. This had us questioning what they are involved in and the implications of being aligned with them." Sterling made eye contact with everyone at the table. "The meeting ended tensely and with a threatening air to it. I do not get a good feeling from going forward with a deal."

Anthony and Matthew were silent after Sterling spoke for a solid minute. Nobody spoke or moved until Anthony did. "Thank you, Sterling. We will consider your thoughts on the matter when we meet with them this week before your fight."

"Yes, thank you for telling us your *feelings* about our business deals," Matthew said with a sneer. Marie hushed him from her seat across from him.

I felt Milo and Sterling exchange a glance over my head. With two glasses of wine flowing in my veins, I felt the need to reach out a hand to both of their thighs and give them both reassuring squeezes. Milo tensed even more under my grip before I let go, and Sterling shot me a wink. I looked down the table to where Devon was glaring at Sterling and Milo, and I sat back in my seat with a defeated sigh.

"Yeah, I see him," Sterling muttered to me.

"He doesn't agree?"

"He didn't know the whole story."

Stephanie stood up and called the women to the kitchen.

Devon nodded at me to tell me I was included in her summons, and I followed. I rolled the sleeves up on my blazer as we passed through the doors and into the kitchen. I didn't want to get my sleeves wet while doing dishes. A slight wine buzz and warm feeling was sweeping through my body and I confidently approached the huge sink and turned on the water.

"Excuse me, do you need something?" an unsure voice asked me.

I turned to see a young, pretty, woman dressed in a black pinafore apron over a white button down and black slacks. Her hair was pulled back into a tight ponytail and her eyes were alight with confusion and worry. She was clearly a member of the house staff.

"No, I was just..." I looked around to see I was alone in the kitchen besides the young girl.

She looked at my rolled-up sleeves, my face, the running water, and then back towards a door to the outside. I had been looking down at my sleeves and hadn't seen the other women go out the door.

"Oh. In my family, all the women do dishes after a meal," I explained hurriedly. "Please, don't tell anyone I misunderstood."

Her posture relaxed as she realized I was a normal person, and a smile grew on her face. "Your secret is safe with me. The women are going to have coffee in the tea garden."

I smiled back and quickly went to catch up with the other women. There was a small, screen enclosed gazebo surrounded by boxwoods just outside the door. In spring and summer this place would be its most beautiful. I could see rose bushes and other foliage surrounding the gazebo and yard. When I stepped into the softly lit gazebo, the smell of coffee and cigarette smoke met my nose. Stephanie turned to me and handed me a lit cigarette and a full cappuccino mug. It seemed like they hadn't minded my brief detour or didn't notice where I had gone.

"Here, sit with us," Stephanie gestured to the white wicker furniture with tufted cushions. The gazebo was warmed by a little fireplace. Thick, furry blankets were available on each chair and Marie and Victoria were already cozied up under them. I joined their little circle around the fire pit and took a hesitant drag from the cigarette when the others did.

"Now, what do we think about Giovanni and Taz returning?" Stephanie asked us as she settled in her own chair.

"I can tell you that this doesn't bode well," Victoria said solemnly. She puffed from her cigarette and her wrinkled upper lip looked natural, as if the lines on her skin were from the repeated movement of sucking on a cigarette. "They left to avoid war with us when Anthony and Matthew took over from their fathers. Giovanni and Taz had recently lost men in a war with another gang, and they were in no position to war with us. They limped off, and we never heard from them again."

"Do you think they want to take over our business?" Marie asked and sipped her cappuccino.

"Of course, they do," Stephanie said. "Why else would they be popping up?"

"I think they planned on killing Anthony and Matthew if they'd shown up that night," Victoria mused.

"Anthony is still insisting that this is a good alliance," Stephanie said warily. "I told him it was a bad idea."

"Yeah, and that's why he sent my brother and Sterling and not Devon," Marie spat.

"Those boys know what they're getting into," Stephanie dismissed her. But I didn't miss the twinge of guilt that flashed over her features.

"Are the guys going to fight, even if we think they're going to be killed?" I spoke up.

"They won't be killed so publicly. It would attract too much attention," Stephanie explained to me kindly. "They won't be killed in the ring. The fight is the least of our worries."

"Can someone really build up a fortune with MMA fights?" I asked.

"Not like what they claim to have." Victoria shook her head. "Back in the day, they focused on prostitution and drugs. I doubt they've let go of that market."

"Well, then they can't stay," Marie insisted. "We don't allow gang run prostitution here."

"In this deal, I have little power. Anthony seems to have already decided," Stephanie said with a sigh of defeat. "It's not often he makes these types of decisions without me."

We were silent for a few moments as we sipped and smoked. I heard a round of male laughter coming from another end of the yard. I looked around and saw puffs of smoke rising into the air on the other side of a tall hedge. Glasses clinked together and there were celebratory shouts.

"So, Emily. Devon told me you were a teacher?" Stephanie asked with a smile.

"Yes, I taught kindergarten," I replied.

"I loved that age when the boys were young," she said wistfully.

"They are great at five and six," I agreed.

"And your ex-husband was a mayor?" she continued.

I nodded.

"Cheating bastard," Victoria added.

I smiled.

"I hope you made him pay," Stephanie said, her tone laced with aggression.

"Well, after he took our home, my car, and had me living out of a motel, I made him pay with his reputation. I told everyone how I caught him screwing his secretary on tax-payer property. And then I disappeared," I replied and took a long drag from the cigarette. I'd only smoked one cigarette in high school. I had hated it and felt so bad after that I cried to my mom about it. She had grounded me for a week. I let the smoke swirl in my lungs before I let it out in a slow, controlled breath.

"You've got balls, I'll tell you what," Stephanie said with a shake of her head.

"I'll toast to that," Victoria said and held out her cappuccino mug. "To lady balls!"

"Lady balls!" we shouted back and clinked our mugs together with shrieking laughter.

"Hey!" A shouted male voice came from the other side of the hedge. "Pipe down over there!"

We dissolved into more laughter and my heart lifted.

I was picked up from the tea garden by Devon and provided with a bag of leftovers to take home by the kitchen staff. Once we were all in the car, Devon whipped around in his seat to glare at both Sterling and Milo. "Why didn't you tell me all that? Why didn't you tell me Giovanni and Taz were threatening you? I thought you agreed to the fight?"

"It was... strongly suggested as our only option," Milo retorted.

"You made me look like an idiot in front of my dad and Matthew. I had told them that the meeting went well, and an alliance will come," Devon snapped.

"Aw, do you look like a poor leader now?" Milo fake whined.

Devon launched himself over the center console to hit Milo, but Sterling caught him and shoved him back into his seat easily. I quietly buckled my seat belt and set my clutch and bag of leftovers on my lap; happy to not be the focus of Devon's anger this time.

"You mentioned at dinner that the new family has different business holdings than your family. What does that mean?" I asked after five minutes of tense silence as Devon drove.

"Our family owns a deli, a salon, a restaurant, a hotel, and a spa," Devon replied, his voice sounding like his teeth were gritted. "Those establishments launder the money from our gambling rings, weapons sales, and drug distribution. We also offer protection to area businesses and individuals. That is where the other family claims to overlap the most."

"That's... basically everything I could think of that a mafia would deal with. What else could they have?" I asked hesitantly.

"There is so much more, Bambi," Sterling said with a smiling glance back at me.

"I think they deal with skin," Milo grumbled as he got back to scrolling on his tablet.

"Skin?" I questioned with a wince.

"Yeah, like prostitution or trafficking," Milo explained.

"That's what Victoria said. If that's the case, would we do business with them?" I asked with a gasp.

"If that's what our leaders want, then that's what we do," Devon said, and Sterling and Milo both looked at him, expressionless other than furrowed brows.

"We are definitely not going to just fall in line when other people's lives are at stake. We can't," I insisted and looked at each of them.

Nobody else chimed in.

"What else did you talk about over in the tea garden?" Sterling asked.

"Girl stuff," I said in response. The wine was less potent in my body now and I was feeling tired.

"Don't be a brat," Devon snapped. "What did you discuss?"

"Stuff," I snapped back, not pleased with his tone.

"And what does that entail?"

"Things."

"Emily."

"I told you. Girl stuff."

"Tell me," Devon insisted.

"No."

"I will stop this car right now if you don't-"

"Fine. Do it," I challenged, interrupting him.

I looked over to see Milo watching me and Devon with amusement as Devon yanked the car onto the side of the road with screeching tires. As Devon shoved out of his door,

Sterling and Milo gave me the same "it's *your* funeral" expressions. I bit my lip as he yanked my door open.

Devon leaned over and unbuckled me, shoving my bag and the food onto the seat. The scent of his expensive cologne mixed with cigar smoke in his hair, and I took a slow breath. He pulled me from the car roughly and slammed my back against the wet car next to the door. I let out a little squeak at the cold and wet surface. He leaned down until we were eye to eye. It was dark, so I couldn't see the honey color of his irises, but I could see his angry brow and clenched jaw.

"When I tell you to do something, you do it," he gritted out at me.

"Why?" I asked in an innocent tone. "What are you going to do about it?"

"I'm the leader of this family," he reminded me.

"Not mine," I said with a shake of my head.

He shoved a knee between my legs, lifting the skirt of my dress as he moved. He was pinning me tight so I couldn't move away from him. He was trying to intimidate me. It didn't work.

"Do you know what I am capable of?" he ground out, his voice low and threatening. A streetlight shone brightly behind his head and caused his face to be in shadow. I didn't need to see his expression to know he was barely restraining his rage. It practically radiated off of him and made the air around us buzz like an old neon sign.

"*Not* the dishes, I'm aware," I said and fluttered my long, false lashes at him.

Sterling let out a sound of amused disbelief. I turned to look at him through the car door, but Devon roughly caught my face and turned it back towards himself. He squeezed so my lips were squished and fishlike. "Don't look at him, look at me. I have you cornered. You are under *my* control. And you will answer me when I ask you a question."

Devon's knee was pressed against the apex of my thighs with enough weight that I could lift my feet from the ground and be straddling his thigh if I chose to... and I chose to. I lifted my feet from the ground and my weight rocked against his thigh as I settled, unintentionally giving my clit pressure I didn't realize it was needing. I did my best to not react to the pleasure. He huffed with anger as he realized I was throwing his intimidation tactic back at him. He let go of my face and slammed his palm down on the hood of the car. I yawned and asked, "What was the question again?"

He swallowed, and he blinked a few times like he was having a hard time remembering his own question. "What did you talk about in the tea garden?"

"We talked about how Giovanni and Taz are going to kill you. But not before you get your ass kicked in the ring for him," I said in a sweet voice and looked up at him with wide eyes.

Devon's jaw clenched, and I felt him searching my face. "Who said that?"

"Victoria. And Marie is mad because she thinks your dad sent Milo and Sterling to that meeting to be killed in his place," I said in a quiet, lilting voice. "Did he not send you because you're too precious?"

Devon stepped back, and I slid to the ground, my feet settling easily. "Get in the car," he hissed.

I wordlessly slid back into my seat and buckled before

I looked up at Sterling and Milo. Milo looked at me like I was an idiot and shook his head. Sterling, on the other hand, was staring at me like he was starving, and I was a perfectly cooked steak. I gave him a small smile as Devon got back into the car and shoved it into drive.

Getting Devon worked up was fun. If I wasn't going to be running from them, I could at least help them with any information I gathered to keep them, and by association- *me*- out of danger. I had been going to talk to them about what I had learned tomorrow, but if pissing off Devon was an option, it was always going to be chosen.

10

Sterling

"Alright, so I'll show you how to wrap your hands for MMA fighting first," I said to Milo as we entered the gym, Emily trailing behind us.

"I always used those inner gloves when we trained," Milo said as he opened his gear bag.

"For MMA you want a more customized fit. Especially in a high stakes fight like this one," I said and took out the new wrap.

"Wait, if you lose, do you miss out on the deal?" Emily asked as she turned on the treadmill.

"No, we just get our asses kicked by professional fighters," I muttered.

"Fucking fantastic," Milo sighed and sat on a bench.

"Here, I'll help you wrap up and you'll see what I mean about a better fit," I said and sat next to him. Our bodies pressed together hips to thighs because I needed to be close to him. He held out his left hand, and I talked him through what I was doing as I did it. His hands were long and pale, unmarred by split knuckles and cuts. His job within our family differed from mine and his hands surely told the tale. Silver and pink scars alike covered my hands where they weren't tattooed. His hands were often our first line of defense, though.

"Oh, I see what you mean," Milo said as he clenched and unclenched his wrapped left hand.

Emily kept up a jogging pace on the treadmill, but her eyes watched us in the mirror, rather than out the window. Her eyes were alight with interest, like she thought I couldn't see her in the mirror ogling us. Honestly, I couldn't blame her. Milo and I were wearing loose fitting, but short fighting shorts, and we looked good. His shorts were a forest green and mine were, of course, black. But our thighs were exposed and spread on the bench. Realizing that I had her attention, my cock twitched. Thankfully, I was wearing a cup and compression shorts underneath my fighting shorts.

Once our hands were wrapped and we were geared up, we got on the mat and did a few stretches. Milo wasn't completely new to fighting. We had trained almost our entire lives. But it had been a while since he had been up against an opponent hand to hand. It had been a bit for me, too. We had gangs that worked for us for that kind of shit. But I practiced with our gangs regularly and trained up new recruits.

Our first move was a jab. Milo scoffed and came at me hard. I blocked him with only a little difficulty. When he let off after a round of sharp jabs, I chuckled. "Alright, alright, I get it. You can do that one. Let me see an overhand."

Milo's eyes glinted with a competitive spark, and I knew he was about to come at me dirty. He hit me with a solid jab, an up jab through my gloves, and then a heavy overhand to my jaw. I stumbled but didn't fall. I glanced up at him for a second with what was probably a mirrored expression of his competitive spark and then used my hunched position to run through him and take him down with a double leg takedown. I lifted him at his thighs and threw him to the ground with my chest and momentum.

He sprawled on his back on the mat, and his chest heaved as the air whooshed out of him. "Fuck!" he gasped with a laugh at the end.

"That's what I thought! That's what I thought!" I pounded on my chest and backed away from him, grinning.

"Cheater!" he called as he stood up.

"It's not cheating, baby, it's using my advantages," I called back as I pounded my chest one more time.

"If your advantage is being bigger than me, then so be it," he chuckled.

"A solid eighty in muscle over you," I taunted.

"'*Muscle.*' Okay," he teased.

Instead of responding verbally, I rushed him, grabbed around his neck and side and had him on his hands and knees with me behind him in a second. "Let me see you get out of this one, little turtle," I grunted as I reached to put him in a choke.

He tried to buck back against me. It did nothing other than to get him further into the turtle position and have his ass pressed harder against my hips. He growled in frustration as my forearm closed around his neck.

"Take your inside leg and wrap it- there you go. Take the same side arm and lift under my armpit- yup. Now use my body to flip over and break the choke- you got it," I coached and then smiled down at him as he flipped around to face me. "Now, unfortunately for you, my base is still open, and I can get past your guard and mount you."

A tripping and scuffing sound came from the treadmill and both of us jerked our attention up to Emily. She was quickly turning the speed down on the treadmill, and she trapped her bottom lip between her teeth. I looked back down at Milo. He laughed at her flustered state and I winked at him as I sat up, holding out my gloved hand to help him along.

We took a water break before working on some jab and kick combos. Emily finished her workout, showered in the gym, and then left. We had warned her that all the doors had sensors installed and would sound alarms on our phones if she left the house. So, I felt confident in letting her remain unwatched for the time being.

When Milo's hits came slower, and a muscle in my back kept pulling tight, I suggested we call it a day. We were silent other than our labored breathing as we took off our gear and did some stretches to cool down.

"Devon's going to get his ass handed to him," Milo said as he grabbed a towel from the rack.

I shrugged. "He knew we were going to train today. He chose to go meet with his dad."

Milo shook his head and took the first shower while I got the sauna going. He was fast, and I washed off quickly after him. I met him in the sauna, where he was sitting with his head back against the bamboo wall. I sat on the other bench across from him. The room smelled like bamboo and euca-lyptus and Milo's soap. It was the perfect combination, and I inhaled deeply as I let my muscles relax with a groan.

He cracked an eye open at me and gave a sideways grin. "I had to sit over here after your latest video."

I snorted and adjusted the towel at my waist. "That's right, I forgot Emily's not allowed to be in here, so it didn't get cleaned."

"You are perfectly capable of cleaning it yourself," Milo scolded.

"Nah, I'd rather leave my mark," I joked.

"There are only two benches, and I like this sauna. I guess I should leave my mark on this one before Devon does." Milo laughed. He hadn't worn his glasses for our practice, and I enjoyed seeing his eyes crinkle at the corners. It was the only sign of his aging. I wondered if I had them, too.

"Go for it, I can close my eyes," I said and settled back with my eyes closed, a smirk still on my lips.

"Shut the fuck up," Milo chuckled.

I shrugged and relaxed in the warm room, listening to the hum of the heater and Milo's breathing. It occurred to me it would not have bothered me one bit if he were to jerk off in the sauna while I was here. Maybe that was weird, but I didn't care. Milo was the only person in this world that I loved. He really couldn't do a single thing to turn me away.

"Speaking of that video," Milo said lightly after a minute of silence. "You got another hundred subscribers. And the comments are feral for your 'unrestrained' moaning."

I shook my head. "I needed to bang one out and I figured

I'd film it. It was spur of the moment. And I wasn't moaning that much. It was... a manly grunt."

"You moaned."

"But like in a manly way."

"I'm pretty sure you said, 'oh yeah, daddy,'" Milo whined in a high-pitched voice.

I kicked at his shin and said, "Shut the fuck up. Some women like it when a man moans in their ear."

"Apparently it's what your subscribers want," he said with a nod.

"Too bad I didn't bring my phone in. I could have repeated the performance with a special guest," I said and watched for his reaction. Getting Milo riled up was a favorite hobby of mine.

"I'm not sucking your dick on camera," Milo said disgustedly as his ears reddened.

"Who said anything about sucking my dick? I meant we could both jerk off. A race or something," I laughed and clutched at my bare stomach.

Milo's face and the top of his chest were tomato red. He was staring at the wall above me and shaking his head. Sweat dripped down over his pecs and I watched the drip. I had forgotten what a tattoo free chest looked like. Inexplicably, my cock swelled to half-mast under my towel. Fuck.

"Do you have a security camera in here? Whip it out," I said and reached for my towel at my waist.

"No!" Milo said and stood up, clearly uncomfortable.

"Fine, another day. I think a special guest star on the channel would be cool," I said.

He shook his head again and left the room without looking at me. Laughing, I followed him out soon after.

"Wait, you said not on camera. So, you'd suck my cock off camera? Milo, that won't make us any money," I teased him.

"Fuck off, Sterling," he grumbled and pulled his t-shirt on over his head, ruffling his auburn hair.

"No, but for real, will you do a guest video? I think it would do well," I said and put my shirt on.

"Don't you think that's like... crossing a line?" He asked.

"Not really." I shrugged. "You've seen all of my videos and I'm pretty sure we all jerked off in the same room when we did our camp outs growing up."

"That's different."

"It doesn't have to be. Consider it?" I asked him as I finished getting dressed.

"Sure, I'll think about it," he conceded. His face was still tomato red over his beard.

We got dressed and went to the kitchen for something to eat. The hard personas we showed Emily were back in place like masks. Emily was plating some peanut butter cookies in her maid's costume. She looked up and smiled when we entered. When she turned away to get something out of the refrigerator, it reminded me of her bare ass under that skirt on Christmas morning. It was certainly a Christmas miracle to get a view of her perfectly rounded ass first thing in the morning. I had needed to physically stop myself from smacking it and turning it pink. She would have run away from us for sure.

She handed Milo whatever he had asked her for, looking up at him through her lashes. Even in the dumb costume, she was beautiful. She was wearing some of the makeup Devon had given her, and it amplified her natural beauty. She had worn a red lipstick last night, and I imagined seeing it on her lips around my cock. Fuck. I was getting hard again. I sat at the island and plucked a cookie off of the plate. Milo was looking down at her and saying something in a gravelly voice, and I was almost instantly fully erect. What the hell?

I needed to get laid. I scrolled through my phone, looking at my contacts for someone who'd be willing to hook up tonight as I chewed the cookie. Nobody was standing out as someone I wanted to call, even after I scrolled through the list twice. I guess I'd just make some more content for my Personal Camera page.

11

Emily

I brought a bag of trash out to the bin just outside the door. Milo had given me permission to do so, and I knew he was watching on a security camera. I had left him and Sterling in the kitchen eating cookies after their workout. Gathering trash and then stepping outside for just a few seconds was a little taste of freedom and I hated that I liked it. This situation was getting stifling.

As I headed back into the house, a man's voice called for me. "Emily! Hey! I have packages here for Milo. Can you bring them up?" I looked around to see a man standing near a little gatehouse by the end of the driveway.

I glanced over at the security camera above the door but figured Milo would know where I was going. I walked down and met the guy halfway where he was holding a stack of packages. A shout echoed from the side door, and both

Sterling and Milo came sprinting out. I startled and almost dropped the packages.

"Where the fuck do you think you're going?" Milo shouted as he caught up with me.

"Sorry, you have some packages," the young guy said, and held his hands up and backed away.

I turned to Milo and Sterling, wide eyed. "I wasn't running away. I was getting your mail."

Sterling looked chagrined, and Milo still looked irritated. I shoved the packages at Milo and stomped back to the house. I washed my hands at the kitchen sink and the two guys set the packages on the island.

"I think I'm supposed to apologize," Milo grumbled.

"Oh?" I asked airily and dried my hands.

"Yeah," he said and shoved the packages towards me.

"I'm waiting," I said, and crossed my arms over my chest.

Milo rolled his eyes. "Devon likes that bratty shit, not me."

"What? I'm just waiting for an apology," I said and leaned back against the counter.

"I did."

"When?"

"When I said I was supposed to apologize."

"That was not an apology."

"Fine. I'm sorry," Milo groaned. Sterling watched on with amusement.

"For?"

"For... not trusting you," Milo continued.

"Next time I'll...?" I goaded.

"Next time, I'll just watch on the cameras," Milo said stubbornly.

"Whatever, close enough," I sighed.

"The packages are yours, anyway. Your clothes. And a phone," Milo muttered.

"A phone?!" I asked. My heart pounded in my chest. It wasn't that I had anyone that I wanted to contact, but it felt like a step towards freedom.

"A phone," Milo confirmed.

"Am I allowed to wear my new clothes? Or do I have to wear this?" I asked and gestured to my maid costume.

"When we're home, I want you in the costume," Milo stated, and his eyes raked over my legs.

"Every day? How about weekends and evenings I get to wear real clothes," I bargained.

"No."

"Please, Milo?" I asked, almost begging. This costume's material was cheap and was not comfortable. Besides being degrading, of course. I clasped my hands together at my chest and gave him the biggest puppy dog eyes I could muster.

"Fine," Milo groaned and turned to open the boxes.

"Folded like a lawn chair," Sterling laughed to himself as he scrolled on his phone again. Milo and I both ignored his comment.

"Thank you, Milo," I said and fluttered my lashes at him as he handed me a box.

"Try this stuff on and let me know if anything needs returned," Milo grumbled, a pink hue to his cheeks.

I happily went up to my room and tried on the clothes that Milo had picked out for me. Most everything was black and white, high-quality brands, and a much more sophisticated style than I was used to. Eventually, I'd convince them to let me wear something I'd picked out. Milo had a good eye and had followed my sizing instructions, but with my curves, it was sometimes hard to gauge sizing. One pair of black skin-tight jeans was a size too small. I repackaged the item and brought it down to Milo in the kitchen. He and Sterling were both looking at a laptop screen, their shoulders pressed together, but jumped away and stopped talking when I entered the room.

"These don't fit. One size up should be good," I said to Milo, looking between the both of them suspiciously. I handed Milo the jeans.

"Alright, come down when you're done with the rest and I'll give you your phone," he said and gestured to the new phone currently plugged into his laptop on the dining room table.

I tried on the rest of the designer clothes and sorted them by washing instructions before heading down to get my phone. I didn't want to seem too eager and therefore seem suspicious. This time when I entered the kitchen, I walked quietly and slowly to better hear what they were saying. While I wasn't gathering information to take to the police upon escape, I was still learning about the family and the businesses they ran. Milo's phone was open to the calculator app and was not watching the security feed to see I was coming.

"Sterling, that's twenty grand! You need to do more of that!" Milo said excitedly.

"I will! I just don't want to lose subscribers who liked the more scripted stuff," Sterling said, and ran his hand through his hair.

"You can do both. I think maybe one of each a week is best

to keep engagement," Milo said and typed out a few more numbers on his phone.

"That's a lot," Sterling sighed.

"Is it? You don't jerk off twice a week?" Milo scoffed.

What? I did not know what they were talking about. I tip toed, so I was firmly hidden out of sight behind them.

"Sterling, at this rate of growth alone, you could make close to four hundred thousand by the end of next year," Milo said, his tone excited and insistent. It was more emotion than I had ever heard from him.

"I need to give you a raise," Sterling said and shook his head, looking sideways at Milo with a smile.

"I'll say," Milo agreed and returned the smile.

They held each other's gazes for a moment before Sterling broke eye contact first. He scrolled on the laptop and I glimpsed the website logo. Personal Cameras. My heart leaped to my throat. That was a website for amateur porn! I had heard of it in terms of celebrities posting content and moms getting kicked off the PTA for having accounts. Sterling was a creator on the site? And he was paying Milo? I bit my lip. Were they doing stuff *together* for the page? I pressed my thighs together at the idea.

"I could even increase it by doing special pay-per-view content. With special guests," Sterling said and waggled his eyebrows at Milo.

Milo shook his head. "Cut that out before I'm tempted by the money."

Sterling gave a dramatic gasp. "Milo Holden, I didn't take you for a whore!"

"Stop it."

"I'll give you half of what the video makes, *plus* your usual cut for being a dirty, dirty whore on camera with me," Sterling negotiated while still teasing Milo.

"Ask Devon," Milo muttered. I could see the red of his ears from my hiding place.

"Maybe I will," Sterling said with a glint of defiance in his eyes.

Just as I saw Milo pulling up the security footage on his phone, I entered the kitchen.

"All done. Just the one thing for the return," I said as casually as I could.

Milo handed me a sleek and cool to the touch new phone. "This is your phone. I'm giving this to you because we are trying to trust you to not fuck us over and call the police."

"I'm not calling the police," I said insistently. "I'm calling the local FBI office that deals with organized crime."

Sterling whipped his head around to look at me so fast that he almost fell off the stool. Milo's face settled further into his scowl and he reached for the phone back.

"I'm *kidding*," I laughed and clutched the phone to my chest. "You guys are too easy."

"Well, who are you hoping to call?" Sterling asked me.

I looked at the phone for a moment. The screen lit up and I thought about calling my parents. Maybe they were worried about me. I wondered if they'd been calling my old phone, looking for me. Was I a missing person now? Would I be if I never returned from my rumored trip to Europe? Tears pricked my eyes.

"Was anyone looking for me?" I asked, not looking up from the lock screen.

Milo let out a breath and turned to his laptop and pulled up some audio. It was a voicemail from my mom. "Emily, Gregory called your father last night and let him know what was going on. He said you broke your divorce agreement? Emily," she scolded over the phone, "you know there could be legal consequences for that. Gregory came round for break-fast and said that you'd disappeared off to Europe, but you didn't take your passport. I hope you aren't in any trouble. Your father and I can't travel anymore, so we can't come and get you when you run out of money. If you just-" Milo shut off the audio with a disgusted look.

"Just my mom?" I asked in a whisper.

"There were a few from your school. But I'm sure you know that you've been fired by now," Milo replied, his tone even and unaffected.

I nodded.

"Gregory and your lawyer both texted you a few times. Nothing of substance. Just requests for a call back. I was going to ask you if you wanted me to send your parents a message from you saying that you're safe and that you're not coming back. The last thing we need is your face on a milk carton," Milo said and watched me carefully. "I can use your old number."

I nodded again, words and emotion clogging my throat. No friends looking for me. My mom left one voicemail scold-ing. That was it. Tears pricked my eyes, and I stared at the new phone again. I almost set it on the counter and walked away, but I wanted that lifeline. If not to my family, to the outside world in general.

"Our numbers are programmed into it as well as the rest of the family," Milo said, and closed his laptop.

"Thanks," I said, and swiped at my eyes as I pocketed the phone into my apron.

Upstairs, back in my room, I messed around on the phone while lounging on my bed. I let the phone choose my usernames and passwords for a few apps like YouTube, TikTok, Reddit, and then signed in using the linked family subscription to Netflix. I smiled to myself as I made a user profile on Netflix next to the guys' profiles. I scrolled for a little while on YouTube and TikTok so that their algorithms could get working. Then I remembered Milo and Sterling's conversation about Personal Cameras. I paused for a moment, resting my phone on my stomach and staring at the ceiling.

Should I check it out? Would I even be able to see any of the content? I checked the time. It was still afternoon and dinner wouldn't be expected for a while. Biting my lip, I opened up a private window on the browser. I typed as quickly as I could with shivering fingers. Would he be using his real name? Once on the site, I used the search bar and typed in his first name and scrolled the first few Sterlings. With a start and kicking feeling in my stomach, I found him. Sterling Steel. Not his real last name, Hawthorne, but I figured that was a good call.

Did I dare open his profile?

I did.

Most of his stuff was behind a pay wall. His subscription was ten bucks a month. But there was a sample video available to tempt new subscribers. Did I dare click on it?

I did.

But first I got under the covers in my bed and blocked the phone from the camera above the door. To Milo watching on the security feed, it probably looked like I was napping. I turned the volume down low so I could barely hear it as the video started.

It was Sterling, leaning up against the dented black metal headboard in his room. His hair was carefully tousled to look like bed head, and he was smiling sleepily at the camera. All that was visible was his chest and face as he pretended to answer the viewers' FaceTime call.

"Hey baby, I just woke up... yeah, you too?" he pretended like he was talking to the viewer. He went on to say that waking up looking at me (the viewer) made him hard. Then he played shy for a minute and pretended like I was asking him to have phone sex. Then he pretended to give in and set the phone down on his nightstand, giving me a side view of his sculpted torso and hips. He coached me through doing the same, praising and complimenting my body.

I gulped and looked around my room, expecting one of the guys to be standing there, looking disappointed. But I was still alone. When I looked back at the screen, Sterling had his boxers pulled below his hips and his penis in his hand. A silver piercing sparkled in the light as he moved his fist up and down. He looked at the camera and spit into his hand. My eyes caught on the cold steel color of his eyes- probably where he got his stage name- and it felt like he was looking right at *me*. I knew this man in real life- had been in that very room- and I was having a hard time separating fact from fiction. Warmth had bloomed between my hips as soon as his shirtless profile picture had popped up on my screen, and now I was rubbing my thighs together like a sexed-up cricket.

Video Sterling groaned and rested his head back against his headboard. "Mmm, baby. I wish you were here with me right now. I'd kiss your inner thighs so gently until you were begging for me to lick your pussy." He let out a long, deep groan. "Then when you were dripping for me, I'd fucking eat you until you were screaming. Oh, fuck, baby, just thinking about the taste of your pussy has me harder than ever."

I paused the video, locked my phone, and flipped it over on the bed. I stared at the back of my phone for a long moment. While watching that video, I had wanted to reach down and touch myself. Sterling was probably in his room right now, just down the hall from me. This was so wrong. I shouldn't even be watching the video.

Here I was, though, watching a video of my roommate, boss, (kidnapper?) masturbating. And I wanted to join him. I mean, that *was* the purpose of these videos, right? People didn't upload videos of themselves getting off for someone to watch with a bowl of popcorn. I'm just doing what was expected of the viewer. Following directions. Opening my phone again I settled further under my blankets.

I reached down and lifted my skirt up to bunch around my hips. I rubbed lightly over my panties as I watched the muscles on video Sterling's arms shift as he moved. His abs clenched and unclenched like a heartbeat as he pumped his fist on his cock. He was practically growling out his words as he continued to describe what he wanted to do to me.

"I'd ease inside you so slow. Savoring the way your pussy

holds me. Squeezes me," he grunted as he kept eye contact with the camera.

My fingers rubbed faster circles over my panties before I shoved the drenched fabric over to insert two fingers into my waiting pussy. I caught a moan in my throat, afraid that even if Milo couldn't tell what I was doing by looking at the security feed, he'd know if I was moaning. I swallowed it down instead. My eyes were pinned on his hand pumping his cock and I matched his pace on my pussy. I matched his pace and imagined his scent surrounding me. He was the only one of the three that didn't seem to wear a cologne, so he always smelled like the soap in the gym showers- an Irish spring soap, and a little like sweat and pheromones. My brain fuzzed out as I watched, and I didn't retain any of the information about his role play he was grunting and groaning out. I laser focused on his hand, his cock, that peek of a piercing, his muscles, the rate of his heavy breathing. I couldn't get enough. The tattoo on the knuckles of his right hand said "PAIN" and I knew the left said "GAIN", but I couldn't see it between his legs as he cupped his balls. My mouth watered as he paused to spit down on his own dick for lubrication. The diamond and pearl necklaces tattooed on the backs of his hands had per- plexed me before, but now, seeing his hand wrapped around his cock, I understood.

He was still talking through the role play, but I didn't have the volume up high enough to hear more than a rumbling, groaning sound interspersed with gasps. I was so close, but I wanted to come when he did. I tapped the video to see how much longer it was- one minute- so I knew he was probably going to come soon. I removed my fingers and traced over my inner thighs and all around my pussy, waiting for it to be time to come. The muscles in his neck tightened and his eyes closed tightly. His mouth dropped open as he panted and chanted "fuck yes, fuck yes" over and over before he stopped and shuddered, biting his lip. I returned my fingers with vigor, rubbing and fucking myself to a climax at the same time come shot from his cock. He covered his chest with come while his hips bucked up off the bed and his hands slowed their pace. He came more than I'd expected- more than I had ever seen from Gregory, and I realized with a start that it would take more than a few swallows to get him down. I couldn't believe that was a thought I was having as I writhed under the covers in the throes of my own orgasm.

It had been weeks, if not *months*, since I'd come last. My body shivered with release and aftershocks wracked my body. I turned the video off and settled on my bed, hoping that Milo hadn't seen anything. My whole body felt pleasantly warm, and I stretched my muscles under the covers. I needed to remember to do that more often as stress release. It felt silly to have not thought of it before.

12

Emily

The door swung open, and Milo entered with a sly grin on his face. My heart had been slowing its pace but picked back up into a gallop. I let out a gasp and sat up. "You scared me!"

"He's pretty talented, isn't he?" Milo asked, that sly grin audible in his words.

"Um, what?" I asked as panic raced through my body. I curled my legs up under me in the bed. They were still trembling.

"Sterling. He works the camera pretty well, don't you think?" Milo asked, coming further into the room.

"I don't know what you mean," I said, trying my best to lie.

Milo scoffed as he approached me on my bed. "You're still flushed and trembling from it." He leaned down and looked over my face and chest, his pupils dilated wide as they left a burning trail over my skin everywhere he looked. "Did you come harder to a video of your boss than you ever did with your mayor husband?"

I swallowed and tried to look away, but he was so close to me it was like he was everywhere. An intake of breath caused my lingering shivers to be audible. I clamped my mouth shut and looked up at him to see him smirking down at me like I had answered his question. He took in a long breath through his nose like he was smelling me. I held still and pressed my thighs together tighter, hoping he couldn't smell my arousal. He let out the breath with a low rumble in his chest.

"How- how did you know?" I stuttered.

"Do you think I would have given you a phone without tracking your activity?" he snorted.

"I used a private window," I said, defeatedly.

He grinned and his face lit up in a way I hadn't yet seen from him. His usual scowl had fallen away. "That's fucking adorable. No, your phone has its own profile on our firewall. I see everything you do on the internet."

"Oh, I'll just use data then," I said dismissively and looked down at my nails, feigning boredom.

If I couldn't beat them, I might as well run away emotionally, so they couldn't kick me while I was down.

"As if I don't also have that protected," he scoffed again and backed away from me. "Now, I had actually come up here to talk to you about something else."

"Did you need something?" I asked and scooted to the edge of the bed.

His eyes lingered on my thighs for a moment. "No. Devon's home. And we want you to see one of the men that was shooting at us your first night here."

"Oh!" I gasped. "He's here? Why are we letting him in the house if he wants to hurt us?"

Milo smiled and a breathy laugh burst from him. "He's not trying to hurt us anymore."

"Why do I need to see him?" I asked as I stood up from the bed.

"We want you to see part of what we do. We need you to understand what our job is before we trust you," Milo said, his expression sobering into something much colder.

"Okay," I said and moved to my baskets of sorted clothes. "I just need to change. I, uh, got this costume dirty."

Milo's eyes raked over me again and his muscles tensed like he was fighting back the urge to go feral on me. Realizing that I had the upper hand, I slipped my soaked panties down over my legs from under my skirt. Milo swore under his breath as I kicked the panties into a pile of dirty clothes. I slid on a clean pair and then looked at him like I had just considered his presence. "Oh, you can wait outside. I'll only be a few seconds."

He wordlessly spun on his heels and marched to the door like he was forcing every muscle to move away from me. There was something about controlling these men that made me feel powerful and like I wasn't trapped here. It felt like the control I had hoped to get from being given a phone or from escaping them. I slipped on a pair of dark wash jeans and a black cashmere sweater.

"Shoes?" I called to Milo through the closed door. I didn't know if we were going outside or staying in.

"The boots," came his muffled reply. The black boots were one of the few things that he gave me that weren't from a luxury brand. I hadn't thought much of them as I opened them, but they felt like heavy work boots. I laced them up and met Milo in the hallway. He had been leaning against the wall outside my door and looking at his phone. He glanced over at me as he stood up.

"Where is he?" I asked.

"Basement," he replied, and my heart jolted.

"Those metal rooms?" I asked, a cold rope of nerves coiled in my stomach.

Milo nodded as we descended the steps to the main floor.

"What's in there?" I asked, my throat feeling tight.

"I guess you're about to find out, aren't you?" he chuckled darkly as he went down the basement steps.

We approached the second metal door in the basement and Milo knocked twice. The sound barely echoed in the door, making me think it was solid metal. Devon opened it and looked me over before stepping back. The room was inky blackness behing him. Milo gestured for me to enter first, and I took a deep breath before I followed Devon. I could hear a wet, gasping, breathing sound as I stepped around the door with Milo's warm hand at the small of my back. The air was colder here than the rest of the house like it had it's own air conditioning and reeked of urine and vomit.

My feet stopped suddenly when I saw what was in the room. A man was hanging from a chain by his wrists in the center of the room. It was dark in here except for a spotlight that shone down on the guy like a disorienting beacon. His pale hands were almost purple from the loss of circulation and blood dripped down his arms. He was naked as the day he was born, and cuts and burns covered his skin. Blood dripped down his body in rivers and his face was so swollen I wasn't sure he could see at all if he wasn't completely blinded by the spotlight. There was a drain on the floor below where his feet dangled and blood and vomit and urine were sloping towards it.

The door closed behind me, cutting off any sound from the house. This room was soundproof, which explained how I hadn't heard the man's screaming in my room.

I stepped backwards and met Milo's body. Sterling came into view at the edges of the light and the animalistic fury on his face had me pushing further back into Milo, towards the door. I choked back a gag and swallowed. My body trembled and Milo put his hands on my shoulders.

"This is what we do, Emily," came Devon's voice from the darkness to my left. "This is what we do to people who try to hurt our family."

I nodded, but I knew he couldn't see me. Milo's hands tightened on my shoulders. My nodding probably felt like more shaking in the darkness. "I see," I said, and my voice sounded raspy and choked.

"Did you know we had a woman with us that day you shot at us?" Sterling demanded in a growl.

The guy shook his head. He gurgled oddly through the blood in his mouth.

I gagged quietly, stifling it with my hand over my lips. The tightness of my throat had the sound of my gag sounding like a whimper. Milo rubbed my shoulders with his thumbs.

"We had an innocent woman in the car, and you shot at us. Your bullets missed her by inches," Sterling said in a voice so full of fury that I was afraid I was in the blast radius for when he detonated. "Devon, turn on the lights. Let this piece of shit see the woman he almost killed."

My knees knocked as I trembled. I heard movement near me as the spotlight went out and an overhead light flicked on. I blinked as everything came into focus. The man dangling naked in the center of the room sobbed at the sudden onslaught of light that wasn't blinding. Devon moved to lean against the wall near a tray of knives, brass knuckles, guns, and other weapons. Many of the knives were already covered in red blood where they sat on a surgical style table. Sterling was pacing around the man like an animal stalking its prey. His shoulders were bunched up by his ears, his arms held away from his body like he was ready to tackle someone, and blood splattered over his exposed skin. His eyes were wild and staring like I had never seen from a man before.

This man hanging before me had tried to kill the guys. He had tried to kill me. If he was untied right now, he would surely try again.

I gagged again, my hand coming up to cover my mouth. This time I whimpered after, fear racing through me.

"Are you about to-" Devon started, but his own involuntary gag interrupted him. "-be sick?"

"No," I said and gagged again.

Devon gagged in response.

"What the fuck is happening?" Milo asked as me and Devon both gagged back and forth.

"Get her-" *gag*, "- the fuck out!"

"I'm not-" *gag*, "-going to get sick! I do it when I'm-" *gag*, "emotional!"

"Look at that, you piece of shit. You made her fucking *sick* by being here!" Sterling redirected the chaos as Milo ushered me towards the door.

Milo shut the door behind us, and he practically collapsed with laughter. He tried to keep it quiet as he gently pushed me up the stairs to the office. Once we were away from the metal room, his laughter fell into howls of amusement. I couldn't help but laugh with him, in the way that laughter can be catching. I hugged my arms around my middle and giggled with him. Not because I found the situation particularly funny.

"You're an emotional gagger and Devon is a sympathetic gagger. This is great," Milo said breathlessly as he sat in the desk chair.

"I actually gagged when I found Gregory cheating. That's how they knew I was there. Me, gagging in the doorway," I said with an awkward laugh.

"That's fucking hilarious. I'll have to see if I can find the footage of that," Milo said and turned to the computer, typing in his password.

I sank into the armchair that faced the desk and let my body come closer to a resting heart rate and breathing. This was a test, and I surely failed. They showed me the ugliest side of their jobs in this family to test me and my potential loyalty. And I messed it up. I was going to be stuck in this house doing their chores and cooking for them for the rest of my life. They would never trust me enough to leave. I watched Milo as he typed. I couldn't see the screen, but his eyes were narrowed in concentration as he worked.

That man in the basement was dangerous. He had shot at the guys and me. The guys were going to kill him before the night was over. Was I comfortable knowing this? Should I call the police with my new phone? Swallowing hard, I looked around the office. I realized that that was how the guys mistreated someone. They tortured and killed people. If I truly thought before that I was being mistreated by these men, then I was delusional. It was an oddly comforting realization. They weren't mistreating me, they just weren't like the mild mannered men I'd been taught to love. If I wanted out of here, I was going to need to fight. But, if I wasn't getting out, then I needed to step up to earn trust and freedom.

Swiping my sweaty palms over my jeans, I stood up. I didn't say where I was going as I left, and Milo didn't ask. I went back down to the basement and knocked twice like Milo had when we first went down there. Devon opened the door and looked at me before looking around for Milo. "He's upstairs," I said in a reedy whisper.

Devon stepped back wordlessly and let me in. I brushed against his body as I entered the stinking, dark room. The room was pitch black except for the disorienting spotlight again. I couldn't see Sterling in the room, but I knew he was there. I heard his rough breathing and his shuffling feet. The dangling man was still alive. A few fresh cuts covered his tattooed chest.

"Let him see me," I demanded quietly to Devon. I heard Devon's hesitance before he moved to the light switch.

The buzz of the fluorescent lights filled the room as we all blinked a few times to adjust.

Sterling was crouched to the side of the man, bloody knife in hand, and looking like a beautifully demonic gargoyle perched on an old building. He was wearing a black undershirt tank top and his black slacks. The silver buckle on his belt shone under the light. The contrast of seeing him like this and seeing his Personal Cameras video was startling. But that was Sterling's specific brand of masculinity. He was barely controlled brutality and animal need wrapped up in a pretty package. His eyes contained a ferocity and anger that sent a chill down my spine until he looked up at me. His eyes softened a fraction.

"What are you doing here?" he asked me.

I didn't respond to him. Instead, I peered up at the man hanging before me. His watery and bloodshot green eyes were swollen and barely open enough to see me. "Are you a bad man?"

He nodded slowly. Blood dribbled slowly out of his mouth at the movement.

"Did you try to kill these men?" I asked.

The man nodded again.

"Why?" I asked.

"He can't speak. He has no tongue," Devon said darkly from behind me.

"Hmm," I said and pursed my lips.

"He owed us money and didn't want to pay," Devon supplied.

I raised an eyebrow at the man in question, and he nodded. A hacking, blood filled cough echoed through the metal room.

"Have you ever hurt a woman before?" I asked him. My voice was quiet, and I sounded as unsure as I felt in this smelly metal room.

The man didn't answer.

"ANSWER HER!" Sterling demanded, standing from his crouch and getting close to the guy with his knife in hand. His feral steel eyes drilled into the shaking man.

The guy nodded and flinched away from Sterling.

"Have you ever hurt a child?" I asked.

The guy didn't respond again. Sterling put his knife to the guy's rib cage, and he tried to flinch away from the blade with a whimper.

"Marcus Kidd, aged forty-three, criminal record includes solicitation, possession of a substance with intent to distribute, four instances of domestic violence, kidnapping of a minor, battery, child endangerment, public intoxication, and more," Devon read out from a paper in a monotonous voice.

He was a bad man. He deserved to die for what he had involved a child in alone.

The guy's head hung, and tears escaped his eyes, mixing with the blood on his face as he nodded. His crying sounded inhuman and unnatural without his tongue.

My stomach soured, and I tasted bile in my mouth. I moved to the tray of weapons and looked over the metal that lay there. I ran my fingers over the cold steel of knives and other items I couldn't even imagine the use for. I swallowed as I settled on a long steel dagger.

"Emily," Sterling said behind me. His voice was unsure and worried.

Devon said nothing, only handed me a pair of latex gloves. I looked up and his amber eyes were searching and understanding. He'd always been the hardest, the coldest, the most professional. He was the intended leader of this family- this mafia. By handing me the gloves, he was handing me his trust. He gave one slow nod as his fingers brushed against mine.

Unless I made a move, I'd also be in chains for the rest of my life. He was going to die soon anyway, I might as well earn some freedom.

"Emily, no," Milo's voice said, and it shocked me to see him in the room by the door. He must have followed me down here.

Milo was breathing rapidly and I could see his muscles were ready to jump in. To save me or to help me, I didn't know.

"He's going to die here tonight, right?" I asked Devon as I put on the gloves.

"He is," Devon confirmed after a momentary pause.

"Does he have a family?" I asked. I picked up and looked at the cold steel dagger.

"No," Devon breathed.

I held the dagger at my side and approached the crying man. I held myself tall and strong despite the trembling of my jaw. "You tried to kill me. You tried to kill... my family."

I heard shuffling behind me, but I didn't turn to look. They weren't going to stop me. They were letting me prove myself.

The man nodded, even though I hadn't asked him any questions. I lifted the dagger, considering where I was going to stab him. Maybe a slice across his throat would be easiest, but he was taller than me and I would be drenched in his blood. His heart was behind too much bone for me to stab at this angle, for sure. I considered for a moment before settling on stabbing up under the ribcage towards his heart. The dagger seemed long enough to do the job.

I stepped closer and pulled back my arm that held the

dagger. The man closed his eyes and braced himself the best he could.

I swung.

It took a surprising amount of force to stab him.

The man's eyes bugged open, and a coughing scream exploded from his mouth with a shower of blood. He jerked and strained against the chains for a moment before he went completely limp and silent in the chains. I didn't check to see if he was dead. He was silent and unmoving other than the gentle swing in the chains. I pulled the dagger out of his body with a wet sucking sound. I gagged at the sound and the emotional wall that shattered within me. After dropping the dagger on the ground, I turned to the guys. It was done. I had proven myself to be capable of this life. My body began to shake so much I could barely take a step. Sterling caught me around the middle as I collapsed.

Black spots crowded my vision as I took in a gasping, choking breath. I felt simultaneously like my own chest was cleaving down the middle and nothing at all. That man had admitted his evil and had deserved punishment, but my heart broke that *I* was the one who had doled it out. My body felt icy cold despite knowing I was being held by Sterling. The black spots overtook my vision, and I passed out.

I had never been in a fistfight. Never even did more than argue. My body had never been used for violence in my life. One time, Gregory and I were robbed on vacation, but we handed over our wallets without a fight. I was pretty sure that if someone tried to rob one of the guys I lived with now, the robber would end up dead in seconds. Devon would degrade the robber so viciously first that the mugger would be in tears before they died. Milo would have hacked their bank information and robbed him right back before he killed him. And Sterling would bench press the robber before snapping his spine.

And me?

New Emily would stab him. Up through the guts with an ice-cold steel dagger. Unflinching eye contact. A trembling lip.

The sound of water running woke me up. I was being held against a body while someone else turned on a shower. My hands felt icy, and I was still shivering. I felt feverish.

"Help me get her stripped," a rumbling voice echoed against my left ear. Sterling.

Someone tugged off my boots that were probably covered in blood. That's why they were more military surplus than designer. Very practical.

I blinked open my eyes and the two guys took note. Sterling sat me on the lid of the toilet and helped me strip to my bra and panties. Then he stepped back and quickly stripped out of his clothes to his boxer briefs. I looked around for a second and noticed we were in his bathroom. Mine still didn't have a shower head. The large shower in Sterling's bathroom was the same as in mine. He helped me stand up, and I accidentally glimpsed my reflection in the mirror.

A strangled gasp escaped me, and he and Milo jerked around to see what I was looking at. It looked like it had rained blood over my face and neck. My red hair was splattered and hanging in limp strands around my face. I gagged and this time bile came with it. I turned around to be sick in the toilet. Sobbing and retching into the water.

I had killed a man.

Killed.

As in forever.

Me, a small-town kindergarten teacher, had just taken a man's life.

One of them swept my bloodied hair back and kept it pinned to my upper back with a warm hand. I used their touch as an anchor to ground myself. I was here. I was okay. I settled my stomach and the sobbing enough to flush and sit back.

"Let's get you in the shower," Sterling muttered softly.

Milo picked up our bloodied clothes off the floor and left quietly as Sterling half carried, half supported me into the shower. He let the water hit me first, and I sobbed more as the water running down my body turned pink and red. My sobbing had my chest hurting right where I had stabbed Marcus. Sterling helped me wash with a masculine but clean smelling shampoo and body wash. I scrubbed at my body until my skin was red and stinging. Even then, I couldn't forget the feeling of blood on my skin, the sound of the man's dying scream. Sterling pried the washcloth out of my fingers, and I looked up to see him looking down at me through water-soaked black hair. His gray eyes were intense and soft on me at the same time, and I saw concern etched into his features.

"Why did you do it?" he whispered and pushed my clean hair back from where it was stuck to my face.

"So that you will trust me. So that you don't only see me as someone who cooks for you and does your laundry," I said, my voice desperate and rough.

"That's not fair, we had no reason to trust you," Sterling argued without fight.

"You brought me here against my will, you could have just let me go." I pushed at his chest.

"We had to take you in, it was a favor by Victoria," Sterling said and it seemed like that was only a small part of the truth.

"Well, I can't leave now, can I?" I spat. "There's evidence of my crime all over that guy. You could turn me in."

"We would never do that," Sterling said and looked at me like I was ridiculous.

"It's hard to tell what you'd do, Sterling! You've had me locked in this house like a prisoner! Maybe if I was treated with respect and trust and allowed some freedom I'd be more inclined to stay here!" I practically shouted.

He sighed and closed his eyes. "You didn't need to kill someone to get us to trust you," he whispered.

"Maybe... I needed to in order to feel like I belong here." I shook my head. "I don't know."

Sobs shook my body again, and I sunk to the floor of the shower. Sterling reached out a hand to rub my back as he sat next to me. I climbed onto his lap, desperate for affection and touch. He was stiff and uncomfortable until he settled on holding me around my torso. His skin was smooth and wet beneath my hands, and I rested my forehead in the crook of his neck. We stayed that way until Milo opened the door to drop off clean clothes for us. The sound of the door startled us out of our embrace and we looked up to see a sheepish

Milo setting clothes on the counter. He left quickly and shut the door behind him.

Sterling chuckled softly. "Alright, let's get dried off and dressed. I think we'll order pizza for dinner tonight."

13

Sterling

"Come on, you gotta be able to take me down faster," I barked at Milo. We were practicing for tonight's fight. We'd been at it every day this week, with no sign of Devon during our sessions. I had pushed Devon to at least spar so we could see where he was skill wise, but he had barely been home since Christmas. If he wanted to get his ass handed to him in the ring, then he was welcome to it.

"Fucking hell," Milo growled as he pulled himself off of the mat from where I had thrown him. He came at me hard, anger and frustration fueling his movements, and was able to knock my sorry ass flat on my back. Air whooshed out of me, but I worked to turn my hips to reverse the position with a roll and mounted him, sitting on his belly. He had been too excited to get me off my feet so quickly he forgot to expect my next move.

He roared in frustration and worked on getting me off

of him, but that eighty pounds of *muscle* (and cheeseburgers) had me sitting pretty and snug. If this were an actual fight, I'd start pounding, but I grinned down at Milo. I bounced only slightly as he tried to buck me off of him.

"If you do a solid double leg take down like that tonight, don't relax and think you're immediately going to ground and pound him. You have to anticipate him to have a counter move. Don't get cocky and excited. If you aren't quick to get past his guard, assume he's coming at you swinging that second. Okay?" I coached, still sitting squarely on his abdomen.

"Get the fuck off me, you fucking *cow*," Milo hissed, his face red.

We'd been working for over an hour and I was already getting sore. We couldn't risk already having tired muscles for the fight tonight. I stood up, helped Milo up, and headed for the treadmill to start my cool down.

"Let's make a deal," I said to Milo as I walked, and he stretched next to me.

"About what?" he asked breathlessly, as he rotated his shoulder with a wince. I made a note to massage it for him in the sauna.

"If you lose your fight, you have to be a guest star on my page. If you win, you get to *choose* if you wanna be in a video or not *and* I'll give you seventy-five percent of the page's earnings for a month," I said as my heart rate slowed.

"Hmm, how about if I win and I choose to be in the video, I get one hundred percent of the earnings?" he asked with a teasing grin.

"Sure. Deal," I said without thinking. It didn't make any business sense, but I wanted it.

"Wait, really?" he asked, stopping his movements.

"Yeah," I said, and held out a sweaty hand for him to shake.

"Then what's your payment for the video?" he asked as he shook my hand.

"Seeing you have fun. You deserve it," I said in a light and casual tone. His face was red again, but this time with a blush.

I meant it, too. In all the years I've known Milo, the only times he'd ever done anything exciting was with me and Devon. And technically, this time he'd also be with me, but it felt different.

Milo didn't say anything as he drank deeply from his water before heading to the shower. While he was in there, I started the sauna and drank my water. This time I set out some warming post workout body oil on the bench for us to use. Tired and stiff muscles before a big fight would not be helpful.

He came out of the bathroom with a fluffy white towel low on his hips, as he dried his hair with another. My eyes caught on his Adonis belt, that V of muscles between his hips. I had seen him shirtless and even in a towel in the sauna and never noticed that he had that kind of definition. Yeah, he'd do great on Personal Cameras. He threw me the towel that he had been using to dry his hair as we passed.

"You used my towel?" I asked, irritated.

"I used your towel," he affirmed cooly without looking back as he opened the door to the sauna.

"Dick," I muttered as I headed into the shower with a pre-damp towel. Once I was out, I hurried to the sauna.

"What's that for?" Milo asked, and pointed to the bottle of oil.

"Massage," I said, inhaling the soothing scent of the sauna's steam. "Pull the bench out so I can get behind you. I saw you working that shoulder and we can't have you tight and sore for the fight."

Milo swallowed and followed directions as I poured some of the oil in my hand. We both straddled the bench, with me behind him. I poured a little of the oil on his shoulder and caught the drips with my hand and rubbed at the muscles. He was smooth skinned on his back, only his chest had hair, and freckles dotted the pale expanse of skin like stars. He hummed as I worked a tough muscle.

His body swayed slightly with the pressure I was exerting on his shoulders and arms, and the knot of his towel came loose. The ends of the towel trailed on the floor of the sauna and it revealed the top of his ass to me. His eyes were closed, so he likely didn't notice the exposure. He had a freckle right at the top of his ass and it seemed to keep drawing my attention. I found myself wondering if it was the lowest star or if there were more. I shook the thought away.

When I hit a bunched muscle just under his shoulder blade in the center of his back, he let out a long, rumbling moan. "Fuck, that feels good."

My mouth dropped open involuntarily at the sound. "Oh, yeah?" I said breathlessly in return. Why was I out of breath?

Milo nodded, his head hanging now as I worked on muscles in the center of his back. I pressed hard on either side of his spine and cracked his back in a few spots. At the sound of the pops, he let out more moans and I found I was trying to make him sound like that again. I was desperate to hear that rumbling, breathless moan again.

"Can I crack your neck?" I asked him, trying not to sound as breathless and husky as I felt.

He nodded again, and I stood up to get a better angle, my towel falling off and landing on the bench behind me. I didn't care. Milo's eyes were closed, and he wasn't facing me. I cracked his neck and he let out another of his rumbling moans before I cracked the other side with an even breathier moan following. Milo let his head hang after and I peeked to see if he was okay (and I hadn't just snapped his fucking spinal cord) only to see that he was fully erect. Fully hard.

My eyes practically bugged out of my head as I sat back down and pulled my towel back on and knotted it at my hips. Realizing I was half hard, too. Fuck.

Okay, I needed to be cool. Be normal. "My turn," I said, and my voice cracked like a pubescent kid. I spun around on the bench and gave Milo some privacy while he put his towel back on. I'm not sure how he could cover up his dick. It was a lot larger than I had expe- *stop*.

I handed the bottle of oil to him over my shoulder. It took him a moment to grab it from me. Presumably trying to tuck his cock under the tow- *stop*. I sat up straight and heard him open the bottle. He poured some on his hand and on my back, catching the drips like I had done for him. At the first slow swipe of his hands, my skin erupted in goosebumps. I couldn't help it.

The guys knew I was really sensitive to touch. I was not a hugged or cuddled child growing up. That boundary had been set with the Bilals very early. So even now, my body was highly sensitive to when someone was touching me. Just a light touch had my brain lighting up with pleasure. I had craved a loving touch for so long that when I got it; I was addicted. And right now, I was addicted to the feeling of Milo's hands on my skin.

"I always forget how sensitive you are," Milo chuckled quietly. Of course, Milo knew my weakness. Milo knew everything about me. Milo was another who grew up without a loving parent, but he got hugs and cuddles from his sister when they were young. He always had Marie. So, he wasn't as sensitive as I was.

"Can't help it, sorry," I muttered as a shiver went down my spine. His hands felt hot and slick against my hypersensitive skin.

"You know, I always found it sad that of the three of us, the one who responds to touch the most is the one who deals in violence the most," Milo mumbled as he rubbed out a tense muscle in my shoulder.

A lump formed in my throat at his assessment. I wasn't about to cry with half a boner while my best friend massaged me, so I swallowed it down with a nod.

"I remember when you got this one," he whispered as he lightly traced a tattoo that covered my shoulder. It was a lily, the flower my mom carried in her bridal bouquet when she married my dad. It was some of my first ink. My back was almost entirely tattoo free because I didn't trust someone spending that much time behind me where I couldn't see them. Apparently, except for Milo. I realized this as he smoothed his hands over my skin. It felt like the hair at the nape of my neck stood on end as he massaged, and my goosebumps continued. I shivered again.

He chuckled. "Are you like this with women, too?" he asked.

I considered. "It depends on if I'm relaxed. If I'm not relaxed and not into it, then no."

"Oh, so you're... into me massaging you?" he teased.

I thought back to his erection from earlier and my own that had grown again. Fuck. I snorted a laugh. "I'm wondering if there's a happy ending or if I have to pay extra."

"You can't afford me," Milo joked with a sigh as he sat back.

"Make that joke again after the fight tonight. I've got some guys placing bets," I laughed as we got up to leave.

"Hey, speaking of happy endings..." Milo taunted with a mischievous grin as we got dressed.

"You want one?" I asked, confused where this was headed.

"N-no," he stuttered, surprised. He turned pink with a blush, and I smirked in triumph.

"Then what?"

"Emily overheard us talking about your Personal Cameras page," he baited.

"Oh?"

"Guess what was one of the first things she did with her new phone?" he lured.

"No way," I gasped and almost fell as I was putting a leg into my pants.

"Caught her seconds after she came." Milo's expression was wicked.

"Fuuuuck." I extended the word for emphasis as I stared bug eyed at him.

"She was all pink and sweaty and biting her lip," he

explained with a far-off dreamy expression. "She smelled fucking amazing."

"When was this?" I asked as I tugged on my shirt.

"Right before she killed Marcus," he said as he tugged on his own shirt.

"So, she rubs one out and comes to the cells all wet and sated, to then kill a man?" I groaned.

"I don't know how wet she was in the cells, because she changed her panties right in front of me and dude- they were soaked," Milo sighed.

"You saw her pussy?!" I stopped short as we were leaving the gym.

"No! She pulled them off under her skirt," he explained with a laugh.

"She was teasing you," I said incredulously as we walked out of the gym.

"Maybe, but she went and cried all over you in the shower later," Milo said in a way that admitted defeat but was accepting of it.

I shrugged as we went down the stairs to grab lunch. I wasn't claiming a victory yet.

"She killed him so we'd trust her, you know," I explained shamefully.

"I figured it was something like that," Milo said with a furrow in his brow.

"I didn't know how to tell her we'd never had someone join our family like she had and we could never trust her fully."

"Then what did you say?" Milo asked, looking warily at me.

"I told her she didn't need to kill someone for us to trust her," I mumbled, and I could feel the heat in my cheeks. "I don't know, man. How much should we tell her about our suspicions about her joining the family?"

"Yeah, I get it. Saying 'Hey, thanks for killing a man for us, but we think you're a spy from Anthony Bilal trying to keep us distracted from his fuckery' doesn't quite roll off the tongue," Milo agreed with a dark tone.

"I don't know. She seems truly clueless. The truth is in there somewhere," I sighed as we approached the kitchen.

Apparently, Friday counted as a weekend in Emily's book, as she was wearing a pair of jeans and a black t-shirt instead of her maid's costume. I wasn't complaining. I had missed seeing the outline of her ass in jeans. She had a hip leaned against the counter as she stared at her phone. Her brow was furrowed, and she didn't even look up when we came in. She absently picked up plates laden with lunchmeat sandwiches and slid them over the island.

"What are you looking at?" Milo asked her.

She glanced up at him with a small blush forming on her cheeks. "Oh, um, just the news articles about Gregory."

"What's the mayor up to now?" I asked, and then bit into a huge turkey and cheese sandwich.

She shook her head and put the phone down on the counter. "It's pretty divided between not caring about his romantic life and calling for him to step down as mayor."

"They should call for his head," I said, and took another bite.

The blush on Emily's cheeks deepened. "Thank you."

"For improper use of taxpayer funded materials," I said in a harsh tone but grinned when she snapped her head up to me.

"And probably his secretary's entire salary. They'd been doing it since he hired her, at least," Milo said casually.

"What?" Emily gasped.

"Oh, you didn't know? Sorry. Yeah, they'd been fucking on city property, in view of security cameras, for almost two years," Milo explained as he ate.

Emily and I both remained silent, staring at him.

"I did some digging," he said, and waved his hand dismissively.

"Two years?" Emily's voice wobbled. Her Bambi eyes were wide and even more Bambi-like as they filled with tears.

"And you're done with him now, so what does it matter?" Milo asked as he ate. "That is assuming he didn't give you any STDs."

Emily's squeak of panicked anguish was cut off by her covering her mouth with both hands.

"We can call in Doc, just to be sure," I said in what I hoped to be a soothing voice. I glared pointedly at Milo. "Dude, social skills," I grumbled to him. He rolled his eyes at me.

Emily turned away at the sink while she gathered herself. Milo and I continued to eat in silence, staring at her ass and then glancing at each other. While Milo hadn't explicitly stated that he was interested in Emily, I was beginning to think he was. I guess I was, too. There was just something about her I found refreshing and interesting. Every other woman I'd been with had only cared about sexual prowess (mine and theirs), power, and money. Emily... didn't seem to care about any of that. Perhaps I had been looking in the wrong places for interesting women. Who would have thought I'd have to check the suburbs?

When she turned back around, she was calm again. "Are you guys ready for the fight?"

Milo groaned and dropped the rest of his sandwich.

"Got it," she giggled.

"I'm going to need to be so drunk," Milo grumbled.

"After," I barked. "I'm not having you stagger around in the ring and get your ass beat even more."

"I'm allowed to come, right?" Emily asked, her eyes flicking between me and Milo.

"Yeah, of course," I said. "You can be our lucky charm."

"Oh, I was thinking I'd be cleaning up your blood after," she said sarcastically.

"That, too," Milo grunted.

"We could probably have Doc here for when we get home," I suggested.

"His number is in my phone." Emily waved me off. "When you guys get home, we can call *if* you need him. But let's not keep this defeatist attitude. Let's think about how we will celebrate *when you win.*"

I made a considering face. "Hmm, alcohol, burgers, and women."

Emily giggled again, and I looked to a blushing Milo for his answer. "I think I'm going to make a lot of money," he said in a sly tone, but his blush above his beard made him seem sweet.

"Are people betting?" Emily asked, clueless to what Milo was implying.

I was too busy beaming at Milo to answer right away.

"Yeah, of course. That's how Giovanni and Taz made a lot of their money. Allegedly," Milo answered her.

"Well, hopefully he lets you keep it," Emily said with a sigh.

14

Emily

Devon met us at the hotel where Giovanni and Taz were staying. Sterling and Milo were both visibly upset with him, but neither said anything to him about it. A mountain of a man named Mack met us at the automatic sliding doors. He didn't say much other than "My name's Mack. I work for Giovanni and Taz. Follow me" and "Show me your bags," before digging through each guys' gym bag and then checking us over for weapons. I was glad I was wearing black skin-tight fake leather pants and a black tank top under my coat, so Mack didn't have to pat me down as much as the guys.

Sterling had a hand at the small of my back as we walked towards the back of the hotel. His head was on a swivel and his other hand gripped his gym bag. It reminded me he typically ran security for the family. Milo wasn't even on his phone as we walked. He was on my left, just slightly behind me. Devon had taken the lead of our group and walked, stiff shouldered, next to Mack. Out the back entrance of the hotel was an empty white ten-seater passenger van.

"Get in," Mack said gruffly and opened the door.

I looked up at Devon. His jaw was tight, but he gave me a curt nod before he climbed into the van first. I wished they had given us the address so we could drive ourselves. I followed Devon in, and he tugged my hand to get me to sit next to him. He was in the first passenger row, where there were two seats. He sat in the window seat, and I was in the aisle seat. Milo hopped up and sat in the window seat behind us, and Sterling sat next to him.

"Do you know where we're going?" I whispered to Devon.

"We have a few guesses, but no," he whispered back as Mack walked around to the driver's seat.

"We all have tracking devices in our shoes and if I don't disable a program by four in the morning tomorrow, an email goes to Matthew and Anthony with tracking information," Milo said just before Mack opened the door.

"Like UPS, only sexier," Sterling joked quietly.

Devon reached around and buckled me into the seat. I was going to do it myself, but he got to it first. His woodsy, spicy cologne washed over me and I breathed it in. It was oddly comforting in this situation. Considering a week ago I had been terrified of him, it was strange to consider these guys as protective. I squeezed his hand quickly and wordlessly in thanks. His jaw remained clenched, and he stared out of the window as if memorizing where we were going.

I peeked back between the seats to see Milo typing away on his phone, his typical furrowed brow behind his glasses. He glanced up when he felt my eyes and arched a brow at me in question. Before I could open my mouth to say anything, Sterling's face popped into view.

"He's busy," Sterling grumbled, but smirked at me.

We hit a bump in the road and my nose bashed Devon's shoulder. I groaned, holding my nose, and the guys chuckled.

"Careful, Devon, that might be the only hit you get in all night," Sterling joked.

Devon quirked his lips in a small smile in response to the dig. He looked down at me through his dark lashes. "I want you in view of the ring while we fight."

"Why?" I asked.

He leaned down so his lips brushed my cheek. "I don't trust them with you."

The slight touch of his lips had me sucking in a breath and my blood going warm. I swallowed and nodded as he pulled away. Sterling and Milo were talking quietly behind us, and all I could hear was the low rumbling back and forth of their voices.

"I'm worried you didn't practice and you're going to get hurt," I whispered to Devon.

His amber eyes flicked up to Mack's reflection in the rear-view mirror and then back down to me. His eyes were intense on mine, his face just inches away. My fingertips tingled with anticipation. "We're all going to get hurt tonight, Emily."

"I packed a first aid kit in Sterling's bag," I replied. "I only know basic first aid, but I'll do my best."

Devon's eyes warmed, and he gave me a lopsided smile accompanied by a long exhale. My response had surprised him.

I realized he hadn't been talking about physical hurt. "What do you mean by hurt?"

"I have some new theories about what's going on," Devon said, his expression hardening. "If I'm right…" he trailed off and shook his head, glancing at Mack again.

We remained silent the rest of the way. Mack pulled the van up to a warehouse in what used to be an area of town dedicated to manufacturing. A few people had been walking up to the building out front where a couple streetlamps lit the area. The back entrance was dark except for a single door propped open. A thin stream of light stained the gravel. Mack parked the van, and the guys grabbed their bags in anticipation of getting out. Mack opened the door and stepped back.

"You'll go in those doors and directly to your right to the hallway. The only door open is your changing room," Mack grunted.

"Thank you, Mack," I said with a polite smile as I hopped out of the van. He stared down at me, a confused expression on his face, like I had just spoken French to him.

Sterling pushed in front of me to be first in the building. He looked around briefly before allowing the rest of us in after him. We walked silently down the concrete hallway; Mack had left us at the back door and didn't follow us in. A faint hum of voices and music in the distance was all that accompanied our footsteps on the dirty floor. I wasn't a fan of horror, but this looked like a set from a gory movie. My chest heaved with anxious breaths, and I worked to keep them quiet. Milo stopped walking and was looking up at the high ceiling. It was a metal rafter ceiling with hanging lights and a plastic and metal box with blinking lights.

He pointed up at the box. "Internet."

"With Wi-Fi?" Devon asked as he doubled back to where Milo had stopped. "That sounds like a security risk for them."

Milo shook his head. "They could have it password protected. But turning on a service bill can get them caught."

"Think you could hack it?" Sterling whispered.

Milo grinned. "Of course."

"Did you bring your computer?" Devon asked.

"No, I didn't want it taken," Milo scoffed, but pulled out his phone and typed for a few moments. He smirked. "We can look it over later when my script is finished hacking in."

"That's my boy," Sterling said through a grin and ruffled Milo's hair as we started walking towards our room again.

Milo was smiling and blushing, and I couldn't help but laugh.

The room that was left open looked like it had once been a staff lounge. Two empty and unplugged vending machines stood next to a sink and counter along one wall. A well-worn wooden table and six chairs were centered in the room, lit by an outdated and yellowing fluorescent light. Gray stained ash trays were on the table, giving the room a stale, ashy scent along with the damp, moldy smell of a leaking sink.

The guys threw their bags on the table and removed their coats and shoes. Their colognes and soaps scented the air and covered up the stink of the room. I took the first aid kit out of Sterling's bag as Devon gathered their coats and draped them over the dusty chairs. I used a small pack of Clorox wipes to wipe down the sink and countertop, planning for injuries.

"Your faith in us is astounding," Milo said sarcastically, noting my cleaning.

I snorted a laugh and shrugged. "Just in case."

Leaning against the counter, I watched them change. I wasn't intending on ogling them. I was worried about letting them out of my sight, knowing they were about to go fight professional fighters. But when I watched the three of them silently stripping out of their shirts and unbuckling their belts, my mouth watered. I kept a passive, mildly concerned look on my face as I watched so they wouldn't know I was outright creeping on them. My arms crossed over my chest and I remembered to remove my coat.

The guys had all worn their compression boxers (or whatever they were called- they looked like a pair of boyshort panties I once bought at Victoria's Secret), so their stripping stopped there. Milo pulled his sweater over his head by grabbing the back and pulling it up and I was treated to the sight of more muscle definition than I had expected to see from the nerdier of the three men. They put on their fighting shorts over top and sat in the chairs to wrap their hands. They were silent except for their movements. When sitting, the meat of their thighs spread on the wooden chairs in a way that would make me self-conscious but looked undeniably delicious on these men. I swallowed and looked up to see all three of them with the same furrowed expressions as they wrapped their hands.

Sterling was the biggest of the three of them. The muscles of his shoulders, chest, and back were pronounced and bulging, but his stomach appeared softer. No less powerful, just less defined than the rest of his body. Milo had definition in his abs and was more evenly muscular. Devon's power came more from the way he carried himself than from visible muscles- though he had those, too. He was lither than the others, like he preferred running to lifting weights.

Sterling checked over Milo's wrap fit before they started to stretch and warm up.

"Wait," Milo said, and pointed to another box hanging from the ceiling. No blinking lights adorned it.

"What about it?" Sterling asked.

Milo shushed him and then whispered. "It's outdated, not powered on, but also not dusty. I gotta get up there."

He stood on the chair but couldn't reach. Sterling crouched in front of him, and Milo got on his shoulders. Sterling gripped Milo's calves as he steadied under the box. Devon stood behind them in case Milo fell and I stood in front, my arms outstretched.

Sterling looked down at me and chuckled. "What are you doing?"

All three guys looked at me.

"In case he falls," I said and realized how silly that sounded as it came out of my mouth. If Milo fell, I'd easily be squashed like a bug.

"Fucking Bambi," Sterling chuckled, and the guys echoed him.

"Why do you call me Bambi?" I asked with an irritated huff.

"Your eyes," they all grumbled together as they went back to their task.

"Got it," Milo said, and Sterling lowered him back to the chair. Milo hopped off the chair and set what looked like the outer plastic housing of a device and a jumble of wires.

We all looked at the pile on the table as Milo picked through it.

"Hm," he said disappointedly. "It's part of a surveillance set up. It's outdated and old, but nothing outright suspicious. They could have been using it to watch us, or it is part of the old factory's set up. It was plugged into power, but I can't tell if they wirelessly connected it to the internet. Typically, these are hard-wired in and this one wasn't."

"So, it's nothing?" Devon asked for clarification.

"Potentially nothing," Milo said.

The door opened, and we spun around to see Anthony and Matthew walk in.

"Gentlemen," Anthony said with a smile as he shut the door behind him. "And lady."

"Hello," I said to fill the guys' silence.

The door opening had washed the room with cold air and a chill ran through me. Sterling and Milo on either side of me stepped closer. It seemed like they were partially shielding me from Anthony and Matthew, but I appreciated their body heat.

"I expect you've all been preparing for this fight," Anthony said cheerfully, but his demand for them to win was clear.

"Yes, sir," Sterling said.

"I know Devon has been practicing. He's shown immense improvement in the ring under the guidance of some of the best instructors in the area," Anthony said casually, but was very aware of the bomb he had just dropped.

Milo and Sterling stiffened next to me but didn't say anything. They had been practicing together and watching videos online and then practicing more all week. They spent all of their free time getting ready for this fight. And the entire time they were worried about Devon, he was getting professional instruction.

"What?" I gasped. Sterling nudged me with his elbow, and Milo shook his head down at me.

"Well, I will see you all tomorrow morning. I want you in my office at nine," Anthony said before he and the silent Matthew left, the door snapping shut behind them.

"What the hell?" I shouted at Devon at the same time Sterling and Milo also shouted something at their friend and alleged leader.

Devon placed his palms on the table and hung his head.

"Seriously, man, what the fuck?" Sterling hissed.

"My dad told me not to tell you," Devon groaned.

"Oh, Daddy said it's our little secret? Fuck you," Milo mocked; his arms crossed over his chest.

"No explanation would make sense," Devon sighed. "I fucked up. I'm sorry."

"I hope you get your ass handed to you tonight," Sterling snapped, his fists clenched at his sides.

Devon only nodded and looked away.

The door opened, and Mack stood in the doorway. "You're up," he said, looking at Devon.

"Keep her in your sight," Devon said quietly to Sterling and Milo as he backed towards the door.

"Oh, we will. And we're all coming to watch you get beat to shit," Sterling practically growled.

The walk to the ring was tense and nerve-wracking. The guys had put their boots back on for the walk to the ring and I was glad once I saw the glittering shards of glass and metal that still littered the floor of what once was a factory. The sounds of the crowd and music grew to a thundering roar as we got closer. I never knew underground fighting was so popular. My heart pounded in my chest as we approached the wide double doors that led to the ring. A rusted forklift stood to the left and men dressed like security stood on either side of the doors. They mumbled into headsets as we approached.

I could hear an announcer speaking about the opening fight for newcomers in town. A deafening roar of the crowd drowned out the name of the guys' opponents and their names being called. Drum beats of a rock song rattled the door and the security guards opened the doors for us with a flourish. Devon walked in, head held high, and slipped his mouth guard in. Sterling went next, swinging his arms and cracking his neck like he was warming up. Milo followed, stretching his arms across his chest and nodding to the crowd. I followed behind them with no flourish or smiles. These people were here to watch my guys get beat up. I understood the appeal of seeing a fight, I just didn't sympathize with it.

At the side of the ring, there was a bench roped off for us. Devon kicked off his boots, bent down and kissed my cheek, and got into the ring. My face burned where his lips touched, and if I wasn't so angry with him, I might have swooned. But that was not the case, so I just glared at his back as he ducked under the ropes.

Devon faced his opponent, and I noted they were similar in height, but Giovanni and Taz's fighter was definitely built like a professional fighter. "He's going to be killed," I mumbled to Milo next to me.

"He fucking deserves it," Milo almost growled back.

I looked around at the enormous crowd. It was mostly

men holding beers and smoking. I could smell smoke from cigarettes, weed, and cigars all mixed with the stench of sweat and beer. They were all cheering as if they were fans of the opponent or Devon, but were likely just fans of outward displays of aggression and testosterone. I didn't see Anthony and Matthew or Giovanni and Taz anywhere in the crowd, but I knew they were there.

A bell signaled the start of the fight, and I looked back at the ring. Devon was skilled in the ring, but the other guy was a professional. A professional in the sense that he did this for money, and not like he was famous and televised. This fight was illegal.

Devon held his own, and it was a brutal fight. Blood dripped from his nose and a cut below his eye. By the time the third round ended, Devon was knocked out with a solid kick. I didn't understand anything about the points system, but I could assume being knocked unconscious meant he had lost.

Part of me felt bad Devon was being dragged out of the ring like trash by two beefy security guards. The other part of me felt like he deserved it. His bloodied opponent was raising his fists and hamming it up for the crowd, and then turned and blew a kiss at me. I paused for a moment in confusion and then realized he was just antagonizing the guys since Devon had kissed my cheek before the fight. I rolled my eyes and then watched what was being done with Devon. Sterling was passively splashing water over his face to wake up his adopted brother. Devon woke up and limped to the bench and plopped down next to me. He didn't ask me for help, and I didn't offer it. None of his injuries seemed serious, besides maybe a broken nose. He could endure. I turned away and watched as Sterling hopped up into the ring.

The announcer hopped into the ring and shouted into his microphone. "Next in the ring is Cleveland local, Sterling Hawthorne, and Akron transplant heavyweight champion Will 'the Boulder' Hess!"

"Champion?" I asked Milo warily.

He only nodded in response, not taking his eyes off Sterling. I gripped Milo's hand, and he squeezed back as Sterling's opponent hopped into the ring to thunderous cheers. The anxiety of the moment made me gag, and I stifled it with the back of my hand to my mouth. Devon spit blood on the ground next to me and wiped more away from his eyes while unwrapping his hands. Someone brought him a bottle of water and he gratefully chugged it as he watched Sterling square up against the absolute mountain of an opponent. This guy was huge and covered in scars and tattoos. His face twisted in a sneer, like he just couldn't wait to paint the ring with Sterling's blood. Sterling was not a small man, but compared to "the Boulder" he looked almost waifish.

The bell rang to signal the start of the fight. If I thought Devon's fight was brutal, then this one was a disgusting display of gore and violence. Sterling and the Boulder fought four rounds and seemed to be tied for the win. Sterling was able to use the Boulder's size and lack of speed to his advantage and got him down on the ground. Bruises were blooming over Sterling's pale skin even as the fight continued. It seemed to go on and on, but couldn't have been over twenty minutes in total. Blood streamed from both men's faces and they both were spitting and heaving breaths as they circled each other.

Blood smeared over their chests and stomachs when they locked into holds. If I had been a squeamish person, I'd be sick at the sight.

The amount of blood reminded me of the man who I had killed in the basement just days before. I had been forcing myself to not think about that day in order to not freak out. But the amount of blood in the ring brought everything back in full force. I swallowed gulps of stale, smoky air and hoped the nicotine and weed in the air would calm me down. The hand that wasn't squeezing Milo's was pressed against my stomach, hoping to settle it.

Sterling had the Boulder on the ground and was on him punching viciously. The man flipped Sterling over, but Sterling didn't let him keep him pinned. Milo, Devon, and I stood at the side of the ring screaming encouragements as the referee counted down until the end of the match. My throat ached from screaming and the stinging, smokey air. Sterling could beat him. Sterling could win this fight.

With a guttural scream of rage and effort, Sterling gained the upper hand again and had the Boulder below him. The referee signaled the end of the match, and the bell rang again. I couldn't tell who won until the referee lifted Sterling's hand and Sterling pumped his free arm in the air. He stumbled on his feet, seeming woozy while he beat his chest and hammered it up for the crowd. He took out his mouth guard and kissed two fingers before pointing them at me and Milo ringside. I beamed at him as much as I could while he was still covered in blood and swaying on his feet.

He stiffly got himself out of the ring and Milo caught him as he stumbled towards the bench. As they approached, I reached out and helped Sterling fall onto the bench. "Let's go get you cleaned up," I said to him.

"No, I want to see Milo," he said through a mouthful of blood. Someone handed him a bottle of water and a towel. He chugged the water, and I gingerly wiped his face of blood. Nothing seemed serious other than a swollen eye, but head wounds bled forever.

Milo stretched while the referee and the announcers cleared the ring for the next match. His jaw was clenched and his eyes glaring as he stretched out his arms. As the announcer got up in the ring and started talking about bets, Sterling reached for Milo. Milo bent to hear Sterling and nodded while Sterling gripped the back of his neck and gave him last-minute instructions or encouragements in his ear. I couldn't hear what Sterling was saying, but his firm grip on the back of Milo's neck while he talked to him inexplicably made my heart swell. Devon was practically vibrating with anticipation and nerves next to me, his knees bouncing as he held his cold water bottle to his face. Milo stood up as the announcer called his name and handed me his glasses. I placed them, still warm from his skin, on my head like sunglasses as he climbed into the ring. Sterling limped to the ringside, and I followed him. Devon joined us soon after, but kept a few feet of distance.

"He can do this," Sterling said and looked down at me. A cut above his eye still bled steadily down his face and his black hair was disheveled and wet with sweat, making him look more fierce than usual.

I could only nod and swallow anxiously. I knew Milo was a trained fighter and I could probably trust him with my life, but knowing that he was up against a professional fighter had my stomach clenched with nerves. Sterling gripped my hand in his still wrapped fist as Milo squared up against his opponent. His opponent wasn't introduced with any intimidating nickname, but he was clearly more muscular and a more prepared fighter than Milo.

The fight began, and Milo held his own. Sterling and I screamed from the sidelines, backing up when the fighters fell against the ropes near us. "Yes! That's my boy! Hell yeah, baby!" Sterling was screaming as Milo straddled his opponent and pounded his fists into the man's face.

Sterling's hand was tight around mine, almost to the point of pain, but I didn't mind. My focus was entirely on Milo. A round ended and Sterling's voice carried the most as he praised his best friend. "Good boy, Milo. You've got this. Just like we practiced."

"Come on, Milo! I know you can do it!" I added.

Milo's eyes cut to us at the side of the ring, and he seemed to get a second wind from our praise.

"Finish this so we can go home, baby boy. Let's go!" Sterling barked up at him and pounded his fist on the ring.

Milo gave a single nod and turned back to the fight to start the next round. While his opponent was undeniably skilled, Milo was sneaky. He faked a right jab and then landed a hammer of a left jab and knocked his opponent out. The man dropped like a sack of potatoes and Milo stood and watched for a long moment with his fists still up, like he was expecting the man to jump back up and fight more.

The crowd was screaming, roaring. Sterling was shaking me and jumping as he screamed. I couldn't make out his words in the thunder of the factory crowd, but his eyes never left Milo. The referee looked just as shocked as Milo was as he lifted Milo's hand to announce his victory. Milo and the referee turned around to each side of the crowd with their hands up before Milo was released. Milo didn't raise his hands for the crowd. He didn't ham it up. He slipped down the side of the ring and limped stiffly towards us. His left eye was swollen, and his lip was bleeding, but he was less bloody than the other guys. Sterling pulled him into a hug by his hair and Milo winced as he folded into the embrace. He pulled his mouth guard out and then pulled me into the hug as he spoke to Sterling. I couldn't hear what he said, but it made Sterling's cheeks turn pink before he laughed and ruffled Milo's hair.

A hand rested on my bare shoulder and I looked up to see Devon, a serious expression on his face. "My father and Matthew just snuck out that back door. I'm going to follow," he said to us, cutting the celebration short.

"I'll go with you," Milo insisted. "Sterling, get patched up. You're still bleeding everywhere."

It was true. Devon's nose and other injuries had mostly stopped bleeding, but Sterling's cut above his eye was still flowing. "Let's meet in the room before we figure out how we're getting out of here," I said.

We separated, and I felt the smokey air swirl up between us, giving an ominous and tense aura to the moment. It was as if the true fights were just the beginning.

15

Emily

Milo and Devon left us and made their way through the crowds to where I assumed was the back door. Sterling grabbed my hand again and led us through the doors we had come in. As soon as we were through the double doors, the roar of the crowd was cut in half. My ears rang in its absence. As we made our way down the empty concrete halls, all I could hear was our ragged breathing and that incessant ringing.

Back in the room that had been dedicated to our use, Sterling collapsed into a chair with a groan. I rushed to the first aid kit and found some antiseptic and butterfly closures. I filled his water bottle at the sink to use to rinse the blood from his face. He leaned forward in his seat as I approached with the water. I poured it over his face to rinse some of the blood clear to see the cut. The bloody water splattered on the concrete ground. His eyes were closed and remained that way even as he leaned back in the chair and his breathing slowed to normal. We were silent as I worked to blot the wound with a paper towel. He hissed in a breath when I brushed the edge of the cut.

"Sorry," I murmured as I readied two butterfly closures on the table. I needed to get closer to him to place the bandages. I stood on one side of his chair but couldn't get the angle right and then tried the other. Still not close enough. I sighed and scooted my feet, so I was standing straddling him. I was centered on him now and at a perfect angle to get the bandages on. He cracked one gray blue eye open as he watched me. He raised the non-bleeding eyebrow at me, and I scoffed. "I need to be close to bandage you."

"I wasn't complaining." His quiet voice was like a growling rumble.

"You raised a judgey eyebrow at me," I said in explanation as I dabbed on antiseptic. The antiseptic was probably not going to do much since he was still trickling blood, but I had to try. He winced at the contact and more blood seeped out. "Stop moving. Honestly, you should probably get stitches for this. It might scar weird if you don't."

"Oh no, a permanent mark on my body," he bemoaned sarcastically and flexed his tattooed pecs so that they jumped, one and then the other.

I giggled. My legs shook with the effort of holding the standing position I was in, and I gave in and sat on his lap. His hands reflexively came to rest on my thighs as both of his eyes opened. I could feel myself blushing as I blotted away the blood on his brow and placed the bandage. His eyes and hands had remained on me as I placed the bandage. When I finished, I sat back and looked him over to see if anything else needed attention, using my hands at his jaw to turn his head this way and that way. He was certainly bruised and would likely hurt for days, but nothing else needed bandaged. I felt his stare almost as much as I felt my thighs draped around his warm legs. The heat from his body seeped through the fabric of my tight jeans. My breathing was heavy again, and the movement expanded my belly and made the crease of my jeans at the tops of my thighs pinch with every inhale.

My eyes finally met his, and I suddenly felt embarrassed to be straddling his lap. This was too close to be professional. His pupils dilated, and I was glad to see them even and not concussed as they smoothly tracked my tongue that I didn't realize was swiping over my bottom lip. His hands slid up my thighs to my ass and my lower back and he quickly pulled me towards him. My heart jumped in shock and my hands slapped onto his chest. His lips met mine just as I gasped at the sudden and forceful movement.

It took a solid three seconds before I realized Sterling was kissing me. His tongue swept into my open mouth and slid against mine. My gasp turned into a whimper as my hands clutched at his bare chest and I gave in to the kiss. The blood in my veins thrummed and vibrated with a fuzzy sort of pleasure. His face was still wet with water and his lips slid against mine easily. He groaned against my lips when I started kissing him back, and he pulled me even closer to him. My heart pounded a rhythm that barely outpaced the needy throbbing in my core. I fisted my hands in the sweaty hair at the back of his neck and rolled my hips against his, arching my back. His hands kneaded the flesh of my ass with a bite of pain. His hands were still wrapped for the fight, so I broke the kiss and scooted back, grabbing for his hands. I held his hands between us with our sweaty foreheads touching and our ragged breathing mingling as I unwrapped him. It was strangely erotic as I unveiled his tattooed hands. Over one set of knuckles the word "PAIN," the other "GAIN" above the black and white jewelry along the back of his hand. I remembered the sight of his hand around his shaft in his video and how that jewelry tattoo complemented the piercing he had in his cock. With a trembling intake of breath, I replaced his now unwrapped hands on my body. One on my breast and one on my ass as my lips came back down to meet his.

His kiss was hungry, but slow. Fierce and dominating, but with an undercurrent of gentleness. It felt like the physical embodiment of how he had treated me the past two weeks together. And it wasn't until his lips were on mine that I realized it was what I had been craving. How long? I didn't know, but the realization glowed in my mind's eye that Sterling had not been cruel to me but had guided me through this transition to this new life. He had watched over me the first few days to make sure I wasn't going to run, and I had framed it as being held captive. Maybe this was the standard definition of Stockholm Syndrome. But I figured if it felt like this, then I didn't care.

He squeezed my breast through my tank top, and I let out a breathy moan. I could feel his arousal under my hips as he lifted the hem of my shirt. I rolled against him, and he groaned, and his hips lifted in reaction. One of his hands slipped under my bra and was gently but firmly gripping my naked breast as he rocked my hips against his with his other hand. His rough fingertips brushed against my nipple, and I almost cried out at the sensation. He smiled against my lips.

The door swung open, and I jumped off of him. Milo and Devon came into the room and looked at us suspiciously. Milo had been walking behind Devon, who was holding a sweating water bottle to his swelling eye, so they had somehow missed the sight of me jumping off of Sterling. We would have gotten away with it entirely had Sterling not been sitting man spread on the chair with an obvious erection straining his shorts and his lips rosy and wet. I tugged my shirt down and cleared my throat.

"Did you hear anything?" I asked, aiming for a more casual tone.

"They're meeting on the first of the year at a neutral location," Devon said with a shake of his head.

"Giovanni wanted to talk right now, but Matthew refused to talk business anywhere not neutral," Milo said and sat down stiffly in a chair. Devon took his cue to sit as well.

I washed my hands while Sterling asked them where and when the meeting was happening. Gathering more paper towels, I approached the guys.

"I'll get Milo. He doesn't need much. Fucking miracle," Sterling said with a chuckle.

"He's our Batman," I giggled and moved to Devon.

Devon was silent as Sterling and Milo talked about Batman's computer and technology prowess and the gadgets they would like to use in a fight. Devon kept his eyes downcast as I worked to clean and patch him up. I poked at his cuts and bruises a little more than necessary, but he deserved it. Despite having been knocked unconscious, he didn't seem concussed. He wasn't vomiting and could walk in a straight line; his words weren't jumbled, and his pupils seemed even and reactive. I would have to check on him later after I did some more Googling to see what I needed to look for.

Once the guys were cleaned up and were changing back into their clothes, I doled out some ibuprofen. They limped out of the building, not wanting to stick around for any celebrations. Or, rather, opportunities to be roped into more fights. We were silent as Devon ordered an Uber and we walked around to the front of the building. We stuck to the shadows of the street as groups of people walked out to their cars wherever they had parked them inconspicuously.

When our Uber pulled up, he was clearly confused why he was picking us up in this location, but didn't say any-thing about it as we settled into his sedan. Devon got into the passenger seat while Sterling, Milo, and I crammed into the back seat. I was wedged between them so tightly that I couldn't even root around for my seat belt without reaching under their asses, so I opted to go without. The drive was silent. Even our driver didn't want to have small talk with three sweaty and beat up guys in the car. I didn't mind the silence; my ears were still ringing.

We pulled up to the hotel where we had left the cars and we tumbled out of the back seat. Devon remained in the pas-senger seat and handed the driver an additional tip, and said something to him. The driver's eyes widened, and he nodded nervously. Devon climbed out of the car, and the driver sped out of the parking lot. Devon had driven separately, so he walked away from us towards his SUV, but stopped and turned back. Still angry with him, I turned away sharply.

Sterling grinned and draped an arm over my shoulders as we walked with Milo towards Sterling's classic Cadillac.

"Shotgun!" I shouted as we approached the car.

"No," Milo grunted.

"I called it fair and square."

"She did, Mi," Sterling chuckled.

"Whatever," Milo grumbled and threw his bag into the backseat and then climbed in after it.

We pulled out of the parking lot and were on the road before anyone spoke.

"So, you won your fight," Sterling said and glanced back at Milo in the mirror.

"I did," Milo said, sounding exhausted.

There was silence. We had all been there for the fight. Was Sterling concussed? That could explain the kiss.

"And?" Sterling prompted Milo.

"And I want one hundred percent of the earnings for the video, and fifty percent for the month," Milo replied.

Sterling gave a whoop of delight and was grinning bigger than I'd ever seen on him.

"What are you talking about?" I asked, smiling at his infectious excitement.

"Mi-Mi is going to be a porn star!" Sterling explained with a laugh.

I blushed. "You guys are gonna..."

"No!" they both shouted at me at the same time.

I couldn't help the snort of laughter that came from me.

"Solo, but... together on my Personal Cameras page. I heard about your exploration, by the way," Sterling said and winked at me.

A blush of mortification rose to my face. "Well, good for you, Milo. I guess?"

"Thanks," Milo said with a yawn.

"When's that to happen?" I asked. "I'll have to subscribe." If I can't avoid the embarrassment, I might as well lean into it.

"I already made you a viewer account. Since you liked it so much," Milo said sleepily.

I laughed. Because, again, leaning into the embarrassment. "I guess I have plans tomorrow."

"And then New Year's, the day after tomorrow, we're having a party," Sterling informed me.

"Oh?"

"Yeah, we do every year," he explained.

"What kind of party?" I asked.

"What do you mean? We have people over, order food and booze, and have a DJ," Sterling sounded confused.

"Oh, so not a formal party," I said.

"No, that's just for Anthony and Matthew," Sterling said with his nose crinkled. "They like that stuffy shit."

"Devon, too," I said rather than asked.

Sterling and Milo both laughed, and Sterling patted my thigh as if to congratulate me for making a good joke.

"You are not wrong," Milo said through his laugh.

I rested my head against the seat with a smile, feeling more comfortable than I had in days.

16

Emily

The guys weren't kidding when they said they were going to throw a party. I had spent the day dodging random people who were coming in and out to set up. There had been caterers, a DJ, and at least ten people removing any valuables in the house and moving furniture around. I walked downstairs to hesitantly join the party in a pair of jeans and an emerald green t-shirt, only to see a group of girls in mini dresses and skirts. I turned right back around and changed into a short, black bodycon dress and heels. I wasn't exactly trying to dress to impress, but I certainly didn't want to stand out by under dressing.

I waded through the crowd of people to get to the kitchen for a drink and something to eat. The atmosphere was the same as any house party: loud music, drinks, lots of people, and pizza. Except, this pizza and these drinks were catered and bartended. It was kind of funny to see girls dancing to the latest pop hits in a living room while sipping expensive drinks instead of looking like college kids drinking cheap beer out of red plastic cups. I wondered if there would be a keg stand later.

There was a bar in the hearth room already, so I imagined the bartender was in there. I picked up a plate filled with fancy finger foods and a slice of pizza and headed towards the bar. A martini sounded great tonight. It was the most crowded in the hearth room and I squeezed my way to the bar. I felt the eyes of a trio of girls before I turned to acknowledge them. And I say *girls* intentionally because they barely looked twenty-one. Giving them a small smile, I turned back to the bartender as he approached me. I ordered a martini and was presented with a drink with gold leaf around the rim. These guys apparently went all out for their New Year's parties.

Turning back, I saw the girls still looking at me. "Hello," I said and smiled again before sipping my drink. It was perfect.

"Who are you here with?" one girl asked. She crossed her arms over her chest.

"Nobody," I replied.

"Which gang?" she clarified, like I was dense.

"None, I guess," I replied.

"We haven't seen you before," another girl said and flicked her perfectly styled brown hair over her shoulder.

"Oh, I'm new," I said and decided that despite their bratty attitudes, I was going to remain kind. I was most definitely not going to start a gang war in the hearth room.

"Who are you going after tonight?" the first girl asked and looked me up and down.

"Right now, just these bruschetta bites," I said with a laugh and gestured with the plate in my hand.

"Well, the trio is ours," the brunette said with a sneer.

"Who?" I asked, realizing just after the words came out that she meant my guys... er, *the* guys. "Oh, Devon, Sterling, and Milo?"

They nodded.

"Here, do you know where they are? I can start up a conversation for you. Get you in," I said and ignoring the pang of jealousy. I didn't want them talking to the guys, but I wasn't about to cock block them, either.

They blinked at me in confusion. I turned back to the bartender and flagged him down. "Hey, do you know where Devon, Sterling, or Milo are?"

"They're presiding over their people in the den," the bartender said with an eye roll. "Good luck getting to them."

I thanked him and turned back to the girls who were talking amongst themselves. "Come on, they're in the den." I led them through the crowds of people through the kitchen to the den and saw that the three guys were presiding literally *over* the people. Before, when the bartender rolled his eyes, I had made a mental note to tell Devon not to hire him again, but now I agreed with the eye roll. Wholeheartedly.

Devon, Milo, and Sterling were sitting in actual thrones on a raised stage that was against the windows. Their thrones looked to be made out of a dark wood and draped with metal chains. The music in this room was heavy metal screaming and lights were flashing white and red. The wall of windows behind the guys was draped with sheer black curtains, but the night sky was still visible. I blinked against the harsh strobe light and ducked around two girls that were making out and grinding to the music. An odd choice, but I was new here-what did I know? The paintings and bookshelves that had decorated this room were gone and more black gauze hung to cover the beige walls. Red uplighting was interspersed along the walls, looking like flames. The general ambiance of this room was like I was descending into hell (when it was just three stairs below the kitchen I cooked in every day) and walking towards three devils. The shadows and flashing lights emphasized the bruises on their faces and scabbed over cuts on their knuckles. They were glaring and looked disinterested in their surroundings, like they weren't the ones throwing the party in the first place. Knowing these guys in their natural states made the theatrics involved seem a bit ... cringey.

I waved cheerfully up at them and turned back to see my three little ducklings following me closely. A large man came out of nowhere and held his hand up to stop me from getting closer. I had been looking back at the girls, so I bumped into his large stomach. He was shaking his head at me and scowling. I leaned around to look at the guys. They were sitting in their silly thrones and watching the dancers and the people making out. Their expressions were dark and their jaws clenched. It didn't look like they were enjoying their party at all. I caught Devon's eye, and he visibly relaxed his posture when he realized I was there. I gestured to the man in front of me and Devon jumped like he didn't realize I was being stopped. Devon tapped the guy on the shoulder, and he stepped away with a nod of apology.

There were a few steps up to the stage and I grabbed one girl's hand and pulled her up with me. She pulled up her friends too, and Devon quirked an eyebrow at me. I had to bend down and shout in his ear in order to be heard over the screaming rock music. "They claim to have dibs on you three."

Devon's head tipped back in a cruel laugh, and he looked the girls over. His eyes were glaring like he couldn't wait to devour them. The bruises around his amber eyes making him look more menacing. I smiled back at the girls, who were looking considerably less sure of themselves now that they were facing the three devils. I realized by looking around that these people *did* fear them. Devon, Sterling, and Milo *did* have power over them. And here I was, waltzing up with a plate of pizza and a drink like they weren't sitting on thrones draped with chains.

Sterling was in the middle of Devon and Milo. When he finally tore his eyes away from the dancers and saw me, he smirked and pulled me onto his lap. I fell almost gracefully onto his lap, only sloshing my martini a little. I leaned up and shouted in his ear over the music, "Where's my throne?"

His face cracked into a laugh, and I smiled back. He reached over and smacked at Milo. They leaned together to talk, and I took the moment to admire their muscular necks and jaws as they spoke back and forth. They were both wearing black shirts and black pants with their black boots. Sterling wore a silver chain around his neck and Milo wore a silver watch and his usual glasses. Sterling's shirt was a t-shirt and his tattoos stood out against his skin under the lights. They both had styled their hair to look intentionally messy, unlike Devon's perfectly in place hair. I wondered if they had all coordinated outfits before the party. The mental image made me smile. He

Sterling looked up at me and saw I was smiling. He cocked an eyebrow at me and shifted so I was sprawled along his body. He was sitting, legs spread on his throne of chains, and I was now facing forward in the seat with the back of my body pressed to the front of his. My feet touched the ground on either side of his left foot and my ass pressed against his thigh. I was sure I was flashing the crowd of dancers my panties, but I found I didn't really care. He took my plate of snacks and set them next to his chair and left me with my martini. Someone came up and gave the guys' drinks, and Sterling gestured to my drink for the guy to get me a refill. He sipped his drink, which looked like whiskey or bourbon on ice, and trailed the cold glass up and down my arm. I shivered, and I felt his chest rumble with laughter.

Looking around at the crowd, I realized people weren't just dancing and kissing, there were people having sex against the wall in the back. I gasped when I saw them. There were three or four different couples, and one group of three, not caring that they were visible to the rest of the room. A few people stopped to watch, but mostly everyone ignored them. I tried not to watch them, but my eyes kept moving back to the blatant show of sexuality.

I felt Milo watching us, so I rolled my head against Sterling's chest to look at him. His face furrowed as he looked at us. He looked almost... jealous? I honestly wasn't sure who he was jealous of, me or Sterling, so I offered him a small smile to gauge his reaction. Before he could react, Sterling reached over and grabbed the bottom of the seat of the throne Milo was sitting on and pulled it towards us. Milo's eyes widened in shock as he caught himself and sat upright again. I looked up to see Sterling grinning contentedly now that Milo was closer. Milo's blush was confirmation enough that he had feelings for Sterling.

Two of the girls I had brought up to meet the guys started dancing on the small stage directly in front of us. I looked around to see Devon with the blonde one on his lap and his tongue down her throat. Anger snapped through my body, and I rolled my eyes. It wasn't fair of me to be jealous of the girl with Devon; I was literally sitting on Sterling's lap.

Sterling was watching the girls dance provocatively in front of us with intense and lustful eyes, and my stomach swirled. I needed air. I pushed up from his lap and made my way to the back sliding door. A fire was lit in the stone fire pit, but nobody was out there.

Outside, the air was crisply cold. I inhaled deeply and leaned against the railing of the porch. The sky was cloudy, with no stars visible. We were probably about to get more snow.

My body felt weighed down with my feelings of jealousy and anger. It didn't make sense. Sure, the guys were all attractive, and it was normal to feel physically attracted to them. Totally normal human behavior. But the jealousy? The anger? Over them looking at or kissing other girls? That's where it wasn't right. These men had essentially kidnapped me. I had no right to feel anything towards them. Sure, I wasn't being kept in the cells in the basement and exploited, but I wasn't exactly being treated with respect. They were still keeping things from me, and I had no clue what was going on most of the time. Hell, I had been shot at and then killed a man.

I stopped and choked on a breath at that thought. I had

been doing my absolute best to not think about the man whose life I had taken. Killing that man was a crazy decision. What had driven me to do it? Never in my wildest dreams had I thought I would kill someone. Never in my wildest dreams had I thought I'd be part of the *mafia*.

Never in my wildest dreams had I thought I'd be a woman capable of making life altering choices without guidance from my parents or Gregory. I sighed and rested my head against my arms on the railing. As soon as I had choices, I used my free will to kill someone. What kind of person did that make me? What did I think I would get out of killing him? I realized with a lurch that I had been hoping for the guys to respect me and maybe even *want* me. Sure, I wanted freedom, but I had looked to get it from male approval and validation. How messed up was that? I groaned as tears formed in my eyes.

The sliding door opened behind me and let out a burst of sound before closing again. Footsteps sounded behind me as someone approached. A dark green hoodie was settled on my shoulders, and I inhaled the smell of clean soap and beeswax. Milo.

"Thanks, Milo," I whispered as he came up next to me and leaned on the railing, mirroring my pose. His shoulder brushed mine, and I felt warmed by the contact.

"Just needed some air?" he asked.

"Yeah," I sighed.

"So, which one?"

"What do you mean?" I asked and looked up at him.

He looked down at me with a knowing look. "Which one pissed you off by giving another woman attention?"

"Is that why you're out here?" I deflected and looked away.

But not before I saw the flicker of fear in his eyes. "I won't tell anyone."

"It seems we're both in the same boat," he breathed.

"Sterling?" I whispered.

He nodded and swallowed.

We were silent together for a few moments, enjoying the hushed, snow-covered grounds. "I think I killed that guy just so you three would like me." I quietly broke the silence.

Milo looked at me for a long time and I didn't look back. I couldn't bear to see his face after that confession. "Are you okay?" he asked softly. I had never seen Milo act anything other than irritated or indifferent towards me. I wasn't going to question him, though.

"Um, I think so," I said with a sigh. "I'm just realizing that when a man wasn't guiding me by the hand like a little girl, I acted out to get a man's approval."

"Ah, that martini was powerful," Milo chuckled quietly.

"No kidding," I scoffed and wiped away a tear.

"And you're out here sulking because you think it didn't work to make us like you?" Milo asked.

I wanted to say that if it had worked, nobody would make out with a random girl or watch a girl dance. Instead, I only nodded with a deep flush of shame.

"Well, if it helps any, those two are completely obsessed with you," Milo said casually.

I wanted to ask if he was, too. Instead, I kept that thought to myself.

"I kissed Sterling after the fight," I blurted out.

He paused and an auburn eyebrow lifted. "Really?"

"Well, technically he kissed me," I babbled.

"That's what you two were doing when we walked in?" he asked.

"Yeah," I said.

"I don't think you have anything to worry about with Sterling," he said with a note of sadness in his voice.

"He loves you," I assured him.

"Sure, he loves me, but he doesn't go for men." Milo shook his head and looked out at the trees.

"I wouldn't be so sure," I said and rested a hand on his arm. "I've seen the way he looks at you. Just wait until you guys make your video."

"Oh my god," Milo laughed. His voice echoed amongst the trees. "We will not be fucking!"

"I know, but... maybe," I said leadingly.

Milo turned to lean his back against the railing and looked at the house. His eyes caught on something and he grinned and leaned down towards me. "Well, if he has even the tiniest bit of feelings for either of us, or both of us, we're about to make him very jealous," he said in a low voice.

"How?" I asked and looked up at him as he was leaning down further to me.

His lips were just about to meet mine when the door opened. I barely registered the sound over the sudden rush of blood and arousal in my body. Up close, even in the dim light and surrounded by bruises, his eyes were electric blue and framed with auburn lashes. Light flashed over his glasses as he cupped my face in his large, warm hands. I anticipated his lips on mine with an excited yearning. Would they be soft? He seemed shy sometimes. Would his kiss feel soft and shy?

Someone cleared their throat. I jumped in shock that we

weren't alone and put a hand to my chest as Milo backed away with a smirk. "Sterling!" I gasped when I saw him standing there, hands on his hips. His face hid in shadow, and I couldn't read his expression.

"It's almost midnight. I didn't want you two to miss the countdown," he said in a voice that did not indicate that he'd seen the almost kiss. I knew he had, though.

I felt hot all over, and I shifted my weight from one foot to the other. "Okay, thanks," I said, my voice hoarse. Milo winked at me as we both moved to follow Sterling into the house.

The guy who had been bringing us drinks earlier stopped us and he handed us each a fresh glass of champagne. I thanked him and took a long swallow. Milo's cheeks were pink as he watched me chug the champagne. He knew he had made me flustered. The guys drank their champagne down with me, all finishing well before the count down toast. Was that bad luck? I hoped it wasn't. The bubbles warmed my belly as I looked around for more champagne. I saw a caterer setting down a bottle she had just opened, and I pushed through a group of people to snatch it up. Sterling and Milo were both watching me as I returned to them, both looking amused.

Once I reached them, Sterling led us back to the den where the red and white lights were still shining and flashing to metal music. We approached the thrones on the stage, and I took Devon's abandoned one. My sitting on his throne gathered a bit of attention from the partygoers, but the alcohol in my system and the adrenaline from the almost kiss with Milo had me enjoying the attention. I'd never been one to enjoy attention, but here I was, sitting on a throne of chains, sipping champagne from the bottle, making eye contact with anyone who dared to look at me.

While my eyes roved over the dancers and the people having sex in the back of the room, my eyes caught on Devon. He leaned against the back wall, his eyes on me, while the blonde from earlier was on her knees in front of him. When my eyes met his, his slack jaw curled into a smirk as he bit his bottom lip. He liked me watching. His chest was heaving as the girl's head bobbed as she sucked him. He gripped her hair and appeared to thrust into her mouth forcefully.

I didn't want to give him the satisfaction of having me watch him orgasm into another woman's mouth, so I looked away before I saw him finish. I looked over to Sterling and Milo. Their thrones will still close together and they leaned towards each other while they watched me clench my thighs. They were grinning hungrily. I gulped down a mouthful of champagne as a heavy drumbeat hammered from the speakers behind us. Sterling stood up and took the bottle from me, tipping it back and swallowing the bubbly liquid. The shadows of the lights emphasized the muscles of his neck as he swallowed. He handed the bottle back to Milo, who also took a few swallows. Sterling reached down for my hand that was clenching the arm of the throne. He pulled me to my feet and down off the stage as he stomped his way towards the back of the room. As much as I was feeling... flirty right now, I was not someone who would partake in public party sex. But, with Milo hot on my heels, Sterling led us towards the office, basement, and garage doors. Another large man working security, stood blocking the short hallway, and nodded as we approached.

The music lessened just slightly as people counted down. "10..." Sterling shoved his hand in his pocket. "9..." he located his key ring. "8..." Milo passed me the champagne. "7..." I chugged two huge swallows. "6..." Sterling fumbled with the lock on the office door. "5..." Milo pushed him out of the way and took the keys from him. "4..." I was giggling as the bubbles and alcohol made the world a little lopsided. "3..." Sterling and Milo were both drunkenly laughing as they pushed open the door to the office. "2..." we crashed into the room and Sterling slammed the door shut. "1..." I was shoved against the door by one of them, I didn't know which. "HAPPY NEW YEAR!" was being shouted throughout the party as lips crashed into mine. Sterling.

His body pressed against mine, and another hard body pressed against my side. I cried out at the pleasant shock of being kissed so ferociously. He kissed me like he was starving for me. His tongue warred with mine and he pulled back to suck at my lips. I groaned as he bit and tugged at my bottom lip. My eyes moved to meet Milo's as Sterling's lips left mine. Milo was watching us intently, a look in his eyes like he was almost feral with wanting. I smiled and reached for him as I dropped the bottle of champagne. The music from the party was still so loud in the office that the door vibrated against my skin, and I didn't hear the dull clunk of the bottle hitting the floor.

Sterling moved back just enough that Milo could squeeze forcefully between us and kiss me. His lips were fuller and softer than Sterling's and he kissed like he was sipping at my lips. He licked and sucked my lips and tongue in little sipping bursts that had me rolling my body against his, desperate for *more.* Sterling had caged us both in against the dark wood door, his arms bracing himself on either side of my shoulders. As I rolled my body to press into Milo, I was pushing him into Sterling. I couldn't hear our breaths and moans in the loud room, but I could feel their puffing champagne scented breaths on my face and neck and feel the vibrations of their voices in their bodies.

My panties were drenched as I was desperately, drunkenly, seeking friction against Milo or Sterling. I could feel Milo's erection against my stomach, but I was too short to rub my clit against him. He felt massive against my stomach, and I wondered if he was bigger than Sterling. I dismissed the thought because Sterling was taller and bigger than Milo in every way. There was no chance Milo's dick was bigger. I arched against him and wondered if Sterling was hard and pressed against Milo. I pulled away from Milo's lips and made eye contact. His pupils were so wide they almost entirely eclipsed the blue. Only an antique floor lamp illuminated the space, but I could see the feral lust on his face. He was beyond hard against my stomach and pressed harder against me as Sterling leaned down to kiss me over his shoulder, pushing harder against Milo. It was a Milo sandwich, and I was ready to lose my mind over it.

Sterling kissed me until I was panting and moaning and even more impossibly desperate for more. He pulled back slightly, and I looked pointedly at Milo. "He needs a New Year kiss, too. He deserves it."

Sterling looked shocked and unsure for a moment before he turned his gaze over to his best friend. Milo was staring wide eyed down at me like he couldn't believe I'd just said that. I grinned mischievously at them. Sterling took a small step back to allow Milo to slide out from his sandwiched position. Milo turned to face Sterling and leaned casually against the wall next to the door, locking intense gazes with Sterling.

My heart was in my throat with anticipation. I was so turned on by both of them I couldn't wait for them to kiss. I clenched my thighs together to reduce some of the ache and they slipped and slid with my arousal under my dress. I bit my swollen bottom lip.

Sterling took the single step towards Milo, so they were almost touching. Milo's breath caught in his throat as he expected the kiss. Sterling bent and brushed a brief peck on Milo's lips. I let out a breath of broken anticipation at the lackluster kiss. Milo remained frozen, but a blush was visible on his cheeks. His eyes had fluttered shut as Sterling got close and they opened now to narrow at him. Sterling smirked at his best friend and then slammed a hand on the door next to Milo's head and dove back in for a fierce, dominating kiss. It was all lips and teeth and tongues and aggression. Milo reached up and was tugging Sterling's hair to control the kiss, but Sterling was having none of it and pressed hard into Milo.

Just watching, I felt like I could combust, and I put my fingers to my lips to chase the feeling. Sterling pulled away from Milo and immediately came at me. I gasped as he pulled me away from the door and spun me until I was walking backwards, his lips on mine, to the desk. He picked me up and Milo swiped an arm to clear off the desk. Everything clattered and crashed to the ground, just audible over the music. Sterling sat me down on the desk and said something to Milo with a grin. Milo came around the desk behind me and bent to kiss my neck. He licked and sucked at my neck, and I moaned and shook against his chest behind me. Sterling watched for a moment before pushing his way between my legs and kissing the other side of my neck and down to my cleavage.

Milo's hands were on top of mine on the desk and it felt like I was being restrained from touching them. It made a thrill run through me. I had caught Gregory cheating on me with his tied-up secretary, and here I was being restrained by *two* men. Two unbelievably sexy mafia bosses. Imagining them using real restraints sent a shiver of lust through me.

The door opened, and Devon strode in, glaring at us. He slammed the door shut behind him, but none of us moved. He looked beyond livid, and I felt worried. Would he kick me out? He gestured for Sterling to move. Sterling shook his head. Devon gestured more aggressively and said something Sterling could hear. Sterling sighed and moved back. I snapped my legs closed as he approached me. Milo's hands were still over mine on the desk, so I couldn't move. Devon stood in front of me and leaned over me, looking over my body and face as if he had the right to. I turned my head away from him and he gripped my jaw in his hand and forced me to face him.

"Off limits," he said when he knew I was looking at him.

I rolled my eyes.

He got closer to my face, and I thought maybe he was going to kiss me. I spat in his face. Honestly, had I not just seen a girl going down on him in the den, then I probably would have wanted to kiss him. As it were, I didn't know where his mouth had been. Devon moved back with my spit dripping from my face. I used the toe of my shoe to push him further away from me. He wiped his face and shook his head.

He looked at the three of us and said, "Cut it out. You're all drunk as fuck." He glared at us all again and then strode from the room.

Devon had effectively popped the bubble of frenzied drunken lust with the slam of the door. Milo let go of my hands with a start, like he had forgotten they were there. We all straightened our clothes and hair, not looking at each other. It was like we were teenagers that had gotten busted doing something wrong. In a way, I was glad it had only been kissing. Devon was, unfortunately, correct that we were all drunk and not able to make good choices.

Sterling opened the door and left, saying nothing to us. Milo followed him out with only a shy, almost apologetic glance back at me. With a disappointed sigh, I left the office and made my way to the stairs. A guy working security was standing guard at the stairs stopped me from going up to my room.

"I live here!" I shouted to him over the pop music that was blaring on the main level.

He shook his head and pulled out his phone to send a message. Presumably to one of the guys. I waited with my arms crossed over my chest for him to get a response. His phone lit up, and he read the message and then looked me over like they gave him instructions that said, "redhead in a black dress lives here" and stepped back for me to go up the stairs to my room. Alone.

17

Sterling

A rolling feeling in my stomach greeted me before I even opened my eyes. I groaned and turned to my side. The blackout curtains on my windows prevented any sunlight from shining into my room, so I did not know the time. I reached for my phone and the blue light felt like fire shooting straight into my eyeballs. It was eleven in the morning. I had gone to bed at about three, so what had woken me up?

A blender sounded in the kitchen. Anger and disgust coursed through me. Whoever was using the fucking *blender* was about to get beat. I was going to get up and beat their ass... at some point today. I groaned again and closed my eyes, waiting for the blender to stop so I could fall back asleep. This house was enormous. How was it so loud? I waited. And waited. And *fucking waited.* It was becoming almost a white noise, and I fell back to sleep.

The sound of a slamming door and an angry female voice

screeching in the hallway had me stomping to my door. I yanked it open to find Bambi clutching a sheet to her as she leaned over the railing to shout to the kitchen. My brain didn't register what she was shouting, but I could note her angry tone. Whatever she was saying, I agreed. Devon was shouting at her from the first floor, the blender still going. I stood next to her at the railing. "Dude! What the fuck, Devon?" I bellowed and stifled a hungover burp.

"It's eleven, and the meeting between Giovanni and Taz and my dad and Matthew is tonight. We need to come up with a plan and I can't do that with all three of you still in bed," Devon scolded with his arms crossed.

He may have had a point, but *come on.* I groaned so hard it sounded like a growl with my sleep hoarse voice. Bambi struggled to hold on to her sheet as she pushed some tangled hair away from her face. She looked pale and her makeup was smeared under her eyes like she had slept in it.

"Oh, it didn't realize this party had a dress code," came Milo's sleepy and sarcastic voice.

I looked over my shoulder to see him standing there, looking at my back and Bambi's. I realized with a start that I was fully naked in the hallway. *Shit.* I looked over to see that part of the sheet had fallen from Emily's hands and her bare ass was exposed. I snorted a laugh despite my raging hangover. Emily blushed as she realized what he meant and hurried to cover herself.

"Well, *there.* Now, you've all seen my butt," she said with a fake haughty tone and lifted her chin up even though her face and chest glowed with a blush.

"Yeah, we're even Steven," Milo said in his sneering,

sarcastic voice. I raised an eyebrow at him. He looked at me, then Emily, and then back at me. He was silently asking if I had spent the night with Emily and that's why we were both naked.

My eyes bugged open, and I shook my head at Milo fervently. He visibly relaxed. After Devon had interrupted us last night, Emily had gone to bed, and we stayed up with the party. We didn't talk about the... situation in the office. We didn't talk about how we both kissed her. And we certainly didn't talk about *our* kiss. I covered my dick with my hands because as the memories of the office came back, I didn't trust my dick to not respond.

"Get dressed and come down here. I'm making breakfast," Devon demanded, and disappeared from the foyer.

I looked down at the still blushing Emily. "Mornin' Bambi."

"Good morning," she said quietly and quickly made her way to her room, shutting the door behind her.

I smirked at Milo, meaning to make a joke about Emily not sleeping in her formal pajamas, but he was blushing and turning away from me. *Oookay.*

Back in my room, I showered and got dressed, hoping there was coffee made in the kitchen. Devon was sitting at the island, dressed in slacks and a button-down shirt, like he was ready for a day in the office. He nodded to the coffee maker, and I sighed in relief.

A huge, greasy paper bag sat on the counter and my stomach both lurched and growled at the same time. I opened it as Milo padded into the kitchen with wet hair from a shower. The bag turned out to be egg and cheese sandwiches with leftover deli meats from Harold at Deniro's and a bunch of salty hash browns. I both wanted to devour it all and throw it all away at the same time as my stomach quivered in unsure anticipation. My face and body still ached from the fight, so the hangover was just salt in the wound.

Milo got plates and set out our breakfasts while I got our coffees. Bambi came in, dressed and with a scrubbed face, but unshowered. I handed her a mug of coffee as she sighed and sat at the island. Devon had, at some point, ordered new barstools that served as seats for the island and had added a fourth. As much as he acted like he hated Emily, it was clear he had accepted her.

We all quietly ate our breakfast while Devon glared down the island at us like we were the biggest disappointments he'd ever seen. But he had drank and behaved unprofessionally last night as much as- if not more than- us, so I ignored his judgmental stares. It was always like that with Devon. He always acted like his behavior was excusable because he was the supposed future leader of our family. It wasn't entirely his fault- he had been silver spoon fed that information his entire life. Which was the only reason I tolerated him this close.

"Alright, let's make a plan," Devon said authoritatively as we cleared the breakfast remains. "The meeting is to happen tonight. Milo, did you find out where?"

"The casino," Milo muttered.

"The casino is neutral?" Emily asked with a shocked expression.

"Yeah, the official ones are too regulated," Devon responded.

Emily hummed in her intrigue.

"They're meeting at ten tonight," Milo said, and poured another cup of coffee.

"Are we invited to the meeting?" Emily asked.

"No," Milo scoffed while Devon glowered.

"Then how are we going?" Emily asked.

"We'll be spying on the meeting," I replied, having mercy on her ignorance.

"I have access to the camera system in the casinos already," Milo explained. "We've monitored people there before."

"Will we be going to the casino or staying here?" Emily asked, as if she was dreading the answer.

"Going," Devon snapped. "I want to be able to walk in there if we need to."

"So, what's the plan you needed us here to make?" she asked with a sigh like Devon was a child she needed to get back on task.

"We need to decide our limits for if and when we walk in there," Milo said, looking at Devon.

"Would that be like taking over from Matthew and Anthony?" she asked. It was a good question. "Wouldn't storming into their meeting seem aggressive?"

I kept my mouth shut and let the others answer.

Devon's face reddened with anger and frustration. Milo shrugged.

"Sure," Milo said. "It could be seen that way, but if Giovanni and Taz have a physical attack planned, us being there for backup is a guaranteed win."

"What if they set up a deal that you don't like?" she continued to question us.

Devon turned away from us and looked out the back

window. I wondered if he knew something that the rest of us didn't. "Then we follow orders until we can convince my dad and Matthew to change their minds."

I snorted a laugh. As if those hardheaded men ever changed their minds in their lives. Especially upon the advice of people they deemed under them. Milo kicked at me, and Devon turned back to shoot me a glare. But they had no arguments because I wasn't wrong.

"So, the plan is that we listen to hear the deal. If there is an attack, we intervene. But not if we dislike the deal. Later we try to discourage the deal," Emily paraphrased.

"Correct," Devon grunted, and then turned to face her sharply. "Wear something nice. We need to blend in."

She rolled her eyes and slid off her stool. "I'm going back to bed."

Devon stormed out of the room not long after Emily, leaving Milo and me in an awkward silence.

Milo turned red and kept his back to me. I hadn't even said anything to him yet. Was he embarrassed about his kissing Emily last night? Or me? It was apparent that he was uncomfortable around me, so it had to be about our kiss. It was nothing. Just a drunken kiss between best friends at the dare of a pretty woman. Totally excusable as party antics. As they say: no homo. But my dick twitched at the memory sitting here, hungover as shit with grease stains on my t-shirt. So, like, maybe a *little* bit homo.

"Hey, let's not talk about last night. That was so crazy and... out of character for both of us. I think we just got carried away with the lights and the music and the people fucking right in front of us. The alcohol and Emily's dress surely didn't help matters. Let's just forget it happened," I mumbled.

He whipped around to face me. "Agreed."

I nodded once in acknowledgement and then looked back down at the dregs of my coffee.

"Let's film our video today," he blurted.

"What?" I asked, shocked. "Why today?"

He shook his head like he didn't quite want to explain. "I just think the sooner the better if we're about to be involved in a gang war."

I exhaled long and slow as I considered what he said. I drained the last sip of my coffee. "Yeah, fuck it. Let's film."

"Where should we do it?" Milo asked, putting on a brave face.

"Somewhere with natural light during the day. Do we want to pretend that we just fought-hence the bruises on our faces- and now we're jerking off?" I asked as I stood up and stretched my back.

"Not that we just fought each other. That would be confusing. But maybe like post fight when we would get that adrenaline cock stand," Milo said with a huff of a laugh. We haven't been involved in a physical gang fight (other than the one in the ring, but we didn't count that) since we shed our first blood and gained respect from the gangs we controlled when we were in our early twenties. But remembering the adrenaline and aggression fueled boners we'd get made me laugh with him.

"Hell yeah," I agreed.

The camera was set up. The ring light was set up. And

Milo and I were standing just out of frame with our hands in our pants to get our cocks ready while the camera on my phone ticked down from ten seconds. We needed to be hard when we sat down for the story of the video. I stroked over my cock to get it to rise, as if it wasn't already achingly hard in anticipation. Even though my most popular video didn't have a story, it felt like we needed one. We needed the story for why we were both jerking off on camera and in front of each other. It felt like armor.

The timer finished, and we crashed into the hearth room and landed on the couch with grunts and groans as if we'd just finished a fight. "I can't believe we won," I groaned.

"Yeah, five against two wasn't very good odds, but we did it," Milo agreed and sat up next to me. He tugged uncomfortably at the crotch of his jeans.

"They sure got in a few good hits," I said and rubbed at the nasty bruise on my jaw.

Our scripting was kind of awkward. Admittedly. But this was the part most viewers probably skipped, anyway. They fast forward until cocks are out, according to the metrics on my previous videos.

I tugged at my cock through my jeans. "I always get so hard after a fight," I said with a chuckle.

"Me, too. My balls will hurt until I come." Milo echoed my chuckle.

"Well, to avoid any more pain, we should probably... you know, come," I said with a not entirely faked shyness.

Milo and I locked eyes as we both undid the buttons on our jeans and unzipped. I chanced a peek at my phone to make sure it was still recording before looking back at Milo. I could tell the moment he had his dick in his hand. His mouth parted on an intake of breath and his lashes fluttered behind his glasses. A blush rose to his cheeks, and I felt my face get hot as I took my dick in my hand, the piercing only slightly cooler than my skin.

His eyes drifted down to my cock, and I could feel his gaze like a physical touch tickling down my skin. I settled better on the couch with my knees spread to allow me to reach down and grab my balls. My eyes, of their own accord, dropped to his dick. I had caught that glimpse in the sauna. But here, sidelong and obvious, he was undeniably huge. I laughed. "You're fucking massive!"

Milo shrugged bashfully as he tugged his pants down and off. I followed suit, and we both stripped off our shirts. Yellowing and aging bruises that decorated our skin were the only visible bluff that we'd not just come from a fight. Now we were both naked on the couch. My skin was pale and tattooed, and he was pale and freckled. While our complexions were similar in color, they contrasted in purity. It was truly fitting in our cases. I was covered in ink and regularly slept with women and had my porn channel. Milo, on the other hand, had skin as virginal as he was. I often forgot he had never slept with anyone. While Anthony and Stephanie had raised me and Devon with an almost abstinence only mindset (it's hard to be a young gangster if you're toting around toddlers), we had rebelled and been promiscuous rather early. Milo had been encouraged to sleep around and had witnessed his uncle's many trysts, leading him to have a different type of outlook on sex and relationships. It was often a joke between the three of us about how we all turned out the opposite of our raising, despite our guardians' best attempts.

"Am I the first to see you?" I asked in a hushed whisper as I slowly stroked my cock. I could always have him edit this out later.

He looked startled for a second before he sobered and swallowed. He tugged slowly and firmly up the length of his cock, moisture pearling at the top. Finally, he nodded.

I could have sworn my heart stopped in my chest for a second. "Oh, Milo," I practically gasped as we locked eyes. We weren't touching each other, but this moment felt more significant than a quick video for my channel. This felt... important.

He gave a quick shake of his head, as if he was telling me to drop it. I looked away from him, only to check the camera before settling back against the couch cushions. I spit into my palm and used it to lubricate my dick. He and I both relaxed into our positions on the couch as we jerked ourselves off. He tried to spit into his own hand. He chuckled, and I looked up to see him struggling to get enough saliva to spit into his hand.

"I'm so dehydrated from last night," he chuckled, and I realized he was also breathing rapidly through his mouth like he was nervous.

Alternatively, I had been salivating since we took off our clothes. I grabbed his wrist and pulled his hand to my mouth. He opened his hand reflexively and I spit into his palm. He yanked his hand back and out of my grip. "Hey, thanks," he said sarcastically.

"Hey, no problem, buddy," I said brightly as I returned my hands to my junk.

He snorted once in a laugh and put his now sufficiently lubricated hand to his dick. I smirked and watched as he smeared my saliva over his cock. It was mesmerizing to know that my spit made his cock shine and glide through his fist. A shiver of something like lust shot out from the base of my spine and I grunted as I fucked my hand.

As we relaxed more in our places on the couch, our legs spread and met in the middle. His bare knee brushed against mine and my eyes fixed on the point of contact. His breath was shuddering and loud, but it seemed like he was stuck in his pleasure. That weird precipice where thoughts and anxieties blocked his release. He needed a push. But not a physical one, because I wasn't about to reach over and touch him without talking to him about it first. I would need to help him in other ways.

I remembered his blush whenever I praised him and leaned into that. "Come on, let me see you fucking lose it like a good boy."

He let out a deep whimpering breath and his head tipped back to rest against the back of the couch. His chest had been tight, and his shoulders closed in, but they relaxed a fraction at my words. I grinned.

"Yeah, that's right. Show me how good it feels," I practically growled out at him as I jerked myself even harder. His chest relaxed more, and his eyes closed. He let out a low moan that resonated straight to my balls. My breath became harsh and shuddering as I watched him. "Slow down. Good boy. Slow, hard strokes. Let me see how well you follow directions.

Hmm, that's good. Stroke that huge fucking cock for me, nice and slow."

A vein stood out in his neck as he arched his back against the couch with low, unrestrained moans. He turned his face towards me, and I saw the sweat on his brow. In fact, a sheen of sweat had formed over his chest and abs, and I suddenly wanted nothing more than to lick it up. I swallowed and resisted the urge. "Are you going to come for me?" I asked him, my voice breathier and more desperate than I expected it to sound.

He nodded and our eyes locked as his mouth dropped open and he moaned long and low. "Ster- Ster- Sterling," he gasped just before he went silent, arching into his fist as he came onto his own chest and hand. His eyes closed as he came in lines over his skin. As his climax started its descent, he swore loud and aggressive as he looked down at his cock. "Fuck!" he shouted with a harsh exhale.

Milo had said my name before he came. He had looked me in the eyes and moaned my name as he came.

The flush that spread over his chest, neck, and face had me fucking my fist with vigor. I stopped to spit in my hand again and reached down to cup my balls with my free hand. I groaned and came harder than I think I've ever come before. Black spots covered my vision, and it felt like an electric shock shot out from the space behind my balls.

When I finally came to, I looked over to see Milo blatantly watching me. I smiled at him and raised my eyebrows. He chuckled and sat forward to look at my chest and stomach. "You know, I've edited all of your videos and seen how much you come, but it's shocking in person."

"You sure know how to make a guy feel special," I said gruffly.

"No, I mean it's..." he chuckled and gestured to my coated skin.

"Hot? Sexy? Amazing?" I prompted with my own chuckle.

"Talented, I guess," Milo said and traced a finger through the come on his own abs. My dick twitched as if I hadn't *just* come buckets.

"Better to impregnate you with, my dearie," I said in my best impression of an old lady.

Milo blanched. "What?"

"Like Little Red Riding Hood? The wolf?" I scrambled. I sat up and I felt the drips of come slide down to my legs. "'What big teeth you have! All the better to eat you with my dear!'" Even with the voices of the characters, Milo stared.

"Sure," Milo said, and shook his head like I was insane.

"Fuck you, dude," I laughed and used my discarded t-shirt to wipe up.

Milo got up and turned off the recording, and his head snapped up to the stairs. He looked back down at me with a sly grin. "I don't think we were alone."

"Devon or Emily?" I asked as I stood and inspected the couch for drips of come.

"Emily."

"Naughty little housewife," I said with a low chuckle.

"I can have this posted before the meeting. It'll give us something nice to look forward to when we get home," Milo said, and gathered up his clothes.

"You're just excited to see all the comments about your monster cock," I scoffed as we headed for the stairs.

Milo blushed again.

18

Emily

I scurried to my room and, as quietly as I could, closed my door. I could hear male chuckles verging on giggles through the wood as Sterling and Milo approached. They separated and went into their own rooms before I relaxed. I had just watched them masturbate next to each other on the couch in the hearth room. I would feel bad except for the fact that they would post it *on the internet* for anyone to see. People seeing them was kind of the point. I, however, just got it for free.

Once the hallway was quiet, I was able to check in on myself. I had been so enraptured by the sight of them together on that love seat I hadn't realized how wet, breathless, and sweating I had become. Now, I fanned myself as I looked around the empty room. To keep my hands busy, I folded a basket of my laundry and put it away. I hoped the menial, domestic task would be enough to stop the sweating. But it kept my mind open to fixate on how their legs had spread out on the love seat until the two large men had completely filled the space. And how they spoke to each other in low tones as they touched themselves. And how big Milo was. And how they both tipped their heads back against the couch as they gasped and came. And how-

Okay.

I needed a shower. Thankfully, the showerhead had been replaced. I only had to ask every single day. I stripped in the bathroom and turned on the shower. I stepped in as the water heated, the cool splash a welcome sensation. The view of frost and snow-covered trees tinged with orange setting sun through the floor to ceiling window helped calm me. I took my time washing my hair and shaving before movement outside caught my attention. The sun was setting and the solar lights along the patio had clicked on, but I could see Devon lighting the outdoor fireplace. He had a bar cart with liquor and ice next to him. He... couldn't see me, right? This wall of windows in the bathroom wouldn't allow for someone to see in, right? When I was out there at night with Milo on New Year's I had been too distracted to look up. Besides, the lights had been off. If Devon looked up, would he see me? He turned and faced the house, but his head didn't tilt up to look at the second floor. I assumed that meant he couldn't see me and continued on with my shower.

I conditioned my hair, finished shaving, and washed with a soft vanilla and coconut scented soap. My mind traveled back to the guys on the couch. I couldn't help it. It was, by far, the hottest thing I'd ever seen in my life. The muscles. The sweat. The groans. The gasps and moans. A shiver went over me as I snaked my hand between my legs and lightly caressed my clit. A small gasp escaped me as I pictured their straining hips and the veins in their necks and the corded muscles in their arms. I couldn't help myself. Pulling the showerhead off the hook, I switched it to the massaging jet function. This would be quick. With shaking, desperate hands, I aimed the water to hit my clit. A prickling sense of being watched entered my body, and I cracked open an eye and looked over the bathroom. Nobody. The washcloth was still covering the camera above the door. Then I swept my gaze to the windows. *Oh no.* Three men stood staring up at me from the patio as I pleasured myself with my newly regained showerhead.

I couldn't see their expressions from here, but I swore I could see a smile on Sterling's face. Well, they had already seen everything, so I might as well finish. Or so my libido shouted. They didn't know I saw them earlier. They didn't know that I knew they were watching me. This felt more erotic knowing that they were watching me. I was going to come in front of them. I watched Devon take a slow drink from his glass. Sterling set his drink down on the railing and leaned against the wood, cupping himself through his pants. Milo stood frozen and staring. It looked like they had gone outside to meet to talk strategy before tonight and I had so rudely interrupted them by having a window in my shower.

These men were entirely at my mercy at that moment. As my pleasure grew, so did the feeling of power. I ran my free hand through my hair and then down to my nipples and gave both of them a pinch. The massaging pressure was a perfect thrum against my pussy. My chest heaved, and I cried out as I came. As I came down from my orgasm, I peeked at the guys. They were still staring at me, not talking to each other. Sterling was gripping himself through his pants and Milo was slack jawed and watching me. I allowed a little smile to play on my lips as I put the showerhead back on the hook. It felt like I could have told those men to kneel at my feet and they would have done it. That feeling of power felt like a warm, sticky pleasure as it dripped through my post orgasm body.

Getting out of the shower, I wrapped a fluffy towel around my oversensitive skin. I could have spent all night with that showerhead, the memories of the guys on the couch, and the lustful stares from the three men below. But I had things to do.

I dried my hair and put a soft curl in it with the newly supplied hair dryer and curler. Apparently, having bad hair was seen as an attack on the family who owned a salon and outweighed their worry I'd use the tools to hurt others or myself. My make up was subdued, but classic. And I wore a black knit sweater and the black leather leggings. I'd never been to the casino, but I knew it was pretty casual. Anything more dressed up would attract attention. Just outside of the casino was one of Cleveland's most popular areas for night-life. Maybe we could hit up a bar or something after.

I was making us something quick to eat before we left for the meeting when Sterling came to the kitchen. They had holed up in the office for a while after they were outside, and I was about to call them to eat.

"Oh, there you are. I was just going to have you come eat before we left," I said brightly to him.

His eyes were dark on mine, and he looked like he wanted to say something.

"What?" I asked him and gave him doe eyes.

He closed his eyes and took a deep breath before he looked at me again. This time, less feral and more focused. "Do you need me to make coffee, or did you do it?"

I smiled. "I made coffee. I was hoping if the meeting went well, we could stop at a bar or a restaurant on East 4th Street?"

Sterling looked thoughtful. "Maybe. I feel like this isn't going to go well and we're going to come home limping. But yeah, maybe we'll see."

"Why do you think it'll go poorly?" I asked.

"Because Anthony and Matthew have been moving around money today," Milo said as he came into the kitchen.

"Is that bad?" I asked and poured myself a coffee.

"They moved it to cash. So... possibly," Milo grumbled, and picked up one of the sandwiches I made.

"Could they buy out the other gang?" I asked.

"Not with that amount," Milo said as Devon came in. "It's definitely not enough to buy them out of Cleveland. It looks more like investment money."

I sighed. "And we don't know what Giovanni and Taz deal in."

"Bingo," Sterling said as he stuffed a sandwich in his mouth.

"Emily, I want you armed tonight," Devon said quietly.

"Armed?"

"Yeah, a knife and a gun."

"I don't think we can bring weapons into the casino," I reminded him.

Milo snorted in a way that suggested I was ignorant.

"Alright, alright," I groaned and rolled my eyes.

"Bambi, I want a foamy tree on my coffee again," Sterling said.

"What's the magic word?" I asked in my teacher voice.

"Um... oh, *please*," Sterling amended.

"Me too, *please*," Milo added with the air of a Good Student.

I smirked as I frothed up some cream and put a taller "tree" on Milo's coffee. I slid the coffees to them without comment and sat back down.

"How come Milo's is bigger?" Sterling asked.

Milo's cheeks turned pink as he sipped his coffee.

"Hm? Oh, Milo *loves* a lot of cream," I said casually.

Coffee and cream sprayed out of Milo's mouth as he exploded with reaction. His eyes were wide on me.

Sterling's mouth hung open in shock as he stared at me while thumping a coughing Milo on the back.

Devon looked at me with a glint in his amber eyes, like he knew exactly what I had implied. I smiled innocently and handed Milo a towel.

After our quick meal and coffee, Devon had me come to the office. There was a tall gun case built between bookshelves along one wall and he opened it. The smell of gun polish and metal wafted over me. I noted someone had carefully replaced all the stuff from the desk from where Milo had shoved it all last night. A bit of shame and arousal distracted me before Devon took back my attention.

"Is this what you're wearing tonight?" he asked me, just above a whisper.

I nodded and shifted uncomfortably in the presence of these weapons.

He noted my discomfort and faced me. "I know you don't like weapons," he said with a hint of kindness to his words. "But it is important that you have a way to protect yourself. I will do- *we* will do everything we can to prevent you from being in danger. This is only a precaution. Now, let's get you geared up."

He pulled out a small handgun from the case and showed me briefly how to use it. It seemed simple enough, and I hoped I wouldn't need it. Devon took out a black holster and then kneeled before me. His exhale ghosted warmly over my leather legging clad pussy. I swallowed hard and bit my lip. He reached to wrap the thigh holster around me and fasten it tightly. Fingertips brushed the areas just above and below the holster and I fought a shiver.

"Is there no holster like you guys wear?" I asked, to push through the tension. The guys normally wore the holsters that go around their backs or chests.

"I like this one better," he said in a low voice as he traced his fingers over where my thigh did a little muffin top over the holster. I did shiver this time, and he looked up at me.

His amber eyes were warm, like spun sugar through his dark lashes. The woodsy scent of his cologne swirled with the lust in the air and took on a toasted vanilla note. In that moment, I wanted him to stand up and kiss me, but I kept myself in check.

"How- um, how was the party? It seemed like you had a good time," I said and broke eye contact. My bitterness at seeing him with that blonde soured the air.

I heard him take a steady breath. "It went well. I had a good time."

It sounded like he was lying, but I wasn't going to call him out on it. "Do all of your parties involve public sex?"

He smiled, but a mischievous edge remained as he slid the gun into the holster at my thigh. "Are exhibitionism and voyeurism not a turn on?"

"Honestly? I wouldn't know," I said and shrugged. I wasn't ashamed of my vanilla sex life despite the nature of my divorce.

"Does that mean you're interested in trying?" he asked as he strapped another, smaller holster to my other thigh. He wasn't looking up at me, so I couldn't decipher his expression.

I shrugged again. "Gregory said our sex life was unfulfilling, so he strayed. I wouldn't want that to happen a second time."

Devon slid a knife into the holster and then stood up. A warm but serious look on his face. "There's nothing wrong with vanilla. There is, however, something wrong with not communicating with your partner that there may be other needs to be met. There is also something wrong with forcing yourself into situations that make you uncomfortable."

Tears welled in my eyes, but didn't fall. I bit my lip to keep it from wobbling. Devon caught my chin. "Emily, your inhibitions were not what caused Gregory to be unfaithful. He never asked, and you never felt comfortable enough to try. I do hope that you feel comfortable... here. In this house. With Sterling and- and Milo."

"To try exhibitionism and voyeurism?" I asked and blushed because... well. Check.

Devon smiled, and it was a genuine smile. Like the man within the armor was right at the surface. "Sure, I guess if that's where you're going to start."

"Okay, because both have already happened," I said lightly.

Devon chuckled and tipped his head back. "I knew you saw us watching you, you little minx."

"That actually wasn't intentional. You need some curtains. Or we can do that Elmer's Glue trick on the windows to make them frosted," I said as we walked to the door.

"We're not crafting on the windows," Devon said.

"Sure, okay. Then let me know when you shower and I'll stand in the bushes outside and watch and you can let me know how that feels," I said with a laugh.

"No need to stand in the bushes," Devon said in a low voice. "You're welcome to be in the shower with me."

We entered the casino through a side entrance with a key fob that Milo carried. This was clearly part of the casino usually more crowded during business hours. Likely human resources or accountants based on a few glimpses into offices. We walked silently to a dark room filled with screens of video feeds of dark, empty rooms and hallways.

"Why is nobody here?" I asked as I peeked back out into the hallway.

"This is security for the administration, not the game floor. The guy who is on duty for overnight security is one of ours. He's off fixing a camera in another room," Milo mumbled as he sat in front of the main computer.

When he sat at the computer, his body simultaneously

relaxed and straightened in the chair. It was like he was most comfortable sitting in front of a computer. He was wearing a black button-down shirt, and he pushed up the cuff up to look at his watch. The glow from the computer screen reflected in his glasses. His jaw tightened as he set his hands on the keyboard. With lighting quick speed, he had the password entered and a black screen centered with the fastest typing I had ever seen.

I opened my mouth to say something, but Sterling covered my mouth and shook his head. Nobody spoke, and I wasn't sure if we genuinely needed to stay quiet to avoid detection or if Milo required silence. A few moments passed and one of the many video screens flashed and settled on the feed of a lit conference room where Giovanni and Taz sat. Not long after, Milo stopped his furious typing to turn up the volume. They weren't talking, all that could be heard was the white noise of the heating and the occasional shuffle of movement or clearing of a throat.

Milo watched it for a few seconds before turning back to the keyboard and quickly bringing up the feeds of multiple entrances, including what looked like the one we came in. He settled back into the chair and sighed. "We just have to wait for Anthony and Matthew to arrive. It should be soon." He checked his watch again.

"I think that was a record," Sterling chuckled and leaned against the desk next to Milo.

Milo scoffed. "It doesn't count. I had the passwords already."

"Oh, is that them?" I asked and pointed to the screen.

It was. Anthony and Matthew walked side by side into

the main entrance of the casino, bypassing security with a nod. They were expected. An employee rushed over to greet them and escorted them off the game floor and to the meeting room.

I moved closer to a tense Devon to watch the meeting. His arms were crossed over his chest and his breathing was rapid. I rested a hand on his forearm, and he looked down at me. A flash of his worry played over his features, and I felt grateful for the trust he gave me by showing me his true feelings. I squeezed his forearm until he uncrossed his arms and held my hand.

The four men on screen shook hands and exchanged pleasantries before sitting down at the conference table.

"Did the fight with our men bring you in the business you were hoping?" Anthony asked as they settled.

"It did, thank you," Giovanni said.

"Did it give you the capital you needed to start up your newest venture?" Matthew said with a bite of disdain.

"It did," Giovanni said again and maintained eye contact with Matthew.

"We would like to join that venture," Anthony said.

"Do you have the means?" Taz barked.

"We do. And we're willing to give up protections," Anthony said cooly.

Devon's hand squeezed mine, and Sterling swore as he leaned on the desk.

"Our concern is that we've not seen the stock," Anthony continued.

"A tour can be arranged," Giovanni said with a nod.

"I need to see your security details and your political connections," Matthew demanded.

Giovanni and Taz exchanged glances with a chuckle. "Once a deal has been met and funds are secured, we can make those arrangements."

"No, before we give you any money, we need to know what security you have in place. We have our own and an overlap would be inconvenient," Matthew said, his tone allowing no argument.

"I can assure you that our connections go beyond local," Giovanni said with a sigh. "It is not likely that our connections overlap."

"They must extend to us. My family will not be your patsy for your crimes. The justice system does not go lightly on human trafficking, no matter how involved," Anthony said sternly.

Everyone in the security room froze. Everyone stopped breathing. My hand in Devon's grew slick with our combined sweat.

"No," I whispered as Devon's hand left mine.

The meeting on the screen continued.

"Giving up the business of protections to us will ensure a cleaner transaction," Giovanni said smoothly. "Many who you have relationships with now will become sources of stock or product. If they know who protects them personally, they are more likely to rebel and ask questions. If they don't know the person who protects them, then they're more likely to assume a freak accident over a design."

"We understand," Matthew said dismissively.

"I need assurance that our family will not be attacked," Anthony demanded.

"Assurance given. Though we hear you're making some political moves?" Giovanni asked.

This time, Anthony and Matthew exchanged glances. "We can't discuss that."

"Understood," Giovanni said easily.

"What is your cost?" Matthew asked, changing the subject.

"Two million," Taz said quickly. "And protections."

"Done," Anthony replied.

They stood and shook hands, chatting about family and New Year parties. On our end, we were still frozen and staring. Devon turned away first and left the room. Milo looked up with a stoney expression as the door swung shut.

I took a gasping breath before I stormed after Devon. He was already out of the exit when I caught up to him. "Did you know?" I asked, my voice strained.

He shook his head and leaned against the car, his hands braced against the hood. "No, but I suspected."

Sterling and Milo burst from the door behind us. "No fucking way," Sterling said to Devon.

Devon didn't respond, only turned to face away from us all.

"Devon, no fucking way," Sterling repeated when his adopted brother didn't respond.

"He knew," Milo said darkly, his arms crossed over his chest.

19

Sterling

I was never under the ignorant impression that our family business was in the Good Guy arena. We were a mafia through and through. Though we never said the M word on principal. Once Devon, Milo, and I were born, our parents "rebranded" to a family business. We ran like a business who just so happened to skim money from liquor sales, run gambling rings, launder money through a deli and a salon, and offer protection to businesses and people. And we controlled drug and weapon sales with our gangs. Matthew had sent Milo away to business school when most kids our age went to college. Milo had come back and told us we had been in business school our entire lives. I guess knowing we operated like a legitimate business eased my mind -and fuck, my conscience- and had me confused as to what we really were at our core. Not anymore. Anthony and Matthew were ruthless mafia bosses. We were their underbosses.

It wasn't that I had *forgotten* my place and my role. But when I heard our bosses say they were going to go against something they had said they'd never do and start dealing in human trafficking, it was like a sucker punch to the gut. I'd killed for this family. I'd beaten men to a pulp with my bare hands. I'd shot a man point blank. I'd washed blood from my skin and tended to the wounds of my brothers. But human trafficking? I couldn't. I wouldn't.

I had to.

That is, if I stayed with this family. My family. The people I'd known and loved my whole life.

Could I give it all away?

Fuck the house and the car and the money.

Could I give up Devon? *Milo?* Anthony? Stephanie? Matthew? Marie?

Emily?

"Devon, this is fucking ridiculous. We're not doing it," I spat.

Devon pounded his fist once on the hood of his car. He spun towards us, his hands in his hair. The security light above the door was bright on his face and he looked pale. "FUCK!" he screamed.

"We need to leave," Milo muttered as he checked his phone. "We only have two minutes until the security cameras are back online."

We all got into the car, and I sat in the back with Emily. She was silent, so I looked at her. She was probably freaking out. I wouldn't blame her if she was. But she was watching Devon, her eyes intent and thoughtful. She picked at her cuticles with her hands in her lap- her only tell that she was nervous.

Milo and Devon mumbled back and forth about directions to somewhere, but I wasn't listening. Emily was watching Devon so determinedly that I couldn't look away from her. Was she planning something? Was she going to run? Had we finally found her limit? Devon liked her and would keep her safe. But would he break rank to defy his father for her?

Devon pulled us into a parking garage on the other side of East 4th street and found parking near the top. He painstakingly parked his sparkling SUV, and I rolled my eyes. It wasn't often we used public parking and when we did, we usually used a smaller and less expensive vehicle. We were mostly silent and watchful as we made our way through the small crowd on the street. While it was New Year's Day, it was a Monday, so the nightlife was limited. We walked, flanking Emily like we had been taught, but I stepped back when I realized we were attracting attention. Three big men in all black flanking a beautiful woman gave celebrity vibes. Not that we have many visiting Cleveland, but it garnered interest from the normies. I stepped back with her in tow, her hand tight in mine as we walked beneath the strings of lights lining the street.

One restaurant was open, and we claimed a table near the back, away from the windows. Emily was sitting beside me, a menu in her hands, but her eyes were on Devon. Was she trying to intimidate him with her Teacher Stare? Devon had always been a teacher's pet, so it would probably work. I nudged her as the server came over.

We all ordered beers, including Emily, and an array of appetizers. I didn't want to be here. This was dumb.

"Why are we here?" I asked Devon after our beers were set in front of us. "We should be at home planning."

Devon shook his head as he gulped down his beer. "No," he said with an exhale as he set down his half empty glass. "I want us to get food in us and a few beers and calm down before we explode."

We were sitting at a four top table with Milo directly in front of me. I had barely looked at him since leaving the casino. But I didn't really need to. I knew him well enough to know what he was thinking. He was thinking up strategies to get the bosses to back down and change their mind. He was also thinking up back up strategies to tank them financially so that they couldn't put down the required deposit. I rested my knee against his as a sign of solidarity.

"That's dumb. We should be exploding. We should be rage destroying everything," I growled at Devon.

"Thank you for proving my point," Devon said coolly. I glared at him.

"Did you really know, Devon?" Emily's soft voice broke our glaring silence.

Devon's eyes shot across the table to her. I grabbed her hand and held it on my lap when I saw she was trembling.

Devon shook his head. "No, I didn't know. But I suspected. I never-" he broke off to huff out a breath and shake his head again. "I never thought they'd agree to this. My dad has always been strongly against it. He has always said he would never stoop to this level."

"Oh, so you think it was all Matthew's fault? No fucking way," Milo hissed.

I pressed my knee against his more strongly under the table. I felt the vibrations of his rage from here.

"That's not what I mean," Devon defended. "I mean, there has to be something causing this change of heart."

"Money?" Emily asked.

Milo snapped out of his rage enough to chime in. "Most likely. We've been having to use more of our profits on our legitimate businesses, the weapons and drugs have increased in price. We've upped our costs to gangs but... well, you saw how that turned out."

"Oh," Emily whispered, remembering her first day with us. Her hand was icy in mine despite the blowing heat of the restaurant. I rubbed my thumb over the soft skin on the back of her hand.

"It doesn't matter their reasoning. We're done with them. We're stepping away after we blow their shit up," I said and drank down my beer.

We paused our conversation for our food to be set down in front of us. Emily thanked the waitress in a bright and happy tone. I raised an eyebrow at Emily. "What? She's working and has nothing to do with what we are all grumpy about."

I rolled my eyes but squeezed her hand.

We ate in a few seconds of silence before Devon spoke. "We can't walk away."

"The fuck we can! What is your limit, Devon? So I know when we hit it," I snapped.

"I didn't mean *never* walk away. I meant-"

"Where do they cross the line for you? When they kill one

of us for not agreeing? When they traffic Emily?" I asked, my voice gruff and demanding.

Emily stiffened next to me, and Milo's knee bumped mine in warning to calm down.

"I will not let anything happen to any of you. They're taking nobody from me," Devon growled, leaning over the table towards me. His eyes flashed with fear and desperation, despite his tone. "We will stay. We will follow orders. And we will take over and stop the trafficking as soon as we can."

"And how many women and children will lose their lives in the meantime?" Emily asked quietly.

My shoulders relaxed when she spoke. She understood what I was saying.

Devon looked down at his partially eaten food. We had all stopped eating. The discussion was too heavy, and it loaded rocks into my stomach.

"We could run," Milo said calmly. "Disappear. Sterling and I have money unconnected to the family."

He slid his phone over to me and the illuminated screen showed a ridiculous number. "What?" I asked.

"Our video was a separate paid video on the site. So, anyone who paid five bucks could see it. And I had a few teaser videos and screenshots on social media and... it was well received." Milo blushed.

"Ten thousand dollars?" My mouth went dry.

"Yes. That's just for the one video. According to the site's metrics, your subscribers have also increased by twelve percent. Just today," Milo said with a grin. "I haven't done that math yet."

"Okay, so you've got some cash," Devon said. "But that doesn't mean we wouldn't be hunted down."

"Sterling and Milo just need to fuck on camera and we'd be able to hire security," Emily said nonchalantly.

I choked on my spit at hearing her use a curse word. I hadn't heard her curse since I'd met her. It made me semi hard in my jeans. I adjusted myself in my seat.

"Jesus, Emily," Devon groaned.

Emily shrugged. "You mean you wouldn't fuck your friend to save the city?"

"This isn't a fucking Power Rangers movie, Emily," Devon scoffed.

"I don't remember much fucking in Power Rangers," Emily retorted absently as she sipped at her beer.

"I meant the 'saving the city' part. It's a bit dramatic, don't you think?" Devon sneered.

"No. You don't know how many people's lives would be destroyed by bringing trafficking into Cleveland," Emily said.

"Cleveland is already a hotbed for it. With or without our involvement," Milo added with a wince.

"Well, I couldn't stomach being involved other than tearing it down and exposing the people making it happen," she snapped. I'd seen her angry. I'd seen her hurt. But this was absolute rage she was keeping carefully contained. "And I'd hope you weren't one of those people."

Devon sat back in his seat and sipped his beer, looking around the restaurant. Our waitress returned to where almost no food had been touched. Emily politely ordered another round of beer and asked for take home boxes.

"Since you're Mr. Money Bags, you get to pay for dinner," Devon grumbled to me as the waitress dropped off our check.

I smirked and paid the bill. We left not long after, quickly getting back to the car. The pedestrian-only street was empty other than a panhandler and a few cops.

"Shotgun!" Emily's voice echoed in the parking garage.

"Shot gun position requires you to be armed with a shotgun," Devon muttered.

"Well, neither of those two have one, either," Emily replied and gestured to me and Milo.

"Then what you should do is call out 'front seat,' so loudly it echoes for miles," Devon corrected sarcastically as we got in his car.

"FRONT SEAT!" Emily screamed before opening the door.

Milo and I shared an amused glance as Devon flinched and angrily got into his seat, muttering, "Brat."

The rest of the drive home was silent and tense. Nobody spoke and Milo typed away on his phone. I leaned over to see what he was looking at so intently. He was checking the security feeds of the casino to make sure we weren't seen on the premises. He glanced over at me before going back to his work. He pulled up another tab containing bank information and selected the "Lost or Stolen Card" option. The addresses listed for the new cards were for the salon and the deli—our most profitable legal businesses. These were the only accounts with enough cash to make the investment money for Giovanni and Taz. He swiped over to a text with Marie and then Harold, letting them both know that he had gotten an email about a potential data leak, assured them that nothing had been affected, but to be safe, he ordered them new credit and debit cards. They would get new cards, but until then, there was a hold on their accounts. This probably bought us a day or two of time before the investment could be withdrawn. He lifted a hand to rub at his eyes under his glasses and an eyelash fell onto his phone screen. I had been leaning over to watch, so I blew the eyelash off the screen for him. He exhaled sharply through his nose, silently reprimanding me. I grinned up at him and rested my elbow on the seat between us to support my lean.

"Please don't breathe your germy breath on my phone," Milo whispered to me.

"But you love my germs," I said with fake hurt.

He rolled his eyes and brought up one of my social media accounts. I had over a million views on a video he posted that was a cropped view of the two of us looking at each other and then it flashes in time with some dramatic music to us with our heads tilted back against the couch and our mouths gasping and eyes squeezing closed in slow motion. He opened the comments and scrolled through them slowly so I could read them.

If the things people were saying about us were making me blush, then I knew Milo was bright red in the dim light of the streetlights. It seemed like the overall consensus was that we needed more content together. I patted Milo's thigh and grinned. "Looks like you're hired."

Milo only grunted in answer before we were pulling into the garage.

We all stood in the kitchen while Emily put away the leftovers. Devon got a bottle of whiskey out of the cabinet and four glasses. He poured us each a measure and passed the glasses around.

Emily looked at her glass for a moment thoughtfully. "Perhaps if we agreed to not talk over each other, our discussion can happen in a respectful and efficient manner."

"Are you about to suggest a talking stick?" Devon spat and his eye twitched in his irritation.

"No," Emily said gently, like she was coaxing a child out of a tantrum. "I don't think we can be safe with our bodies and our hands if we are holding a talking stick."

Milo and I smirked at each other again. Something about this woman repeatedly putting Devon in his place was so poetically perfect. Sure, she put us in our places, too. But *Devon* deserved it. And right now, he was leaning his palms flat on the granite island top and glaring daggers at her. She took it in stride and sipped her whiskey. Her right eye fluttered as she fought against the taste assaulting her mouth. She gave no other indication that she didn't like the whiskey as she stared Devon down.

If we burned the business down and left town, would she come with us? Or would she go back to her mayor? I could see us all moving somewhere tropical. I bet Emily would love swimming in crystal blue water in a little string bikini. Full curves on display. Milo would still have his laptop under an umbrella at the beach and he'd be wearing those short swim trunks guys had been wearing lately. Or maybe somewhere cold and rainy. Emily curled up with a book and some tea. Milo would wear a cozy knit sweater vest and drink a frothy cappuccino. Oh, and Devon would be at both places, too.

I looked out at the backyard while everyone was quiet. It

was the calm before the storm, I knew. This wasn't the first disagreement between the three of us by a mile. But this was the first one of this caliber and with another person's life involved. Well, many other lives if I thought outside of this house. Emily would leave us, surely. And there was no guarantee that Milo and Devon would come with me. Despite our differing ideas on what to do, I loved them and didn't want to split up from them at the same time I left the only family I'd ever known.

Turning back to them, I said, "Let's blow it all up and then form our own new business."

"Just us, no money, no alliances, no connections, nothing to build up from? Hell no," Devon snapped at me with a dismissive shake of his head over his glass.

"Hear me out," I started and slammed my glass down. "We sever our own ties from them, get them caught, and then bring on our own-"

"I'm not getting my dad thrown in fucking prison, Sterling!" Devon shouted. His glare was firmly fixed on me and rage filled me.

"Fuck your dad for getting us into this!" I yelled back. I felt my heart pounding in my chest and it was hard to breathe a full breath. I was so fucking sick of having to follow Devon's every word just because his dad was the only one of our dad's surviving mafia life long enough.

"Hey, now-" Milo tried to settle us, his hands outstretched like he was calming a wild animal.

"No!" I shouted over him. "Fuck Anthony and Matthew *both* for getting us into this. For making the choice without our input. And for sending me and Milo to meet Giovanni and Taz, knowing that it was probably going to be an attack."

Devon's eyes shifted from anger to a conflicted expression. He leaned his elbows on the counter and hung his head. "We're going to stay here and we're going to go along with it for now." His voice was muffled, and he held his hand up to stop my interruption when I opened my mouth to speak. "*For now.* And as soon as we can, we take over. Not violently. Not against their will. We get them to give us power and control and we stop the trafficking."

"No," Emily said firmly. "No, we're not letting innocent people get hurt just to save face."

"Let's just run away. Disappear. Let's fuck all of this up. I've already got the financials held up for a few days, but I can take it all out in a minute. We get Giovanni and Taz locked up, Anthony and Matthew financially ruined, and we get the hell out of here," Milo said, and my chest swelled. He got it. He understood.

"And do what, Milo?" Devon scoffed. "Go be porn stars until we get saggy?"

I shrugged. "Sure."

Devon roared in frustration and threw his empty rocks glass at the wall. Emily squeaked in fear and ran around the counter towards me to avoid the glass. She came towards me on instinct. She stood between me and Milo now, and I stood up straight. Devon saw he had scared her, and his boiling rage crested.

"I'M NOT GIVING UP THIS FAMILY!" Devon bellowed. He slammed his fists on the counter with each word, a vein pulsing in his temple.

"WOULD FAMILY DO THIS? WOULD FAMILY GO BEHIND OUR BACKS AND MAKE THIS DEAL? WOULD FAMILY MAKE US RUIN LIVES AND HURT CHILDREN?" I screamed back and got in his face. He met me chest to chest, his angry breath puffing over my collarbone. But I was bigger. I was taller. I could kick his ass. And he very well knew it.

"THAT'S MY FATHER!" Devon shouted.

"NO, that's our BOSS!" I yelled in his face.

"Guys," Emily's voice was pleading, and a soft hand gripped my elbow.

"I'M THE LEADER. YOU LISTEN TO ME. I'M THE HEIR!" Devon was shouting, and I saw red.

My arm wound back, and soft fingers caught my fist before I could knock Devon's lights out.

"No!" Emily ground out through clenched teeth as she pulled my fist down with all her might.

Milo's arms reached under mine and his hands pulled back on my chest. I stumbled back into him and away from Devon as Emily rushed to push Devon back from me.

I shook Milo's hands off of me and grabbed the bottle of whiskey from the counter. Without looking at any of them, I left out the back door to the patio. I needed air. I needed to cool down.

The crisp outside air had only just bitten my sweaty skin before I took a long drink from the whiskey bottle. The door opened behind me, and I looked back, anticipating an attack from Devon but finding Emily instead. Her Bambi eyes were wide and worried. She crossed her arms over her chest. "I was worried you'd drive off to kill Anthony and Matthew right now."

"No, they have too much security," I grumbled and picked at the crooked label on the bottle.

She gave a soft snort of a laugh and leaned against the railing next to me, looking at me up and down. She bit her bottom lower lip in thought, and I remembered the way it felt against mine. Her lips were as soft and plump as they looked. Why hadn't I kissed her again today?

"See something you like, Bambi?" I tried to give her a flirty grin, but I was sure it looked strained.

She smiled. "Yes, I like you, Sterling."

"Do you like me or like like me?" I asked, looking down at her with lowered lids. A blush hinted at her cheeks.

She shook her head and smiled softly. "You sound like a student."

I crouched on the patio where our footsteps hadn't disturbed the soft snow. With an extended index finger, I wrote in the snow, exposing the darkened cement underneath. "Do you like like me? YAH or NAH."

She giggled when I stood back and admired my handi-work. I sipped from the whiskey again, a smaller sip this time. More to have something to do with my body rather than from wanting the buzz. I watched as she bent to circle her answer. I couldn't see what she had done until she stood up and stepped away from the note, brushing snow from her leather leggings.

YAH was circled.

I set the whiskey bottle down and wordlessly crowded her into the railing. She bit her lip again, but looked up at me with those big blue eyes. I watched as her pupils dilated when my body brushed hers. I cupped her face in my hand and tilted her head up to me. Her eyes fluttered closed in anticipation and her soft lips opened expectantly. Pliable, responsive, and eager were her lips. She tasted like whiskey and smelled like warm cotton and lavender shampoo. I drank her in as my cock swelled against the zipper of my jeans. Her soft hums made the blood in my veins go hot and electric as I fucked her mouth with my tongue. Her hands clutched at my hair and gave me a little tug. My chest rumbled with pleasure, and I returned the favor, gripping her hair tight in my fist. I saw when it became painful when the corners of her closed eyes tightened. She didn't ask me to stop or pull away, so I held just the smallest bit tighter, and she gasped against my lips. I pulled back and kissed down her throat. I found a spot just above her softly curving collarbone that made her whimper when I licked my tongue over it.

"Sterling," she whispered, but it came out lustful.

"Mm?" I replied as I sucked at that spot.

She moaned and her fingers in my hair clenched. "Are you going to leave me behind?"

I jerked upright at her words. "No." I shook my head. "I thought there was no way you'd run away with us. You'd want to stay here. That's the only reason I said we could build our own business here after we take out the leaders of these two."

She laughed, loud and suddenly. "I was trying to run away before, remember?"

"Okay, so don't hate me. But we kind of thought you were a plant from Anthony and Matthew," I admitted and rubbed at the hair she had released from her grip.

"For what?" She asked, her mouth gaping.

"Like to spy on us or something. Especially with the new family popping up," I explained and stepped back.

She stared, openmouthed.

"You have to admit, it is a weird coincidence," I added. "We've never taken someone on into the business like this before. Or ever, really."

Her mouth snapped shut as she processed what I'd said. "Okay, I see it."

I shrugged at her, trying to dismiss the negativity that was attached to my confession. I didn't want to stop being allowed to kiss her.

"Is that why Devon's so mean to me?" She asked.

"Hmm, nope. That's just Devon. He's an idiot," I replied confidently.

"Well, I'm not a spy," she said firmly.

"I was leaning towards that conclusion, yeah," I said with a nod.

"Thanks for believing in me, I guess," she huffed.

I grinned at her. "Come on, it's late. And it's freezing out here."

"Yeah, we need our rest so we can go vigilante Power Rangers on two mafias tomorrow," she said as we walked to the door.

"Is Milo or is Milo not the absolute most perfect Blue Ranger? Like from the original Mighty Morphin' ones," I asked as we went up the stairs.

She giggled. "Milo is. Billy the Blue Ranger was always my favorite."

20

Emily

Sunlight shone through my eyelids and woke me up early the next morning. I stayed in bed, looking out the window as the sun peeked through the trees. Reflecting on the events of last night, I felt conflicted. While my kiss with Sterling was amazing, I was worried about what we were going to do about Anthony and Matthew. All I knew was that there was no way I'd stay with them if they participated in human trafficking. I wouldn't just leave; I'd go to the authorities. My affection for these guys didn't outweigh that decision.

I showered before heading down to make breakfast. Devon was already in the kitchen at the island. An empty plate with toast crumbs sat before him and he sipped from a coffee mug. When I entered, he straightened in his chair and smoothed the front of his button-down shirt. "Good morning, Emily."

"Good morning, Devon. Have you already eaten?" I asked him and gestured to his plate.

"I did," he replied and finally looked at me. The armor was down in his eyes, and I saw the exhaustion and fear behind those amber irises.

"Devon, I–" I started to tell him I was counting on him to make the right choice. But he reached out a hand and pulled me towards him.

"I'm going to do my best to not create a war with Anthony and Matthew. Please know that my actions are towards the same goal as Sterling and Milo," he said with a touch of desperation to be understood.

"I can't be around a crime like that," I whispered. "Not even for a minute."

Devon's head hung, and he looked at my hand clasped in his. His skin was warm on mine, and I could see his pulse pounding at his throat.

Milo and Sterling entered the kitchen, talking low to each other. Milo went to grab a cup of coffee and Sterling met me in front of Devon. He stooped slightly to kiss me in greeting and then looked down to where Devon was still gripping my fingers. "What's up?" Sterling asked.

"Since when do you two kiss good morning?" Devon asked, a harsh bite to his words. He let go of my hand.

"Last night," Milo said for us. "They kissed again."

"Third time's the charm," Sterling said brightly as he made his coffee.

I rolled my eyes and moved to the fridge to make breakfast.

Some ricotta and lemon pancakes, bacon, and two pots of coffee later, everyone was better fortified for planning and problem solving. We settled in the office where Milo sat at the desk and typed away on the computer. I sat in the plush and straight-backed chair and wished for a whiteboard to write on.

"Should we go over our options?" I asked the silent room.

The guys all shifted, knowing there was going to be another fight once we got started.

"Do we have a whiteboard or some big paper?" I asked.

Devon opened the small closet near the door and pulled out a posterboard size note pad of lined paper. He handed me a pack of markers and returned to his seat. I uncapped a fresh black marker and sighed at the sight of a perfectly chiseled tip. The smell of marker ink swirled around me in a comforting hug. Maybe I missed teaching a little. I leaned the notepad against the desk and squatted down to write on it.

"Option A: Do nothing and be participants in human trafficking," I read aloud as I wrote it.

I felt Milo get out of the desk chair and come around to sit where he could see what I was writing. I fought a grin of triumph.

"What do we think the most likely outcome of Option A is?" I asked the guys over my shoulder.

"Do we have to raise our hands?" Sterling asked.

I looked back to see all three of them raising their hands while they waited for my answer. I smiled and all three of them smiled back. "No, you don't have to raise your hands."

"Most likely with Option A, we would be responsible for the ruined lives and deaths of a lot of innocent people. We would probably also get caught," Milo answered.

I wrote "Outcome: Ruined lives, deaths of innocents. Prison." I moved to the next line. "Option B: Stay and wait to inherit business, stop trafficking."

"What do we think the outcome is for Option B?" I asked and stood to face them.

"We get what we want. We stop trafficking and we still get to keep the business and our family," Devon said and crossed his arms over his chest.

"People would still be dead," Sterling snapped.

"Stop," I interrupted any more argument with my Teacher Voice and wrote on the page. "Outcome: Keep family and business, responsible for lives ruined and deaths."

"Option C: Forcefully take over business, stop trafficking," I read aloud and faced them again. "Outcome?"

"Family is dead or in prison, severed connections and loyalties," Milo reasoned.

I wrote, "Cut family ties- death or prison. No trafficking."

"Option D: Run away."

"It wouldn't save anyone but us," Sterling said.

"Option E: Blow it up and run away."

"Everyone in jail or dead but us," Devon said and shook his head.

"Option F: Try to reason with the leaders to cancel the deal."

"War with Giovanni and Taz and trafficking still happens," Sterling muttered.

"I think that's all of it," I said as I finished writing.

"What do you think?" Sterling asked me.

I looked at the options again. "I think it should be a mixture of more than one."

"How so?" Devon asked.

"I think we should put a stop to the deal and the trafficking with the least amount of death involved," I said and flipped the marker over and over in my hands. "So maybe we should talk to Anthony and Matthew about backing down first."

Milo shook his head. "If we did, they would never trust us again. We were spying on them. They haven't talked to any of us about this yet."

"Who knows if they were ever going to tell us?" Sterling grumbled.

"No, they would have to. We would have to have an entirely new infrastructure. One that could handle security, transportation, law enforcement, product management, and sales. All of that takes work and multiple people. We would be the ones to oversee it," Devon explained sourly.

"If you gave up protections, would that leave many people?" I asked.

"Protections doesn't mean bodyguards. Well, not typically. It's mostly a scam to get businesses to give us money monthly, and we pretend to keep them safe from gangs. But we control most of the gangs," Sterling said with a shrug.

"People pay for that?" I asked, shocked.

"Yeah. Sometimes we have a gang member rough them or their businesses up a little to motivate them to use our protections. Sometimes they do piss someone off and they ask for bodyguard protection. Most of the time, it's just a way to get money," Sterling finished.

"That's so shady," I said.

"That's business, baby," Sterling said brightly.

"We can't fully incriminate my dad and Matthew without getting ourselves in trouble for other things. We need to consider that," Devon said, getting us back on track.

Everyone was quiet as we digested this information.

"So, we have to leave," Milo said. It's what he had been wanting from the beginning.

"Or we step in, take over for Anthony and Matthew and shut it down on our side and get Giovanni and Taz caught," Sterling said. "And I mean take over *right now*, not whenever they decide to step aside."

"There's nothing to say that our connections and our gangs would still be loyal when we take over like that," Devon said angrily. "Everything we've worked for would be for nothing."

"Is being in charge that important to you?" I asked coolly.

Devon's face reddened and his nostrils flared. I maintained eye contact in challenge.

"Okay, okay, before we fight again," Milo interjected. "Let's see if we can get Matthew and Anthony to talk to us about this. If they tell us the plan, then maybe we can get them to go back on the deal. We have to at least *try* before we go ahead with any other plans."

"Make the call," Devon said and gestured his allowance to Milo.

Sterling nodded.

"I think we're all in agreement," I said calmly.

Milo called Matthew and said he needed to talk about some cyber security stuff with him and Anthony. I heard Matthew's voice on the other end agree and suggest a meeting at seven. He invited us all over for dinner. Once Milo hung up, we all exhaled with relief.

"Sterling and I will do rounds tonight, so we will meet you there after we're done," Devon said. "I don't imagine you'll get much information over dinner. You can get them drinking and give them ego boosts until we get there so they're comfortable and happy."

Sterling looked at me worriedly. "I don't know about that."

"We'll be fine," Milo assured him. "It's Anthony and Matthew."

"I can pretend to ask about what businesses the family operates and bring up trafficking as one of my questions. Maybe it'll be a segue into them telling you about it. And then we can try to talk them out of it," I suggested.

"And if that opportunity doesn't come up, one of you can ask about Giovanni and Taz's ventures in town and in Akron," Devon said with a stressed sounding sigh.

"I don't like this. We shouldn't be sending in Emily," Sterling said and rubbed his hands roughly over his thighs.

"She was the wife of a politician. She can handle it," Devon said, his eyes locked on me.

"I think getting five-year-olds to do what I want them to do is better practice for this," I said and smiled confidently.

Milo snorted. "Don't let his quietness fool you. Matthew could eat you for breakfast."

"Good thing we're going for dinner."

We spent much of the rest of the day apart in the house. Everyone was in a quiet contemplation of the meeting tonight and I was over it. I cleaned a little, used the treadmill, and even made a loaf of bread to pack Sterling and Devon sandwiches for rounds. Getting antsy, I found myself outside Sterling's bedroom. I could hear music playing, a dark and ethereal sounding metal song. I hesitated only a moment before knocking.

It wasn't that I didn't trust Sterling- I had found that I did trust him. I trusted all three of them with my life. To whatever end, apparently. Since hearing about the deal, the guys had asked for my opinions, respected my insights, and treated me like an equal. It was startling to realize I'd never been in that position before. I'd never been a valued voice in the room before. Gregory and my parents chose almost everything in my life for me and made it seem like they were taking care of me. But I was a capable and intelligent woman. I hadn't really accepted that about myself until these men turned to me and said, "Emily, what do you think?" Part of me hated it took a man (or three) to get me to realize my worth. But it took a patriarchal upbringing to get me to devalue myself, so maybe having men show me that was wrong was the poetic justice I needed.

The door opened and Sterling's eyebrows rose. "Oh, hey Bambi."

"Hey."

"Come in, I was just cleaning some... tools," Sterling said, a velvety and dark tone to his voice.

"Tools? I didn't think you to be a handyma- oh." I ended with a weak gasp and almost choked on my tongue.

"Depends on what needs to be fixed," Sterling chuckled and stalked behind me.

The music sounded haunted but sensual at the same time. Very much like Sterling himself. On his long black dresser was an open black box with a pillowy black interior. The contents carefully placed along the slightly dented wood of the dresser top were two glinting silver daggers, silky maroon rope, a soft black blindfold, what looked like a harness with leather handcuffs, two red vibrators, an unopened package of a set of anal plugs, a new bottle of lube, and a box of regular and magnum condoms. A small jug of isopropyl alcohol sat next to the daggers, and the smell of new plastic and alcohol filled the air.

I tried to suppress a shiver as he came up behind me and his breath ghosted along my neck.

"Was that a shudder of disgust or...?" he trailed off, the question hanging.

"No, your breath tickled me," I half lied in a whisper.

I heard his smile in his words. "I'm touch sensitive, so I know how that goes."

"What do you mean?" I asked, thinking of the sensory sensitive students that had come through my classroom over the years.

"Any touch like... lights up my brain. I don't know how to describe it. I- uh, wasn't hugged much as a child. So, when I got touched by anyone, I'd be like... hungry for more," Sterling explained shamefully. "It kind of stuck around. Even now when someone touches me even in passing, I'm hyper aware of it."

I turned around to face him. "Can I touch you?"

"Yes."

"Anywhere I cannot touch?" I asked and looked at him through my lashes. I traced my fingertips up his arm from the back of his hand, circling the inside crook of his elbow, and up to where his biceps pressed against his faded black t-shirt.

"No," he whispered back, but his breath hitched, and goosebumps rose over his skin.

"Sterling, you beat people up for a living," I said, trying to hide the desperate sadness that pitted in my stomach for him.

"I won't hurt you," he rushed to promise, his eyes bright and wide.

"I know, I just mean... you touch people all the time with aggression and violence. It's touch, but the worst kind," I said, and my throat closed at the idea of little Sterling just wanting to be pet and coddled with love still inside the man in front of me.

His body seemed to relax as he let go of some of his burden. He gave me a small smile. "You and Milo are the only ones to think like that."

"The only ones to care about you?" I asked, anger sharpening my words.

He shrugged. "Two people who care are better than none. And there's Devon, he half cares."

I paused. I guess he was right. There certainly weren't any more people in my own life who cared about me. I trailed my fingertips lightly up to his neck and jaw. His eyes fluttered closed, and he took a long breath, just enjoying the sensation of touch. I would ask about the "tools" later. They seemed counterintuitive to the touch he craved.

"Sit down and let me touch you," I said, more command in my tone than I meant to use.

He listened and sat on the edge of his bed. I lifted his t-shirt off of him and marveled at his tattoos. They were all well done and entirely black ink. He watched with heavy-lidded eyes and parted lips as I ran my fingers over his chest and abdomen. Goosebumps rose on his skin, and I could see his pulse hammering in his neck. His muscles tensed and relaxed as my hands touched him. His chest rose and fell in stuttering breaths, and I smiled. He really was sensitive to touch. I bet I could make him moan like in his videos.

I slid onto his lap, so I was straddling his hips, and he smirked and leaned back on his hands. Feeling emboldened, I kissed his lips. The music surrounded us, and the sensual beat directed our lust. The kiss deepened, and I felt him harden under me. His tongue caressed mine, and I pulled back to nip at his lips. He groaned. I smiled as I trailed kisses over his jaw, neck, and chest. When I licked over a nipple, he practically jumped at the sensation, making us both laugh. I licked and sucked until he was reaching for me and stroking back my hair. I kissed and licked a tickling trail down his stomach and his breathing became heavier and he watched me closely.

Sliding off of him and to the floor, I slipped my fingers beneath the waistband of his sweatpants and tugged. He lifted his hips and bit his lip as he watched me. He wasn't wearing any underwear, so his cock stood proudly before me. My mouth watered, and I licked my lips. He stroked back my hair as he watched my mouth.

Blow jobs were something Gregory was very particular about and often claimed he didn't like. Maybe I was just bad at them. I would let Sterling decide for himself, though. I wasn't sure about the bar piercing through his cock, so I started with a long flat tongued lick from the base to the tip and around the piercing. A shuddering moan resonated from Sterling, and I felt more confident. I took him into my mouth and gave him a suck, enjoying the warm and salty taste of him. I bobbed my head and then swirled my tongue around the head and flicked the metal piercing. When I lightly caressed his thighs, I felt the tickle of his hair as I made my way to join my mouth on his cock. I squeezed the base and stroked up to meet my mouth with one hand and held his balls in my other. He was groaning with each upward stroke and suck, and he tipped his head back. When I tugged at his piercing just the slightest, he cried out and beads of pre-cum met my tongue.

He sat up suddenly and pulled me onto the bed, and I squealed in shock. He grinned at me as he forcefully pulled off my pants and demanded my shirt to come off. I stripped off my shirt at the same time he yanked down my pants, leaving my soaked panties askew on my body.

"So fucking wet for me," he groaned, just audible over the music.

I could only "Mhm," in agreement, feeling worried about him going down on me. It was another thing Gregory claimed to not like. But maybe he just didn't like anything with me. He had only ever done it once and used his fingers for fore-play after that. I was always jealous when a friend got bold and talked about her husband's or boyfriend's oral prowess. I had a feeling Sterling had no similar qualms as he buried his nose against my wet panties and inhaled.

I giggled as he moaned out his exhale and pulled down the soaked cotton. He smirked up at me with dark eyes as he discarded my panties. He settled between my open legs and kissed the sensitive and soft skin of my inner thighs. My heart pounded with anticipation as he kissed and nipped and licked my thighs, the mound above where I needed him, and the cleft where my thigh met my hip. Slowly, he used his thumbs to spread me open as he held me under my hips, his fingers digging into the globes of my ass. I was quivering with need and desperate lust. A sweat broke out on my forehead. I was just about to reach down and shove his face to my pussy when I felt arousal drip down and his mouth swiftly chased it.

A sound burst from my mouth that I was sure I'd never made before. It was wanton and unrestrained. He licked and sucked and *devoured* me in a way that I had never thought I would experience. He growled low in his throat as I grabbed hold of his black hair and rolled my hips for *more*.

"That's my good girl, Bambi. Let me see you lose control. Fucking ride my face," he demanded, low and sultry.

Warmth crept through my limbs, originating from where his mouth sucked at my clit while massaging it with his tongue. The warmth became a scorching, electric heat that felt like buzzing bees in my arms and legs.

"Come on, baby, come on," he coached in that same deep voice.

I heard my voice keening and crying out as my pleasure crested and ended with an explosion so sweet, so large, and so perfect I wished I could live in it. My back arched and my entire body shivered and shook, my voice high and shaking with it. My eyes were shut tight until I was coming down from my high and I opened them to see Sterling kneeling between my legs and rolling on a condom. I moaned as he lined himself up, lubing up with my wetness. He looked at me with a raised eyebrow, asking permission, and I nodded vigorously. His mouth fell open and his head tipped back as he eased into me. The stretch to accommodate him burned for a moment, as it had been a few months since I'd had sex. I hissed in a breath and my body tensed, and he stopped and looked down.

He gave a quick nod in understanding and let me settle for a moment before he started slow, shallow thrusts until my muscles relaxed again and I moaned.

Sterling leaned down and groaned against my neck. "You feel so good. Your pussy is so delicious, and it's gripping my cock so tight. I want to feel it strangle me when you come," he murmured.

I was beyond the ability for speech, so I only nodded and moaned. Wrapping my arms and legs around him, I bucked up against him to make him thrust harder.

He chuckled, low and dark, before almost taunting me. "Tell me what you want, baby."

I opened my mouth to speak, but he gave two sharp, deep thrusts and I couldn't say a word.

"What was that? What do you want me to do?" he laughed breathlessly against my neck.

Again, I opened my mouth to speak but he thrust deep and tilting upwards and I saw stars and a sobbing cry came out of me instead.

"Wha-" he started, but I interrupted him.

"More!"

"More what?"

"Everything. Harder. More," I shouted at him, feral and cave woman-like.

"That's not how we- OW!" he laughed because I smacked his ass. Hard.

He grabbed a pillow down from the top of the bed and set it next to my hips on the mattress and then pulled out of me and flipped me over, so my belly was on the pillow. He did it so effortlessly, and I was thankful for his strength. I was not a particularly small woman. He knocked my legs apart with his knees and slammed into me. I bit my lip to keep in a scream as he pounded into me with fierce, snapping thrusts. When I buried my face in my arms on the mattress, he grabbed my ponytail and hauled me up, so I was on hands and knees.

"Let me hear it. I want to hear you scream for me. Don't cover it up. I want the guys to know you're mine. I want them to know you're stuffed full of my cock, and you love it." His voice was breathless and grunting as he fucked me.

I was shy to scream now, but he smacked my ass so hard I cried out.

"Good girl," he chuckled. "Let me hear it."

He stopped fucking me and I tried to push back onto him.

"Uh-uh," he said and held my hips still.

"Sterling! Fuck me!" I screamed in frustration.

He let out a loud laugh and smacked my ass again before resuming his thrusting. "There. Good job. Thank you."

I rolled my eyes, and he pulled me up by my ponytail so that my sweaty back slid smoothly against his sweaty chest. He reached one hand to circle my clit and the other up to grip my throat. I'd never been choked before, but I was open to the experience. He gripped hard and my breath became thin and strangled. I trusted him to know when to stop, so I let him continue as long as he was about to make me come. I reached up and wrapped my arms around his neck behind me in a steadying embrace, my fingers in the soft hair at the nape of his neck. At this angle, he was consistently slamming my g-spot while also swirling his fingers over my clit. I felt the liquid pleasure of an orgasm roll through my body like a tidal wave. I felt his hand tighten around my throat and I was completely cut off from oxygen just before the orgasm fully hit. Black spots danced before me. My body tensed and shook, and he loosened his grip. As I gasped for air, my orgasm took over. The adrenaline from being choked and the pleasure from his cock blended in my veins and had me screaming and sagging against his muscular body. He praised and coaxed me through it. My thighs were trembling and wet as he settled me against the mattress again and fucked into me hard and fast.

Still shaking, I reached my hand back and clutched at his flexing thigh, my nails digging slightly. He hissed and rested his forehead against my neck as his breath became gasping moans. He pushed into me so deep and I felt wave after wave of come even with the condom as he groaned against my neck. He had to be completely filling the condom, and I made a mental note to call that family doctor about birth control.

He collapsed us to the bed and against my back before rolling off of me. I turned over to cuddle into his side, and he wrapped a sweaty arm around me. We were both panting and our hearts pounded loudly in our chests. I looked up at him and he looked sleepily back down at me.

"Do we have time for a nap?" I asked him, my voice hoarse.

He craned his neck and reached to touch his phone on his nightstand. "Yeah, we've got about two hours until you need to leave."

"Good. Time for an hour nap," I said contentedly with a stretch.

He chuckled and got up to dispose of the condom. When he came back, I shuffled to the bathroom to pee and wipe up. He set and alarm and tucked us into his bed for a quick nap.

An hour later, the alarm on Sterling's phone woke us. The sun was set already, so we got up in darkness. Sterling sleepily kissed me before heading into his shower. Tugging on the t-shirt he had been wearing earlier, I darted down the hall to my room. I showered quickly and dried my hair, focusing on my tasks. I dressed in a pair of black jeans and a cashmere white sweater, swiped on my red lipstick, and headed to meet Milo.

Milo and Devon were in the office, and I let Devon know there was dinner packed for him and Sterling. He thanked me but wouldn't look at me. I rolled my eyes at his behavior. Sterling came into the office and plopped down in a chair. I stroked his wet hair, so he had some more positive touch before he went to do his work.

"If you two are finished, we have work to do," Devon snapped.

"Are we not on time?" I asked.

Devon didn't respond, but Milo and Sterling exchanged amused glances.

Milo finished typing on the computer. "I sent it all to your phones, so you're set to go."

"Are you taking Harold?" I asked.

"He's driving them because I'm driving you," Milo replied.

"Well, let's get going now. I'm going to need an expensive coffee before I talk to the leaders of the mafia," I said brightly.

Milo's car was an old Toyota sedan, and I looked at him suspiciously when I got in. "Is this the car you transport dead bodies in?"

He laughed and started the engine. "No, I don't want my

car to have computer parts in it. All newer cars have computer elements in them."

"Oh, I would have thought you'd have like a high-tech electric vehicle or something," I said and looked around. The car's interior was incredibly clean and well kept for its age.

"The opposite, actually. I want as few computers in my life as possible. No high-tech cars, no wi-fi thermostats, no wi-fi washing machines," Milo said as he drove us down the street.

"Why? Is this like the baby monitors getting hacked thing?" I asked.

"Sort of. I have a secure network at home. I trust my work on the network. But that security only goes so far. Those devices use the internet to connect to a service. That service is something that I don't control. Do you know how many times I've hacked into people's thermostats to turn their heat or A/C down to see if they're home? How many times I've hacked into security feeds? Emily, I have the footage of you catching your husband cheating on you and that was on a government run server. I don't trust anything that the internet can control."

"Got it," I breathed.

"Sorry," he said with a blush. "That was a lot."

I giggled. "No, it's just the most you've spoken to me, and I was kind of shocked."

Milo laughed and shook his head. I enjoyed seeing him smiling and laughing. I watched his blue eyes as they crinkled at the corners. A light shone in our direction, and it caught my attention. All I saw was headlights swerving and heading directly towards us.

"MILO!" I screeched, and he jerked the wheel to avoid the collision.

A horrendous cacophony of crunching metal, breaking glass, car horns blaring, and our screams surrounded us. The airbags exploded into our chests and faces, and it obscured my sight of Milo. There was the distinct feeling of spinning and free falling as we screamed. I tried to reach out to him. I tried to hold him. A wrenching pain in my side was the last thing I felt before all was black.

21

Emily

There was a tire swing on the riverbank on the back property belonging to the Garfield family near my home growing up. Teddy was in my grade at school and had parties in the summer before senior year, where his older brother would buy us all cheap beer and we'd swim and play in the water. The first party of summer was the biggest. It was not long after school let out and we were just beginning to soak up the freedom of our last summer before graduation and the beautiful sunshine. I remembered the smell of all the girls' lathering up in tanning lotion and Sun In hair spray like it was yesterday. I remembered strutting out in my first bikini- bought without my mom's knowledge- with heart pounding and tummy fluttering nerves. It was early in my relationship with Gregory, still fresh and delicate, and I wanted to impress him. In that way that adolescents most desperately want to be seen as unique, I was determined to do a flip off the tire swing and be the Talk of the Summer.

The boys all stood around the plastic table laden with barely cold beer with puffed out bare chests. They were flexing so hard as they drank their tepid, shitty beers that they were almost inadvertently crunching the cans. They would pretend to not be watching the girls as we lathered our skin in practiced and intentionally vaguely sensual but not overtly sexual ways, while we pretended like that wasn't the entire point. I remembered Gregory winking at me as I slipped out of my little denim shorts and flowing top to show off my new red bikini. That feeling of budding womanly power would stay with me for the rest of my life.

The feeling of flipping off of the tire swing, soaring with a huge grin, and... splash landing on some submerged rocks would stay with me longer, though. Shooting pain, accompanied by a full, temporary paralysis of my spine, was the most pain and most fear I had ever felt. The flow of the river in the early summer heat was thankfully slow, so I didn't go far downstream. The boys had been watching me jump in my new bikini, hoping for a strap to slip, and had seen me hit the rocks. When my head broke the surface for a second as I was limply carried away, I saw them all sprinting towards me, shouting to each other to organize my rescue.

When I could open my eyes again, I felt the burn and prick of hot stones on my back, accompanied by the searing pain in my right arm. Lips pressed against mine as Hallie, a friend who was also one of the local pool's lifeguards, blew air into my lungs. Once I was sufficiently drained of river water, we determined my arm was broken.

After that single flip off the tire swing, I retired from my daredevil summer, and settled into my Sun Hats and Ankle Wading Summer. My cast was signed by everyone and gently kissed every day by a young and fresh-faced Gregory. I never thought I'd feel pain and fear like that again.

"EMILY!" a bellowed voice shook me from my dreamy, sunny memory.

I groaned and tried to turn over in my bed. But I was not in my bed. And that pain I was remembering was not just a memory. A scream caught in my throat as I fought to keep my tenuous hold on consciousness.

A roar of effort echoed near me, and I struggled to open my eyes. I was being dragged away from the sound of fighting and my back burned as I was scraped against the gravelly road. I groaned again in protest as my eyes landed on Milo. He was limping around the front of the car towards me and trying desperately to fight off a man while bleeding heavily from his head. If Milo was over there, then who...?

I looked up to see a man I didn't know, dragging me away from the smoking, destroyed car. Sirens began in the distance and other motorists had stopped around us. Cries of "I've called for help!" and "Stop fighting, the police are coming!" rang out around me.

"Please," I tried to beg, but blood had filled my mouth and it sputtered from me as I tried to speak. Something told me that this was not a good Samaritan trying to help me get to safety. The gritted set of his jaw and uncaring eyes made that apparent.

He ignored my plea, and I struggled to find purchase on the road with scrambling feet. My right arm hurt so bad I was sure it was blown to pieces, but a quick look down proved it to still be present, although limp and useless at my side. I tried to stand, but I was being dragged too quickly.

"Milo!" I screeched out, spraying blood from my mouth.

He looked up from fighting one handed to see me. His glasses were missing, and he was bleeding into his eyes, but I could see the fear and desperation on his face. Before anything else could be done, a loud pop came from the car just before it blew up. I screamed, desperate and hoarse, as they shoved me into the back of a white work van. I landed flat on my face and the pain in my mouth had me seeing stars and stuck in a silent scream until the surge of pain passed. Scrambling towards the door, I tried to get up, but my right arm was entirely useless, and I was feeling dizzy and sick.

The door was ripped open and a shouting, fighting Milo was thrown in with me. The guy who had dragged me came in on his heels. I sat back on my ass and lifted my legs up to kick out as soon as he got close. Milo was back on his feet and had his right arm up, ready to punch the guy, while his left arm hung as uselessly as my right. The guy approached Milo with a quick jab to his ribs, which made Milo cry out and bend over. Raising a gun over Milo's head, the guy brought the handle down to Milo's skull and knocked him out cold in a heap on the floor of the van. I didn't have time to scream before the guy came at me. I got one solid kick to his thigh, missing his dick, before he caught my other foot. He yanked my foot towards him and gave my skull the same treatment as Milo's.

The next time I regained consciousness, I was freezing cold and wet. I heard a growling, teeth clenched scream, that sent my adrenaline spiking. Heavy panting followed the scream, and I sat upright. Something kept me anchored in place by my left wrist and I bit off a scream before it came out. I looked around. My eyes had a hard time clearing and focusing, and I shook my aching head.

Milo was shirtless and strung up by his wrists in front of me. His black utility boot clad feet barely touching the ground. He tipped his head back between his arms in pain, and sweat and blood ran in rivulets down his pale skin and soaked into his dark jeans. His abdomen and chest were mottled with bruises and a few bleeding cuts. As he panted, his chest and stomach inflated and deflated back to tense and shivering abs.

A man came out of the darkness behind him, holding a wooden baseball bat. I flinched as he raised his arms back to swing it. Milo's head hung down to his chest as his entire body tensed up, anticipating the blow. The man swung, and the bat hit Milo's back with a sickening sound.

I screamed at the same time as Milo. I couldn't stand the sight of someone hurting him. The older man was Mack, the guy that drove us to the fights at Giovanni and Taz's building. Mack returned to the darkness again and Milo looked to see me sitting up.

"Milo!" I sobbed.

"Emily," he said, and it sounded like he was begging me. "Look away."

A retching sob broke from my chest. My arm was still a blinding pain and my head felt like it had been split open. Everything tasted and smelled like blood and bile, and I wanted nothing more than to get us out of here.

"No, Emily," Mack snapped. "Watch me slowly kill your boyfriend for not telling me what I need to know."

"What do you want?" I asked after I could open my mouth without the fear of vomiting. I clenched my jaw shut after speaking to hold down the gag that was in part because of the blow to my head and the other part an emotional reaction.

"Who are your family's political ties?" Mack asked Milo, close to his ear.

"I don't know," Milo growled.

Mack stepped back and swung his bat, hitting Milo on the side. Milo's scream had tears running down his face and his voice giving out.

"Who are Anthony and Matthew working with?" Mack asked.

"I'm just the IT guy, I don't know," Milo tried to explain breathlessly.

"No, I know your uncle has been training you to be a leader since he adopted you," Mack said. "Tell me who they've got, and I'll spare your girlfriend."

Milo's blue eyes snapped to me. "I'd give you *anything* for you to spare her, but I truly don't know what you're talking about."

Mack stepped back and looked at me and then back at Milo. He studied us for a moment and then leaned the slightly bloody bat against the wall. Silently, he unhooked Milo's handcuffs from a long chain that ended on a metal hook hanging from the ceiling rafters. Milo collapsed to the dirty, rough cement floor with a groan. Before he could do anything, Mack roughly dragged him to the wall down from me to another chain that he locked into the wall. I looked up and saw I was chained similarly, but with only one arm. The windowless room was large, and Milo was far enough down the wall that we couldn't touch each other.

Mack turned to me and before I could finish my scream, he hauled me to the chain and strung me up by my left arm, as my right was useless and hanging at my side. It had to be dislocated as well as broken, and I fought another gag.

"Emily, close your eyes. I'm so sorry, baby. I'm so sorry," Milo begged me from the wall.

I was hyperventilating and shaking with gasping sobs before Mack even stepped back. "Please, I don't know anything. I've just joined them."

"I know," he said simply. "And I know who your husband is."

"Gregory knows about this?!" I gasped between sobs.

Mack recoiled his wrath to let out a guffaw. He stepped back one step and swung his reclaimed bat at my side. A blinding, searing pain covered my ribcage on my left side. The force had knocked the breath out of me, and my next inhalation pinched.

"No, fucking Gregory Ambrose doesn't know about this," Mack answered. It took me a moment to register his words.

"He's the only connection I know about, and he doesn't know where I am. I ran away from him after the divorce," I wheezed in a rush.

Mack looked at me for a moment before swinging the bat again and hitting my hip this time. When I could finally take in my surroundings again, I was being hooked back to my chain against the wall. My own hoarse whimpering echoed around us as I breathed.

Mack strode out of the metal doors at the far end of the room without another word. The door slammed shut behind him and I heaved and retched until I was almost passing out from a lack of oxygen. There was nothing in my stomach save some water, so nothing other than watery bile soaked into the concrete.

I slumped against the cement brick wall and fought to breathe when every big inhale felt like a knife poking my lungs. Milo shuffled and groaned from his place against the wall.

"Emily," he said in his ruined voice. "Are you awake? Can you hear me?"

"I'm... awake," I said between pants.

"Oh god, Emily. I'm so sorry."

"It's... not... your... fault."

"I should have listened to Sterling and had you stay home," Milo growled through his pain.

"It's... so... cold... and... it... hurts.... I'm... going... to... sleep."

"No, Emily! Don't-"

22

Sterling

Just after our second pickup, my phone and Devon's phone chimed in unison. We glanced at each other before Devon looked at his message. "It's my dad telling us to come to the house after rounds," he said.

"Milo and Emily must have been successful," I said, my chest tense with nerves.

Devon lifted his eyebrows briefly, as if to say, "We'll see."

"Send Milo and Emily a message and ask so we know what we're in for ahead of time," I suggested.

Devon exhaled sharply through his nose as if he didn't like being told what to do, but was doing it anyway.

We finished our last few stops, deposited the cash with our bank handlers, dropped off Harold, and switched to my car at the house before heading towards Anthony's place. There were no replies from Emily or Milo and no more information from our leaders. I wondered if they were just having a good time or if Milo and Emily were in trouble.

"Hey, wait," I said as I pulled onto Anthony's street. "I thought they were going to Matthew's house."

Devon shrugged. "Maybe they came here after. You know how my mom liked Emily."

He was right. Stephanie had loved Emily and was so glad to have another woman in the family. Emily had even gotten an invitation to the tea garden the first time she was at the house. I tried not to think about the change of venue again until I pulled into the driveway. Milo knew the rules of No Second Location and Always Drive Yourself, even when it involved our family. And his little shitbox car was nowhere to be seen, but Matthew's car was haphazardly parked in the driveway.

I felt Devon tense next to me as I threw my car into park and killed the engine. We wordlessly ripped off our seatbelts and practically raced to the front door. Our boots stomping at a jogging pace were the only sound on the street. Devon got to the door, and a house staff member opened it before he could reach the handle.

"They're in the office," the girl said quietly, without looking at us. Her eyes were downcast, and she rolled her shoulders in. Not the usual posture of the well paid and well-treated staff.

My heart sank through my stomach and landed somewhere by my feet. Or so it felt as Devon and I stomped our way to the office.

I heard the soft sobs of Stephanie and the clink of ice in a crystal glass. Devon slammed open the door and looked around fiercely. Anthony stood facing the window behind his desk, his hands in his pockets. Stephanie was sat, sobbing into a tissue in one of the leather chairs. Matthew was sitting in another leather chair, his elbows on his knees, head hanging, and a glass of liquor in his hand. My heart disappeared from my body all together now when I realized Milo and Emily weren't in the room.

"Where are they?" ripped from my mouth like a demonic growl.

"Oh, Sterling," Stephanie wailed and threw herself at me. She pulled Devon towards us, but he shook her off. I stood frozen, awaiting answers. Her tears soaked into my sweatshirt, and I wanted to push her away.

Devon stormed to the desk and slammed his palms down on the glass top so hard everything rattled. Anthony turned around, an unfeeling expression on his face. "Where are Emily and Milo?" Devon demanded.

"Sit down, both of you," Anthony said in a calm voice.

"No," I said harshly.

"They're dead," Matthew said, finally looking up from his hunched position. His eyes were puffy and he clenched his jaw like he had been crying for a while.

My blood turned to ice in my veins and my breath halted in my chest.

"What?!" Devon gasped and whirled to Matthew.

"They were in an accident. Another car hit a patch of ice-" Matthew started. His face was lined with grief and pain, and he clutched the glass of liquor like it was his lifeline.

"NO!" I pushed Stephanie off of me and she stumbled back. I approached the desk next to where Devon was still frozen. His face had gone pale and sickly, and his eyes were wide. I stared right at Anthony with his stone face and business as usual posture. "You fucking BASTARD!"

"Sterling, it was a car accident!" Stephanie wailed behind me.

"NO!" I bellowed and flipped Anthony's desk. He only stepped back like I had spilled a drop of wine on the carpet. "They were *mine*, and you KILLED THEM!" I heard the crack in my voice before I felt the tears on my cheeks.

"When?" Devon whispered.

"Just after they left the house, we presume. Witnesses say another vehicle spun out of control and struck them," Anthony said, as if I wasn't staring him down like a wild beast.

"They're in the hospital and they'll be fine," Devon insisted.

"No," Anthony whispered, his face still stone.

"They're waiting to be discharged from the hospital right now. I'll go pick them up," Devon tried again.

"No," Anthony whispered a second time.

"Dad," Devon begged his father.

Anthony looked down at his shoes, the only sign of emotion within that stone armor.

Devon bent over and put his hands on his knees as a cry of anguish erupted from him. He was all I had left. My pseudo brother.

The door opened again, and Victoria and Harold came in, followed closely by Marie and her husband, Brendon. She had a confused, worried expression on her face. My heart shattered anew, and I knew I couldn't be there when they told Marie. I couldn't say anything. All I could do was run. I ran from the room and was at the bottom of the stairs when

Marie's piercing scream echoed down to me, finding a twin torment in my chest.

Devon stumbled from the room, looking like he was drunk, and half fell, half ran down the stairs. His soft brown skin looked alarmingly green as he pushed me and the maid out of the way to get to the front door. He made it two steps outside before he was heaving into the boxwoods. I went up beside him and held him up from falling into the bushes while he heaved and heaved.

"She trusted us," Devon said with gravel in his voice when he stood up.

"I know," I whispered.

"He loved you," Devon added.

"I know," I choked out.

"They're gone," Devon said and wiped his face with the hem of his cashmere sweater.

I couldn't say anything. My throat had closed painfully on a sob. I gripped his arm tight. What were we supposed to do now? Go home? Go sit with the assholes upstairs and have a cry together?

A car door echoed in the driveway, and my body jolted as we both jerked up to see who it was. Doc walked towards us, a somber expression on his face. "Gentlemen. Are you staying or leaving?"

"Leaving," Devon answered, and I was thankful for his decision.

Doc nodded. "I'll drive you."

I walked towards Doc's car with shaking legs and Devon was not better off. We both sat in the back seat, and Doc glanced at the unused front seat before disregarding it. I didn't want to be far from Devon, and I presumed he felt the same. We were breaking my rule and letting someone else drive, but I didn't care anymore.

Doc cleared his throat as he drove. "I went to the scene."

"Did they suffer?" Devon whispered.

Doc was quiet for a moment. "The car exploded after the accident. A witness said both individuals in the car were unconscious when it happened. I don't believe they suffered."

We didn't speak again until Doc pulled into our driveway, waving to the guards at the gate. Devon and I got out and Doc stopped us. "Boys," he said, and we turned around. "I'll be here in the morning with you."

"We're not sick," Devon grumbled.

"No, I know. But... you're not alone," he said solemnly.

We nodded and entered the silent house. I went straight for the kitchen, removing my shoes and coat as I walked, leaving them where they landed. Devon was not far behind me, but he tidily put his coat on the rack by the door. I pulled out a bottle of bourbon and poured us each a tall glass, neat.

Devon and I stood stoically, drinking until our glasses were empty. I refilled them with a belch and a shaking hand.

It wasn't long before Devon disappeared to the office, and I heard screaming and crashing. He was destroying the office with one roaring scream of effort after another. I left him to his destruction and went to my room. I laid on my bed for a moment before the smell of lavender vanilla encompassed me. My chest felt like it cracked open at my ribs, leaving my guts exposed to harsh winter air. The urges to both destroy the room to get rid of her scent and also to bury my face into the cotton to absorb the last remnants of our time together warred in my body, leaving me paralyzed.

I settled for laying on the floor and chugging the rest of my liquor. The alcohol soon had me numb to my grief and blacking out on the floor.

A burning smell and a smoke alarm woke me up from my drunken slumber. I stood up as quickly as my aching, creaking, hungover body could get me vertical. I stumbled down the hall to the stairs, where smoke was curling up to the second floor. Downstairs, Devon was staring at a burning frying pan as flames shot up to the ventilation hood above the range.

"Hey!" I called out in a hoarse voice as I approached him. He was stooped over like he couldn't stand up straight and wearing his white tank top undershirt and his black slacks from last night. His hair was disheveled, and it looked like he'd been awake drinking and raging this whole time.

He barely looked up when I approached to check the situation. The fire needed to be put out, and I reached under the sink for the fire extinguisher. With a few bursts of the foam, I got the flames under control. I coughed at the smoke and fumes and used tongs to turn off the burner.

"Dev," I grunted. "Dude."

"I'm sorry," he rasped like he just woke up.

"It's alright. I got it," I said and patted him on his shoulder.

He scrubbed his face with his hand and groaned. "God. Fuck. What are we going to do?"

Devon swayed on his feet, and I gently pushed him down to sit on the floor, leaning against the island cabinets. I opened the kitchen window and the back door to air out the room before returning to sit in front of him against the oven. We were silent again, just breathing in the icy cold fresh air that blew into the room. Eventually, Devon's head drooped on his shoulders as he fell asleep or passed out. His legs fell to rest against mine as his body relaxed and I was comforted back to sleep by his touch.

My phone chimed in my pocket some time later. I jumped and looked at my screen to see it was Doc. He said he dropped off breakfast but didn't want to disturb our sleep, so he'd be back later. As I read the message, the smell of greasy bacon met my nose. I looked around and saw he had closed the window and door as well before he left.

My phone chiming had given me a desperate false hope that it was Milo and the recoil had me feeling sick. I watched Devon sleep as I tried to settle my stomach. He was the closest to family I had left, and he was the one I fought with the most. Would I stick around for Devon? Could I look at him without thinking of what I'd lost with Milo and Emily?

Sighing, I reached up onto the island for the bottle of liquor that was sitting mostly empty on the cluttered granite. I took a long swig directly from the bottle and rested back against the oven door. I opened my phone and stared at the messaging app, desperately willing a text from Milo or Emily to come in. Nothing came in for the two hours I stared at my phone and sipped the bourbon.

Eyes swirling in my head, and my thoughts pickled by alcohol, I texted Milo.

"Please come home."

"Please, I need you."

"Milo."

I was dry of all tears and I stared blankly at my phone. Scrolling through my home screens, I searched for some kind of human connection. Opening a social media app, I scrolled for a second before being disgusted by how few faces I recognized as a friend. My accounts were more business related for my Personal Cameras page rather than for actual human connection. I exited out of the app and saw the Find My Device app. With a roiling stomach I realized that if I opened that app I would see the stupid Air Tag trackers that Milo used pinging two of us at the house and two at the morgue. Maybe it would show them still at the site of the accident because the trackers broke in the crash. I actually never heard where the crash happened. I wanted to know. I *needed* to know where they died.

I opened the app.

Two emojis in the house, my black spider and Devon's pink worm. And two... not at the morgue, Emily's pink bow and Milo's little laptop. Where were the trackers? I zoomed in on the map and the building was large and unmarked, far on the east side of Cleveland. My heart pounded so hard I thought it would come out of my mouth.

I nudged Devon, and he snorted awake. "What?" he grunted.

I showed him my phone screen.

He shrugged. "It's probably a junkyard. It's probably where they took the car."

"No, those trackers are in our shoes, remember?" I urged him, my voice tight in my throat.

He stared at my phone for another moment. "Nobody else knows about these trackers."

"Nope, it was just us. Not even Anthony and Matthew knew," I insisted.

"Do you think they're..." Devon swallowed the rest of his sentence.

"I have to see. I'll never stop thinking about it if I don't see for myself," I said.

Devon took in a big breath. "Well, we have to sober up before we do anything."

With a burst of energy, we got up, forced down a few bites of the food Doc dropped off, chugged a glass of water with Alka Seltzer each, and split up for showers. We reconvened with wet hair and aptly dressed in sweatpants and t-shirts for more food and water. After some more greasy food, water, and coffee, we were closer to human shaped. I tried not to get too excited at the prospect of them being alive. The emotional whiplash would be doubly devastating after false hope, so I kept myself under control as much as I could. We got into Devon's car and saw that mine had been dropped off this morning. I cringed, thinking that someone else drove my car, but I had other things to worry about. I had ghosts in my mind to put to rest.

23

Emily

A bright light was shining in my eyes, and I woke as if from dreamless death. I scrambled up painfully and took a sharp breath as if to scream, but the stabbing pain in my side cut the breath off. Milo was slumped against the wall and his eyes were closed. His bare chest had taken on an icy white hue where he wasn't covered in bruises and blood. Only his chest moving up and down told me he wasn't beaten and frozen to death in this cement room. The bright light that woke me was actually from the sun that shone through the high windows. I had thought the room window-less last night, but now I knew there were windows high on the wall that were seemingly long missing their glass panes. An icy wind blew in with the sunlight. Last night, the only light had been from a light outside the windowed door that Mack had exited.

"Milo," I whispered.

He jumped awake, and I saw the tear stains on his face. "Emily," he said, shocked. "You're alright."

"I don't know how alright I am. But I'm alive," I moaned in pain as I resettled against the frosty concrete.

"Stay strong. We're going to get out of here," he whispered determinedly.

"Do you know where we are?" I asked.

He shook his head.

My heart fell to my stomach. "Then how are Sterling and Devon going to find us? We can't get out without help. There's no way!"

"Shh," Milo hushed me and glanced at the door. "We have Air Tags in our shoes. Devon and Sterling just have to open an app to find us."

"Air Tags? Nothing higher tech that, like, won't break?" I asked desperately.

He scoffed. "They work just fine as long as we're not stuck in a room lined with fucking lead or something. Besides, have you seen how many pairs of shoes Devon has? Anything higher tech would cost a fucking fortune."

I shook my head. We just had to wait until Sterling and Devon noticed we weren't at home. It was morning, and they were supposed to meet us after dinner last night- they had to know by now.

We fell into a silence for a while before the door swung open. Giovanni and Taz entered with Mack. Both leaders were wearing suits and jewelry, and Mack was wearing slacks and a white tank top. He carried his trusty bat and a briefcase.

"Good morning, Milo, Emily," Giovanni greeted us coolly.

We didn't respond.

"I'm sure you've been made aware of the information we're after?" Giovanni asked and clasped his hands together at belt level.

"We don't know Anthony and Matthew's political connections," Milo spat fiercely.

"I believe you don't, Milo. But something tells me that Emily here does," Giovanni said and approached me. He stood just out of kicking range and bent to look me in the eye. I glared up at him defiantly.

"I only know my ex-husband. He doesn't know where I am," I said gruffly, but ended panting.

Giovanni smirked. "Oh, Gregory has been quite vocal about not knowing where you are. First, I thought he was just trying to smear your name as some runaway adulteress to clear his own reputation. But now, I believe he protests too much to not know where you've been."

I shook my aching head. "No, I ran away from him."

"Right into the comforting arms and home of the underbosses of the mafia," Giovanni added with a hand wave. "Yes, yes. How very... coincidental."

I gulped. Sterling had said something similar to me about what the guys thought when I first came into their lives. "I went to a salon and got approached by a woman who gave me a number to call. That's all." I didn't want to name Victoria and Harold in case they would be in danger, but I didn't want these men to think it was all intentional. "I'm telling the truth. I wanted to run away, so I called the number she gave me."

Giovanni smiled. "Do you think Victoria didn't know exactly who you were before she approached you? Do you think they didn't keep the only salon appointment in the tri-county area the weekend before Christmas open for you? As if every woman after a divorce doesn't change her hair?"

If I could have taken a full breath, I would have been hyperventilating. There was no way he was telling the truth.

Taz chuckled with Mack behind Giovanni. My mouth was hanging open in shock and I likely looked ridiculous.

"You think Gregory was part of this?" I gagged. "You think my husband sent me to be with the mafia as a political tool?"

"Gregory has no clue. He's not with us. I know that for certain," Milo said. "I've been tracking him since Emily came to live with us."

"Let me ask you this," Taz said, stepping up to Giovanni's side. He looked at Milo and me. "Since when does a newcomer come in at this level? Since when does someone entirely un-affiliated come in at underboss seniority? Without blood?"

Milo shook his head. "You're not entirely wrong. But they brought her in to produce heirs for us. Not run any part of the business."

My heart stuck in my throat. Milo wouldn't look at me.

"It's so all the heirs are related and equal in inheritance. Like me, Devon, and Sterling were supposed to be," Milo continued.

"So much for that plan, if it were true," Giovanni said boredly. "Anthony and Matthew are the ones who sanctioned your deaths today. It was supposed to be at the site of the accident, but I thought we'd get some... information before the job was done."

I gagged convulsively. Milo pulled on his chains.

"YOU'RE LYING!" he bellowed.

"Perhaps you were in the way," Giovanni said to Milo. "Perhaps you were bad stock," he said to me. "Perhaps they were taking out the competition for the only proper heir." Giovanni shrugged. "Either way, if you don't have any information for me, you'll be disposed of as promised."

Milo tugged more on the chains with a growling scream of anger and frustration.

The men left before Taz turned back to us. "I'll give you some time to decide if you're dying quickly after giving us information or slowly and with your secrets."

The door slammed shut behind them. Milo screamed again and tugged on the chains, his muscles straining. "FUCK!"

I was crying in a heap and trying to calm my breaths to not puncture my lung. Though drowning in blood would likely be better than anything they could torture me with before I died.

"Emily..." I heard tears in Milo's voice. "If Anthony and Matthew tell them we're dead, they'll have no reason to open the app to track us."

"We have to hope they will," I whispered through my sobs.

"You weren't brought in as breeding stock, Emily," Milo said with a sniff. "I just wanted you to know that."

I let out a breath. "Then why was I brought in? They have a point."

Milo shook his head. "I don't actually know. Their theory about trying to get your political connections- Gregory or any friends- could be accurate. Other than the part where you and Gregory were in on it. I know that's not true."

"It really felt like a coincidence. I feel so stupid," I said with a whimpering whine as I tried to stifle more painful sobs.

"You're not stupid. You had no idea," Milo insisted.

"And now we die because of it," I choked.

"I'll be right here with you," he soothed. It was a moment before he sighed and mumbled to himself. "Dying as a fucking virgin."

"What?" I asked. "Did you say you're a virgin?"

"We're literally awaiting our slow and agonizing deaths and you fixate on that?" Milo snapped with a blush.

"Um, yeah," I said. "It seems like a better thing to focus on. Tell me what you said."

"I said that I'm dying as a virgin," Milo mumbled.

"You're how old?" I asked.

"Are you judging me right now?"

"No, I'm just shocked."

"Judging."

"Perplexed. I watched you jerk off on camera with Sterling and you're a *virgin?*"

"You still sound like you're judging me."

"Milo," I stretched out his name as far as my pinched lung would let me.

"Fine. Yes, I'm a thirty-three-year-old virgin," he groaned with frustration rather than pain.

"Are you... saving yourself for marriage?" I asked as judgement free as I could. It really wasn't a bad thing to do, but... in this line of work? Isn't half the fun of being a mafia underboss all the girls?

"No. Just someone- male or female- who wasn't trying to sleep their way up the mafia ladder. Or someone who wanted money. Or a woman who wanted a child support check," Milo explained.

"You sure have a high opinion of women," I grumbled.

"No, I love women. Just not the ones that throw themselves at me for the wrong reasons," he said.

"What's the right reason a woman throws herself at you, then?" I asked.

He chuckled despite our situation. "Why? Are you considering?"

"Milo, I'm... something that can throw itself. I can't think of a metaphor right now," I grimaced in pain.

He chuckled again. "I should have taken you in the office on New Year's Eve."

"With Sterling there?" I let out a breathy laugh that pinched.

Milo moaned and tipped his head back against the wall. "Yes, absolutely with Sterling there."

"When we get out of here, I'll pop your cherry," I promised Milo. "And I'll make Sterling watch."

"In another life, baby. In another life."

24

Sterling

I t's right up here…. There. That building on the right," I
said and looked up from the map on my phone. It was a
large building, with cars out front and a few guys smoking
just outside some open garage doors. If I still had a heart, it
would have frozen over with grief again.

"A chop shop," Devon said with a sad sigh as we drove
past. If Milo's car had been totaled like we had been told,
it's possible a chop shot was scavenging parts. In fact, it was
likely. It didn't explain the Air Tag trackers pinging in the
building unless their shoes were still in the wreckage. I felt
sick thinking about it.

We drove a block in a heavy silence before Devon pulled a
U-turn and had us pass it again. I stared at the car up on the
lifts and it wasn't Milo's. I don't know what I was expecting.
A miracle, maybe.

"Wait, what the fuck?" Devon muttered, staring out his window.

A man, smoking a cigarette and walking towards the building, looked familiar. What was his name? He was from the fight. He was the one who picked us up and drove us... *Mack*. What was he doing there? Didn't he work for....

"Giovanni and Taz!" I blurted.

"Where?" Devon asked quickly.

"No, that guy works for them!" I explained, pointing.

"Oh, yeah, I know. It's, uh, Mack, or something," Devon said and backed into an alley a few buildings down and across the street. He positioned the car so we could still see.

We watched as Mack approached the building and greeted the guys who were just outside the garage doors, smoking. We watched them finish their cigarettes before going into the garage. One guy was wearing a mechanic's jumpsuit and showed Mack something on the sedan up on the lift. Another showed him a clipboard while he answered a phone call. He didn't seem like he was a customer. In fact, it looked like he ran the place. There were too many people standing and walking around for it to be simply a legitimate repair shop, though.

"Signage is new," Devon muttered. "MT's Autobody and Towing."

"I'm going in there," I said and opened the car door. I had one foot on the ground when Devon grabbed my arm.

"No, you dumbass! We can't go barging in there, no weapons, and no plan. Let's think this through."

I growled and slid back into the car. If there was a chance that Milo and Emily were still alive and in that building, then

I needed to get to them. Now. They could be counting on *me* to save them. Unfortunately, Devon was right. We needed a plan if we wanted any of us to survive.

"I think Giovanni and Taz set this all up," Devon said once I was back in my seat.

"But why?" I asked. "Why would they want Milo and Emily?"

"Maybe because the money fell through with my dad and Matthew. Maybe it was retaliation for the deal not working out how they had hoped," Devon mused, his eyes still locked on the building.

"There's no way for us to ask Anthony or Matthew without giving away what we know and possibly fucking up our rescue," I grumbled. "So, it's up to us."

"Only us," Devon exhaled. "Alright, let's sober up the rest of the way, clear our heads and make a plan."

I nodded. "Doc can give us some IVs if we ask. He was coming back today."

Devon shook his head. "Turn him away, tell him we're fine. We need to plan alone and without questions."

"Let's get going," I said, glaring at the building, looking for any sign of my people. There were none and I tried to stay reasonable.

After drinking more coffee and some Gatorade, finishing up the greasy food, copious ibuprofen, and another round of showers, we came up with a plan. Just after sunset, we armed ourselves to the teeth under our winter gear and knit hats low on our foreheads. Our plan involved being unrecognizable from a distance in case we encountered someone who knew us.

The building was previously abandoned but newly leased by a Mackenzie Teller, or "Mack" for short. Mack had a business permit and multiple operator's licenses to his name. It was difficult to get this information, as it was most often Milo's job, but we had managed the basics. A realtor's listing was still archived online and listed the place as an auto body shop with onsite storage, offices, and a scrapyard. I couldn't find the blueprints; my skills didn't go as far as Milo's did. But we had enough information to begin.

We drove one of our cars that was registered to an alias (another job by Milo), to a bar a few blocks away from Mack's garage. I quickly jammed a long roofing nail into the tire and then Devon drove it hard enough into a newspaper box that the front end crumpled. He got out of the car, rubbing his neck.

"Aw, poor baby," I chuckled at him.

He punched me lightly in the side while I dialed the number for the garage.

"MT's Autobody and Towing," a gruff voice answered.

"Um, yeah, hi. Me and my roommate just crashed our car," I said in what I hoped was a breathless, shaken sounding voice.

"Have you called an ambulance?" the gruff voice asked.

"No, we're totally okay. But we need a tow and then some repairs," I said and looked around at the empty, but still open bar. An older man had hobbled to the door to see what was going on.

Devon went to meet him to assure him we were alright and just waiting for a tow and that we weren't drunk, we'd just hit a nail and popped a tire.

I gave the guy on the phone our location based on the bar and said that MT's was the closest tow and repair shop according to Google.

"Yeah, you're right down the street. Give me twenty minutes," he said before hanging up.

I nodded to Devon as he said goodbye to the old bar owner and handed him a stack of cash to forget he ever saw us.

We waited in the frosty night air until a tow truck rumbled around the corner. There was only one guy I didn't recognize in the cab. It would be easy to take him out. As soon as he hopped out, I slid my knife across his throat and shoved him into the back of our alias car as he bled out. Devon hopped into the tow truck, and I followed him.

"We didn't need to crash the car," Devon muttered, still rubbing his neck.

"Well, there was only one guy, it was easy," I said and wiped the blood off my knife onto the cloth car seat. "It was worth it to see you flopped around like a rag doll, though."

"What a rich comment to make just after Emily and Milo died in a car crash," Devon muttered nastily.

I stopped for a moment. He was right. But I felt comfortable making that joke because my hopes were officially up. In my heart, I was convinced that Emily and Milo were alive. I swallowed around a lump, realizing that if we found out that we were wrong, and they were dead this whole time, it was going to kill me.

"Sorry," I whispered.

Devon didn't reply as he drove the rumbling tow truck back to the garage. Another guy was opening the door with one hand and the other hand holding his phone. He was watching something on the little screen and barely looked up as we pulled into the space next to where the car had been up on the lift earlier today.

"Did they not have any money?" the guy asked, eyes still on his phone.

I opened the door and hopped down, slicing his neck the same as the first guy. He gurgled through his blood and his phone continued to play The Office.

There were considerably fewer people in the garage at night than there were during the day, a fact that we had been assuming and counting on. We disabled two more idly lounging and almost sleeping guys before we entered the building from the garage. Everyone we had encountered so far was relaxed and not expecting an attack. I would have felt bad for taking them unaware, but Emily and Milo were here. Somewhere. They *had* to be. And I would take out everyone in this city to get to them if I had to.

We knew from the Air Tag map they were near the back of the building. Or so we hoped it was that accurate as we moved through the building. The concrete hallway was empty of people, and dirt and trash littered the cement floor. We walked silently and peered carefully into each room. Another hallway towards the back was locked, and I knew that if they were here, they were in that hallway.

A growing desperation fueled me as I looked around for a guy with keys while Devon attempted to pick the lock. Peering into the last room, I saw a scrawny guy sitting at a desk playing a video game on a laptop while computer monitors displayed our crimes right in front of him. The guy I killed in the garage was literally front and center of one screen, but the security guy wasn't even looking.

The guy at the desk was bashing at a computer key, his tongue sticking through his lips, when I opened the door. He didn't even look up as I came around behind him and slashed his throat. He had uttered "What do you want?" as if he were talking to a coworker when I approached him. Huge eyebrows practically covered his eyes, and acne scars riddled his face. For a second, I worried he was a teenager, but then I realized he was just an ugly adult. At least my IT guy was sexy.

Objectively speaking, of course.

Not like I thought Milo was sexy.

Well, I did, but not in a sexual way.

Right?

Fuck. Now was not the time for a little queer awakening.

I searched the ugly IT guy for a key. He had one key ring, and I hoped it contained the key I needed. I unplugged the surge protector from the wall and all the computers went dark except for the laptop that still played a game. Returning to Devon, I found him standing over another dead guy.

"He was on the phone when he came in here. We have very limited time," Devon said quickly, his eyes flashing with panic.

I looked at the lock. It was a relatively standard commercial lock. Steel and new. I looked at the key ring. Finding one silver key without blemishes or grease, I slid it into the lock. I had a sudden and vivid memory of New Year's Eve when we were drunk and struggling to open the office door before midnight. I kissed both Emily *and* Milo that night.

"You need to work on your lock picking skills. This is a normal lock," I grumbled to Devon as I pushed the door open.

"I haven't had to pick a lock in years. Give me a break," Devon defended and looked around, checking for more guys.

We crept down the hall past two small storage rooms. There was only one door. I took a deep breath, ready to be shattered with disappointment and grief. I didn't know what to expect. A few pairs of singed and bloody shoes? A storage box of crap recovered from the accident? Was it a total coincidence that Mack was the one to get Milo's car?

A male scream sounded from the door we were both staring at. It was blood curdling and sent a chill to my bones. I grabbed at Devon as we both ran to the door. Someone had propped this one open with an empty plastic Coke bottle, as if someone who didn't have a key had gotten through. The door led to dusty concrete steps and to a dimly lit basement hallway. Our boots echoed down the steps, as we were not bothering to be quiet anymore.

Ignoring the other doors we passed, we ran through a propped open door to a dark room. My eyes took a moment to adjust before I registered what I was seeing. A man I didn't recognize was purple faced and choking, kneeling before a sprawled-out Emily. A shirtless, bruised, and bleeding Milo was holding chains wrapped around the man's neck. I jumped in and sliced the neck of the guy Milo was choking while Devon dropped to his knees next to the bruised and bloodied Emily.

Milo was swaying on his feet, steady streams of blood flowing down his pale skin. I helped him to sit, but he was fading out of consciousness quickly. It didn't even seem like he knew

Devon and I were there. I laid him down and checked his pulse. It was light as a flutter under my fingers, and I turned to Devon. "He's alive, but he needs to go to the hospital."

The chains Milo had been using to choke out the guy clattered to the ground, and I saw they handcuffed him. I looked around and saw two holes in the concrete wall, like he had pulled the chain from the wall. One arm cuffed Emily to the wall and Devon was inspecting it.

"She's unconscious and chained up," Devon said and looked up at me. He was pale, like he'd seen a ghost, and his eyes were wide and fearful. I pulled out my wallet and found the handcuff key I kept in there. Most cuffs used the same universal master key, and I'd been cuffed enough times to know I needed one. I freed both Emily and Milo quickly.

With shaking hands, I scooped Milo into my arms, ready to carry him out of this hell. Standing, I met Devon at the door where he was holding Emily. Footsteps pounded on the steps, and we exchanged glances before moving to pull out our guns. We had been stealthy when getting there, but we were ready to blast our way out of this stinking basement. I shifted Milo over my shoulder to carry my gun, and Devon did the same with Emily. We stepped out of the room as the footsteps approached and raised our guns to fire as Giovanni and Taz came into view.

I was just about to take Giovanni out when a gun clicked behind me, and I felt the presence of another person. Looking over my shoulder, I saw Mack, grinning darkly, and pressing a gun to unconscious Milo's head.

Fuck.

"Good evening, gentlemen," Giovanni greeted calmly like it was any other day. "How nice of you to drop in!"

25

Emily

I woke up with the distinct, weightless feeling of being carried over someone's shoulder. My broken arm was pinned between someone's neck and my hip, and my good arm was dangling towards the floor. I had woken up like this once before when Sterling was carrying me into the house after the guys had kidnapped me. Inhaling as deep as I could without puncturing a lung, I did my best to gather myself. If I surprised this man, I might have a fighting chance at getting out of here before they killed me. The pain in my hip from the beatings with Mack's bat and my broken bones would have to wait. But on that inhale, I smelled a familiar woodsy cologne. I peeked open one eye, despite my throbbing head. Blinking away sweat and blood, I saw a dark denim clad ass.

Devon.

My heart trilled in my chest, and he clutched me harder

around the thighs. If he had felt my heart pounding, he might know I was awake. We were going up a flight of stairs now, and the air became drier and warmer as we went up. We must have been in a basement. I looked up and was about to tell him I was awake when I realized the fancy snakeskin loafers just behind us didn't belong to any of my men. Quickly, I went limp again until I could assess the situation. Luckily, the man behind us hadn't noticed me lift my head a few inches.

At the top of the stairs, we walked through a cement hallway. Were we leaving?

"Where are you taking us?" Devon growled.

Fear surged through me again. Devon wasn't rescuing me-someone trapped him just the same.

"To the junkyard. Mack here forgets to feed his dogs and I've heard they're hungry," came Giovanni's sly reply.

I turned my head just the slightest bit to see if Milo was there. The last I saw of him, he was screaming at that stupid guy who had come down to take advantage of me being tied up. The man had raised his fist to hit me just as Milo had broken free from the wall, chains and all. He got in a blow to my head before Milo could reach him and I was unconscious for the rest of it.

There, being carried by Sterling, was Milo. He was still bleeding and unconscious over Sterling's shoulder, and I wanted to cry out for them. Sterling's black long-sleeved t-shirt was stuck to him where Milo's blood soaked through. When Devon stepped down out the door to what I presumed to be the junkyard, my cheek bounced against his lower back. Or what would have been his lower back if he didn't have a gun in the holster along his back. As soon as the guy behind us (I was assuming Taz without looking) had moved to be by Giovanni, I lifted Devon's black knit sweater to remove his gun from his holster. My shaking fingertips grazed his warm, smooth tan skin, and I heard him take a sharp, shocked breath of recognition. I tucked the handgun in the stained white cashmere sweater at my neck above my hopeless, broken arm.

"Search them," Giovanni demanded levelly.

Devon gently placed me on the icy ground next to Milo as he and Sterling were searched for weapons. I heard the *thump* and slight *clang* as they deposited their weapons on the ground. All but one. They didn't need to search me or Milo. We'd been checked over before they tied us up in the basement. I calmed my shivering body as much as I could. I was freezing cold after wearing wet clothes in an unheated basement for two days. If I shivered too much, it would surely draw attention to me. The ground below me was covered in snow and ice and it pressed cuts into my cheek before the ice melted. The cold felt soothing against my sore and likely bleeding head until the cold started to bite. But I wouldn't move an inch.

When the guys were stripped of their weapons, Devon spoke up. "What do you want with Emily and Milo?"

Taz and Giovanni chuckled. I watched from beneath my lashes as much as I could see. In my limited field of view, I could see Sterling desperately looking at me and Milo, and then back to Giovanni and Taz. His eyes were bright with fear- so much that he couldn't keep his face carefully schooled like usual. It was tearing Sterling up to not come to us. It was tearing me up he was here in danger with us.

"It's a funny story, really," Giovanni said. "It all started when we came back to Cleveland to expand our operations. We found out that your family still had the city within its grasp, and we thought, 'Well, if we can't beat them, let's join them and take them down from the inside.' Right, Taz?"

"Right."

"We did our research, watched you three fight, and learned about your little pet here, Emily. And I thought it odd that a mayor's ex-wife was suddenly living with all three under-bosses of the mafia. What were the chances it was coinciden-tal, right? I thought 'there must be some political connections being made here.' And those connections could be detrimen-tal to our business, you see." Giovanni stopped to chuckle again. "It's amusing, really. We were going to kill you soon. But your pet, Emily, and Milo must have pissed Daddy off. We got a call offering us quite a bit of money to take these two out."

"That's not true!" Devon spat.

"Oh, it is, little heir. It is. Your daddy called me up and said these two would be heading to Matthew's home and we would be looking at three million for doing the job," Giovanni explained. "You have to understand that expanding our businesses to Cleveland costs quite a bit of cash. It was a straightforward decision."

"He would never!" Devon shouted, his voice cracking with his rage. If my ribs weren't already broken, I feared my chest would crack open at the pain in this realization. Not only for myself, but for my men.

Giovanni and Taz laughed at Devon's reaction.

This wasn't new information for me, but my heart ached hearing Devon's ragged breathing.

"No?" Taz asked, still chuckling. "That father of yours has done it before."

"And like you haven't ordered a hit?" Sterling snapped, his eyes still wild and desperate.

Giovanni sobered. "I've never ordered the hit on one of my own's children. Adopted or otherwise," he said, referring to Matthew and Milo. "And I've certainly never ordered the hit on my fellow leaders, and the mothers and fathers of young children."

"What?!" Sterling rasped, understanding something I didn't.

"You know, it was such a shock to see you and Milo at that first meeting," Giovanni said with a reminiscent sigh. "After all, Anthony had Owen and Kristen killed... and not long after that, Michael and Meredith."

I didn't know those names, but Sterling and Devon did. Sterling let out a breath like he'd been kicked in the stomach.

"I figured you'd all have known that by now and only one heir, Devon, would remain," Giovanni finished.

"No," Devon whispered. I saw him shove his hands through his hair, his head turning from Giovanni to Sterling and back.

"Truly, it is a sad story," Giovanni said. "One that shocked even me to hear. I was glad to have left Cleveland by that time, that's for sure. Because it showed me that Anthony would stop at nothing. I wonder if Matthew is the same?"

"You're lying," Devon whispered.

I could see part of Sterling's face as he bent over, hands on his knees, and breathed. He looked devastated and like his world had just exploded in front of him. Were those names Milo and Sterling's parents? My head throbbed from the multiple hits I'd sustained, and I had difficulty forming full thoughts.

"Why would I lie? I'm about to kill you. What good would a lie do?" Giovanni said like it was ridiculous.

Devon and Sterling were quiet and tense.

"What can we do to get out of here? Do you want money?" Devon asked, his voice shaking.

"No, I'm afraid we have to kill you," Giovanni said with a sad sigh. "What a shame to kill off an entire generation of a rival gang."

"Our leaders will never work with you again if you kill us. They'll know it was you. And they'll kill you," Devon ground out.

In a split second, there was the loud bang of a gunshot. The sound echoed between the buildings and out into the junkyard. I felt the reverberations in my spine. Devon cried out and fell and Sterling rushed to him with a shouted, "Dev!". They were out of my line of sight on the ground, so I couldn't see them. I couldn't see if Devon was alright. I couldn't stand the thought of another shot being fired at one of my men. This needed to be over.

Now.

I grabbed the gun from my once beautiful sweater and clicked off the safety. Ignoring the dizzying flush of blood through my head, I sat up and fired left-handed at Taz, who was still holding the gun aimed at Devon. The bullet sank into his arm. The momentum and shock turned him to face me. This opened up his body to me and I fired again, missed, and immediately again and got him in the chest. He fell and dropped his gun with a clatter. Giovanni and Mack, who I hadn't realized was here, were both aiming guns at me. I knew I was about to die, but I was going to do my best to take at least one of them out with me. Giovanni was not only the closest, but the one I was looking forward to killing the most. A buzzing in my head blocked out the screams of the men around me.

It focused me. It steeled me for murder.

For vengeance.

Hearing only the buzzing of blood and adrenaline in my broken and battered head, I aimed and got him in the jaw. He stumbled back, unintentionally dropping the gun.

Mack fired off two shots at me. One sunk into my already useless arm, so I couldn't feel it, and the other hit the frozen dirt next to me. I had shocked him, and he was unprepared. That was my only advantage. Sterling was at my side now, bloody handed and vibrating with lethal rage. He pulled the gun from my hand, stood, and shot Mack dead between the eyes in one well-trained movement. Then he turned to where Giovanni was screaming through his destroyed face and sunk a bullet in his forehead identical to the shot in Mack's.

The buzzing in my head dimmed slightly and nausea swam as I gagged.

Devon let out a clenched teeth groan of pain as he clutched his left shoulder. I saw blood on the snow all around me, illuminated by a single floodlight. Sterling dropped to his knees before me and said something to me. He reached for me, and his hands came back covered in blood. My vision doubled and danced, and I couldn't process any of the words he was shouting at me. Was he even speaking English? I felt myself drain the last dregs of energy, adrenaline, and fear out with the blood pouring from my arm.

"What?" I tried to croak, but my mouth was full of blood and bile.

My eyes closed to dark, inky unconsciousness *again.*

I had always hated the word "trust." I had never heard it used in a way that actually deserved it. The word grated on me every time someone said it.

"*Trust me*, you don't need dessert after the dinner you just ate."

"*Trust me*, that green dress looks better with your skin tone and the pink one looks better with mine."

"*Trust me*, I know you don't want to go out of state for college."

"*Trust me*, I'm your husband and I know what's best for you."

It was always used to manipulate me into doing whatever the other person wanted. Sometimes I knew it was happening and sometimes it wasn't until later. But what was I to do about it? Say no? Make someone I loved mad? Strain relationships over something trivial?

It wasn't until I met these men- these dark, kind of twisted, murderous men- that I understood the word "trust." I trusted they would do their best to protect me. I trusted they would value my opinion. I trusted they would keep my own dark, murderous, and kind of twisted secrets. Real trust was mutual and not a manipulation. And I wholeheartedly trusted Sterling, Milo, and Devon. I trusted we would live through this.

26

Emily

"E mily? Emily, dear, can you hear me?"

I was warm, dry, and laying on something soft. My mouth was bone dry, and I moved my tongue around, trying to find moisture. A dry moan came up as I tried to move my body and open my eyes.

"Don't move yet, Emily," the gentle voice said again. It was a man's voice.

I forced open my eyes, expecting to see the face of Giovanni or Taz.

Wait, hadn't I killed them? Was that just a nightmare?

Blinking, my eyes focused on the family doctor I had met when I first came to live with the guys. I tried to speak, but only a squeak came out. He smiled kindly and reached for a cup of water with a plastic, bendy straw and held it to my lips. I drank a few sips, wanting nothing more than to gulp it all down. Little straw be damned. He pulled it back.

"Just a few sips for now. I need to see you keep it down," he said warmly.

"Where are they?" I croaked and then coughed.

"I'm right here," Sterling said from my left, and he gripped my hand in his large, warm grasp. My eyes had a hard time focusing on his face, but his steel-gray eyes were wide and bright. "Milo and Devon are in their own rooms."

I blinked again and looked around to see I was in my bedroom at the house. I was hooked up to monitors and an IV like I was in a hospital bed. Sterling pushed me back down when I tried to sit up. "No, you're all bandaged up. Stop."

Tears welled up in my eyes as memories came back to me, one by one, swimming through my foggy mind. "I feel loopy. I can't think right."

"You have a pain medication drip, I can turn it down for now," Doc said as he changed something on the IV. "Let me know if you need it turned back up. Do you have questions?"

"What happened?" I asked and waited for my mind to clear.

Doc and Sterling exchanged glances. "I don't know, Emily. I'm just here as your doctor to help you heal. But I can say that you have a broken right arm, and a gunshot wound to the same arm. You've sustained multiple head injuries, you have one broken rib and two fractured ribs, and your hip is extremely bruised. Despite all of that, you'll be just fine, Emily."

"Milo?" I asked. "Is he?"

Sterling squeezed my hand. "He's going to be alright. He woke up this morning and is resting down the hall."

I nodded, tears leaking out and into my hair at my temples. "Devon?"

"Devon's just fine. He's been patched up and pissed off since we got home and Doc removed the bullet," Sterling said. His annoyed tone suggested that there had been no worry about Devon's health.

I tried to smile, but it wobbled. Doc held out the water glass to me again, and I sipped it carefully. As my brain cleared of the drugged fog, I asked to sit up. Doc and Sterling helped me with pillows and gentle hands. Once I was settled in more of a reclined sitting position, I could see that my arm was not in a plaster cast but was carefully wrapped and bandaged. A plaster cast would block access to the healing bullet wound. I made sure not to move that arm from where it was resting on a pillow.

"How did you get us out?" I asked.

"After Giovanni, Taz, and Mack were down, we just walked out. Well, I carried you to the car and then had to come back for Milo, since Devon couldn't carry you anymore." Sterling unconsciously rolled his shoulders as he spoke, as if thinking of the muscle strain. "And while we sped out of there, I called Doc and told him to meet us here with as much of his medical supplies as he could carry."

"This is not the first time I've been called to bring someone back from the brink of death," Doc said jovially.

"How can you do this here?" I asked the doctor.

"Oh, that second room in the basement is an operating room," Sterling said. "We can't typically go to the hospital. They ask too many questions."

"Do Anthony and Matthew know we're alive?" I asked Sterling.

"No," Sterling said and shook his head. A dark expression

overtook his features and his jaw clenched. I stroked my thumb over his hand that held mine. "And I trust you won't say anything?" Sterling was looking at Doc as he spoke, eyes glaring and focused.

Doc shook his head, looking at Sterling. "I've learned long ago to not question or discuss most things that happen within your family, Sterling. Not because I don't care, but because Anthony and Matthew are leaders of a mafia and will stop at nothing to protect what they feel is theirs."

Sterling hung his head and sighed. "You're the second person to say this to me recently."

Sadness crept into Doc's face as he watched Sterling. "Please don't take my continued employment with this family as complacency in any crimes you think they've committed."

"No, it's because there's no leaving this family. It's stay here or death," Sterling said angrily.

Doc exhaled and changed a setting on my IV again and checked my vitals. "I'm going to change Devon's bandage and make a broth soup for you."

He left quietly, leaving me and Sterling in my dark room. "What time is it?" I asked.

"About ten at night," he replied after checking his phone clock.

"How long have I been sleeping?" I asked and yawned.

Sterling swallowed. "Three days."

"What?!" I tried to exclaim, but my voice cracked.

"Milo just woke up today, too," Sterling said and rubbed the back of his neck. He looked exhausted. "I've been bounc-ing back and forth between the two of you. I tried to get Doc to put you both in the same room, but it could have been too much on you two to move."

A lump formed in my throat. "Thank you, Sterling," I whispered.

He gave a lopsided, exhausted smile. "Yeah, no problem."

"No, really Sterling. Thank you for saving me," I said, my voice choked. I squeezed his hand tight in mine.

"Well... I'm falling in love with you, so of course I saved you," Sterling said self-consciously.

"What?" I squeaked. My heart pounded in my chest so hard it made the monitor beep next to me.

Sterling smirked at me after glancing at the monitor. "You heard me."

"I think Doc upped my pain meds rather than reducing them," I whispered dryly.

Sterling smiled. "No, I'm starting to love you."

I wasn't sure if I was ready to say it back. He'd saved my life, and I was so very thankful, but I wasn't sure if I was in love with him yet. It had only been a few weeks since we'd met. And we'd met under dubious circumstances at best.

"It's okay," Sterling said with a cocky grin. "You'll catch up."

I giggled at his confidence and sipped my water. "Well, you should tell Milo, too," I said and watched him from under my lashes.

His face blanched white before reddening with a fierce blush. All the while, he kept his eyes off of me. I smiled as I watched him go through emotion after emotion. His usually hard to read face was now like glass to his thoughts. He inhaled deeply before letting it out between pursed lips.

His eyes were back on me as he expected my answer. "Am I allowed to love you both?"

"Yes, because I have feelings for him, too," I said, my voice hoarse with emotion now.

Sterling opened his mouth to speak, but the door swung open and hit the wall, making us both jump. Sterling whirled around and stood up to see Milo limping in with his arms around bandaged ribs. His bright blue eyes landed on me, and relief washed over his features. "Emily."

"Milo," I smiled at him and reached out my good hand towards him.

Sterling moved out of the way and helped Milo stiffly sit down on my bed. "Milo, you're not supposed to be out of bed yet."

"Doc said it was fine," Milo said with a wave of his hand. "Who do you think told me she was awake?"

"How are you?" I asked him as he reached to stroke my hair. He winced at the movement, but didn't stop.

"I'll be fine," he said and shook his head. His eyes bounced all over me in the bed, like he was checking to see if I was really alright. "Just a couple of broken bones."

I realized that his left arm was in a cast that bent at his elbow. His arm had probably been broken in the crash, or so we had suspected when we were locked in that basement together. Remembering how he had still been strung up by his arms and beaten while having a broken arm made tears come to my eyes. I gripped his right hand in my left in a tight and shaking hold. I choked on a sob.

He leaned forward and pressed his forehead against my chest, and I felt his hot tears soak my thin hospital gown.

I hadn't noticed what I was wearing until then. Milo was shirtless and wearing cotton pajama pants and I was in the gown. Sterling sat down on my other side and rubbed our shoulders as we cried and clutched each other. We held each other like we had been desperate to in that basement and in those chains. I stroked his hair and his body covered mine almost protectively as the reality of our being safe finally crashed home.

Eventually, he pulled back, and we wiped our eyes. Sterling wiped his own eyes discreetly and gave a big sniff.

"Milo, thank you for all you did in the basement." I hiccupped.

He shook his head as he looked down. "I didn't do enough."

"You did. You talked to me while they hurt me, and you took beatings for me. You saved me when that guy-" I broke off for a gasping sob.

He held me again and kissed my forehead, murmuring to me. "Always. I would always try to protect you, Emily."

Overcome with emotion, I leaned back slightly and placed a tear-soaked kiss on his lips. His eyes had fluttered closed, and I went back in for another kiss. This one pulling his plush bottom lip into my mouth with a slow suck. His breath ghosted across my face as I kissed him slowly, lovingly, and reverently. He returned the kiss with a trembling hand, lightly tracing my arm.

"Oh, fuck," Sterling groaned.

I giggled and pulled away from Milo. Sterling's eyes were dilated and full of pure need as his gaze raked over us. "Sorry, Sterling," I said through my giggles.

"That was the hottest fucking thing I've ever seen," Sterling said with a sigh.

Milo blushed. "Including New Year's?"

Sterling let out a long moan. "I've thought of nothing other than that since it happened."

Milo's eyebrows shot up. "Oh?"

"Yeah," Sterling said, his dilated and hungry eyes fixated on flustered Milo. Milo didn't have time to move more than an inch before Sterling hopped over my legs on the bed to be next to Milo. He grabbed Milo's face and kissed him hard.

I'd be lying if I said that my heart wasn't pounding in my chest and my arousal wasn't dampening my hospital gown. I fought the urge to shift and rub my thighs together as I watched them devour each other's lips.

They were breathless and moaning as they kissed desperately, like they couldn't get enough. I knew that this sight would live in my mind forever. They clutched each other like they were afraid to let go and lose each other. I watched as years of emotions, trust, and devotion poured through their lips and tongues and teeth. Despite the intensity of the kiss, I didn't feel jealous or left out. I felt lucky to bear witness to their adoration and lucky to be included.

As the kiss slowed, Sterling lowered a hand to my leg over the blanket and rubbed my thigh soothingly. Someone cleared their throat, and I looked around Sterling and Milo as they broke apart. Devon stood in the doorway, staring expressionlessly at the three of us. "About time," he said.

Milo looked sheepish, but Sterling looked confused.

"You two have been dancing around this for years." Devon rolled his eyes.

I giggled again. The last bit of pain medication was making Devon's annoyance funny.

"Not a chance," Sterling scoffed.

"Absolutely," Devon replied.

"Well, if it helps any, I noticed right away and I've only just got here," I said happily.

Sterling and Milo both turned glaring eyes on me, and I shrugged innocently.

"Anyway," Devon said dryly. "I'm glad to see you're awake, Emily."

I reached for him, and he smiled slightly as he approached me on the side of the bed that Sterling had vacated. He sat, minding my propped-up arm. He frowned at my arm after he settled. "I'm sorry this happened."

"It's not your fault. Not at all," I replied.

"It might have been my dad, so I feel partially responsible," he explained in a voice so quiet it was almost a whisper.

"You are not your dad," I said strongly, feeling choked at the thought of his situation.

He nodded, his head still hanging in shame and sorrow.

"How are you alive?" I asked with a whimpering sniff. "I saw you get shot."

"It missed my heart," he explained. "It missed the important stuff. I think he tried to do it quickly, so we didn't have time to stop him."

I nodded, and he pulled away. "I see I interrupted something by coming in here," he said, shaking off the emotion of the room. "I'll go help Doc make food."

Devon left quickly, and we all looked at each other before

laughing. "And to think I was worried about what Dev would think about me loving you," Sterling chuckled.

"Wait, what?" Milo asked, his eyes wide.

I laughed again. Milo, being just as confused at Sterling L-wording him as I had been, was hilarious and validating. "See? It's not just me!"

Sterling shrugged and grinned cockily at us. "Maybe I just like seeing you both go all pink and open your mouths all wide."

Milo snapped his gaping mouth shut. We settled, smiling and safe, into my bed and reveled in our security of each other. Sterling flipped on the TV I'd rarely used in my room. It was only moments of him changing channels and mumbling about nothing good being on before I fell asleep.

27

Sterling

I settled on a rerun of a reality show about tattoos before looking over at Milo and Emily. They were both asleep, leaning against each other. Smiling, I tucked Milo under a spare blanket before giving up on the TV and turning it off. I left the small bedside lamp on before leaving them to their rest. I had been at their sides since we'd gotten home, having only taken a quick shower to wash off their blood when Doc said they were stable. Now, having seen them awake and talking and *alive*, I could let out the breath that I'd had trapped high in my chest since I heard about the accident.

Stepping into the hot shower in my room, I let the panic go. Hands splayed on the tile and the stream of water on my head, I let myself hyperventilate. I let myself explode with the anxiety and fear and grief I'd been living in for the past week. It came out jagged and sharp and had me leaning against the wall, staring out of the glass of the long windows at the starry night sky until the water got cold. It hadn't occurred to me how much I loved Milo and was beginning to love Emily until I thought I'd lost them. And it hadn't occurred to me how far I'd go for the ones I loved until I was infiltrating an enemy gang's compound with only Devon and a few guns. No plan, no backup, no escape route. Just determination and rage. We'd been successful, and now... now what? Now I would love them both? Now I would spend the rest of my life protecting them from the world? Honestly, I would do that and more. I washed quickly and stepped out, eager for food and to squeeze in beside Milo and Emily in the bed.

Doc was waking Emily and Milo up for some broth and a few pieces of bread when I walked in with my food. Milo glared at my deli meat sandwich, and I promptly left before I was physically and emotionally hurt. I ate my middle of the night dinner and waited in my room until Doc finished checking bandages and vitals. But exhaustion overcame me and I fell asleep on my bed.

It was late the next afternoon when I finally woke with a start, hearing Emily's laughter drifting down the hall. I got up, brushed my teeth, and put on a shirt that didn't have a mayonnaise stain on the front. She and Milo were sitting in her bed, both showered and clean and with color in their cheeks from good rest and food. My heart bumped against my ribcage harder than usual. I rubbed my chest and felt eerily like the Grinch after he returned all the Christmas presents. I was considerably less musty than the Grinch, but I could see the resemblance in our situations.

"Hi," Emily said with a shy smile.

"Hey," I said, my voice still raspy with sleep. I ran a hand through my hair and Emily's eyes tracked low where my skin peeked out between my shirt and pants. I looked over to Milo and saw he also locked his eyes on my skin. Like that, was it?

"Did you sleep well?" Milo asked and visibly swallowed.

"Yeah, how are you two feeling?" I asked, looking them both over.

"Great, now that Doc had us shower and gave me a sling," Emily said and pointed with her chin to her right arm.

"I see that," I said and sat at the end of the bed. They were both icing their respective broken arms and were holding hands on their non injured sides. "Together, you two make one functional person. Wait, how did you shower?"

Emily and Milo smiled and exchanged glances. "It probably would have been easier if we helped each other, honestly," Emily said and giggled. "Doc insisted he helped us in case we fell."

"Did he line you up and hose you off?" I asked and leaned back in the bed, my hands behind me.

Emily gulped as she looked over my body. My cock twitched. "No, nothing like that," she said distractedly.

"Just tell me next time and I'll help," I offered in a deep voice. I would help both of them, no issue there. And I could be respectful and good, too. But the way they were both looking at me right now called for dirty insinuations.

"You know, I didn't thank you for saving my life," Emily said, her eyes hooded.

"You did," I affirmed. "It was pretty much the first thing you said after asking if everyone was alright."

"No, I mean... I didn't *thank* you," she said and let go of

Milo's hand to crawl, one handedly towards me. The ice pack tumbled from her sling.

"You were, uh, drugged and in pain," I said as she kissed along my jaw. I hadn't shaved in a week, so I was nearer to a beard than stubble.

"I'm not drugged anymore," she said against my throat. Goosebumps erupted on my skin and shivers ran down my spine.

"Are you in pain?" I asked, knowing this was important, but wanting to do nothing other than to flip her around and slam into her.

"Mm-mm," she breathed her negative as she licked my Adam's apple. My body hummed with the pleasure of being touched.

"We both took ibuprofen," Milo elaborated as he came up behind me and kissed along the other side of my neck.

I moaned and relaxed as they both kissed my neck, jaw, and lips. They took turns kissing my lips, and I kept my eyes shut. Soft and small lips with a sweet tongue that traced my lips and tongue gently- Emily. Plush and warm lips that sipped at mine with a light and teasing tongue- Milo. I could play that guessing game all day, every day. Even more so when a hand, not sure who it belonged to, cupped me through my sweatpants. My hips jerked involuntarily, and I let out a rasping groan.

Emily giggled and my pants were ripped down my thighs quickly and aggressively. My eyes sprang open to see them both working together to get my pants down. "One functional person, I told you," I joked.

"Here, I'll do it first and you can copy," Emily said to Milo.

"I know how to do it," Milo said with a roll of his eyes. He tossed his ice pack to the nightstand.

What were they talking about? I quirked an eyebrow at them both and my cock twitched at their expressions. I was, perhaps, in trouble in the best way.

Emily swooped down and spat over my bobbing cock, making the silver jewelry sparkle. Milo watched with intense focus as she licked her lips and took me into her mouth. She was warm and wet, almost scorching, as she sucked. My breath left me with a *whoosh* and I lifted my shirt hem. I held it between my teeth, so it didn't get in the way as I watched her lick up the underside of my cock and then swirl around the piercing and tip. She took me all the way and gagged around my cock, and the unforgiving squeeze of her throat had me gripping the back of her head and panting. Emily pulled off me with a strong suck and sat back. "Now you try."

Milo didn't hesitate before kneeling before me. He looked up at me and our eyes locked as he lowered his mouth to my cock. My abs constricted in anticipation as his mouth took me in. His mouth was bigger and hotter, and he sucked even harder. A sweat broke out over me as I watched him lick and suck me into his mouth. My focus was singularly on my dick as he worked to pleasure me, and I almost didn't see Emily laying down next to him. She wiggled until she could cup my balls in her hand and lick the base of my cock that Milo couldn't fit down his throat.

It was too much.

It was perfect.

My shirt fell from my mouth as a moan ripped from my throat and I tipped my head back. I fought to look back at the two of them licking and sucking in turns. My cock was red and wet as they sucked me down and gagged and sucked some more. I bunched my hands in the blankets, and I was swearing incoherently. I heard my voice saying their names and begging as I had never begged before.

I felt the familiar pull just behind my balls as my orgasm ripped through me. With a final hiss and a cry of *"Fuck yes!"* I came. Throbbing wave after wave, I pushed up into Milo's mouth, gripping his hair tight. Come dripped out of his mouth around my cock, overflowing, and Emily licked it up greedily.

Laying back on the bed as I caught my breath and the twitching of my limbs subsided, I looked at them. They were grinning and wiping their mouths. "How'd he do?" Emily asked.

I laughed. The sound came out breathless and hoarse. I have a thumbs up. "A plus, Teach."

"I've seen porn," Milo said defensively. "I knew what to do."

"Oh, yeah?" I asked, sitting up. "Let's see you find Emily's clit."

Emily giggled as I gently pushed her back against the pillows. She was wearing a pair of pajama shorts and a camisole. I hadn't noticed how well the dusty pink complimented her blush before. But now, sated, I could see her beauty more clearly. Her red hair fanned against the white pillowcase, and I pulled down her pajama shorts for Milo. I sat back and gave a flourished gesture to her spread legs and exposed pussy.

He snorted a laugh and fell onto her pussy like a starving man at a buffet. She gave a high-pitched, delighted squeal and her mouth fell open. Her eyes rolled back, and she bucked against his mouth. "Found it! He- oh, *god!* Found it!"

I patted Milo on the back in congratulations. I let him go to town on her pink and gleaming pussy while watching for anything to suggest. When she cried out for more, he rested flat on his belly on the bed to use his right hand on her. He licked his finger before inserting it slowly into her. My cock was hard again, watching his glistening index finger pump in and out of her. He crooked his finger, but it was in the wrong direction. "Wait," I said huskily. "Like this." I aggressively shoved my index and middle fingers into his mouth to get them wet. He sucked and swirled his tongue around them, and I could have come again right there. Instead, I pulled my fingers out with a pop and slowly pushed them into Emily's waiting pussy. She keened high and sweet, and I curled my fingers up towards her belly button. "See? Up."

I reluctantly pulled my soaking fingers out to let Milo try again. He, open-mouthed and breathing hard, held his two fingers out to me. I smirked and leaned down to suck them into my mouth the same way he had done for me. Holding eye contact, I sucked hard and long before popping off. Milo's eyes had fluttered but remained focused on me while I'd done it and I suddenly couldn't wait until I had him moaning my name.

"Oh, my god that's so hot," Emily panted just before Milo slipped his fingers back into her. Her back arched off the mattress, and she cried out. Her legs trembled as Milo pumped his fingers, the muscles in his wrist showing me he was quickly tapping her g-spot.

I saw an opportunity, and I took it, stooping until I was

sucking her clit while Milo fingered her. She screamed as she came wetly against us. Her thighs trembled as she writhed on the bed. She bucked away from us when she became over sensitive, and I stopped before it hurt her. I tapped Milo on the shoulder, and he sat up, wincing slightly as he moved his cast.

"Can I touch you?" I asked him huskily.

Milo paused for a moment, looking from me to Emily. He swallowed and wiped his mouth with the back of his hand.

Emily's face lit up at the prospect. "Sterling, when we were in the basement, I made Milo a promise."

"Oh?" I said, fully intrigued now.

Milo bit into his lower lip and his blue eyes looked almost black as he looked at her.

"Yeah," Emily said. "I told him I would take his virginity... and make you watch."

Fully, painfully erect, I stared pointedly at their cast and sling wrapped arms. I wanted nothing more than to watch them, but... not right now. "Mmm, that's a good promise. I would have pulled my chains out of a cement wall with a broken arm for that, too."

Milo rolled his eyes and smile scoffed like he hadn't pulled the most superhero stunt I'd ever seen.

"But as much as I want to see that- and I mean *desperately* - I want you both whole first," I said.

"Which hole first?" Emily asked innocently.

I almost swallowed my tongue.

She grinned, letting me know she knew what she'd said and what I'd meant.

"On that note, Milo, let me see that monster cock," I

demanded and watched as he scooted his sweatpants over his hips one handed. Bruises and healing cuts marred his hips, much like Emily's. A conflicted bunch of feelings rose in my chest at seeing their twin bruises side by side. Anger that it happened. Grief and self-loathing that I'd not been there to protect them. Lust at seeing Milo's cock standing at attention for me. And a warm fuzzy feeling of safety and love knowing that they were *here* and *mine*.

"Oh my god," Emily whispered, leaning forward to get a better look at Milo's dick.

Milo chuckled, and his abs rippled. Fuck, I needed to work on my own abs. I wanted to look like that. I also wanted to lick his abs.

"It's seriously not fair," I grumbled and pushed him back against the pillows. He curled his good arm up and used his forearm as a pillow. Looking down at us with dark eyes and wet, swollen lips, he was the sexiest I'd ever seen him.

Emily traced her fingertips lightly over his cock and it jerked in her hand. I watched Milo take a deep, long breath. Emily gripped him in her fist, and he moaned as she stroked. Nobody had ever touched him like this. His eyes closed.

"Open your eyes, Milo," I demanded softly.

He obeyed, and I hummed my approval. Emily stroked a few more times before lowering herself down to lick him from root to tip. He fought to keep his eyes open as he moaned long and deep. "So good," he whispered.

She took him into her mouth and sucked slowly and stroked him at the same time. Milo swore and moaned and panted. I watched every muscle twitch, breath, and eye roll like I'd never see it again. Cataloguing all the dirty things

Milo said, the roll of his hips, and how his tongue kept poking out to lick his lips.

"Suck it slow again," he begged. "That's so *fucking* good. Mmm, let me see your tongue on it... yeah. Fuck."

"Move," I demanded of Emily, and she whimpered in protest before giving Milo one last suck.

I held a dark and challenging eye contact with Milo as I lowered my mouth to him. I let my breath whisper over his wet, hard cock and he shivered. "Suck my cock, Sterling," he snapped, breathless and irritated.

I sat up and slapped his thigh. That feral desperation was what I had been waiting to see. I grinned. He sucked in a sharp breath and, just as he was about to cuss me out again; I took him into my mouth as far as he could go. I'd never done this before. I'd never touched another man's cock, let alone swallowed one. But I knew what I liked, so I did my best to emulate and watch his face and body for clues to what he liked. He apparently liked me to flick my tongue on the underside of his head. He thrashed and gripped my hair painfully when I did this. Emily wiggled in next to me, trying to get back to Milo, and I turned on my side to make room between his legs. We worked in tandem until he was groaning our names and bucking into our mouths. He looked down at us again and watched with his mouth open and a long groan on his lips as he came. I held his balls as they drew up and emptied. I hesitantly licked up some of his come as Emily swirled her tongue in it. It was bitter and salty and not what I expected it to taste like. Not that I'd thought much about it before.

And I realized in that moment that I'd never wanted this

with another man before, but... *Milo*. And not just now that I've almost lost him. It was always there. Only for Milo.

And now I had both Milo and Emily.

I knew I'd feel pain in my life. I knew I'd feel loss.

But I never knew I'd get to feel this kind of love.

This kind of peace.

As Milo's breathing slowed, Emily sat up and winced after lying on her stomach. We might have overdone it for two people who had been beaten almost to death just days before.

"Did you love it?" Emily asked Milo and stroked his thighs with her fingertips.

Milo chuckled. "Yes, absolutely." He pulled her hand up to his mouth and kissed her fingers. "How are you doing? Both of you."

"Perfect," Emily sighed, with a dreamy expression.

Wordlessly, I nodded around the dumb emotional lump in my throat. I helped them sit up in bed and hurried to the bathroom. I provided aftercare for Emily and Milo, cleaning them with warm washcloths, giving them painkillers and water, and helping them rest. Aftercare was usually needed after the sex I typically had, but this was different. When they scooted over to make room for me, I realized I needed some aftercare, too. And finally, I was with people I trusted to provide it.

28

Sterling

When everyone woke up and gathered around the dining room table under the direction of Doc, I knew we were well enough to discuss what had happened and to make plans. Doc had us all eat incredibly bland eggs with wilted spinach, denied us coffee, gave us whole grain sandpaper toast, doled out medications, checked bandages, and then finally left. As soon as the door shut behind his old ass, I shot up from the table. Devon was cranky now that he was only taking ibuprofen for pain and hadn't had any coffee. Emily and Milo weren't better off than him, but I tolerated them more than I did Devon on account of the orgasms. I snatched the nasty dry toast away from Emily as she tried to eat it. Stomping into the kitchen, I made regular toast and an enormous pot of coffee.

Everyone murmured their thanks as I handed them new toast and steaming mugs of coffee. While their grumpy asses waited for their ibuprofen to dull the edges of their pain, I started thinking. We had to do something about Anthony and Matthew. It was going to be ugly. It was going to hurt. It was going to start fights. But we needed to do *something*.

"So," I said and set down my now empty mug. The porcelain clunked against the wooden table, and everyone looked up from their solitary thoughts. Milo set down his tablet that he'd been staring at with a furrowed brow.

"So," Devon echoed.

"We need to talk about what happened," I said.

"Um, your dad and your uncle tried to kill us," Emily said, looking at Devon and Milo.

"Something tells me it was just my dad," Devon grumbled and glanced at Milo. "Matthew was distraught."

Milo blinked, but showed no sign of relief. I didn't blame him. There hadn't been a single decision made by Anthony that Matthew didn't know about and cosign on for our entire time in the business.

"Regardless, none of us are safe," Emily said and pushed her toast crust around on her plate.

"What do you want us to do? Show up and go 'Surprise! We're alive!' and give them all heart attacks?" Milo scoffed.

I frowned, considering. "I hate surprise parties, but that would be *amazing*."

"No," Devon said. "We need to figure out how to get us out of here."

"What?! Now you say that? After Emily and I almost *died* trying to compromise with you?" Milo spat.

"Stop," Emily demanded sharply before the guys could fight.

"Yes! Yes, okay? Yes, I want to run away now that I almost lost you two. I thought we could reason with them. Maybe they'd respect us and our decisions enough to listen. Because *why else* would they have spent our entire lives training us? Just to kill us off? Ignore our potential? Single us down to *one* leader? No, he was ready to have you killed. There's no respect there. There's no love there. It's business. And a business I can't be a part of anymore," Devon said, his eyes wide and expressive. This was the most emotion I'd seen him display other than when we found out about the crash. As much as he drove me fucking crazy, I knew there was a good heart in my foster brother.

Emily sniffled and reached a hand to Devon. He exhaled and took her hand across the table. She squeezed for a moment before speaking. "I think we're all on the same page. Time to leave?"

"And go where?" I asked.

She shrugged, and the guys shifted uncomfortably.

"Anywhere," Milo said. "I can get us new IDs and passports."

"Why do *we* have to run, though?" I asked. "Shouldn't we run them out?"

"Are they still going to have business in human trafficking?" Emily asked.

We all shook our heads. "With Giovanni and Taz dead, their immediate connection to an established ring is gone," Milo explained. "They'd have to build their own from the ground up or find another. It's not impossible, but very unlikely."

"If we can get them to step down, or really, we push

them out, would we want to take over operations here in Cleveland?" I asked them.

Devon considered. "In a perfect world, yeah."

Milo exhaled but didn't agree or disagree out loud.

Emily sat back in her seat and looked at each of us. "Why?"

"I've been taught to lead since I was a baby," Devon said. "Without this family, my skills are moot."

"I don't think it's that dramatic, Devon," she said. "Your leadership skills are transferable."

"Well, maybe I don't want them to be," he snapped back.

I shot him a warning look for talking back to Emily.

"Why don't we plan a time for a coup? And we can surprise them with me and Milo being alive. But I think it needs to be done soon before anyone comes to the house or you two are called to a meeting. And... before someone tries to kill Sterling, too," Emily reasoned.

My blood went cold. I hadn't even thought of that. "Yeah, the sooner the better."

"Do they know about Giovanni and Taz yet?" Emily asked.

Milo shook his head. "I've been monitoring the news and their incoming calls and emails. No mention of it and no movement of money. They got the money they needed for the original two million buy in. The rest of the money that was used to pay for our deaths was likely done in gold bullion."

"Gold bars?" Emily laughed.

"Yeah, it's not traceable and is more stable than money," Milo explained as he poked around on his tablet again. "I can see that Anthony typed in his code into the vault at his house, but I don't know how much he took out."

"Why didn't they do that original deposit with gold?" Emily asked.

"They try to use cash as much as possible," Devon explained. "It's more accepted by other families. If money is regularly moving in the banks for actual business expenditures, the less reputable stuff gets ignored more easily. It's really a very delicate system. The gold is for when they need to be entirely untraceable."

"And an investment into human trafficking doesn't warrant it?" Emily continued.

Devon raised his eyebrows in acknowledgement. "Good point. It was likely explained as an investment in one of Giovanni's and Taz's legitimate businesses. I'm wondering if that gold was always meant for getting rid of family members."

Milo and I both shifted at the reminder of our parents. I extended my leg to rest against his across from me.

"Was... was Giovanni talking about your parents?" Emily asked softly.

I nodded. "He said Anthony had them killed."

"Do we think that's true?" Emily whispered.

"I do," Devon replied hoarsely.

"What?" Milo snapped.

"I don't know for sure. But when I was fifteen, I had a short period when I didn't want to be in the mafia. I didn't want to be the leader of our business, legal or otherwise. I wanted to be a doctor, a family physician. I even asked to shadow Doc for a while one summer. When I showed interest in pursuing it outside of the ways our family would need a physician, my dad had me sit down for a conversation. He told me that our family was different than other people's families. He said that

I was born into this life, and this is where I'd stay unless I wanted to look down a barrel. I knew he was threatening me. I knew he was saying he'd kill me if I left. He said he'd done it before and he wouldn't be able to stop it from happening to me," Devon said, his voice struggling to remain even. "I never realized he meant... fuck, I never thought he meant your parents."

"Can I kill him?" Emily asked.

We all snorted and chuckled. "Sure, Bambi," I said.

"I can still hold a gun in my left hand," she said defensively.

I smiled proudly, remembering her shooting Taz and Giovanni. "Yes, Bambi, you can."

"Please don't patronize me. If it weren't for me, you'd all be dead," she snapped and crossed her arms.

We were silent and humbled. Asses thoroughly chapped.

"Are you our leader now, Emily?" Devon asked in a quiet voice. His voice was deep and soft, but couldn't be ignored. His eyes were dark with challenge and lust as he leaned forward with elbows on the table. Devon never took consequences or scolding well, even as a child.

I glanced at Milo to see him just as amused as we both watched.

Emily mirrored his body language and maintained her stubborn eye contact. She was such a brat. Devon wanted a game of cat and mouse, but Emily would never willingly be his prey. It was straight up Tom and Jerry.

Devon arched one eyebrow at her. She tilted her head.

I rolled my eyes and stood up. "Let's go, Milo. Mommy and Daddy are fighting again, and I don't want to get in the middle when the spanking happens."

Milo stood up and turned his tablet around to show us something on the screen. "There's a meeting on Friday at Harold's."

"The deli?" Emily asked, breaking eye contact with Devon. He blinked away the sting rapidly, and I grinned. He almost didn't win the staring contest. Fucker.

"Yeah, there's a conference room above it. It used to be an apartment, but now it's the room we use for bigger meetings," Milo explained. "People have good excuses to come in and out of the deli, especially when they leave with leftovers."

"Meetings with people outside of the family," Devon specified. "People we wouldn't invite into our homes to conduct business."

"So, a bad time to undertake a coup?" Emily asked.

"Um, for them. For us, it might be the best. They might meet with our major contacts and gang leaders to discuss the new leadership organization without me involved. Since they think I'm dead," Milo said. "And it would be nice and tidy if we were to bust in and take over. It would be a lot fewer visits and threats later if they're all there for it."

"Friday it is," I said and looked at my bandaged and injured family. "Unless we aren't ready."

"We'll be ready," Devon said. "We have to be."

"Now, sit back down," Emily tutted at me and Milo as we were about to leave. We obeyed. God, that Teacher Voice was no joke. Having not had a typical education, I figured we'd be impervious to it. I was incorrect, I realized as my ass hit the chair.

"Tell me why I'm here," Emily demanded primly.

The three of us looked at each other, silently communicating our wariness.

"We don't actually know. We truly know as much as you do at this point," I said carefully.

"Giovanni and Taz seemed to believe I was to be used as a political pawn. Milo said it was for breeding," Emily listed. "Sterling once told me he thought I was a spy for Anthony."

"Breeding?" Devon hissed at Milo.

Milo shrugged. "It was a working theory. And my saying so may have saved her life."

"Breeding how?" I asked with a wrinkled nose.

"Like she would have a baby with all three of us so our kids would be equal in the hierarchy," Milo explained, a tint of red above his beard.

"Oh, because three equal heirs worked out so well the first time around." Devon snorted and sat back in his seat.

"Yeah, well, like I said, it was a *theory*," Milo snapped.

"Milooo," I crooned. "Do you have a breeding kink?"

Milo opened his mouth to retort, his eyes flashing with anxiety and anger at my slyly grinning face, when Emily spoke up. "We are not discussing our fetishes at the dining table."

"Yes, Mrs. Ambrose," I said with a salute.

"Ugh," she said. "I forgot I wasn't able to change back to my maiden name."

"I did it for you. You're legally Gardener again," Milo said casually.

Emily looked taken aback. "Oh, I would have liked to have known that. Maybe I didn't want that name anymore."

"You're welcome," Milo said, ignoring her irritated tone.

"What name would you have chosen?" Devon asked, his eyes narrowing at her.

She sat back in her seat and looked up thoughtfully. "I don't know. Something cool. Emily is so common; I would like something interesting as a last name."

"You can take Hawthorne, baby," I said with a lusty grin.

"Emily Hawthorne does sound nice," she said and pretended like she wasn't blushing crimson.

"Maybe Emily Holden would be better," Milo added.

"No, Emily Bilal is clearly superior," Devon insisted, his voice like silk.

Emily rolled her eyes with a sigh, as if we weren't making her hot and flustered. "You're all getting me off track. Please, tell me: why am I here?"

Devon straightened up in his chair and gazed at her intently. "I think they brought you in for your political connections. But when Gregory went on a smear campaign to save his image, the people who were your political friends turned on you. This may be hard to hear, but your school colleagues and some of Gregory's friends in local politics have come out with stories of your unfaithfulness and a history of mental issues." Devon paused to let Emily gasp before continuing. I held Emily's shaking hand as tears filled her eyes. "I believe my father saw that as your ties being severed, so he felt he no longer needed you."

"Giovanni acted like a political alliance was being made with our family," Milo said casually. He was always oblivious to the emotions of the people in the room. "I've been through their emails and phone calls, and I've seen nothing to suggest it was happening."

"They seemed very threatened by it, yeah," Emily sniffled.

"I wouldn't think too hard if Milo's had no clue about it," Devon said dismissively. "It's likely Giovanni and Taz knew you were involved with us now and got nervous since they were involved in trafficking. They were probably just looking to cover their asses."

"But what about Milo?" Emily choked out. "Why would he want to have Milo killed?"

"I had their accounts frozen when they tried to move money for that initial buy in with Giovanni and Taz. I think there was a suspicion that I had been spying and knew what they were up to," Milo said, barely above a whisper. "I had only been trying to buy us some more time. I didn't mean to put a target on our backs."

"Nobody blames you," Devon said. My chest warmed at hearing Devon be the one to say it. He was supposed to be our leader, and regardless of Milo's struggles to accept his second place standing, it meant a lot to have Devon's continued approval.

Milo looked down at his hands. I wrapped my foot around his and pulled it to me under the table. Locking his leg between mine, I squeezed it like a hug.

"I certainly don't blame you," Emily said and squeezed his hand on the table.

Only then did Milo look up at me. "Not your fault, My-My," I said with a smile as warm as I've ever attempted.

Later, I went from bathroom to bathroom, helping all three of them bathe. I behaved myself as much as possible and only copped a couple of feels with Milo and Emily.

Devon could squeeze his own butt cheeks if the mood struck him. Being the only one without injuries was odd. I almost felt guilty for not having been shot. If we went anywhere in public, people would think I was abusive or something. An abusive pimp. I was sure as hell working for it, though. They all needed to be bathed, bandaged, medicated, and brought drinks and snacks.

It wasn't until I was working out after tucking their sorry asses into bed for healing naps that my brain caught up. What would I do if I found out that Anthony and Matthew were responsible for my parents' deaths? If what Giovanni had said about them being responsible, and what Devon said about people leaving the family were to be believed- could I be led to believe that they wanted out? I let the thought bloom for a moment and my chest ached with the old sadness of losing my parents so young. Had they wanted out after having me? Had they wanted a better, normal life, but Anthony didn't let them? Was it the same for Milo's parents? Had Matthew been a part of his brother's death?

A sick feeling rolled through my body, and I stopped my chest presses. I rested on the machine for a moment while I caught my breath and let my stomach settle.

I couldn't change the past.

I couldn't bring them back.

But I could do my best to protect the people I considered my family now.

29

Emily

I can't move. I'm bound to the wall in chains again. Pain in my broken arm reverberates though my entire body like a thunder clap every time I try to move. A whimper escapes my mouth when I hear the pained groans from Milo next to me. It's cold and wet in the basement and I wonder if I'll become hypothermic. How long before I die? My head spins and I heave. I'm concussed, too. The man comes towards me, unzipping his fly. He's finished beating Milo to a pulp and now it's my turn to suffer at his hand.

I cry out-

"Emily!" a voice startled me awake.

I scrambled back away from the man who woke me up. His hands came down on my shoulders and I tried to knock his hands away, but my broken arm stung with pain. A high-pitched but hoarse scream tore from me before my eyes processed what I was seeing.

"Emily, wake up!" the man's urgent voice said, as he stilled my flailing hands in my lap. He held my arm in the sling gently.

Finally, my brain made sense of what my eyes were seeing. "Sterling!" I gasped as I gulped in air. The air here was clean and smelled like my shampoo and laundry detergent. It didn't smell damp and moldy like the basement.

"You were having a nightmare," Sterling supplied and rubbed over my arms. My skin was raised in goosebumps after remembering the cold of the basement.

I nodded. I'd had nightmares every time I slept since I got back. They weren't always as vivid as that one, but I'd woken up with a start every night. I figured my dreams were tamped down some while I was taking more pain medication and antibiotics. I had stopped taking the narcotics and finished the antibiotics. My brain was free to swim and roam on its own.

It was Thursday night, or technically Friday morning, before we were set to storm the meeting at the deli. We'd spent the last few days quiet and... together. We watched movies, we tried to work out around our injuries, and we relaxed. It was a really enjoyable time and everyone got along. The only fight was about what movie to watch and it was so *normal.*

"Do you want to, uh, talk about it?" Sterling asked awkwardly and looked behind him at my open bedroom door.

I gave a weak smile at his effort. "Maybe. I don't know. You'll probably think I'm crazy for dreaming about it."

"If it's any help, I have dreams about the stuff I've been involved with too," Sterling said vaguely. "The fights, the death. All of it. I think-" he stopped to swallow. "I think if we didn't feel at least a little disturbed by the violence we dole out, then we'd be really sick."

"I don't regret it, though. I don't regret killing them," I whispered and looked down at my hands in his pale tattooed ones.

I felt Sterling nod. "No, I get it. It's like… you regret you were ever put in that situation, not that you were the one to survive. I've felt that my entire life. The shit that Anthony and Matthew had me do simply because I was the biggest, the strongest, and the best fighter is disgusting. But it was kill or be killed. And not just by my targets. Apparently, it was our leaders, too."

"Oh, Sterling," I said and stooped to kiss his hands. I kissed his hands slowly like I was kissing away the violence. Cleansing his bloodied hands with affection.

When I came back up, I felt more comfortable telling him about my nightmare. "It's almost always the same nightmare. It's the basement we were in and the chains." I stopped for a deep, steadying breath. "I can still feel the chains on my wrist, the cold dark room, my wet clothes. When I wake up, it takes so long for my body to feel *mine* again."

"I'm not a therapist or anything," Sterling said but paused for both of us to snort laugh. "But you need to reclaim your body. Take it back from your nightmares."

"How do I do that?" I asked.

"Well, I think you'll feel better when you're healed and there's no more pain in the same places you had pain in the basement. I think your body keeps reminding your brain," Sterling explained with an unsure shrug.

"No, you're right. I think it's because I'm not taking so many medications and now my brain is free of the drug soup," I said and sat up better in bed.

"Hm, I can think of another way to cover up the feeling of the basement," Sterling said slyly after a moment of thoughtful silence.

"How?" I asked.

"Do you trust me?" he asked and stood up. He held out a hand for me to take.

"Yes," I whispered as I took his hand. His hand was warm in mine, and I stood up with him.

He smiled and led me down the dark hallway to his room. I breathed deeply when we entered. It smelled like his soap, deodorant, and smoky incense. He shut the door behind us and led me to the black box that rested on the dented and scuffed surface of his dresser. Sterling opened it with a flick of his wrist, and my eyes bugged out. It wasn't like I had forgotten his... tools, but I hadn't been thinking of them as we walked down the hall.

"You said they chained you up?" he asked quietly, his voice both soothing and a threat at the same time.

I gulped. "Yes."

"I don't have chains, but I have this rope," he said and ran a finger along the satiny maroon color. I shivered with fear and anticipation. "Have you seen rope like this before?"

I nodded. "On Gregory's secretary."

He paused for a second before turning eagerly toward me. "Take it back. Let's take it all back right now. Reclaim it."

I bit my lip. "Okay."

"Okay?" he questioned.

"Am I supposed to say 'Yes, sir?'" I asked with a roll of my eyes.

"Only if you want me to come in my pants. Now, get on

the bed on your knees in the middle," he directed and turned me towards the bed in question. His sheets and blanket were balled in the center. I shook them out, and he *tsked* before helping me make the bed.

Once the bed was made, I followed directions and kneeled on the bed. "Don't forget my ribs and my arm are broken," I reminded him.

He stared blankly at me. "I have heard nothing but where all of your sorry asses have been hurting for a week now. I know, Emily."

"Okay, jeez," I giggled.

Sterling put on some music low so it played softly. It was that same ethereal metal band from the last time I was here. He lit incense, and the smoke curled before drifting to the ceiling. It smelled like roses and a wood I couldn't place. Maybe cedar? Maybe Palo Santo? It smelled nice, and I took deep breaths to relax as he gathered what he needed. He placed two coiled bundles of ropes on the bed before switching the lights to two lamps rather than the overhead light. The room was now bathed in a warm glow, and I felt my body relaxing despite not knowing what was about to happen.

I silently watched as he stripped down to his black boxer briefs. He faced away from me for a moment while he brought his clothes to the hamper, and I realized he had no tattoos on his back. His large, muscled, pale back was free of any marks. I thought about this as he stood next to the bed and uncoiled one rope. He helped me undress slowly and traced his fingers over my skin lightly. I was shivering again, but with the anticipation of pleasure and something new. He wrapped rope around my unbroken arm gently. He kissed my hand and wrist as he wound it tightly. His lips were soft and warm as his breath feathered over my skin.

"You're doing so good," he praised. "Your safe word will be... Devon's polka dotted underwear."

"That's a sentence," I giggled.

He gave a sharp slap on my bare ass. "I didn't tell you to speak."

"Sorry," I apologized reflexively. My ass stung where he slapped it, and I itched to rub at my skin.

He stopped his movement to stare at me disapprovingly. I bit my lip to keep back a smile.

"Devon likes brats. I like good girls who take directions," he said blandly, and went back to his work of stringing me up.

He hummed thoughtfully a few moments later. "This is difficult to do only using one arm and no chest."

"I have a chest," I said defensively.

He smacked my ass again. "Again, I didn't say you could talk. Yes, I know you have a chest. A great one at that. But I meant I'm not putting any pressure on it because of your ribs."

I remained silent, with two stinging ass cheeks, as he wrapped and tied my left arm. There were multiple knots and a pretty cool design. It was tight, but not so tight that I thought my arm would lose circulation. Just enough to feel constricting like a comforting hug. He seemed to tie off the end of the rope, but I couldn't see what he was doing behind me. A moment later, he was in front of me and standing on the bed. I looked up to see a hook on the ceiling. It was painted white like the ceiling, so I'd never noticed it there before. He uncoiled the second rope and secured it before lifting my arm to attach the ropes. I didn't watch what he was doing; the Adonis belt V directly in front of my face distracted me. I swallowed.

I heard a male shout down the hall and we both paused and looked towards the door. Sterling hopped down off the bed, paused the music, and poked his head out of the door. He listened for a moment before shrugging and coming back in. He shut the door and turned the music back on, coming back to me on the bed. Sterling stood again and finished tying me up.

"Let me see the hold. Go limp for a second," he said calmly. I obeyed and felt the support of the ropes. He gently set me back on my knees. "I won't let you swing for very long if you go limp. It'll hurt your good shoulder. When you're healed though... that's a whole other story."

Just then, the door burst open, and we both jumped. Sterling spun around and jumped off the bed, ready for a fight. Milo stood in the doorway, looking white as a ghost, with his glasses askew and hair disheveled. He was wearing a white undershirt and pajama pants, one sleeve cut to fit over his cast.

"What?! What?!" Sterling asked him and pushed him into the room and looked down the hall again. Still ready for a fight.

Milo's eyes were stuck on me, tied up in Sterling's bed. I blushed.

"Who's here? What's wrong?" Sterling asked urgently as he shut the door.

"Um, nobody," Milo said and walked over to me, his brow

furrowed. "I had a nightmare and needed to see Emily. She wasn't in her room."

"Oh," Sterling said as his muscles relaxed.

We were silent.

And awkward.

"Welp. She's right there," Sterling said and gestured grandly to where I was artfully tied and hanging from the ceiling.

"I see."

"Hello," I said, feeling my entire body flush with heat.

"Hello. What are you doing?" Milo asked and finally tore his eyes from my naked and tied flesh to Sterling, who stood with his hands on his hips and his lips in a flat line.

"I think the term is *bondage*," I supplied helpfully and did a little swing on my ropes.

"No shit," Milo said dryly.

"I also had a nightmare," I explained. "Actually, I've been having them every night since we... got back. And Sterling said I should reclaim my body. Take back control of my body's memories."

Milo frowned thoughtfully. "No kidding. I'm in."

"What?" Sterling asked, his eyes wide and his hands sliding off of his bare hips.

"Let's do it," Milo said and stripped off his shirt.

He was pushing his pajama pants down over his thighs before Sterling's brain caught up.

"Wait, are you serious?" Sterling asked and seemed to swallow around a dry throat.

Milo hopped up on the bed next to me and kneeled, naked. "Yeah, string me up, Rope Daddy."

Sterling wiped the back of his hand over his now sweating

brow and I grinned. He rested his hands on his knees and seemed to take deep breaths before he stood up. "Alright, let's do this."

Milo and I exchanged amused glances as Sterling rummaged through his room, muttering to himself. He emerged with another hook, a few screws, and a screwdriver. He hopped up onto the bed and kneed Milo out of the way. Milo reclined, naked on the pillows. He watched Sterling screw the hook into the ceiling with hooded eyes. I bit my lip and clenched my thighs.

Sterling hopped down and gestured for Milo to reclaim his kneeling place next to me. Milo complied and narrowed his eyes at the hook. "Are you sure that's in a stud?"

I knew his mistake before he did. I made sure I was watching as Sterling's palm came down on Milo's ass with a resounding slap. Milo jerked away from Sterling and into me compulsively as he hissed.

"No talking. Emily, tell him the safe word," Sterling demanded, his voice taking on that soft but deadly tone again. He started wrapping Milo's unbroken arm the same as he had done mine. Though, where my flesh bulged slightly over the top of the rope, looking soft and doughy, Milo's bulged less and looked more muscular. My thighs felt wet as our skin brushed at our hips as Sterling tied him.

"The safe *phrase* is 'Devon's polka dotted underwear,'" I informed him.

"It's weird that you involved Dev- *ow!*" Milo complained, but was rewarded with a second hard slap to his ass.

Once Milo was strung up, a mirrored twin to my own ties, Sterling stepped back. He looked at us like he was a lion and we were fresh steaks hanging just before him. As he paced slightly, looking over our bodies, I amended my animal comparison. He was a jaguar. I shivered.

"You said you were bound in that basement," he said, his voice low and threatening. "You said it was dark."

He turned to his box of toys and came back with two black silk blindfolds. A quiver of fear settled in my stomach. I let him see my fear in my eyes before he put it on my face.

"I've got you," he said and caressed my face.

With my eyes covered, I relied on my ears to tell what was happening. I heard him move to Milo's side of the bed.

"Be careful with my glasses. Those are already my back ups and I can't- *ow*! Okay, okay."

I smiled.

A moment later, the door opened and shut, a gust of air cutting through the incense smoke.

We remained silent, save a few chuckles, as we wiggled and bumped into each other in the ropes. After our chuckles settled, I started to feel nervous. Sterling wasn't kidding when he said my body was reminding me of what happened. This felt too much like the basement we were kept in. I felt my pulse pound in my wrist against the rope and I took deep breaths and focused on the incense and the smell and feel of Milo just next to me. A ragged inhale and a shuffling sound was my only clue that Milo was feeling the same.

When the door opened and shut again, we were on our best behavior. I knew it was Sterling. I knew I was safe. But the pounding of my heart and my rapid breathing told of my body's fears. Milo pressed his body against mine as much as he could in the ropes. I felt his shaking almost like it was my own.

"You said it was cold," Sterling said in almost a whisper. I heard the clinking sound of maybe ice in a glass. I couldn't tell. The music started back up with a desperate voice screaming out lyrics.

Something freezing cold trailed down my body from my neck to the apex of my thighs. At first touch, it was such an extreme temperature that my body wasn't sure if it was hot or cold until the air hit the melted water that trailed behind.

"It's cold, I know. Good girl, let me make it warm again," he said in a reverent whisper.

Next to me, Milo hissed in reaction to the cold. Sterling's tongue came after, trailing the cold water on my skin in a scorching path. Humming, my body heated with pleasure. I heard Milo's unsteady exhale next to me when Sterling's mouth touched his skin at his turn. I wished I could watch.

"Milo, let me warm you," Sterling whispered. "Let me fix it for you. Good boy."

Ice trailed from hip to hip and down over my outer labia. I spread my legs eagerly, my thigh pressing firmly against Milo's, as I anticipated Sterling's tongue to follow. The tickling of Milo's leg hair against my smooth skin only added to the sensory experience. When Sterling's tongue followed the ice, my head tipped back as I moaned. Milo's groan rumbled in his chest as he trembled in the ropes.

We were so quickly undone. So weak. So desperate for Sterling to give our bodies back to us. To shove our minds back into our skeletons, where they belonged with the violence and desperation with which they were ripped out of us.

Ice and his searing tongue trailed over our flesh unforgivingly. Lovingly. Achingly soothing.

I heard Sterling get off of the bed. Milo and I heaved breaths next to each other. Leaning into each other's skin like we couldn't in the basement.

"You said they beat you," came Sterling's hoarse voice. His words cracked on the last word. He was as desperate as we were to be whole again. A young boy who had been neglected was now the man tasked to provide. To defend. To rebuild.

Something stinging came down on my lower back. I squeaked out a scream and arched away.

"That's my girl. Take a breath, that's it. This is your body, take it back," Sterling said in an awed, hushed voice as he trailed the whip between my legs. I whimpered and tears filled my eyes.

I heard the slap of the whip hitting Milo's skin. He hissed and groaned.

"Let out your breath, Milo. Just like that. This is your body. Take it back," Sterling continued in the same tone to Milo.

I tensed, waiting to be hit again. It came again, but this time across my ass. He wasn't hitting very hard, but it still stung. He praised us and soothed our skin after every strike. After a few strikes, I stopped tensing up, and I relaxed into it with moans. I felt my arousal drip down my thighs and I heard Sterling chuckle.

"What a good girl. You're so strong," he praised and dipped his fingers into the wetness, smearing it around.

"Milo's been a good boy, too. Open," Sterling directed.

I heard a soft sucking sound and more arousal dripped.

"Doesn't she taste so sweet?" Sterling asked.

Milo moaned his agreement.

"You're both dripping," Sterling rasped and brought fingers up to my mouth. I obediently and greedily sucked Milo's pre-come off of his fingertips. "Spread your legs. Both of you."

We followed directions eagerly. We were rewarded with Sterling's hands and mouth on us. He was everywhere at once. Licking over my nipples, fingers on my clit, dipping into my ready pussy. I heard Milo moan next to me. Our bodies trembled and sighed side by side.

"This is yours," Sterling said worshipfully as he ran his hand flat over my body from pussy to my neck. "This is your body. You are safe. You are home and in my hands." I heard Milo's breath hitch next to me and the slick sound of Sterling's hand on him.

Sterling kept his hands on both of us, pleasuring us. He had me dripping and desperate and at the precipice of an orgasm for what felt like hours. I was sobbing in pleasure and emotional release, the mask and my face sopping wet. Feeling Milo's shaking and breathing against my body, I shifted to hook my leg in his to show him I was there. We were together. Sterling was putting us back together like Lego people and when we eventually came out the other side, we would be knitted together and stronger for it. I felt Milo's orgasm vibrating at the edge just like my own as Sterling played our bodies like instruments.

Just as my orgasm was tipping over the edge, Sterling pulled back, ripped my blindfold off, and returned to my pussy. My hair was all over the place from the blindfold, but I watched him through the copper strands.

"Look at me!" Sterling demanded breathlessly. His gray

eyes blazed with emotion. "You're *mine*. I love you, you're both *mine*. You were mine before they stole you away and you're *mine* again."

He brought me right back to that edge and let me tumble off just as Milo did. He bucked against the ropes with a strained moan. The orgasm was so strong it almost hurt, and I screamed, limp in the ropes. The only thing that kept me from swinging was my leg wrapped around Milo's. His blindfold was also on the bed right in front of us at Sterling's knees.

The pleasure was so strong I coasted on it for a long time. I let it hold me even as Sterling gently unhooked me from the ceiling. I only came back to awareness when Milo gripped me with his sweating, quivering arm and pulled me to him. We lay in a crumpled, breathless, and sobbing heap as Sterling made quick work of our ropes. I clung to Milo's sweaty skin, and he clung to mine.

When the ropes were off, Sterling tapped at us until we sat up enough to fold him into our arms. "You both did so good. I'm so proud of you. Oh, God, I'm so proud of you." He kissed us over and over as he clutched us to his sweaty chest.

He praised us absently as our heart rates and breathing returned to normal. A faint grumbling sounded from somewhere in the pile of limbs.

Milo chuckled.

"Shut up. That was a lot of work. I worked up an appetite," Sterling said, muffled against Milo's chest.

"Want me to make some grilled cheese sandwiches?" I asked. My throat was still dry from exertion.

Both guys lifted their heads eagerly with cheerful expressions. *Puppies.* "Grilled cheese?" Milo asked.

"Yeah. Is it just a girl thing or do guys just have to Grilled Cheese about it sometimes, too?" I asked as we sat up.

"You're speaking in tongues," Sterling said.

"You know, after an emotional day, you just need a buttery, cheesy grilled cheese sandwich to process the events," I said with a shrug.

"Oh, you mean beat it and meat it?" Sterling said as we tugged on t-shirts.

"Don't tell her-" Milo groaned as he stepped into his pajama pants.

"Please tell me," I laughed.

"It's when you jerk off and then eat a cheeseburger," Sterling explained. "Solves all emotional ills."

"I regret asking for clarification," I sighed as we left the soft, safe, smoky atmosphere of Sterling's room.

30

Emily

Milo and Sterling were bent over one of Milo's laptops in the den and murmuring to each other about Sterling's Personal Cameras page. I was perusing the bookshelf for the millionth time. There was nothing but leather bound classics that were there for decoration, not reading. I had read over the spines so many times that I had the order memorized at this point. Devon stepped out of the office and gestured for me to come in with him.

"What's up?" I asked as he shut the door gently behind me.

I could hear loud and dramatic kissing sounds as the door shut. Biting my lip, I pretended not to hear Milo and Sterling's teasing and Devon gave no sign he had heard it either. "I wanted to speak with you before we go to the meeting," Devon said and moved to lean against the desk. He crossed his ankles in front of him and placed his hands on the desk, gripping the edge behind him.

"About what?" I asked and sat in the leather chair in front of him.

He looked down at me and seemed almost sad. I was sure he was not looking forward to taking over the mafia by force from his own father, but this felt different. "I want to apologize to you, Emily."

"For what?" I asked, still just as clueless as when I walked in.

"For getting you involved with us. With this family. This... business," he said and then ran a hand through his dark hair.

"Oh."

"I know you didn't come to us willingly. I'm sorry for being a part of that," he said, his eyes uncharacteristically gentle.

"Um," I whispered, and swallowed hard. "Thank you for apologizing."

He tipped one side of his mouth up in what would have been a smirk if it didn't seem like there was more to his apology. He took a big breath. "It's not in my nature, and I'm sure you've noticed, not in Milo and Sterling's nature to kidnap women. We- I- was only following orders from people that I thought had our best interest at heart. It turns out that I was wrong. I'm sorry for not letting you go when you fought us at the deli."

"I don't know what to say." I shook my head and trained my watering eyes on my hands in my lap. It had been a traumatic event. I hadn't wanted to be kidnapped. I hadn't wanted to be shoved into the life of a mafia member. I hadn't wanted a life of killing and death and fighting. As much as none of the recent events had been a part of my life plan, I was oddly glad they had happened. Did I begrudge the guys for taking me? A little. It was a shitty move, after all. But I really liked Milo and Sterling. Devon was okay, too. Were they good people? No. But I realized that I really liked the color gray.

"You can leave if you want," Devon finished in a rush. His words came out so quickly I had to replay it in my head to decipher what he'd said. An important skill I'd developed in my time with five-year-olds.

"What?" I asked, even though I'd sufficiently translated his jumble of words.

"You can leave. Go home. Go back to Gregory... or your parents. Anywhere. You could disappear like you'd wanted to," Devon said, not looking at me. "I'll help you get a new identification, passport, money, anything."

"Do you want me to leave?" I asked him, watching for any tiny sign on his face that he wanted me gone.

His eyes locked on mine. Their color looked more like warm honey than the hard, fossilized amber I'd thought them to be. Black lashes framed his eyes so beautifully, like eye liner, even on the bottom lash line. His expression was barely restrained desperation. His jaw clicked as he swallowed. "No."

"Well, good. Because I'm not leaving," I said, maintaining eye contact.

His hands slapped down on the armrests on either side of me in the chair. A gasp left my lips as he leaned down. I couldn't help it- I blinked first. "I'm offering you mercy," he said, his voice a growling rasp.

"I don't need it." My voice was quiet but belied my weakness.

"Tonight..." his voice was so much of a rasp it was almost a whisper brushing over my cheeks. "Tonight, we steal power from the men who stole power from their fathers... and their brothers before we'd even cut our teeth. Tonight will be the fire and brimstone of our world. Tonight... we will not be good men."

"Devon," I whispered and then gasped. He had grabbed the crimson hair at the base of my neck in his fist and squeezed. I couldn't tell if he wanted me to run with his devil's mercy or submit to him. I couldn't tell which I wanted, either. "Devon, if you're a bad man, then I don't want to be a good woman."

His face took on a look of pained devastation as he groaned, low and growling, and kneeled hard before me. His hand remained gripped in my hair almost painfully. My mouth opened to pant through the pain. My nails sunk into the leather of the seat, likely leaving little half-moons in their wake.

"It's going to be dangerous," he growled.

"I know."

"*We* are dangerous."

"I know."

Something broke behind his eyes, and he pressed his forehead against mine. He was sweating and his heat made the scent of his cologne surround us like a hazy summer morning. "You're a stupid, *stupid* woman." He said, his tone suggesting that he thought me anything but stupid as he lightly banged our foreheads together with his grip on my neck. His breath was hot against my face, and I was desperate to steal it from him with a kiss.

"I know."

A timid knock sounded from the door. "Uh, Mommy and Daddy?" came Sterling with a high-pitched imitation of a child's voice. "If you're done, um, reading the Bible and praying, it's time to go to Grandpa's."

I smiled and heard Milo's laughter in the den. Devon exhaled all the tension and emotion he'd been holding in his chest and shoulders. He let go of me and stood up. "Hold on," he called to Sterling. "I'm going to arm Emily."

"Dirty!" Sterling called back.

Devon rolled his eyes and opened the weapon case, pulling out the knives and gun I'd worn before. I was wearing a pair of black, high-rise jeans. They'd become the favorite pair Milo had picked out for me, and I often chose them. My sweater was a deep maroon cashmere. It was the same as the white one I'd been wearing in the accident, and I decided I wasn't going to let that deter me from wearing a beautiful sweater. Devon quickly strapped my thigh holster on and placed a soft, reverent kiss on my thigh just above the strap. I breathed evenly and slowly as I watched him almost worshipfully kiss the denim.

Without thinking, I stroked his hair back from where it had fallen over his forehead. He looked up at me from his place on his knees, his eyes more expressive than I'd ever seen. I realized he'd never let me see him before. His hardness was an act to protect himself. Inside, he was just as soft and gooey as any human.

"Fire and brimstone," I whispered.

He stood up now, close and towering over me with strength and power. "Fire and brimstone, baby." He said and stroked my cheek.

My lips parted, and my eyes closed, expecting a kiss, but none came. Cold air rushed against my face, and I opened my eyes to see the closed weapons case instead of Devon. I turned around to see he had left the office, leaving the door open for me. I swallowed the rejection and followed him out the door.

Sterling and Milo were standing near the door, and Milo was poking around on his ever-present tablet. Sterling was looking over his shoulder with a furrowed brow.

"What's going on?" Devon asked as he shrugged on his coat and handed me mine.

"Anthony and Matthew arrived at the deli. Stephanie's there, too. No Marie, but Brendon's there. Victoria and Harold are in the kitchen. Harold looks like he's still working, but Victoria is just talking, fixing her makeup. Nobody else is there yet," Milo informed us as we headed towards the garage.

"Why weren't you two invited?" I asked Sterling and Devon.

"They assumed us to still be grieving. They were asking Doc about our status, and he covered for us, saying we needed privacy," Devon said as we approached his car.

I was about to get into the back seat on the passenger side, but I heard Milo and Sterling fighting over who would sit next to me. I heard their feet shuffling and their grunts of effort. Ignoring them, I got into the front passenger seat instead. Devon smirked at me and started the car. He rolled down his window. "Gentlemen, if you're quite finished, we have a meeting to get to," he said in his clipped, posh tone.

I snorted as Milo and Sterling stopped fighting and saw me in the front. Sterling had been holding Milo's tablet out on the side of Milo that was impeded by his cast and lightly kicking him, so he kept turning away. They glared at each other before sliding into the back seat.

As we drove, we planned. "When we get there, I want to walk in with Sterling at my side," Devon said. "And then Emily and Milo come in. Emily, I want you walking on the left, so both of you have your broken arms on the inside. I need you both to have arms free for defense."

"Do you think there will be the need to fight?" I asked him, a pit of unease in my stomach.

Devon pursed his lips and gave an unsure shrug. "I know there will be security. But they'll know us and won't fight us unless they're directed to by Anthony or Matthew. That's why as soon as we get in the room, Sterling will take your six."

"Anthony and Matthew will call for us to be subdued, but probably not *killed* right in front of my mom and everyone else," Devon explained.

"I'm seeing a few cars pull up, but nobody I recognize. Hard to tell if they're actual customers getting dinner or they're there for the meeting," Milo said.

"Hey, look at that! Having a meeting room above a deli works!" Sterling said.

Milo put the tablet down for the rest of the drive. It didn't matter who was in the building. This was happening.

We pulled up and parked in the employee lot behind the deli. "Won't they see us parking on the security cameras?" I asked.

"If they knew how to access it. Their IT guy is dead, though," Milo said blandly, meaning himself.

"Too bad. I heard he was hot," I said with a sigh and a grin.

We hopped out of the car and checked over our weapons behind the car.

Sterling looked us over and shook his head. "I look abusive. Everyone's going to think I beat you all at home like it's some sort of domestic issue."

"I look perfectly healthy," Devon said haughtily and smoothed his white button-down shirt. We had left our coats in the car, not wanting the bulky material to impede our movements.

"Oh yeah? Raise your left hand above your head," Sterling taunted. Devon glared. "That's what I thought, bitch."

Milo checked the tablet one more time to get an idea of where people were in the building. "There's probably fifteen people in there around the table. I think that's the back of Victoria's head, next to Stephanie. Um, I can't really see who anybody else is with the angle of this camera. They moved the table back maybe five feet, so it's not centered anymore. Anthony and Matthew are both standing at the head near the second door."

"We'll go in the first door and face the room. I'll stand to the right so we sandwich you two," Sterling said as we walked to the building's back entrance.

"Mm, a muscle sandwich, my favorite!" I said brightly, earning me one annoyed look from Devon and a lusty smirk from the other two.

"Anyway," Devon said as he opened the door with a code on the handle. "We're walking into something huge."

We were silent as we walked through the kitchen to the stairs. I could hear the normal bustle of business from the other side of the swinging door. I assumed someone other than Harold was working at the counter now. The stairs to the second level were chipped red brick like the outside of the building and looked original. Our steps were quiet on the stairs, and my heart thrummed in my chest with anxiety.

This was it. Fire and brimstone. A full severing of the guys' family ties to their guardians and leaders. I looked at the three of them. They set their jaws hard, nostrils flaring as they all privately panicked. Their eyes were glaring and focused ahead as we emerged from the stairs. I saw Devon's shoulders broaden as he stood up tall. I followed suit, not wanting to look like I didn't stand with them. With searching fingers, I touched the cool metal of my knives at my thigh and my gun at my hip. Sterling glanced back at me and Milo, checking we were still there, as he topped the stairs. I nodded to him with a small smile that I hoped to be encouraging.

"Oh, hey Devon," I heard a younger man's voice say. "Sterling. I didn't know you two were-" His voice cut off as he saw me and Milo emerge from the stairs. His face visibly slackened like he'd seen a couple of ghosts.

"Move aside," was all Devon said. His voice was strong and deep.

The young gangster did as he was told, wide eyes taking us in. Devon opened the door and strode in confidently. Sterling followed a second after. Devon had a tall, silky, devilish air, while Sterling's boulder strength and rippling muscles showed his power. He had worn a black shirt, but even the dark color could do little to disguise the power and rage housed in his muscles. I heard Anthony's voice stop speaking mid-sentence as they entered.

"Devon, I-"

I entered, followed immediately by Milo. Milo's breathing was rapid, but he stood with his chest strong and his feet shoulder width apart. Sterling had come in just behind Devon at the head of the room, and now he swung around to stand next to Milo. Gasps and a few choked cries were heard around the table as people who thought we were dead learned otherwise.

A strangled male shout of "Emily!" happened at the same time another voice shouted, "Milo!"

Who knew me? I looked around at all the faces. There were certainly over fifteen people there. Probably closer to twenty-five. A few people looked vaguely familiar. No, they wouldn't-

I choked on a breath.

Gregory.

Gregory was at the table.

Gregory was at a meeting with Anthony and Matthew.

I covered my mouth as I stifled a gag.

"You're alive?" Matthew was shouting as he rushed around the table to Milo. Milo, who stood stoically next to me took a shaking breath.

"Why is he here?" I asked Devon, my voice squeaking.

Devon looked down at me before looking around the room. I saw the muscles in his face relax in shocked recognition once his eyes landed on Gregory, who was slowly standing from the table.

Milo pushed Matthew away and Sterling shoved him the rest of the way to the ground. Matthew stood up, looking hurt and upset. Devon grabbed my hand as my knees wobbled. His firm grip was the only thing keeping me upright.

There were shocked whispers and a few sobs around the room. "Alright everyone," Anthony was trying to calm the room, his arms outstretched and his eyes manic.

"No," Devon said, his voice booming. Everyone instantly stopped. "You've done enough."

"Devon," Anthony said in a patronizing voice, like he was talking to an unruly child. "We are in the middle of a meeting and-"

"NO!" Devon shouted, his eyes ablaze. "You put a hit out on Milo and Emily. You paid for their deaths. Just like you paid for the deaths of Owen Hawthorne, Kristen Hawthorne, Michael Holden and Meredith Holden."

More gasps and choked sobs. My eyes were glued to Gregory. He had sat back down and was glancing between me, Devon, and the door. He wanted to run. But not before I had the chance to ruin him. Rage burned through the shock in my blood, and I saw red.

"You've killed and betrayed your own," Devon continued, and I fought to listen through the buzzing in my ears. "You've destroyed for your own greed. And now we are here to seek vengeance and take control."

"Vengeance? Control?" Anthony scoffed. "Boy, who do you think you are?"

"Fire and brimstone," Devon said quietly now, but loud enough in the silent room that Anthony heard him.

There was a screech of someone getting up from the table, their chair scraping back. I looked up to see Stephanie rushing to her son. She stood just next to Devon, facing Anthony.

Anthony's face fell.

Matthew was rushing toward Anthony, and I thought

he was taking his side. Instead, he landed a hard punch to Anthony's jaw. "You killed my brother?" Matthew screamed.

"He wanted out!" Anthony screamed back. "They wanted out and there is no *out* of this life!"

Matthew gave a wrenching scream and hit Anthony again. Anthony was reaching for a weapon as Sterling and Milo were rushing toward the fight. Someone shouted "Gun!" and all the people who were at the table ducked under the long wooden slab. A few were crawling to the doors.

I made quick eye contact with the young gangster we'd shocked earlier at the door and shook my head in response to his questioning gaze. He blocked the stairwell so nobody could leave. He had looked to me for direction and had listened as if I was a leader. A feeling of power flowed through me before I was startled back by a gunshot.

Milo screamed, and I thought he'd been shot. "NO!"

I rushed to him to see that he wasn't bleeding as he dropped to his knees at his uncle's side. Sterling and Devon were tackling Anthony to the ground and wrestling the gun from his hands.

In the crush of people, I was knocked to the ground. I came face to face with a large man I knew I'd seen before but couldn't place. His terrified eyes and piss soaked pants threw me off, but it clicked. He was the mayor of the town next to the one I'd lived in. He was friends with Gregory. I couldn't remember his name, but I'd had dinner next to his wife at Gregory's celebration dinner.

Giovanni and Taz had been right. Anthony and Matthew were making political alliances. Gregory was here. The mayors of other towns were here.

I was supposed to be a pawn in this game.

Well, fuck them. I stood up and searched for Gregory. He was looking right back at me. I advanced toward him, and he backed up towards the door. He made it out the door before I could stop him and there was a crowd of terrified politicians in the hall, all squawking like chickens.

"Listen up!" I shouted. Power and rage flowing and making my fingers tingle like I was full of electricity. Everyone turned, squeaking with fear, to look at me. "The business you came to conduct today is gone. I will let you go home, but I want you to know who granted you mercy. Remember our faces. Remember our control. We run this shit now and you'd be wise to fall in line."

The gangster gave a nod to me and stood aside while the terrified local politicians scurried like rats down the stairs. I didn't watch them go, instead I looked for Gregory. I hadn't seen him since he'd left the meeting room and I didn't see him here now. Had he snuck past the gangster working the door?

I needed to get back to my men. Gregory would have to wait. He wasn't a priority to me anymore. I knew where to find him, anyway.

I returned to the shouting in the meeting room. Sterling's eyes were wide and searching, looking for me. When I came back in, he relaxed slightly.

Matthew was dead on the floor, his blood spreading on the floor. I approached to see Milo kneeling at his side, head bowed.

Anthony was shoved against the back wall by Devon, who was snarling in his face. I couldn't hear what he was saying to his father, but Anthony looked scared. A warm hand grabbed mine and pulled me away. Stephanie's face was tear streaked and blotchy as she pulled me away from the men. She hugged me and I was stiff in her arms.

"Emily, I'm so sorry. I knew something was going to happen. I just knew it," she sniffled as she held me.

She had suspected that Giovanni and Taz were going to kill the guys. "Giovanni and Taz are dead," I said to her, my voice even and unfeeling with the shock of the afternoon. "They told us about Anthony."

She shook her head. "I can't believe it. I never knew. And I knew everything." She looked over at Sterling and Milo. "Oh, those poor boys."

I wanted to scream. I wanted to burn the building to the ground.

"Go!" Devon shouted as he stepped back from Anthony.

Anthony rushed to Stephanie, but she crossed her arms over her chest and turned her head away from him. He stopped. "Stephanie," he murmured, heartbroken.

"You heard our son; go!" she said steely.

Anthony took one last look around and left.

Harold, Victoria, and Brendon remained in the room and came together. Sterling pulled Milo to his feet, murmuring something in his ear. Milo nodded and gritted his teeth. The four of us faced the four remaining people of the original mafia.

Devon stood breathless and manic eyed as he wiped blood from his lip with the back of his hand. "So... are you with us?"

The story continues in Book 2…
Spite comes November 24, 2023

Cat Austen is an emerging romance author based in Ohio. She lives with her husband and their two boys. She enjoys gardening and baking and is a voracious reader of romance novels.

You can find Cat on TikTok, Instagram, and Facebook and her website catausten.com.

Subscribe to her newsletter for updates on her books and opportunities for Advanced Review Copies.